"Then you know about 21," Brianna said.

Jase gave a curt nod. "It made national news. A bizarre ritual killer usually does. And, of course, I was on the crime beat, so he intrigued me. I was in Savannah at the time, but I kept up."

"He scared the hell out of me."

"He scared a lot of people."

"He still scares me."

"You don't think they," he hitched his chin toward the police station, "got their man."

"I'm sure of it," she said, and her thoughts turned dark again. "At least 99 percent. You eavesdropped on the conversation, so you know the details."

"I heard part of it. Why don't you fill me in?"

She studied him for a second, decided she had nothing to lose. "The long and the short of it is that I think 21 has come to New Orleans. Why? Probably to show off for Bentz, but who really knows? A couple of girls are missing and we . . . their mother and I, are worried sick that he may have targeted them." Staring into his eyes, she felt the now-familiar lump form in her throat when she considered the fate of the Denning twins. "But I hope not. God, I hope this is all a mistake and that I'm just a paranoid conspiracy theory nut who's got it all wrong."

"But, you don't think so."

"No," she admitted. "I don't . . ."

Also by Lisa Jackson and available from Hodder

The New Orleans Novels

Hot Blooded
Cold Blooded
Shiver
Absolute Fear
Lost Souls
Malice
Devious

The Montana Novels

Left to Die
Chosen to Die
Born to Die
Afraid to Die
Ready to Die
Deserves to Die

The Savannah Novels

The Night Before
The Morning After
Tell Me

Standalones

Running Scared
Twice Kissed
Deep Freeze
Fatal Burn
Almost Dead
Without Mercy
You Don't Want to Know
Unspoken
Close to Home

About the author

Lisa Jackson's books are number one bestsellers in America. She now has over twenty million copies of her books in print in nineteen languages. She lives with her family and a rambunctious pug in the Pacific Northwest. You can visit her website at www.lisajackson.com, become her friend on Facebook or follow her on Twitter @readlisajackson.

LISA JACKSON

NEVER DIE ALONE

MULHOLLAND
BOOKS
HODDER

First published in the United States in 2015 by Kensington Publishing Corp

First published in Great Britain in 2015 by Mulholland Books
An imprint of Hodder & Stoughton
An Hachette UK company

1

A CIP catalogue record for this title is available from the British Library

B Format Paperback ISBN 978 1 473 61749 0
A Format Paperback ISBN 978 1 473 61750 6
eBook ISBN 978 1 473 61748 3

Printed and bound by Clays Ltd, St Ives plc

Hodder & Stoughton policy is to use papers that are natural, renewable
and recyclable products and made from wood grown in sustainable forests.
The logging and manufacturing processes are expected to conform
to the environmental regulations of the country of origin.

Hodder & Stoughton Ltd
Carmelite House
50 Victoria Embankment
London EC4Y 0DZ

www.hodder.co.uk

CHAPTER 1

D*rip.*
 Drip.
 Drip.

The noise was constant, nearly rhythmic, little droplets falling and falling and . . .

Zoe's eyes flew open.

She blinked in the semidarkness.

What the hell was that noise and . . . Oh, Jesus, where was she?

She squinted, straining to see in the semidark. Dear God, was she naked and lying on some kind of cold, hard slab? No, that couldn't be right. Her head pounded as she tried to think, to figure out if this was real or all part of some macabre dream, or worse yet, a prank.

She and Chloe were about to turn twenty-one, and with the help of fake IDs they had gotten, the party started long before midnight, downing drink after drink, laughing, talking, drinking some more. In a sharp-edged swirl of memories she recalled the neon lights and noise of Bourbon Street, the drinks, everything from Hurricanes in their special glasses to margaritas in oversized plastic cups and Jell-O shooters and . . . Her stomach roiled at the thought of what she'd downed; all to prove she was becoming a legal card-carrying, alcohol-swilling adult. Her head felt as if it were in a vise, the handle of which was being twisted by some he-man.

At least she was no longer reeling. She did remember that, how the world had spun in wild, crazy colors before . . . before . . . what?

Had someone laced one of the two-for-one shots? Given her something to make her lose focus? Had one of their "friends" pranked her and hauled her here to strip her and leave her on the cold stone floor or whatever it was she was lying atop? And what about Chloe? Where the hell was her twin sister?

For the life of her, she couldn't pull the last few hours into sharp focus.

But here she was.

In the darkness.

Stripped bare.

Her arms pinned behind her.

Lying in some dark room where the dank, earthy smell was overpowering, as if she were buried alive. Her bed was a cold, hard patch of concrete. She twisted a bit and something rough dug into her throat, cutting into her skin.

What the hell?

With effort, she tried to pull her arm up to loosen the tension, but even the tiniest movement made the binding around her neck cut deeper. A noose? For the love of God, what the had happened?

In an instant all the fuzziness fell away.

She was in trouble. Big trouble.

If this was a prank, it was a sick one. A dangerous one. If not . . . she shuddered at the thought. Struggling, she attempted to move, but discovered that her hands were bound behind her, tethered by the same scratchy cords surrounding her neck.

Shit! Cold to the bone and shivering, she tried to move, then stopped as a searing pain scorched a ring around her neck. When she nudged a shoulder up toward the throbbing wound, it caused a brutal, cutting tug on her ankles. She realized her hands were bound to her ankles.

Hogtied and naked. That's what she was.

"Happy birthday to yooouu."

She nearly jumped out of her skin when she heard the whispered words, a lifeless, growling monotone. But sung, not spoken. "Happy birthday to yooouu."

This had to be a dream. Right? A nightmare. She swung her head around and saw him, a big bull of a man at some kind of workbench, bare-ass naked except for a black bib apron. Hairy arms, a hairy butt and legs. The back of his thick neck glowed dimly from one of those battery-powered dome lights used in attics, closets, and basements that didn't have power or sunlight. Just beyond the bench, a clock ticked loudly on the wall.

From the dank smell, she suspected she was underground, that this man who looked like an NFL lineman had captured her, though she couldn't remember her abduction. She tried to move, but her restraints held her fast to some kind of ring cemented into the floor. Blinking again, her mind clearing from the shot of adrenaline suddenly singing through her blood, she focused on one of the walls. Again, cement. With dark stains running down it. Water she hoped. Mixed with rust.

Please don't let it be blood.

She wanted to scream, but bit any sound back. Instinctively she knew it would be best to let him think she was still passed out, still stuck in a fetal position, as he worked. Jesus-God, what was he doing? Cutting lengths of red ribbon, measuring them over and over again, and then snipping them. The sound of his god-awful singing and something else—some other noise—caused her skin to crawl.

Mewling.

The soft, frightened cries were slightly muffled, as if whatever was issuing them was trying to hold back the sobs.

An animal?

No.

Some other person.

So Zoe wasn't alone. He'd captured another prisoner.

Her heart dissolved.

Chloe. Her twin sister. In a flash, Zoe recognized Chloe's voice, the choked sobs she'd heard as a child whenever Chloe was scared or being punished or whatever. Chloe had always been the weaker of the two Denning girls, the more sensitive. It had been Chloe who had held funerals for their pets, or run upstairs, footsteps banging on the wooden steps, when their parents fought. Chloe had stayed on her knees for hours, eyes shut, hands folded, as she'd prayed that the discord in the family would be quieted by the Holy Father and that their ever-quarreling parents would stay married.

"You should try it sometime," she'd told her minutes-older sibling. "A little prayer can solve a big problem."

Or not. Mom and Dad had gotten divorced, and Mom was still not over it.

Zoe only hoped that Chloe was praying now, that her presumed connection to the Lord God Almighty would garner them both some quick salvation because, as her mind cleared, Zoe realized the situation was more dire than she'd wanted to believe. No college prank. No mistake. Somehow, some way, this huge sicko had been able to subdue and abduct them both.

How?

For a second she thought she remembered it happening. In a kaleidoscope of jagged images, she recalled fragments of her abduction.

A voice behind her, whispering her name over the din of the crowd. "It's your sister," he'd said, his words cutting through the noise of pedestrians. "She's hurt."

"What?" Zoe had turned toward him, then searched the crowd. Where the hell was Chloe? Her twin had been right beside her . . . hadn't she? Then she'd felt a sharp prickle of pain, like a wasp's sting at first, then more intense as a needle had been plunged into her neck. In a quicksilver second she'd panicked, searched the faces of people teeming on the street, hoping to see Chloe or a cop or anyone who might think she was more than someone who'd had too much to drink. She'd stumbled and started to fall and tried to scream, but only a whimper had left her lips. On her way down, someone had caught her. The lights of New Orleans swirling, the cacophony on the street fading, she'd heard "happy birthday" whispered into her ear before she'd passed out.

Sweet Jesus, it had been this freak who had captured Chloe and her, and somehow brought them here, wherever it was. Chloe's sobs were louder now.

He quit singing, glanced pointedly at the clock. "Shut the fuck up," he said, his voice gravelly as he shouted away from Zoe, toward the opposite corner of the darkened room.

The sobs stopped for a second. "Let me go," Chloe begged, her voice trembling. Zoe's heart nearly stopped. *Don't,* she thought desperately. *Oh, Chloe, don't get him mad.*

Chloe didn't get the mental message.

"I . . . I don't know what you want or who you are, but please just let me go."

"I said, 'Shut the fuck up.'" This time the words were said harshly and tightly, as if his lips were clamped in rage.

Oh, God, this was no good. No good!

"But—"

"For the love of Christ!" He yanked something off the table where he worked. *Zzzzt!* Then a jangle. "I don't have time for this!"

What?

Quickly he raised one hand, his shadow looming against the far wall. A snake seemed to curl and writhe from his fist as he gave it a shake.

Chloe screeched in fear.

A belt, Zoe realized.

He cracked his wrist and the leather sizzled through the air.

Chloe shrieked and Zoe had to bite back her own scream.

Stop it, Chloe. Don't piss him off! Use your head!

"I mean it!" he roared, and snapped the belt loudly again, close, it seemed, to the spot where Chloe was most likely tethered against the far wall. Though it was too dark to see into the corners, Zoe guessed her twin was also tied up.

Bastard!

It was all Zoe could do not to say a word, not to betray the fact that she'd come to and her mind was clearing. She wanted to shout out to Chloe, to warn her, to comfort her, but Zoe bit her tongue. Instinctively she knew it was best to stay silent, to lull the freak into believing she was still sedated and unconscious, not a threat. Let him focus on his work, whatever it was, until Zoe could come up with a plan, some way to get them out of this horrific situation.

Barely making a sound, she once again tried her bonds and was rewarded with a deeper cut into the flesh of her throat.

Damn!

Again, Chloe pleaded but her cries only incited him further. The man was a psycho. Well, duh. Only a true whack job would abduct twins off the street, drug them, and torture them. And his quick-triggered temper indicated he was volatile. Dangerous. Tied as she was, Zoe had only one weapon: her wits.

Crap!

Once Chloe was subdued, the near-naked bastard resumed his off-key singing. Never had the birthday song sounded more like a funeral dirge. And that was, no doubt, his intent. She was certain of that one heart-stopping fact. Gone was any thought of a prank gone wrong.

"Happy birthday, dear twinsies," he crooned in his

horrid scratchy voice, still concentrating on his work and not sending a single glance her way.

Good.

"Happy birthday to yooooou."

Her stomach convulsed. Vomit rose in her mouth, but she fought the urge to spew.

And then he started over, repeating the verse, like a broken, ominous record. She hated to think what would happen when he stopped. Because she knew. As certainly as she knew this day was her twenty-first birthday. He was going to kill her. And kill her sister. This sicko was just waiting for the right moment.

No effing way.

"Do you know what time it is?" Olivia's voice called softly from the bedroom, and Rick Bentz, seated at his desk where he'd been for the past two hours, glanced at his watch. "It's after midnight," she said groggily, and he imagined her in the bed, wild curls splayed on the pillow, her eyes at half-mast. "Come to bed, honey."

Bentz's jaw tightened. She was right. The digital display on the face of his watch read 12:14 in the damned morning. And he'd like nothing more than to strip off his clothes and the worries of the day to settle into bed with her. The baby, Ginny, eight months old, was asleep while their aging dog, Hairy S, was curled up and snoring softly. Even the damned parrot wasn't making a peep.

Too bad. He couldn't shut it down for the night. Not yet.

Streaming live from his computer was a radio program with Dr. Samantha Wheeler, who took calls from lonely hearts. Their voices were a soft drone of conversation. Dr. Sam, as she called herself, gave out psychological advice over the airwaves late at night on her show, *Midnight Confessions.*

Bentz was listening in.

So far it seemed as if all of tonight's callers were legit: lonely or confused people seeking advice. It hadn't always been so. Years ago, before she'd married Ty Wheeler, Dr. Sam had attracted the attention of a sadistic serial killer, a man who was sick enough to dress in priest's robes, pretend to be a man of God, and then with horrifying determination went about his grisly business. She'd been his ultimate target and had barely escaped with her life.

Bentz retrieved a bottle of beer from the six-pack he'd picked up at a convenience store on his way home from work. Hesitating only slightly, he cracked the longneck open and pushed aside all thoughts of days, weeks, and years of sobriety as he twisted off the top and caught a glimpse of the other five bottles tucked inside the cardboard container at his feet.

He wasn't tired.

"Rick?" Olivia called again, this time sounding a little more awake.

In the darkness, the only illumination in the house came from his computer screen. He stared at the frozen frame of the video link as Dr. Sam's calm voice ran a soothing counterpoint to the image of a gray prison cell. "Be there in a sec," he said, turning his head so that his voice would carry into the general direction of the bedroom before he took a long, calming swallow. A balm, the cold beer slid down his throat easily.

Then he turned back to the monitor and clicked on

the Play arrow once more, putting the video from the prison security camera in motion for the umpteenth time. This time, maybe he'd see something important. A clue. God, he hoped so. In the days since the prison homicide, he'd been steeped in fury and disbelief. It just couldn't be.

"You can't force him to love you," Dr. Sam was saying in her melodic voice. "But you can love yourself," she advised. The same psychobabble BS she'd peddled for years.

"But he promised me," replied the woman, a girl in her teens, Bentz guessed. "Nathan promised me we would be together forever and then . . . and then"—she sniffed loudly—"I saw a picture of him with Rachel. I mean, it was all over Instagram and everyone texted me and were, like, dude, what's going on with Nathan?"

"I know, but you can't control Nathan," Dr. Sam advised. "You can only control yourself."

Bentz listened with half an ear. He didn't really care about the caller's boyfriend problems, but he did want to listen to all of the people who phoned the radio show. Even though the producer of *Midnight Confessions* had assured him that the calls were being screened and recorded, you couldn't trust that crew to weed out a psycho.

This psycho. Bentz had watched the damned video from the Department of Corrections so many times, he might as well have it on a loop.

The familiar image showed a prison cell. A female prisoner sat on the edge of her cot as a priest stepped inside the cell, the shadow of the bars striping his cassock. The prisoner looked up expectantly, ready to give her confession to the man of God, whose back was to the camera. As he stepped closer, she bent her head in prayer, probably hoping for absolution or some other damned thing. The priest appeared to say something softly to the confessor and then in one quick, sure movement, he reached down as if to bless her, but quickly, expertly snapped her neck.

She slumped quickly and Bentz noted that the priest didn't use his trademark sharpened rosary beads to kill her. This time his actions were on camera; his image might be splashed on a monitor in the prison's security hub, and he probably couldn't risk his slower signature kill. The guards would have been upon him before he could finish. Instead of strangling the life out of her with a rosary constructed of piano wire and sharpened glass beads, he broke her neck, then left the rosary dangling between her fingers, the blood red beads sparkling as he glanced up at the camera he obviously knew was mounted near the cell door. Smiling triumphantly, he revealed himself.

Bentz's stomach turned.

The sick son of a bitch actually grinned into the camera's eye before disappearing from the cell.

Bentz's jaw hardened.

Father John was back.

CHAPTER 2

Biting her lip, Zoe tried to figure out a way to save herself. To save Chloe. Somehow. Some way. First she had to get herself free.

While the whack job worked at his bench, she silently worked on the rope that bound her wrists and ankles. She had to make good her escape. *Their* escape. She wouldn't leave Chloe. Not ever.

Once again, she tried to pull her hand to her abdomen. The tension on the rope intensified, so she relaxed. That wasn't going to work. *Think, Zoe, think. There has to be a way.*

Again she tried to move. Again the bite of rough cord into her neck.

Damn!

She heard Chloe crying. Softly now, careful not to interrupt the freak from his task, she kept her gaze steady on his blocky body and the shadows he cast on the wall and tried again. This time, almost counterintuitively, she pulled her wrist closer to her naked back and upward toward her shoulders. It allowed her a range of movement, awkward though it was. She had trained as a gymnast in high school and also had double joints or hypermobility in her shoulders, elbows, and fingers—talents she assumed her abductor didn't realize.

Still, it was hard work. But as she rotated her shoulders she felt the rope around her wrists give just a bit. She tried again, contorting, picking at the knot with her fingers. Noiselessly, knowing that time was running out, she gritted her teeth and kept picking.

Was it her imagination or did the rope move slightly?

Hope swelled. Heart thudding, she worked at the knots and remembered her capture. God, how could she have been so stupid to have been lured by him, to believe that her twin was in trouble?

She'd paid for her mistake, but she wasn't going to docilely wait for whatever horror he meted out. No way! With an effort, she attempted to think clearly, to goddamned act despite the fear, deep and penetrating, cutting to her soul.

You have to get yourself free, Zoe. No one else is going to help you.

Silently, her jaw set, she picked at the huge knots in the semidarkness, working at the rope restraining her wrists, determined to break free.

Before it was too late. The clock on the wall counted off the seconds of her life.

Tick. Tick. Tick.

And still his sickening voice chanted the fateful song. "Happy birthday, dear twinsies," he warbled tonelessly, then chuckled to himself, a freak to the core. Chloe's sobbing continued, almost a countermelody to his grumbled refrain.

Shut up, Chloe! Don't irritate him. He's going to kill us, maybe torture and rape us first, so don't hasten the process.

But her twin kept whimpering.

Zoe couldn't see Chloe. She had tried, but the room was too dark; when she slid her gaze toward the sound of soft crying, she saw only a deep umbra.

If only she had some other means of escape aside from her own wits. A weapon. A club or a knife or a saw or a rake or an ax or . . . God, what she'd do for a damned gun. But as she squinted, her gaze scraping the walls and floor, there was only a meager array of tools on the wall and a cell phone that never seemed to ring, even though he talked on it often enough, always, it seemed to the same person. Now, he was using scissors, and she thought she spied screwdrivers and a crowbar on the wall, but she couldn't be sure. The twilight was pervasive, the stale air close as she noiselessly picked at the knots. Feeling the rope shift, she tamped down a ray of hope that rose in her heart. No time to get ahead of herself. And she was sweating. Beads of perspiration rolled down toward the hard floor, her fingers slippery as she plucked at the braided nylon, her joints straining.

The rope shifted.

Loosened.

Or was it her mind?

Oh. God.

She pulled again on that end of the cord and again she felt the tension on her bonds lessen.

Chloe sniffed loudly, sobbed again.

Stop, Zoe wanted to shout. *Don't give this sicko the*

satisfaction of hearing your fear. Be strong. You can. You know you can.

But that was a lie, wasn't it? Deep down Zoe had always known that she was the strong one, that her twin was weaker, always had been. Hadn't Zoe played the role of protector since the day they were born, twenty-one years ago? Zoe had come into the world first, and according to their parents had let out a yowl that nearly shook the concrete and steel of the hospital. Minutes later her younger sister had entered this life with barely a peep. Chloe had been so quiet the maternity staff had to double-check to make certain the smaller baby had been breathing, her little heart beating.

Right now Zoe's younger sister was certainly making up for that quiet entrance into St. Anthony's Hospital, and it wasn't a good thing.

Be quiet.

Please, please, please!

Be brave.

I'll save you.

Zoe let go of the breath she hadn't realized she'd been holding.

If I can.

She, too, wanted to cry but knew it wouldn't help. She, too, felt the need to scream and rail at the heavens, but again, that would do more harm than good. Zoe didn't want the bastard to know what she was thinking or even that she was aware. She could not let him know she was plotting her escape. Let him believe her to be compliant and either still groggy from whatever drug he'd injected her with or so scared out of her mind that she couldn't fight back. Let him think that she would be easy to deal with, that she would do exactly what he wanted without a fight.

As if!

Now, if she could just break free . . .

Somehow save herself and her twin. Jesus, could her sister please stop with the pathetic little sobs?

In the darkness, she stretched, trying to lengthen the cords holding her fast. She froze. The off-key singing was getting closer.

Her stomach crumpled in on itself and she almost gagged to think that the nut job had stopped whatever he was doing at the workbench and was drawing near. His footsteps padded on the ground, soft and frightening, but at least she had some idea of where he was in the gloom.

From the corner of her eye, she saw him reach for something on the wall above her—some new tool. Dear God, were there weapons just beyond her reach? Again, her heart leaped with hope as he turned back to the bench.

Come on. Come on.

Sweat drizzled down her back as once again she began to loosen the knotted cord.

"Hey!" His gravelly voice cut through the darkness. Sharp. Angry. The stupid song momentarily forgotten.

She froze. Oh, dear God, if he figured out that she was trying to escape—

"Quit that!" he yelled.

She was doomed! Drenched in her own sweat, she didn't so much as draw a single breath.

"All that cryin' and sobbin'. Stop it. Won't do no good anyhow. Besides," he said, the edge in his voice giving way to a jovial tone. "It's almost your birthday, so you should be happy. Right?" he cajoled Chloe, the evil in his voice dripping over his words.

Zoe's skin crawled at his personal tone.

He glanced at the clock again and grunted. "Damn, the time."

What the hell was his fascination with the time? Did he have to be somewhere? Was it important? Why was a clock mounted in this austere cave of a room?

"No more wailing!" And then he was back at it, humming and singing as he tinkered at the bench, working on . . . what? Nothing good, she thought. She didn't want to go there, didn't want to imagine what horrid, twisted fate he had plotted for Chloe and herself; the hollow pit in her stomach warned her that whatever he had in mind would be more horrible than she could imagine. A sick, slow torture and probable rape, considering the fact that he'd stripped her. No, she wouldn't think of the possibilities, couldn't go there.

With renewed conviction, she worked at her bonds, feeling the cords on her wrists slacken a bit more. She didn't have a plan. She knew only that the first step was to break free before he realized what was happening, somehow get the drop on him. Get herself and her sister out of here. Maybe lock him inside if it were possible.

But first, the rope. It cut deep into her wrists, rubbing her skin raw, stinging as she plucked at the knot. With her back to him, she could only hope her movements were veiled by the darkness. Her sister sobbed a little more softly now, though it was still enough to distract him.

"I said knock it off," he yelled angrily over the steady ticking of the clock. "Fuck!"

Snap!

Her heart stopped. The earthy-smelling room seemed to close in on her.

Oh, no!

She hazarded a glance over her shoulder and again saw the thin belt in the dim light that fell softly over his massive shoulders and back. Looming in a pool of gray light, still holding the horrid belt, he placed his hands on his hips and stared into the darkness, no doubt toward her twin.

"Didn't you fuckin' hear me?"

Oh. Dear. God. Chloe!

Snap!

He moved so quickly to crack the belt again, Zoe nearly jumped. In the silence that followed, Zoe wanted to cry for her sister, who had probably just received the worst whipping of her life.

"Don't make me use this again," he warned, his voice low and gravelly. He raised his arm again, and the leather snaked from his clenched fist.

Her throat turned to sand.

Fear slid through her blood.

Frantically she worked, watching him while the rope began to give. A little. Then a little more. She could move her hands more freely, felt the blood pumping through her veins again, sensation returning to her tingling fingers.

And then, almost magically, the cord gave way. The tight manacle fell free into a loose braid, and the tension on her neck relaxed.

Hallelujah!

Shaking her hands free, she wondered—should she try to unbind her ankles? Crap! She had to. It was necessary if she wanted to walk out of here on her own. Adrenalin firing her blood, she bent over a little more, the fetal position a cover as she studied the cord on her ankles with her fingertips, finding the knots.

And still he sang, though he kept checking the clock as if it were important. What did it matter what time . . . oh, God. Suddenly she understood; he was going to do *something* to them at the exact time of their births. That had to be it. The clock displayed prominently. The song. Both of them here . . .

And there wasn't much time left.

She'd been born at 1:21 a.m. Chloe had come along seventeen minutes later at 1:38.

Oh, God. Another look at the clock.

1:14.

If she was right, she only had seven more minutes to make a move! Frantically, she tore at the loosening knot. It began to unravel.

Come on, come on!

Viper-like, the braided cord slid from her ankles. Finally! Zoe held fast to one frayed end and pulled, wincing as the rope slid round her neck and fell away. She gripped the rope. Now she had a weapon.

". . . *birthday, dear Zoe,*" he sang, striking fear into her heart as he singled her out. Of course. She was the firstborn. *"Happy birthday to—"*

She sprang!

He started to turn just as she landed on his back.

"Hey!" he yelled, startled. He dropped the scissors, then bellowed, "What the fu—"

He shifted, trying to throw her off, but she held on

with a steely desperation and wrapped the rope around his neck. Roaring, grunting, jumping like a bucking bronco in a rodeo, he tried to fling her from his back. But she held on tight, anchoring the cord over her fingers and winding it around his thick neck. To anchor herself in place, she had to clench her legs around his gross, naked waist. The stench of him reached her nostrils as he tried to free himself, whipping his head back and forth.

The rope burned her hands but cut deep into his flesh. Clenching her jaw, she twisted it tighter, imagining a crushing force on his windpipe. He dug frantically at it with his fingers.

Chloe's mewling turned to terrified screams.

Die, freak! Zoe thought as he twisted and turned, gasping, falling against the workbench, sending his scissors and ribbons, wire, and a stack of clothes—her damned clothes, the dress she'd been wearing when he'd abducted her—flying and scattering onto the floor. One of his arms flailed, hitting the domed light. It fell from the ceiling, skittering across the floor and cracking, giving off a sick bluish hue. Still he bucked. Jumping up and down, he clawed at the rope with one hand. The other big paw flailed backward, his fist swishing the air over his head in a wild attempt to connect with any part of her.

No way! No frickin' way!

She threw her weight backward, pulling with all her strength, trying to cut off his air supply or sever his windpipe or break his damned neck.

Letting out a garbled growl, he stamped his powerful legs, then threw them both back against the wall, squeezing her body between his muscular back and the rough cement.

Bam!

Pain jolted down her spine.

Her teeth rattled.

The breath was forced from her lungs in a whoosh and a groan.

She felt her grip begin to slip.

No!

She held on as he pounded her, taking a step forward, then throwing all his weight backward once more as he clawed at the rope and gasped.

"Die bastard!" she hissed.

"Zoe?" Chloe cried.

Crack! The back of her head slammed against the wall.

Pain exploded through her skull. Lights flashed behind her eyes. She thought she might pass out and the rope began to slip in her hands.

For the love of God, just die!

As Chloe cried out again, Zoe snapped back to awareness and yanked hard on the rope. She wound it tighter until her shoulder muscles screamed and the nylon cut into her fingers.

The beast responded by clawing at the rope. Sputtering and moaning, he staggered away from the wall, a little less steady this time.

She braced herself, pulled back so hard that her arm muscles ached.

His muscles bunched. With a muffled roar, he threw himself backward again. She banged against the wall and he pinned her, squeezing her against rough concrete. Every bone in her body rattled and her bare skin felt scraped raw.

She felt the rope slipping. *No, no, no!*

Desperately she clung on. Tried to breathe.

"Zoe!" Chloe screamed from the shadows in the corner. "Help me!"

Oh, Jesus, what do you think I'm trying to do?

Zoe's fingers were cramped and bleeding. She dragged in a breath, determined to hold on.

The monster's back slackened. He stumbled slightly and then caught his balance as he gasped and sputtered. He was strong, but his knees were giving out.

Good! Gritting her teeth, she wound the rope around her fingers and yanked even tighter. Both his hands were on the noose, scraping and pulling. He rocked to and fro, his legs wobbling.

That's it, you sick whack job. Die! Take your last damned breath.

Wobbling, he sank to his knees.

Still, she clung to the rope as his throat rattled, a hiss of air still escaping. *Damn it!* With all her strength, she wrenched the cord so hard she was certain the bones in her hands would break. She didn't care. "Chloe!" she yelled. "Get yourself free."

More wailing.

Sometimes her twin was such a wimp!

"Pull yourself together! The scissors. Cut yourself free! Come on, Chloe! Do it! Do it now!" She was barking orders as the big man teetered on his knees. "Die you son of a bitch," she growled into his ear as gravity dragged him to the ground. "Just frickin' die!"

As he slumped to the floor, pinning her leg, she didn't

let go, wasn't about to take any chances. Still holding tight to the cord, she searched the gloom and ignored the pain screaming up her thigh. Damn it all to hell, he was a heavy bastard.

With difficulty, she unwrapped the cord from one hand, then in the gloom, gripped both ends with the other. Slapping and sweeping the floor with her free arm, she frantically searched a weapon.

When he moaned, she tugged the rope again, but her strength was nearly zapped. Chloe was still whimpering in a far corner. Shit! As usual, Zoe had to do everything. Scrabbling wildly with her free hand, she hit something sharp. Metal. The scissors!

She slid backward and kicked at the beast of a man with her free foot to roll him off her leg. Finally, she let go of the cord around his neck. Then she curled her bloody fingers through the eye ring of the scissors, turned, and with all her might, stabbed him in the throat. The blades went deep into the soft tissue, right into the welt created by the cord.

Chloe screamed.

Zoe wasn't finished. With an effort she pulled at the eye rings of the scissors and forced the blades open, trying to slice whatever tissue she could. Then, she slammed the scissors shut again.

The beast roared over a sickening slurp of blood and muscle and tendon. Zoe hoped to high heaven that she'd severed something important—the carotid, his jugular, his spine. The ensuing sucking sound curdled her blood, but she couldn't think about it. She only hoped the bastard bled out quickly, for both their sakes.

Zoe crawled across the floor toward the sound of her sister and found Chloe naked, bound, and trembling against a wall. Her eyes were wide, her breathing shallow and rapid.

"Oh, God, oh, God, oh, God," Chloe babbled, quivering and pale. "You killed him."

"I hope so."

Chloe started crying.

"Pull yourself together!" Zoe ordered and started cutting her sister's hands free with the scissors. Her fingers cramped and she, too, was shaking, but she forced the bloody blades open and closed, then sawed with them as Chloe stared in horror. "Come on, come on," Zoe ordered herself, and shot a glance at the motionless blob that was their abductor. The cords were tough, and part of her longed to crumple into a pile like her sister, but adrenaline and fear spurred her on.

And Chloe was no help at all. "I can't, I can't, I can't," she chanted, her eyes wild and teary. "Oh, no . . . no, no!" She began to pant, gasping for breath.

"Shit." Zoe winced, working one prong of the scissors into the coils of a fat knot.

The cord over Chloe's wrists weakened and finally gave. "Come on, help me with your ankles," Zoe ordered, but Chloe was shivering and wild-eyed, panting and damned useless.

"Chloe!" Zoe gave her twin a sharp shake, then worked at the ropes around her twin's ankles. "Come on. We have to get out of here. Now!"

"No. Oh, God. He . . . he!" She was staring petrified over Zoe's shoulder, and for a split second Zoe thought the freak had awakened and was dragging himself up to pounce again. A quick look confirmed he was still unmoving. Hopefully dead.

Still, her twin was frozen in place. "I . . . I can't . . . he . . ."

"Stop it!" Zoe ordered.

"I . . . I . . . I can't." Chloe sobbed, staring at the naked man prone on the floor, blood still pumping in a dark pool blooming around his body. "I—"

Slap! Zoe swatted her twin on the cheek.

"Ow!"

"You can and you will," Zoe insisted, finally untying the rope around Chloe's ankles.

As Chloe started unwinding the cord from her neck and kicking her feet free, Zoe spied a ladder propped upward, extending through a hole in the ceiling.

Zoe pulled Chloe to her feet. "Come on, let's go!" Even in the garish half-light she could see a red welt rising on her sister's cheek. Zoe didn't have time to care. Served the ninny right. Propelling her sister toward the ladder, she took one last look at the freak still bleeding out. "Get going!" she commanded. "Up!"

"Geez, you didn't have to hit me." Chloe was rubbing the red spot above her jaw.

"Yeah, I did. Now! Up, damn it. Climb!" What was wrong with her twin?

With maddening slowness, Chloe began the climb up the teetering ladder. *Come on, come on, come on!* Zoe mentally urged, right on her sister's heels. Impatient, she pushed her upward on the unsteady rungs. As Chloe reached the top, the great unknown, Zoe heard a pained groan come from behind them, an ugly noise rising from the shadows.

Her heart sank.

The freak wasn't dead.

CHAPTER 3

"What's wrong?" Olivia's voice was a balm, always had been. Soft and sensual, with a bit of a Southern drawl. Sexy as hell.

Bentz sat on the edge of their bed, felt the mattress beneath the thin quilt sag. He'd tried to enter the bedroom quietly so as not to disturb her, but of course that had been impossible. "A case."

"Father John." Not a question.

"Yeah."

Sighing, she rolled over and hit the bedside lamp. In the soft illumination he saw the concern in her large eyes, the dusting of freckles over her nose. "Want to talk about it?" Yawning, she swept a few blond curls from her face.

"Nah."

"You never do."

He chuckled, leaned over, and brushed a kiss across her cheek. God, she was beautiful.

"You've had a beer?" No judgment. Just a question asked as she pulled herself onto her elbows and cocked her head to one side.

"Or two."

"So the case is really bad."

"I hate that bastard."

"I know. We all do." She was wearing an oversized T-shirt but was still incredibly feminine.

He chuckled at her pout, unbuttoned his dress shirt, peeled it off, and became serious again. "This guy, a fake priest of all things. I thought he was dead. I mean . . ." He pulled his T-shirt over his head and yanked off his pants. "What the hell? Couldn't he have had the decency to die in that damned swamp?" Angrily, he balled the dirty shirt. "I mean, all of my cases are bad. You know that. Hell, I work homicide. But some of them, some of the killers, like this one, make it personal."

"You'll get him," she said, smiling up at him in the shadowed room with its gauzy curtains, huge bed, and coved ceilings. "You always do."

"I thought I already had," he muttered, tossing his shirt into a darkened corner where a hamper stood near the closet. He missed, of course, the T catching on the side of the hamper. Not that he cared. He thought of all the cases that he hadn't closed, the killers who'd gotten away. There were several where he'd known who the criminal was but hadn't been able to gather enough evidence to put the bastard away. And there were a few where a criminal was convicted, the case against him sufficient, but still Bentz had wondered if the right man had ended up behind bars. Those, thankfully, were not even a handful.

"Hey, can't you forget about it for a few hours?" Olivia said. She'd let one long leg slide from beneath the quilt, and reached up to touch his cheek. With a gleam in her eyes and a lift of one already arched brow, she added, "I'm awake, and the baby's asleep."

He couldn't help the grin that grew from one side of his jaw to the other. "Why, Mrs. Bentz," he asked, "are you trying to seduce me?"

"Never," she said, but dropped the hand from his face, slowly tracing his neck and chest to fall into his crotch. "Uh-oh." Feigned innocence.

Jesus, he loved her.

She let a finger trail between his legs.

His erection, already at half-mast, stiffened.

"You're wicked," he said, and leaned over to kiss her.

"Only for you," she said into his open mouth as he scraped back the blankets with one hand and stretched out beside her. Her arms surrounded his neck and she kissed him with a passion that had been with them since the first time they'd made love. Yes, they'd had their bumps in the road. Their relationship had been far from perfect. But the heat between them, that raw lust and deep yearning, had never faltered. And now, as her hands sculpted his muscles and his blood quickened in his veins, he closed his eyes, lost himself in her, and wished that the lovemaking would never end.

"Come on, hurry!" Zoe said, pushing her sister from that hellhole. The ladder had opened to the stone floor of a small one-room building that was more shed than living space, and she'd had to push her sister up and out. After they had made their way up the metal rungs, Zoe had taken the time to pull the ladder to the ground floor of the darkened shed. If the psycho in his rubber apron somehow had the grit and strength to wake up and try to follow them, he'd be trapped in his own lair.

Fitting, Zoe figured, as she knocked over a chair and tripped while ushering Chloe outside to the darkness of the night.

"What about him?" Chloe asked, her voice tremulous with fear.

"He's dead."

"You killed him?"

"Yes! Move it! "

"Good. Twisted psycho-freak!"

The old door scraped as Zoe tugged it open. Then she led her sister into the dark night. The cabin was dilapidated, ready to topple onto the sparse, weedy clearing around it. A forest surrounding the small patch of ground seemed to block out any light. From here, there were no visible neighbors, no signs of civilization. If only she could hear the hum of traffic on a highway or the clack of a train on tracks or the deep moan of a foghorn on the river. But there was no sound beyond their tattered breathing, the steady patter of rain, and the sough of wind rushing through branches of nearby trees. Then a dog, as if disturbed from slumber, gave a sharp "woof."

"Where are we?" Chloe whimpered, sounding as if she might start crying again.

"Don't know. Come on!" Grabbing her sister's hand, she started running along what seemed to be a path cutting through a dense thicket of trees. The night was warm and wet, rain falling softly, summer in Louisiana evident in the earthy smell and dense vegetation. From somewhere in the distance she thought she sensed the roll of a river, the smell of water.

There was no moonlight. Clouds blocked some of the stars and snuffed out most of the light.

"We . . . we need to call someone," Chloe said as they sprinted.

"Good idea. Got your cell?"

"No, but—" The slumbering dog was now awake and barking wildly.

"Neither do I. Just keep moving."

"But my feet . . ."

"Yeah, I know." Zoe's feet hurt, too. They were running barefoot through the woods, not a stitch on, probably getting bitten all over. Although the lane was now overgrown with tall grass, the gravel long driven into the ground, the twin tire tracks were still visible. Zoe stubbed her toe and bit back a curse. The weedy lane had to lead somewhere, she figured, to a county road or private drive or something. Their only course was to follow its winding path through the looming trees.

Every once in a while she glanced over her shoulder, worried that somehow the freak would escape from his own prison and break free, running them to the ground. *Impossible,* she told herself. *You killed him. You're a murderess.*

"Good."

"What? What's good?" Chloe asked in the darkness, her fingers still clutched in Zoe's hand.

"Nothing."

"Oh." Disappointment. "Shit!" Chloe squealed and ducked as a creature of the night flew by. "Oh, God, was that a bat?"

"Don't know. Don't care."

"An owl. That was it. Tell me it was an owl."

Who cared? "Sure. An owl. Don't worry about it. We've got to find someone to help us."

"We're naked!"

"I know. That's the least of our problems right now." Zoe kept pressing forward, hoping beyond hope that they would find safety and that the abomination who had captured them was dead. Why the hell had the freak kidnapped them? What was he doing at the workbench, cutting up the wire and ribbon? And why did he sing that stupid birthday song? Nothing made any sense. How did he even know it was their birthday? Who the fuck was he? "Come on," she stepped up the pace, her mind racing faster than her bare feet. Obviously they'd been targeted because of their birthdays. He had known. How? Had he been following them? Stalking them?

Happy Birthday, dear twinsies . . . Wasn't that what he'd sung? As if the two of them being twins and sharing a birthday was significant. Holy shit, what was going on? "Hurry, Chloe," she whispered urgently as the forest seemed to close in on them. It was her twenty-first birthday and, for the first time in her life, Zoe Denning personally felt the presence of evil in the world.

Pain screamed through his neck and throat.

An even deeper anguish came from the knowledge that the bitches had escaped.

For the first time ever, he'd lost both victims. He closed his eyes for a second and gathered himself. Willing the fire around his neck to subside, he reached up and felt the blood drying on his throat. He'd been lucky there. That cunt Zoe had tried to kill him with his own damned shears and rope. His lip curled in disgust at his weakness. But he wasn't dead yet.

Wincing, he rolled over and climbed to his feet. His head was clearing at last. A quick survey and he saw the devastation in the basement, the cracked light, the scattered ribbon, the bloody scissors that had been meant to end his life.

He let out a hard growl as rage engulfed him. Didn't they know he was doing them a favor? Taking their lives before they turned into adults? Saving them from the horrors of being separated, wrenched apart?

He'd been careless. Complacent.

And Zoe had gotten the drop on him.

Un-fucking-thinkable.

Blood had crusted down his neck, and he knew he was lucky to be alive, but the fury that consumed him didn't allow him time to give himself a pat on the back. Not when the twins had gotten the better of him, left him for dead and found a way to break free. Fuck. Wait until Myra found out. Shit, he could already hear her taunting him, reminding him of what an idiot he was.

"Son of a bitch!" he roared, but his voice emerged as a whisper, a painful mew. He realized whatever that bitch Zoe had done to him with the rope around his neck and the scissors thrust into his throat was going to keep him from speaking very loudly, at least for a while. Not that it mattered, but it pissed him off.

Furious, his blood pumping, he pounded a heavy fist on his worktable.

She'd get hers.

He'd see to it.

He had to get them. Chase them down. Bring them back. Finish his work. He checked the clock. There was still time.

But a headache pounded behind his eyes and his throat felt as if all the demons in hell were gnawing at his flesh, chewing on him from the inside out. With difficulty, he staggered for the ladder and found it missing. "Goddamn it!" he hissed, then closed his mouth as pain exploded in his neck. With difficulty he peered upward and saw the foot of the ladder visible in the open door of the crawlspace.

How had he let down his guard, letting them escape?

Despite his wounds, he found the stool near his workbench and placed it under the opening in the ceiling. Standing on the stool, he reached up, took aim, and swung his belt over the protruding leg of the ladder. Eventually he was able to hook the buckle over the bottom rung. Slowly he pulled, but the belt slipped, fell back, the clasp nearly hitting him in the face.

"Shit!"

Again he swung the belt upward and hooked it. This time the connection was more secure. He tugged. The ladder moved. Gently, he pulled, forcing the ladder to the opening and levering it through. One final tug and gravity took care of the rest; the ladder slipped down to him. He secured the feet and a second later he was clambering up and checking the small cabin for signs of the twins. Nothing.

Outside the darkness was thick, no moon glow or starlight. A misting rain filled the air. He closed his eyes and strained to listen to the sounds of the night. Over the pounding of his own damned heartbeat he heard a hoot of an owl and the steady croak of a bull-

frog and the rush of wind through the trees. But no
frantic footsteps. No hushed voices. Nothing to indicate the twins were nearby.

Fuck!

Frustration burned through him with a savage heat,
and even though he was stripped bare, wearing only the
damned apron, he began to sweat. Had he lost them?
The twin girls who could ID him? His teeth ground together as he searched the darkness. They couldn't be
far. He hadn't passed out for that long, less than fifteen
minutes, and they were both naked and on foot.

He didn't think twice as he rounded the shed where
his dog was going ape-shit, barking and howling loud
enough to raise the dead. For a second, he thought
about releasing Red, but he didn't want to take the time
and his van would be so much faster. He reached into a
deep pocket of his apron and found his keys. There was
only one way out of this place, and the lane was long.

"Hurry!" Zoe stage whispered, still yanking on her
twin's hand. The rain was coming down harder now,
fast and furious, so loud that she could barely make out
the rush of the river. The sudden noise of a dog barking
wildly in the distance alerted her senses. "Come on."
She couldn't get away from that horrid cabin fast
enough. Sure she'd left their captor bleeding out, probably dead already, but the all-consuming fear that they
somehow wouldn't escape kept her racing on the uneven track.

"Ow! Shit!" Chloe stumbled and let out a groan.

"What?"

"I think I cut my foot. Goddamned rock."

Too bad. "You'll be all right." Zoe kept pulling on her sister, forcing her to run.

"I . . . I don't know." Chloe's whiney tone was back. "How did this happen?" she demanded, breathing hard. "Who was that psycho? What did he want from us?"

"Who knows? As you said he's a psycho." But whatever his sick plans were, they included their birthdays.

"Jesus, he was going to kill us, Zoe. I know it!"

"Just keep going," Zoe said, tugging her sister along as a new noise cut through the night. A rumble of sorts. "Wait!" She skidded to a stop, wet grass and gravel sliding beneath her feet.

"What? But I thought—"

"Shhh!" Over Chloe's complaints and her own breathing, Zoe thought she heard the sound of a motor, a car's engine. Trying desperately to locate the direction, she closed her eyes, straining to listen. "You hear that?"

"What?"

"A damned car or truck or—oh, shit! Maybe it's him!"

"What? No, I thought you killed him."

"I thought I did, too."

"Where is the car?" Chloe looked over her shoulder, one way and then the other. Even in the dark night Zoe saw the wide whites of her sister's eyes, felt her fear. "I don't see anything. No headlights, no—"

"Just run!" Zoe yanked hard on her sister's hand. They had to leave the road. Zoe couldn't believe the freak could have survived her attack, but maybe he had an accomplice. Chloe was right, no headlights shined in the wet night, but the uneven growl of an engine bore down on them, and it was coming from the direction of the cabin. "Come on!" Zoe tore through the dark woods, dragging her sister with her. From the way Chloe lagged behind it was clear that Zoe had always been more athletic, while Chloe more of a student. Tonight it didn't matter. Chloe was going to have to dig deep and push herself if they were going to escape this living nightmare.

Panic reigned as the sound of the vehicle's engine came nearer. Oh, God, please let him drive past. Let him think we're long gone. Maybe they should hide, just stop and use the cover of darkness as their cloak, but that seemed like inviting danger. No doubt he had a flashlight or lantern and some kind of a weapon. A gun or machete or whatever.

Run, run, RUN!

Dragging her sister, Zoe veered off the road, over a berm of weeds and grass. Finally the rain was letting up a little, clouds moving, a bit of moonlight offering some visibility.

"We should've listened to Mom," Chloe said as they stumbled and raced to the edge of the woods. "We should've gone to her apartment."

Shoulda, woulda, coulda.

"Then this dickwad wouldn't have found us." Chloe was breathing hard, panting.

"Too late."

"Or I should never have broken up with Tommy. If he were here, he would know what to do—"

"Tommy's a prick and we don't have time for this!" Why the hell was Chloe thinking about her ex-boyfriend now?

"But he loves me!"

"Oh, for crap's sake, just hurry!" Together they scrambled through the undergrowth. Thorns pricked, nettles stung, the sharp edges of pinecones cut into their feet as they hurtled blindly through the trees. Chloe thought she heard and smelled water ahead, maybe a creek or river or—

Thunk!

"Ow! Shit!" Chloe yelped, her hand sliding from Zoe's as she fell. "Damn it all to hell."

"Shh!" Zoe ordered, sliding to a stop and turning back toward her sister. The hairs on the back of her neck prickled and she whipped around. Was there someone else here? Suddenly she felt dozens of pairs of unseen eyes watching her. Which was crazy. No way. She took a few steps toward the sound of running water. Aside from the lunatic she'd left in the cabin and whoever was driving the car, they were alone . . . right?

Craaack.

A twig snapped.

Zoe spun quickly, searching the darkness. "Chloe?" she whispered.

No answer.

"Chloe!" Which way was her sister? She had to be nearby. "Where the hell are you?" Her voice was a raspy whisper as she squinted into the shadows. "Chloe?"

"Over here!" Her sister shouted from the suddenly quiet copse. But her voice came from a few yards off, as if she were moving away from Zoe.

"Where are you?" Zoe whispered.

"Here!"

The engine had quit running and now . . . Oh, God, Zoe saw the sweep of a flashlight's beam flickering through the foliage. How the hell had he found them? *It's not the freak. He's dead. You killed him. You had to have killed him. He couldn't have survived.*

"Maybe it's help," Chloe ventured.

"No!" Zoe wasn't convinced. "We've got to get out of here," she shrieked, her arm scrabbling in the air, searching in the direction from which she thought she'd heard Chloe's voice. "Run!"

"Don't leave me!" Chloe cried.

Zoe turned and plunged into the dense growth, racing toward the sound of her sister's voice. A few steps in her legs met the resistance of something heavy and cold. By the time she realized it was a fallen log, she was going down.

Crap! She tumbled down, rolling to a stop against a stump. "Oooph!" Sharp pain splintered through her ankle.

"Zoe!" Chloe cried as the beam of the flashlight strobed through the trees, searching.

No!

They were seconds away from being discovered, and Zoe couldn't let the searcher find her twin. No way! Zoe stood a chance against whoever was hunting them down, but she had to think fast to save her sister. Forcing herself back onto her feet, she tried to keep weight off her tender ankle as she waved and yelled and screamed to divert the hunter's attention from Chloe. "Hey!" she shouted at the beam of light. It moved quickly, bouncing as if whoever was holding it was running. "Hey! Over here!"

But the light didn't swing in her direction. Instead, it veered over into the brush many yards from her, toward her sister. Horrified, Zoe watched the watery beam shift and circle, homing in.

Suddenly the beam landed on Chloe. Cowering and ghostly in the light, she seemed rooted to the spot, frozen in fear.

"Chloe, run!" Zoe screamed as she struggled to see the hunter in the thin moonlight. It was a big, hulking form. The hairy man in an apron. The monster was alive! Somehow he'd survived!

Sick inside, she screamed at the top of her lungs for her sister to get on her feet and escape. "Go! Run!"

But it was too late. In the next instant the freak pounced on his prey, springing with the agility of a lion.

Chloe let out a shriek as the light cut out.

Oh, God!

"There's still time!" he growled, his voice a gravelly whisper in the damp night.

Instinctively, Zoe had lurched toward her sister, but now, trapped in the muddy darkness, she froze. She'd lost her bearings! She stared into the night, willing her eyes to focus in the moonlight. As her eyes adjusted she saw him hovering over her shocked twin. It looked as if he were striking her again and again, but as her focus sharpened Zoe realized he was tying Chloe up. The beast was subduing her, trapping her, just as a spider traps its prey . . . for later.

Zoe sank onto the wet ground, her fingers scrabbling over the earth and mud, searching for a weapon—a rock, a stick, anything. What had he said? *There's still time?* As if there were a deadline. Her fingertips located a root, but she couldn't dislodge it. Damn it, there had to be some stone or . . . nothing!

"Help!" Chloe cried, and Zoe sprang to her feet only to feel an excruciating pain skitter up her leg. Jesus!

"Zoe! I can't—"

And then Chloe's voice cut off, as if she'd been gagged.

"Let's go," he croaked.

"No!" Zoe screamed, hobbling toward them. Terror rushed through her as she watched him haul her sister to his shoulder and begin walking toward the road. "I'll be back," he growled in that horrid voice. "Don't worry. The party won't start without you."

Zoe took a step forward, intent on chasing him down, on somehow maiming him and saving Chloe. After all, she'd done it before, but his chilling words echoed through her brain.

The party won't start without you.

The party?

And then she knew for certain that this was all about timing—about their mutual birthday. Whatever his twisted plan was, it involved both sisters, not just one, otherwise he wouldn't have taken the time or chance to kidnap them both. The bastard needed both of them to do his sick work, and that gave Zoe some power. The only way to save Chloe was to save herself first.

With a sick feeling in the pit of her stomach, Zoe pressed into the forest. The pain in her ankle was crippling and her chances of outrunning him were nil, but she had to try to escape and lure him away from Chloe. She had to make sure the clock kept ticking. Then she'd double back and save her sister. There wasn't much time, but this, she felt, was her only option.

As she ran, she heard him give chase.

She had a head start because he'd taken the time to

put Chloe into his vehicle. Dear God, if Chloe had the brains and the ability, maybe she could drive away and get help! But those thoughts were futile. Chloe was too passive, too introverted, too damned weak to help herself. Chloe was the classic victim. *That's why it's up to me to save her,* Zoe thought as she hobbled through the dark woods.

Closer he came, crashing through the underbrush.

Oh, Jesus!

He was gaining on her!

Over the rush of water and the rasp of her own ragged breathing she heard the pounding of his footsteps, snapping twigs as he rushed forward.

Her heart froze.

Keep moving. Just keep running.

Lunging forward, she brushed branches from her face. Thorns scratched against her bare legs, but she kept moving, plunging through the darkness. Her heart was beating frantically, pulsing in her ears when she heard his breath coming in hard, fast gasps.

So near!

So damned close.

Even though her twin was tied up, she hoped Chloe was using this distraction to try and escape.

Hurry, hurry, hurry!

"It's no use, bitch," he said, his voice so close to her she flinched. Oh, God, he was right behind her! Adrenalin spurred her legs faster just as she felt fingernails swipe over her bare shoulder and fall away. "I've got you!" His foul stench told her that he was close, inches away. He took another swipe at her, this time grabbing her arm. Zoe leaped, trying to break free of the pincer of his grip. Her shoulder wrenched as she yanked her arm back and his moist hand, sweaty and probably bloody, slipped away.

"Shit!"

The force of evading him sent her airborne. She landed hard, and her ankle gave way. Letting out a groan, she began to roll down a steep hill, her body bumping and sliding over mud and leaves. Picking up speed, she kept traveling down, down . . . away from him. She surrendered to the momentum and let herself tumble like a stone.

Above it all, somewhere beyond her violent descent, she heard the far-off rev of an engine.

Chloe? Oh, God, please. Let her save herself.

Splash!

Zoe slid into the water.

"What the fuck?" the freak cried from the top of the embankment. "Shit!"

As she felt the current tug her downstream, she silently prayed that her twin would get away.

CHAPTER 4

"It's happening. It's happening again!"
Arianna's voice came from the mist. A whisper.
Please, no. "Where are you?" Brianna demanded.
She stood in a dark thicket cloaked by rising fog. Although unable to see into the darkness, she knew her twin was nearby. She could feel it. "Arianna?"

"Help them."

"Help who?"

"The others."

"I don't know who you mean."

"The ones like us, silly. Help them," Arianna said, and in that moment Brianna found herself alone in a desert under a broad blue sky and parching bald sun. Cacti stood guard over acres and acres of sand. "Arianna?" Brianna said again. The only answer was the rush of wind and the cry of vultures circling overhead. When she looked down at the ground she saw them: two bodies curled in fetal positions, mirror images facing each other. Pushed by the gusting wind, sand scattered away from their bones: hollow-eyed skulls with *long teeth and empty nasal cavities, rounded, exposed ribs, and knobby vertebrae bleached by the intense sun.*

With a sickening spasm, Brianna understood that she was staring at what remained of the missing twin brothers, Garrett and Gavin Reeves, both originally from Phoenix. She had to call the police, to alert the authorities that she had found them, but before she could make a move, one of the skulls twisted on its chalky vertebrae to stare at her. "End this," it hissed over the rumble of the wind.

"What?"

"End this, or there will be others." The wind was picking up, growling over the flat landscape, whipping up sand as it moved. "Their blood will be on your hands."

"I don't understand."

"Oh, you know, Brianna." The skeleton raised a bony hand to stroke the unmoving skull of its twin. "You know." The wind roared as a sandstorm arose and swept over the area. As Brianna watched helplessly, the second set of bones was blown from the gravesite and scattered over the desert plain, leaving the remaining skeleton intact and untouched and very much alone.

Overhead, the vultures circled again, screeching loudly.

Brianna's eyes flew open. For a second she was disoriented and blinking in the darkness. The dream, so vivid and real, receded as her cell phone rang again. Automatically she reached onto the nightstand where her phone glowed dimly as it jangled again. Tanisha

Lefevre's photograph and number appeared on the screen.

Tanisha was a friend whom she'd met through the support group Brianna managed, a group for people who were struggling with the loss of their twin siblings. "Twinless twins," some called them. Tanisha had been one of the first members to join. As Brianna reached for the still-ringing phone, she had to push St. Ives, her overweight cat, off the pillow. No doubt his purring had been the source of the rumbling in her dreams.

"Hello?" she answered, blinking and trying to shove aside the disturbing images from her nightmare. "Tanisha? Are you okay?"

"No," was the quick answer. "Not really and I, uh, I know it's late."

Brianna glanced at the clock. Nearly two a.m. "Real late."

"Yeah, yeah, I said I know. But I couldn't sleep, kept having weird dreams about Allacia. I'm sorry, but I had to talk to someone."

"No problem," Brianna said, scooting up in the bed and propping a pillow behind her. She flipped on the bedside lamp while St. Ives hopped down and padded over to the glass door overlooking the patio of her small house. "What happened?"

"It's just that I've had this weird vibe tonight, like it was happening all over again. You know, the separation thing." Before Brianna could say a word she launched into her story. "Allacia and I, we were teenagers, but we weren't living with Mom and Dad. We were on our own and we went on a double date or something, I can't remember all the details. Anyway, Allacia she gets mad at her date and takes off. I didn't want to leave my date, but I chased after my sister and she slipped out of sight. Disappeared. Bam. I couldn't find her. Then it all mixed up and I was in college, but I kept seeing her. She was like texting me all the time, asking me to meet her and I'd go, but she'd never show. In between the dreams I'd wake up, calm down, then go back to sleep and dream about her all over again. Y'know, it's kinda freaky. Like somethin's happening."

Tanisha believed that in the universe of twins, there was an invisible aura connecting them. She thought that a traumatic event experienced by one twin could also be felt by the other. Tanisha also claimed to be sensitive to the pain of other twins she had met. Brianna found Tanisha's beliefs to be more than a little extreme, but hey, hadn't she, too, had a weird nightmare about her own twin tonight?

"What do you think is happening?" asked Brianna.

"Separation," Tanisha said decisively.

"To whom?"

"I'm not sure. Just close twins."

"Someone you know?"

"No . . . well, maybe. Someone I know of. Look, I know you think I'm a little out there with all this twin stuff, but trust me, it's true. I can't tell you what's going on with twins in Berlin or Moscow or Capetown, or even here in New Orleans if I don't know them or of them, but if I do, I just feel some strange vibe."

"If they're separated."

"Yeah, oh yeah. I mean, it's not like I can read their thoughts or any strange stuff like that. And complete strangers? Forget it. But if there's some thread linking me to them, no matter how thin, I'm tellin' you, I get this weird feeling, kinda like a spider crawling up your bare back, y'know? And then I can't sleep and I end up calling you in the middle of the damned night."

"It's fine," Brianna assured her as St. Ives began batting on the door wanting to go wandering in the night. "Anytime." She considered admitting that she, too, had dreamt about her own sister, but decided against it. She dreamed so often about Arianna, Brianna didn't think tonight's dream was significant.

"Thanks. I guess I just had to get it off my chest, and I'm not sure I want to share it with the group tomorrow."

"That's what group is for."

"I know, I know, but . . . well, maybe. Depends on who's there, I guess, and the whole discussion." With a sigh, she said, "Look, I'd better go. I have an *early* wakeup call in the morning. I'll see you tomorrow." She groaned. "Well, technically later today." She hung up, leaving Brianna telling herself that her dream had nothing to do with Tanisha's.

Twins thought about each other often, and even if one moved away or died or disappeared, the remaining twin could be consumed with memories, dreams, even the need to converse with the missing person. Not all twins were close, but Brianna believed that all twins had a deep connection, one that went beyond the simple genetic link of biological siblings. "Or maybe you're just kidding yourself," she said aloud as she threw off the covers and walked to the door. She opened it a crack and let the cat slip through.

A gust of summer wind blew into the room, ruffling the curtains and carrying the sweet scent of magnolia. Brianna stepped outside and watched St. Ives slither through the bushes lining the enclosed patio with its uneven stone floor and broken fountain. The breeze stirred leaves in the magnolia tree and she heard a distant siren piercing the night, far beyond the walls of her private garden. She shivered as she scanned the perimeter of the small, enclosed veranda. There weren't many hiding spots, no little nooks and crannies where someone could hide, and still she felt a prickle of dread, her skin pimpling.

No one's out here. Get over yourself. There's no maniac in the shadows, no killer on the prowl in your garden, no damned monster in the closet.

But she couldn't shake the feeling. Ever.

Since Arianna had died, Brianna had never felt truly safe, never truly whole.

Swallowing back her fear, she noticed the gate to the garage was latched; the bolt on the inside was in place, locking it to the concrete. Good. Taking a few deep breaths, she felt a little calmer. "Come on inside," she called to the cat, who blatantly ignored her and went about his nocturnal hunting. "Okay. Fine. Suit yourself. You've got five minutes. Hear me? Five." She actually raised her hand and spread her fingers in the tabby's direction, then told herself she was genuinely nuts for thinking the cat understood vocal commands or her gesture or the concept of time. Feeling foolish, she went back to bed and stared up at the ceiling. The door remained cracked, a stick propped to keep it open wide enough for the cat to slip through. As she lay staring up at the ceiling, she wondered about Tanisha's dreams of separation and how they related to her own nightmare.

"Just a coincidence," she said aloud, and glanced at the picture she kept on her night table. Picking up the silver frame, she studied the snapshot taken nearly thirty years before of identical twin girls, toddlers in shorts and matching T-shirts. Their arms were flung around each other as they stood at the prow of a fishing boat, the sea and sky sparking behind them. Brianna traced her finger along the small face of her identical sibling and her heart cracked a little. Arianna had been gone for so long, and yet she still missed her intensely. Especially on nights like this.

And though she was loathe to admit it, Brianna did believe there was something to Tanisha's feelings about disturbances in the twin universe. Hadn't she, too, experienced the pain of separation? And to be honest, she had to admit that separation played a part in her dream, in which one twin's bones had scattered away through the desert.

She thought about the two skeletons she'd seen in her nightmare, how she'd known they belonged to the missing Reeves brothers. She had no idea how she knew that fact; she simply did.

Worse yet, deep in her heart, she knew more. She knew that he was out there, and he had made another move. She squeezed her eyes shut against the knowledge that filled her with dread: the 21 Killer had struck yet again.

Exhausted, Zoe swam with the current, faster and faster, trying to put as much space between her and the freak as she could. Chloe had escaped, she felt sure of that. So in the chilly water Zoe bolstered her own spirits by telling herself that her sister was okay. Now it was her turn to find safety.

Any normal person would give up chase at this point, but Zoe couldn't be certain how the freak would act. So she let the current carry her on farther downstream all the while trying not to think of the alligators that lived in these murky waters. It would be awful to have escaped the naked pervert only to become gator bait.

Don't go there.

Don't freak out.

You've come this far, just keep going!

When she considered her ordeal, she felt safer facing gators than him. To think that she and Chloe has actually been kidnapped and stripped naked and held by a madman for some bizarre birthday ritual . . . it was crazy. But they'd thwarted him. Well, at least for now. Since she and Chloe could identify the psycho, he would probably keep hunting them down.

No, the ordeal was far from over.

She'd never make it; not without rest. A cold-blooded chill pervaded her body and every muscle ached. She fantasized about a warm bath, her own bed. As she rounded a bend in the river, she spied lights in the distance. Hope glimmered in those lights—a town on the shores of the river. There, she hoped, she would find a Good Samaritan to call the police. She would tell the authorities what had happened to her, reconnect with Chloe, and hopefully end this madness. She headed toward civilization. She hoped.

Oh, God, please, she silently prayed as she felt something slithery and wet slide through her legs.

For the love of Mary. She brushed at the object, kicked away from it, and tried to maintain a steady stroke in the water. Her ankle was throbbing, her muscles beginning to weaken, but she kept swimming, putting distance between herself and the freak's lair as she eased closer to the town.

Just a few more strokes.

She stretched her arm forward and felt something slimy and wet just before the heavy object struck her head.

Bam!

Pain slammed through her brain.

She slid under the surface as a fat, rough log rolled over her, threatening to pin her down.

Frantically she thrashed in the darkness.

The air in her lungs came out in streams of bubbles as she shielded her head and pushed away from the log. She managed to free herself, but which way was up? She needed air. She gasped, taking in river water as she tried to surface.

Her lungs recoiled and she shot upward, barely missing the heavy log again.

Fight, Zoe, fight!

Sputtering and coughing, she tried to expel the water in her lungs as she gasped for air.

The world spun.

She didn't know up from down, night sky from inky black water.

Instinctively she reached forward. Her fingers collided with a narrow end of the log and she grabbed on, wildly clutching a fork in the limb. This could be her raft, her lifesaver. She hung on, letting it pull her downstream. She blinked and coughed, aware of her vulnerability in the black river. She knew it would be easier to just let go, to let the river and the night swallow her.

Don't!

Surrender was seductive, but she couldn't allow herself to let go now. So she hung on, clinging to the log and the hope of life, battling to keep unconsciousness at bay, all the time praying that Chloe had gotten away.

A gate? There was a gate blocking her escape? Chloe couldn't believe it, but the beams of the headlights washed upon the obstacle.

After she'd slipped her hands from his loosely tied bonds and while he was desperate to track down Zoe, Chloe had managed to yank off her gag and take advantage of the keys he'd moronically left in the ignition.

Now there was a gate blocking her escape?

Damn! Chloe couldn't believe her bad luck. She stood on the brakes of the van and climbed out. She had to get away. Had to! It was her only chance. And Zoe, oh, Jesus, what about Zoe? She'd had to fight the urge to stay at the river and find her twin, but Zoe, always the bolder of the two, the planner, the leader, had ordered her to escape. And Chloe was not going to let her sister down. She'd get help, of course she would, and she'd return to the river to rescue her sister, and Zoe would be okay. She was cagey and smart and athletic and . . . Holy shit, why did there have to be a damned gate?

She scrambled out of the van, leaving the driver's door open, the interior light glowing, the damned seat belt alarm dinging. Her headlights were trained on the aluminum slats of the gate, where she fumbled with the padlocked latch. A damned padlock.

Really? He'd locked them in? Now what? Think, Chloe, think!

With all her strength she yanked on the lock.

Nothing.

Again, she threw her weight against it and again she failed. Well, of course. What lock would give way to a girl?

But maybe he had a tool in the van, a hacksaw or . . . or a key! Maybe there was a key on the ring that held the van's ignition. She ran back to the van and thought she heard something in the trees. Twigs breaking. An animal on the prowl? Or could it be him?

No!

Leaping onto the driver's seat, she fumbled for the keys, found that only a single key was attached to the ring. "Shit!" Quickly she searched around the front seat, the glove box, and the console, looking for another set of keys or a saw or—

A quick glance in the rearview mirror. Beyond her own image, she saw him. Huge. Naked. Covered in blood and dirt. Dark hair plastered to his head.

Hell! She didn't think twice but pulled the driver's door closed, slapped on the automatic locks, threw the van into Drive, and hit the gas. Wheels spun, spitting dirt and gravel. The Dodge hurtled forward and crashed into the gate. With a groan the aluminum twisted and bent, but didn't give. Damn!

Chloe rammed the van into Reverse and, spying the man running forward, didn't hesitate. "Die, fucker!" she said through gritted teeth, and punched it. The van's engine roared, the huge vehicle streaking backward.

Thunk!

Oh, God, she actually hit him!

Too bad.

Or not.

Her stomach revolted and she fought the urge to gag. She had to hold it together now. Throwing the gearshift lever into Drive, she punched it, hoping there was enough distance for the acceleration necessary to break through the gate. Tires whirred as the Dodge spurted forward, hitting the gate and stopping so quickly Chloe was thrown against the steering wheel. "Ooof!" She caught her breath. Had to keep moving. "Come on, come on," she moaned through her pain, and tromped on the accelerator again.

Whining, the tires dug deep into the lane.

Thunk! That same awful sound she'd heard before when she'd run over the bastard. But the van wasn't moving. No matter how hard she stepped on the gas. Frantic, she rammed the Dodge into Reverse again to take another run at the gate.

Thunk!

What?

Crash!

The passenger door window shattered.

Glass sprayed.

A beefy hand shot through.

Chloe screamed.

The door flew open.

The huge whack job stood in the frail light cast by an interior lamp.

Clutched in one of his massive hands was a heavy stick, most likely the branch he'd used to thump against the van.

"No!" Terrified, she scrabbled for the door lock. She had to get out. To run!

Cowering against the driver's door, she tried to find the handle, but the evil smile that crawled over his bruised and bloodied face petrified her. He knew she couldn't escape.

A weak, mewling sound slipped from her throat.

He yanked the keys from the ignition and opened the glove box.

Her fingers found the door handle.

She pulled.

Her door gave way, but as she dove to the left to escape the van something closed over her arm. He had grabbed her with one meaty hand.

"Not so fast," he muttered against her ear as she fought, flailing and clawing at him. She tried to wrench free, but the sound of a metal click matched the manacle he was tightening over on her wrist.

Handcuffs. He'd taken them from the glove box.

Before she could react he yanked her over his lap and twisted her arms behind her. Over her own cries, she heard the horrifying click of the second cuff locking, and she knew it was over.

He would never let down his guard again.

She was as good as dead.

CHAPTER 5

After a fitful night's sleep, Brianna showered, then scraped her curly hair into a loose dark knot before throwing on yesterday's faded jeans and her favorite cotton T. While St. Ives preened himself, she went to the kitchen to make coffee and clean a few dishes that seemed to have multiplied on their own in her sink.

Last night's dreams still lingered with their disturbing images, but in the predawn hours she had convinced herself that her dreams were hers to own, period. It was silly to think that skeletons in the desert had any connection to Tanisha's nightmares. "It's all just some weird cosmic coincidence," she muttered as the doorbell pealed.

She glanced at the clock on her stove.

The sun wasn't even up yet.

No one stopped by this early.

Wiping her hands, she made her way to the front door, peered through one of the sidelights, and spied Selma Denning on the front stoop. Selma stood in a cloud of smoke, pulling hard on a cigarette.

Brianna felt a chill deep inside. Selma had given up

smoking years ago, and it wasn't like her to drop by so early in the morning. Pale as death, her graying hair pulled back into a sloppy ponytail, Selma looked unkempt and stark under the porch light. Dawn was breaking, fingers of gray light crawling through the city streets, chasing away the shadows, but from the looks of Selma's rumpled shorts, T-shirt, and cardigan sweater, Brianna suspected that she hadn't slept a wink.

As Brianna unlocked and opened the door, Selma quickly squashed her cigarette.

"Selma?"

"It's the twins," Selma said before Brianna could ask any questions. "Zoe and Chloe. They're . . . they're missing!" Her face was twisted in pain, her eyes red behind her rimless glasses.

Brianna held the front door open. "Come in, come in . . . please. And start over at the beginning."

"It was their birthday. I mean, it *is* their birthday and oh, God." Selma didn't budge from her spot on the porch as her eyes filled with tears. She dropped her face into her hands and hiccuped a sob. "I know it hasn't been all that long, but I just know something has gone wrong. I can feel it in my bones, you know?"

Brianna nodded. Although she wasn't a mother, she did understand the invisible connections between people. Now Tanisha's call and her own dreams of a disturbance, a separation in the universe, took on a new significance. The soft ping of alarm deep inside her began to swell.

"Something's happened. Oh, God." Selma clamped a bony hand over her mouth for a second, then let it fall. "You don't think . . . I mean, it's impossible that the two of them together were . . . *kidnapped*." Her voice trailed off as she considered the horrible possibility.

Brianna's heart turned stone cold. "I don't know what to think," she said, half-lying. "But come in, come in." She waved Selma inside and stepped out of the doorway, casting a quick glance to the still-dark street. Saw nothing out of the ordinary. She pulled the door firmly shut. "Let's go into the kitchen."

Sensing the dread in her new companion, Brianna ushered Selma past the living area to the back of the house where a pot of coffee was brewing, the last of the water gurgling through the grounds. St. Ives was stretched out on a rug near the French doors, which gave the tabby a view of the backyard. Brianna imagined the cat looking forward to the day's activity in the yard, where birds would flit across the stone paths and splash in the fountain, and squirrels would tease from the twisted branches of the live oak trees that shaded a small café table. Such a simple life.

"Coffee?" Brianna offered, opening a cupboard and scrounging inside to locate a cup that wasn't chipped. "Black, right?"

"Yes, that's . . . that'll be fine." Selma struggled against tears as she dropped onto a barstool at the counter.

"So why don't you start over? At the beginning." Ignoring the icy feeling seeping through her blood, she tried to convince herself that this was just a coincidence. That was all. Of course Selma's twin daughters were fine. Right?

"As I said, today is their birthday." Selma's voice was a dry whisper. "Their twenty-first."

Oh, God.

That was why the fear in Selma's pale eyes was so real, so visceral.

Brianna tried to keep calm. "Just because they were turning—"

"Don't!" Selma ordered, her voice surprisingly fierce, her blue eyes sparking. "Just don't . . . don't patronize me. Okay?" She sniffed and ran the back of her hand under her nose. "We've been friends too long for that."

Fair enough. "Okay."

"Good. We both know what this could mean." Her chin wobbled and she closed her eyes. "You, especially."

That much was true. They both knew that Brianna had been studying the 21 Killer for years. Dubbed "21" by the press, the killer had terrorized Southern California a few years back. The police had finally arrested Donovan Caldwell, who had been tried and convicted as the killer.

But Brianna didn't believe Caldwell capable of the ritualistic murders, and she feared that 21 was killing again, broadening his hunting ground. But here, in Louisiana? She held her tongue as she poured coffee into two cups. "Let's not go immediately to the worst-case scenario," she said, even as her mind was leaping ahead.

"Didn't you go there? Sweet Mother Mary, they turned twenty-one and I can't find them!" Selma's voice cracked. "And what if . . . what if he's out there? You've worked on this for years, right? You don't believe that monster they call the 21 Killer is Donovan Caldwell. You've said as much."

Brianna couldn't argue the fact. Plenty of people

knew that she had been studying the 21 Killer and pur-
suing the possibility of Donovan Caldwell's innocence.
A psychologist, she'd tried to "look into the mind" of
21, at least from a psychological perspective, based on
any information she had found on the crimes. What
most people did not know was that Donovan was her
cousin. The Caldwells were on her mother's side, a
California branch of the family she had barely known
growing up. However, when she had learned that 21's
first victims were her own cousins, said to be murdered
by their brother, Brianna had felt a personal stake in
the case. Over the years she had followed the develop-
ing details of the murders, investigating as a concerned
family member and twin, and later a psychologist. She
had always tried to hide her family connection to the
murders.

That was about to change. It was time to go public
with her concerns about his imprisonment and what
she now knew. During her last visit to the California
prison, she'd told him that she would take care of
things. She was going to make sure the truth was
known. But her campaign did little to bring Donovan
out of his depression.

"No one will ever believe I didn't do it," he'd said
morosely on the other side of the thick glass in the
prison, the phone pressed to his ear. "It's true, I didn't
like my sisters. I admit it. But I didn't kill them. I didn't!"
For a second there had been fire in his eyes. "And the
others that they think I murdered?" Phone pressed to
his ear, he'd let out a bone-weary sigh. "No way. I didn't
even know them."

"I know. I know. I believe you and I swear, I'll help,"
she'd promised, but the look in his eyes had been that

of a doomed man, one without a sliver of hope. "You just have to be patient."

"I can't. I'm going crazy in here."

"Please, just hang on," she'd said, her heart heavy at the thought of leaving him penned up for God knew how long.

"I don't know if I can," he'd said before the guard had ended their short conversation.

With fierce disappointment, Brianna had left California without any real progress on Donovan's case. The state bureaucracy seemed impenetrable, and the LAPD was not interested in reviewing the case against one of the state's most notorious serial killers.

Now, Brianna chose her words carefully as she handed a cup to Selma. "Yes, I saw Caldwell in prison. I hoped to have his case dismissed, or at least appealed."

"Because you think he's innocent, right? And that means the killer is still out there. What if he's out there and somehow he knew my girls were turning twenty-one and targeted them and . . . oh God! *He* couldn't have found them, right?" Her eyes hardened as she stared at Brianna for reaffirmation.

"It's unlikely that the killer would have come here," Brianna said, though the words seemed a lie. She went to the fridge and pulled out a half-empty carton of milk. "Come on, now. You were going to start at the beginning."

"Yes, right." Selma rubbed her eyes, as if lost for a few seconds. "As I said, it's their birthday, you know, the big one and"—she cleared her throat—"I was hoping to celebrate with them this weekend, but they had other plans. They were going to meet up with friends,

go out on Bourbon Street, and didn't want their mother
tagging along. I get that, and told them we could do the
family thing later. Dinner and drinks out another night,
you know. They seemed cool with that. Of course, I
have no idea if they were going to see their father . . ."
She pulled a face at the mention of Carson Denning,
her ex-husband, then stared into her untouched drink.
"I'm *not* in *that* exclusive circle." There was a bite to
her words.

The Denning divorce had been far from amicable.
Though it had been five years since Carson and Selma's
initial split, Selma wouldn't or couldn't get over it. The
scars, she said, just ran far too deep. Carson's betrayal
had been devastating; no coming back from that. Brianna understood; she knew all about heartache.

Sighing, Selma glanced out the window over the
kitchen sink and focused on a middle distance. Brianna
doubted that her friend noticed the morning light
streaming through the branches of the magnolia tree,
or the birds flitting near the fountain. No, Selma's gaze
was turned inward to her own private hell. Although
Selma had spent years trying to heal from the broken
relationship, she hadn't been particularly successful.
Since Carson's remarriage to his girlfriend of a year
had occurred less than a month after the divorce was
final, Selma had been left reeling. The fact that Carson's girlfriend had been Selma's niece had amplified
Selma's pain and feeling of betrayal. Though Selma
had been in therapy ever since the breakup, she was far
from moving on. Every family event seemed to send
her into a new level of emotional hell.

And now this.

"What happened?" Brianna asked again.

"I wish I knew."

As Brianna took the stool next her, Selma explained how Chloe and Zoe, students at All Saints College in Baton Rouge, had come to town with plans to spend the evening barhopping with friends in New Orleans. It was, after all, in between terms. Selma hadn't liked the idea much, but they'd laughed her off, claiming as always that she was a super-controlling mother. They had ignored Selma's suggestion that since she lived in New Orleans, they crash at her place, an apartment on Lafayette Street. Although she had promised they could come in late with "no questions asked," her twins had declined to spend their first night as legal adults in their mother's guest room. "But I did have them leave their car with me. They share a car. It's in Carson's name. He bought it for them a while back. I didn't want them getting back behind the wheel, you know. I insisted they get a designated driver, one of their friends to drive them back to Baton Rouge. They were supposed to get a ride and come back and pick it up, but . . . the car is still there and . . ." She shook her head sadly. "I don't think they made it back to the college."

"But it's only been a few hours," Brianna argued, thinking her friend had jumped the gun on her worries. "And they were partying," Brianna argued, feeling a little better. "Maybe they had a late night."

"Why aren't they answering their cell phones? Not even a text message." Selma frowned, eyebrows pulling together behind her glasses, lips trembling a little. "No one has heard from them this morning, and I found out that Chloe didn't make it into work. She was supposed to be at the coffee shop at five-thirty. She didn't show. Zoe is due at her part-time job at the accounting firm by seven, and you can bet I'll be calling her there, but . . . but I have a feeling I won't find her."

In Brianna's mind, it was still too early to be alarmed. "They're young adults. I'd say this is most likely the result of a wild night out."

"I want to believe that, but I just can't. I know something's wrong." The cup started trembling in Selma's hands and she set it on the scarred butcher block counter. "Christ, I'm a pathetic excuse for a mother."

"Selma, quit beating yourself up. You don't know that anything's wrong, and you're a great mom."

"Didn't I ask you not to patronize me?" she demanded, anger spiking only to immediately dissolve. Balling a fist, she placed her curled fingers to her lips as she struggled with tears. "I'm sorry. I know you're just trying to help. The last I heard from them was last night, a text after I had dinner," she whispered, guilt clouding her features. "And you know what they say about the first forty-eight hours after a crime has been committed?" Meeting Brianna's eyes, she added, "After that short window of time, if the crime isn't solved, if a person is still missing or the perpetrator disappears, the trail goes cold fast." Tears slid down her cheeks and she angrily swiped them away.

"Whoa, slow down. You're not sure there's been a crime," Brianna said, but even to her own ears her argument sounded patronizing. Placating. "Have they ever been out of touch with you before?"

"Oh, yeah. Sure. Of course. They're always pushing me away, telling me that I'm a freak show because I worry about them. Once they turned eighteen and went off to school, they would go for days without letting me know where they were. They're still in college. Seniors in the fall. So they resent my need to mother them." She sighed loudly. "I guess . . . I guess I'm ultra-protective because I know what it's like to lose someone close to me." Her voice cracked a bit. "God, I wish Sandra were here," she admitted, bringing up her own sister. Selma, like Brianna, was a twinless twin, part of the support group that included Tanisha.

"It's normal to want to protect your child, no matter what the age."

"Really? Because their father never seemed protective." Selma shook her head, her graying ponytail brushing the back of her shoulders. "He certainly gives them their freedom, but then he's pretty preoccupied with his new family." She said it bitterly, referring to the fact that Carson now had two sons, one four, the other less than a year. Brianna knew the history; she had heard it often enough in their group sessions.

"Have you gone to the police?"

"I called the Baton Rouge Police Department before I came here. But they weren't all that interested. Because it hasn't been that long and, you know, the girls *had* been out celebrating."

"Have you talked to Carson?"

"Their father doesn't communicate with me." She closed her eyes for a second and sighed. "But I had to get in touch with him. I mean, what if the girls had gone there? So I texted his sister and she was going to call him. But have I heard back? No. No surprise there. He'll probably think . . . oh, that it was some kind of ploy for me to, I don't know, gain his sympathy or attention, but that's just nuts. Hopefully Bette can get through to him." She lifted her cup to her lips, then set it down before taking a sip. "Of course I've contacted everyone I could think of. I left messages for the Dean of Students at the college. I spoke with the Resident Director at their dorm, Harmony Hall."

"They're still in a dorm?" At twenty-one, the twins had to have been older than most of the students residing in campus housing.

"Yeah, I know, most kids move to an apartment after their first year, and believe me the girls lobbied long and hard for their own place. They called living on campus 'archaic,' and—what was term Zoe used?—uh, Machiavellian. But it's the one thing their father insisted upon. If he was going to pay any part of their schooling, then the deal was that they had to stay in a dorm or a co-op or some other type of campus-run housing and go to school in the summer to make sure they graduated on time. I went along with it. Carson hasn't been exactly generous with his daughters, you know, and he owes them at least part of their education. Besides that, I thought it would be safer." Her lip trembled at the irony of it. "Turns out I was wrong. There is no safer."

Despite the morning sunlight beginning to stream through the windows, a pall had settled over the house.

"What about boyfriends?" The Denning girls were beautiful and smart, and they'd always been socially active in high school.

"Oh, I tried the old boyfriends. Left messages and texts, none of them have gotten back to me yet."

"That's not surprising, considering that it was the middle of the night."

"But neither of the girls is dating anyone that I know of right now. Chloe just broke up with Tommy Some-thing-Or-Other." Selma paused. "Wait, his name was

Tommy Jones, like the singer my mother had a crush on, like, a hundred years ago. Chloe went with him for nearly a year, I think, but a while back she called it off." Selma's eyes darkened. "She didn't tell me why. Didn't want to. Accused me of 'prying,'" she said, making air quotes with her fingers. "She also pointed out that her love life was really none of my business."

"What about Zoe?"

Selma shook her head. "Nothing serious since her sophomore year when Zach broke up with her. Zachary Armstrong. He was her high-school boyfriend. It was a big deal at the time. Zach and Zoe, the two Zs. But the breakup hit her pretty hard. Took her a while to come to terms with the fact that he's a jerk. Lately she seemed to have gotten over him."

"Maybe there was someone who wasn't a serious boyfriend?" Brianna sat on the other stool at the counter. "A new guy."

"I don't know." She shrugged. "The girls were shutting me out, growing up, so I wouldn't be the first on their lists to tell about a new relationship." Blinking against tears, she gripped her cup and finally took a swig. "I'm trying to reconstruct what happened, but it's all a haze. Their two best friends say that Zoe and Chloe had dinner with them around seven, then planned to meet at a bar down on Decatur, the Hootin' Owl, later, but my girls never showed. So the friends weren't all that worried. They thought they'd hook up again back in Baton Rouge at that bar near campus. The Watering Hole. Their friends closed the place down, but my girls never showed." She glanced up at Brianna, her expression somber. "The twins would never have done this intentionally."

"And when was the last time anyone heard from either girl?"

"Around eight forty-five, when Zoe texted her friend that she'd see her at the Hootin' Owl." She swiped at her tears. "That would indicate that they stopped partying before nine p.m. I don't believe that. Do you?"

"It doesn't seem likely," Brianna admitted as dread replaced the hope in her heart.

"I know it sounds crazy, but it's got all the ingredients for disaster, especially if the 21 Killer is out there, like you said."

Brianna did not want to admit that her friend was making perfect sense. "Maybe they'll turn up," she said.

Biting back a sob, Selma shook her head. "The thing I don't understand is why he would strike here? I mean, he committed all those murders in Southern California, right? Why would he come here? Why New Orleans?"

"That's a good question," Brianna said, tamping down the rage she fought daily when she thought of 21. Rather than meet Selma's gaze again, Brianna climbed from her stool and walked to the far counter. She placed her cup inside the microwave and punched in thirty seconds to reheat her coffee. As she counted down with the timer, a plan began to form in her brain. If Selma's fears proved to be founded, it was time to get tough. *Really* tough.

Suddenly, the bad dreams and omens of the night melded into Selma's frightening story of her missing girls to create a terrifying matrix. Twins, celebrating their twenty-first birthdays. Brianna's hours of rationalization, all the suspicions she had dismissed as paranoia, now solidified into mind-numbing fear.

She could barely look at her friend.

Why New Orleans? Selma had asked.

The answer was simple: Because of frickin' Rick Bentz.

"You have to go to the police," Brianna said. "I'll come with you."

CHAPTER 6

"That wasn't the deal." Jase Bridges stared his older brother down, but Prescott only shrugged as he stood in the living room of the old house where they'd grown up.

"The deal changed."

"How?"

"Lena doesn't like livin' here," Prescott said with a shrug. "Says there's too many ghosts."

"Ghosts?"

"Ghosts. Memories. Spirits. Whatever." Prescott, an inch taller than Jase, was a bigger man all around. Thicker in the middle, wider shoulders, heavier face. His hair was near black where Jase's was a lighter brown. Prescott had been a defensive tackle on the high-school football team, all-state with offers of full rides to several small colleges, while Jase, a running back three years later, hadn't garnered the notice of college scouts. Now Prescott raked back his black hair and scowled through the window at the surrounding acres of what had once been a large sugar plantation. Over the centuries the farm had been cut into smaller plots, which most recently had been used to produce soybeans and raise cattle. Now the fields had gone fallow, the barns empty, the sheds filled with unused equipment that was rusting. Jase and his brother had inherited the place with the death of their uncle, who had never married or fathered children. The plan had been that Prescott, who had lived here with his family for five years, was to buy out Jase. Now, with payment finally due, the deal had just gone south.

Prescott placed a hand on Jase's shoulder. "See, what's happened is that Lena, she wants to live in town near the school so she can keep an eye on the kids and help out. And now that I'm selling insurance, I don't have time to mess with this place. We need to move on. You understand about that, brother." Then as if a sudden thought had struck him, he asked, "You run into Brianna since you've been back?"

The muscles in the back of Jase's neck tightened, but he didn't answer.

"She's in town now, has a little a place in the Garden District. Come home to roost, just like you." He sent his brother a look only the two of them could understand. "From what I gather, she's a psychologist now. Been back nearly a year. She has a practice and runs some kind of group for twins."

"How do you know all this?"

"Come on, you're the reporter. Figure it out."

Jase waited.

Prescott shrugged. "Hell, I'm in insurance. Always pressured to get new clients, so I checked. Who knows, maybe she could use some term life?"

Jase let further conversation about Brianna Hayward slide, didn't want to go there. "You're already looking to move?" he asked, following his brother down a short, familiar hallway.

"It's gone a little farther than that."

In the kitchen, where the old linoleum curled and the counters were scarred by decades of use, Lena was pouring cereal into bowls. Pale hair had been scraped into a loose bun on the top of her head, and she was wearing a T-shirt that hugged her large belly, a white skirt, and flip-flops that snapped as she moved briskly around the kitchen.

A short woman who had once boasted an hourglass figure, Lena was in her eighth month of pregnancy and appeared squat. She glanced over her shoulder at her brother-in-law. "Pres told you we're moving, right?" she asked, slipping the tab on the top of the Cheerios box into its slot.

Jase nodded.

As if needing to explain, she said, "I can't stay here. I just can't. I won't bring another child into the world to be brought up out here in the middle of nowhere." She walked to the pantry, stuck the box into the cupboard, and yelled up the back stairs. "Kids! Come on! We're gonna be late for VBS! Trinity? You hear me? Caleb, you come on down here! Pronto!"

Hearing the shuffle of feet on the floor above, Lena walked to the refrigerator where she pulled out a carton of milk and placed it, along with two spoons, on the small table pushed against the wall opposite the sink, the same spot where Jase and Prescott had sat during all of their years growing up on this farm.

"Prescott said the place has too many ghosts for you," Jase said.

Lena shot her husband a glance, then automatically

rubbed the cross that hung from a chain at her neck. "Shhh!" she warned as her children thundered down the staircase and clambered into the room.

"Uncle Jase!" Trinity's brown eyes lit up when she saw him. She raced across the room, blond hair flying, and flung herself into his arms. "I didn't know you were here!"

"I snuck in," he teased, juggling her onto a hip.

A moment later, her younger brother barreled into the room with a squeal of delight. "Hey!" Caleb cried, shooting across the floor to jump up.

Jase caught his nephew with his free arm. "Hey yourself, little man." Jase had never considered himself much of a kid person, but when his niece was born seven years earlier, all that changed.

Lena scowled. "Hay is for horses, and we don't have a lot of time to mess around here," she advised her brother-in-law and sent him a don't-mess-with-me stare. Then she glared at the children. "Kids, hurry up. Eat your breakfast. Miss Suzy won't like it if we're late, and Reverend Tim has a special treat for you all."

"I *hate* Bible school," Caleb complained, and his sister's eyes rounded.

"Don't you say that!" Lena hissed, looking over her shoulder as if she expected Satan himself to appear. "You love Vacation Bible School, you know you do. Now, come on, get your things."

Rolling her eyes, Trinity slid out of Jase's arms. "Okay," she said on a sigh that would have made a petulant teen proud, then climbed into her seat.

Caleb, too, wriggled to the floor before scraping his chair back as his mother poured milk over his cereal, then handed the carton to Trinity. As the kids dug in,

Lena motioned to her husband that he was in charge before walking into the front hallway. With a hook of one finger, she indicated silently that she wanted Jase to follow.

Out in the hall, Lena pulled her daughter's pink jacket from the hall tree as if by rote. Then, glancing outside to what promised to be a scorcher of a day, she replaced the small windbreaker on a hook.

"Listen, Jase," she said, her voice low. "I know you expected us to buy you out, but we just can't. Okay?" Her eyebrows launched upward, but she didn't wait for his response. "It's too isolated out here for the kids and for me. They run me ragged. Have no boundaries. No friends. And with a new baby on the way, I can't stand another minute here." Frowning, she swept a glance around the entry with its massive but marred staircase, high ceilings, dark walls, and ancient windows, some of which were cracked and needed to be replaced. "We can't afford to fix this place up. It would cost a fortune. All the wiring and plumbing needs to be replaced, and don't get me started on the roof. Anyway, it doesn't matter. I don't want to mess with it. Too much time. Too much money. Too many headaches. I want new. Clean. Bright. Light. Close in."

"I thought you wanted the kids to grow up in the country."

"Well, I was wrong, okay? I changed my mind." She crossed her arms over her ample belly and glared up at him. "We've already found a place in town that isn't haunted by . . . well, you know." She gave him a knowing look.

"No," he said, wondering just how much his brother

had confided in his wife of eight years. "Haunted by what?"

Lena's blue eyes narrowed. She looked about to say something, but pressed her lips together firmly instead. "Everything," she said evasively, throwing her arms wide. "This place, it just won't work for us. I want to be close to the church." As if to close the conversation, she rounded up two backpacks, one pink, the other blue, and hauled them back to the kitchen.

Jase followed.

Trinity was dutifully carrying her near-empty bowl to the sink. Caleb, not quite finished, lifted his dish to his face and started drinking the remains of his milk.

"Caleb Prescott Bridges!" Lena snapped. "What do you think you're doing?" She shot a disgusted glance at her husband. "Did you see this? Did you? Do you let your son eat like a pig at slop time?"

Prescott snorted. "Honey, it doesn't matter if—"

"It does matter, Pres. Of course it matters. That's the problem. Out here you let these kids do whatever they please. No restrictions. I've had it." She whipped Caleb's bowl from his hands and tossed it into the sink where it clattered against a stack of dirty dishes.

Trinity jumped and Caleb, rather than incur any more of his mother's wrath, slithered from his chair.

"Get in the car. Both of you!" Lena ordered, and her kids scurried out of the kitchen and out the back door leading to the garage. With a finger pointed at her husband, she said, "Deal with him!" Then pointed at Jase. "I'm losing it." Snagging her purse from the counter near the microwave, she hurried out the same way her children had taken and let the screen door bang loudly behind her.

Only when he heard the car's engine cough to life did Prescott speak. "She's always a little nuts when she's pregnant."

"A little?"

"She's got her eye on a house not far from the Garden District," he said, walking to the sink and staring out the window. Through the dusty glass both men watched the silver Ford disappear down the drive. "A bungalow," Pres continued. "Three bedrooms. Big yard. Space for a garden. One block from the church. Actually, we put an offer in and the people accepted, so it's ours as long as the bank approves."

"Will they?"

"Should. But we'll have to sell my interest in this place." He shoved his hands down the front pockets of his khakis. "We're moving out." A beat. "And moving on."

"What's that mean?"

Prescott turned and faced his brother. His tanned hands gripped the sides of the counter on either side of him and he suddenly looked older than his thirty-eight years. "Maybe we both should sell this place, Jase. Just cuz it's been in the family a few generations, so what? We don't need it. Hell, you were going to sell to me anyway."

"Because you have kids."

"So what's the difference if I sell to someone else? Either way, you're out."

Prescott had a point, but it didn't sit well with Jase. They both knew it. Because of the ghosts.

"Or," Prescott said, as if the thought had just crossed his mind. "You could buy me out. I'd give you a deal, and we wouldn't have the Realtor's cut. Clean and simple."

There it was. The reason Prescott had asked him to stop by so early in the morning. It was so like his brother to beat around the bush, hint, and sneak up on a topic rather than say what he wanted outright. In this case, Jase suspected it was because of Lena.

"This is just the opposite from what we agreed." And Jase had ambitions associated with his job; he didn't need a ranch to distract him from his goal. Already he had his application in at the police department.

Prescott lifted a shoulder. "Got to keep the peace, y'know? Besides, things change."

"Do they?" Jase wasn't so sure as he walked outside to the back porch and stared across the rolling acres to a rise. Past the drying grass and a few sunbaked outbuildings, a tall oak rose in the distance. Less than a hundred yards beyond the tree's spreading branches was the property line and the slow-moving river.

Images seared through his brain: scenes from his youth, like photo-graphs in an album shuffled quickly past, and he shut his mind to that part of his life, a past long buried that he'd tried like hell to forget.

He heard the porch boards creak as his brother came out to join him.

"In a way, Lena's right, you know," Prescott said, following Jase's gaze down toward the river. "There are just too many damned ghosts here, y'know?"

Jase did know. Though he'd never admit it to anyone.

"I'll beef up the patrols on your street," Bentz said as he cradled his cell phone to his ear and rolled his chair closer to the desk. Immune to the noise of the other detectives and staff, he focused on the voice on the phone and the image of the killer on his computer screen. Obsessed with the footage, he watched the video of Father John for at least the twentieth time, but this morning, instead of beer, he was downing his third cup of coffee and hoping the caffeine would stave off the headache that throbbed near his temples.

All the while, the station had come to life around him. Phones jangled, voices buzzed, and footsteps shuffled amid the rows of desks. Somewhere a printer chugged out pages over the constant rumble of the air-conditioning unit forcing cool air through the vents. Still, the rooms were warm. Barely ten in the morning and already the heat of the day was permeating the windows and walls of the old building.

"Thanks," Samantha Wheeler said from the other end of the telephone connection.

"I listened to your show last night."

"Then you know that he didn't call in. Maybe he's not interested in me any longer."

I wouldn't bet on it. The killer had blamed Dr. Sam and her advice for causing the death of someone dear to him years before. He had targeted Dr. Sam, plotting out his revenge step by step, taunting the radio psychologist, teasing her and ultimately nearly killing her. The fact that he'd been thwarted should have only intensified his rage.

Unless he'd fixated on someone else.

"Don't worry, Detective," Samantha said. "I'm pretty sure I would recognize his voice. It made an impression."

She seemed certain, but it had been years since Father John had called into her talk show and stalked her as steadily as a hunter searching out prey. Now, as Bentz ended the call, reminding her to be careful, he couldn't shake the bad feeling. Still holding his cell phone, he stared at the screen of his computer where the frozen image of Father John leered up at him.

"I thought that bastard was gator bait," Montoya said, eyeing the monitor as he cruised into Bentz's office.

"So did I."

"Maybe he tasted so bad the gator spat him out."

"Yeah, that's it," Bentz said sarcastically, then reached for his shoulder harness and sidearm. "I thought I'd run out to his place on the bayou. See if there's any indication that he's moved back in."

"You think there's a chance?"

"Probably not. But, you know. No stone unturned." He slid the harness into place. "You comin'?"

"Why not? I'm in."

No surprise there. Montoya was always "in." Though he'd mellowed a bit over the years, settled down, married, even had a kid, Reuben Montoya would always be the same cocky kid Bentz had been partnered with for years. Montoya still sported a goatee, diamond stud earring, and black leather jacket despite the thick New Orleans heat. No strands of gray had yet dared invade his black hair, and his body was fit and toned due to regular gym workouts and a regimen of running the city streets late at night. But maybe, just maybe with the reintroduction of one of the worst criminals in New Orleans history, even Montoya might start to age.

Together they walked down the stairs and out of the building where the Louisiana heat hit them full force.

As it was late June, the temperature was hovering near ninety. Only the barest of breezes rustled through the leaves of the live oaks planted near the parking lot.

"I'll drive," Montoya said, as if he'd ever missed a chance to sit behind the wheel, foot to the floor, fish-tailing around corners.

Bentz didn't argue. It was useless. Together they crossed the parking lot. "I've already called for a boat to meet us at the old pier near the spot where Father John camped out. You remember where it is?"

"Like it was yesterday." Montoya's face was grim, his voice low as he slid into the driver's seat of his Mustang.

Bentz took the passenger seat. Before he could pull the door shut, Montoya fired up the engine and threw the car into Reverse.

"I can't believe that bastard is still alive," Montoya said as he wheeled out of the parking lot.

Bentz clicked on his seatbelt and cracked his window as Montoya merged into traffic. "If I hadn't seen his face, I wouldn't have bought it either."

"But there he was, big as fuckin' life."

"Yep. Not a copycat. Not this time." Bentz glowered out the window and slipped a pair of shades over his eyes. So far, the headache that had been his companion all morning hadn't abated. Last night, his one beer had slid into two, then three, and so on until the six-pack he'd picked up at the local convenience store had been downed, full bottles replaced with empties. Reaching into his pocket, he found a travel-sized bottle of ibuprofen, tapped out two capsules, and tossed them back. Dry.

"Feelin' rough?" Montoya asked as he drove out of the

city, leaving the sluggish Mississippi and the skyline behind. He, too, had slid a pair of sunglasses over the bridge of his nose, but Bentz figured the colored lenses were more for effect than to cut the glare—all part of the Detective Reuben Montoya too-cool-for-school image.

"I'm okay," Bentz said, and thankfully his partner didn't press the issue. Bentz had been sober going on twenty years. Aside from a couple of slips, one of which had been last night, the worst yet, he hadn't even been tempted. He decided to clamp down on himself. Just because a serial killer that he'd thought he'd taken care of had returned was no reason to start sliding. If anything, he needed to be smarter than ever, at the top of his game. Booze, even light beer, was out.

"Give any more thought to turning in your resignation?"

"Not much."

"Good."

Bentz could retire. Between his years with the LAPD and his time here in New Orleans, he'd be okay financially. But he wasn't old enough to completely throw in the towel, and he felt younger than his age. He watched the city disappear through the passenger window. From time to time he'd considered leaving the force. He'd suffered through some near-fatal injuries and put himself and his family at risk, which wasn't good. And now he was the father of an infant.

Olivia was all for him quitting; she claimed it would give them more time together with the baby. But his grown daughter Kristi thought the idea preposterous. "Oh, yeah? And what would you do?" she'd asked, her eyes twinkling. "Stay at home and play pat-a-cake with

Ginny all day? *That* I'd love to see." She had chuckled at the mental image before adding, "You know you'd go out of your friggin' mind within a week. Right? You're a cop's cop, Dad. You live to be a detective, and don't argue with me," she'd warned, wagging a finger at him. "You know it. You love the chase and live for the arrest, sending all those bad boys up the river. Otherwise you would have given up before." She'd held his gaze. "You fought hard to win back your badge after the Valdez incident."

"Not an 'incident,' Kristi," he'd reminded her. "I killed a kid."

"Who you thought was aiming a gun at your partner."

"Nonetheless—"

"Nonetheless nothing. You didn't quit then and you're not quitting now. Face it, Dad, you'd curl up and die reading *Pat the Bunny* and *Goodnight Moon* for the ten thousandth time. Give it a rest." She'd flashed him that incredible smile, the one that reminded him of his first wife. "You can retire when you're old. I mean *really* old."

He'd let the subject drop. Until now, when Montoya brought it up again.

"Not sure what I'm going to do." He tapped a knuckle on the window and considered his future as they sped past a lowland farm.

"Well, let me know, would you?" Montoya gunned the car, speeding around a slow-moving hay truck with bales that looked as if they might topple at any second. "If you're really going to quit, give me a heads-up, okay, so I can request a new partner. Damn, but I'd hate to get hooked up with Brinkman."

Bentz didn't blame Montoya. Brinkman was a pain

NEVER DIE ALONE   83

in the ass and a know-it-all at that. A decent enough
cop who had been with the department for years, Brinkman was a loudmouth who always knew the worst off-
color jokes and never passed up a chance to put the
screws to his fellow officers. Yeah, Brinkman had all
the social skills of a water moccasin on a bad day. "You
could request someone."

"Sure." Montoya squinted through the bug-spattered
windshield. "Because you know if I ended up with
Brinkman, I might just kill the son of a bitch."

"You'd be doing the department a favor."

"That I would." Montoya laughed. "And end up in
jail. Look, just stick around, Bentz. Come on, man, now
you have a real reason to stay. Father John. We need to
take him down. Whether you like it or not, the sick bastard just made our job a lot more interesting."

Montoya made a grim point. Lately, things had been
quiet. Aside from the usual domestic violence cases
and gang-related or booze-fueled fights, the city had
been calm. Not since a killer had stalked St. Mar-
guerite's Cathedral had there been any unusual homicide cases. Which had suited him just fine. Or so Bentz
had told himself. But, as proven by Bentz's obsession
with the tape of Father John murdering the woman
prisoner, Montoya was right. Bentz's investigative juices
were definitely flowing again.

How sick was that?

Frowning, he heard his partner swear as Montoya
turned onto an overgrown lane leading to the remote
bayou. Dry grass and weeds scraped the undercarriage
of the low-slung car as Montoya followed the twin ruts
that marked the old driveway.

By the time they reached the area of the bayou

where Father John had once lived, the mosquitos were out in full force and the midday heat shimmered in waves. Tall cypress trees gave a little shade, but the air was still and humid. Oppressive. Sweat collected around Bentz's neck and he tugged at his collar as they walked down the overgrown path toward the water. The dilapidated dock listed to one side, its rotting boards bleached from the intense sun. The brackish water stretched wider here.

Squinting, Bentz stared across the expanse to the thicket of trees that used to shelter a cabin set upon pilings. A killer's lair where, over the drone of insects and croak of bullfrogs, Father John had tuned into Dr. Sam's show as he sharpened the stones of his rosary and plotted his next grisly crime. Years had passed, long years that had lulled Bentz into believing the killer who had cloaked himself as a man of God had died in this very swamp.

Bentz swiped at the sweat beading at the back of his neck and wondered if Father John's cabin still existed.

Maybe Montoya was right about this after all.

Maybe this trip to the bayou was all a huge waste of time.

CHAPTER 7

Brianna pushed the speed limit. With Selma fighting tears and nearly collapsed against the passenger door, they tore up Highway 10.

Brianna's Honda was fifteen years old, had nearly two hundred thousand miles on the odometer, and was in serious need of detailing, but it responded without complaint. The trip to All Saints should take a little over an hour and a half, but Brianna hoped to shave time off the length of the journey. Time was of the essence because the more Selma had talked about her daughters' disappearance, the more Brianna feared that the 21 Killer was at large here in Louisiana.

She thought back over her recent trip to California, where she'd run into so many dead ends. The LAPD hadn't been responsive, the officer who had arrested Donovan Caldwell for the crime having retired, and the DA who had prosecuted the case was no longer with the department. His replacement, a stern woman of around fifty, was not interested in anything about the case other than keeping the convicted man known as the 21 Killer behind bars. The LA bureaucracy saw

Brianna as some relative of the convicted killer who wouldn't accept the truth.

As if!

She slid a glance at Selma whose eyes were closed, her arms wrapped protectively around her thin body. Was it really possible? Could it be that Selma's two precious daughters, on the cusp of becoming adults, had been kidnapped by 21?

If so, it was far too late.

The killer would have ended their lives precisely twenty-one years from the time Selma had brought them into the world.

Heart filled with dread, she drove into the city of Baton Rouge and turned onto the street that would lead into the center of All Saints' campus. Brianna and Selma had decided that they needed to begin their search in the girls' dormitory. Brianna tried to picture Chloe peering out from under the covers of her bed or Zoe answering the door, telling her mother to mind her own business. She hoped those images were not just a fantasy.

To that end, as the car nosed its way under the archway at the college's southern border, Brianna sent up a small prayer for the Denning twins' safety.

At the sound of an outboard engine, Bentz turned toward the water to watch as an aluminum craft appeared, rounding a bend in the bayou.

Leaving a small wake, the boat sidled up to the old pier. Ray Calloway, a barrel-chested African American who was manning the tiller, cut the engine. With a nod at Bentz, he found a rope and looped it over a post sticking up from the dismal dock.

"Ray," Bentz said, stepping aboard the gently rocking boat. "Thanks for coming."

"Any time, any time. You know it. Good ta see ya, Bentz." The boat's owner was an ex-cop who spent his days fishing these bayous. "No trouble at all," he said as Montoya took a seat on the bench already occupied by Bentz. "Been too long."

"That it has." Bentz made quick introductions, then Calloway unhitched the boat, started the engine, and guided the craft across the murky water. Bentz didn't like the feel of the area where alligators slid slowly through the swamp and water moccasins made their home.

"I hate this place," Montoya admitted.

"The bayou?"

"No, *this* place." He motioned to the shadowy thicket where Father John had resided during his reign of terror. His eyes darkened to nearly black. "Evil lived here."

Bentz said, "A long time ago."

"Doesn't matter. I figure it still exists."

Calloway nodded, his bald head speckled with sweat as he guided the boat's bow between trees rising out of the water. "The spirit stays, you know. It lingers, even after the perp is gone. Y'know, like a bad smell."

Bentz didn't buy into Ray's theory of lingering evil, but he couldn't deny the sudden coolness at the back of his neck, like the breath of a demon prickling the hairs at the base of his scalp. The chill was at odds with the heat of the day. He told himself it was all his imagination. Montoya wasn't right. Evil may have existed in this bayou where a musty smell rose from rotting vegetation, but no malingering spirits lurked in the deepening umbra.

The dinghy slipped further into the woods, where shafts of light glinted through the branches overhead, sparkling the water. An ibis, disturbed by the watercraft, took off. White wings stretched, the bird disappeared in the higher branches.

"Here we go," Calloway said, cutting the engine. Sure enough, the remains of a cabin came into view in the nest of foliage. Rotting on its pilings, the wooden structure sagged. Its roof had collapsed, and some of the floorboards of the porch surrounding the structure were missing.

"No one living in this mess," Montoya observed; he seemed relieved.

"Yeah, I figured." Bentz squinted at the dilapidated building. "This would have been way too easy, and nothing about Father John ever was." He thought back to the time when the serial killer had been terrorizing the city. Long before Hurricane Katrina had meted out her punishment, Father John had stalked the streets of New Orleans, choosing his victims and leaving them with a necklace of bruises around their throats and a mutilated hundred-dollar bill nearby. A fake priest, serial killer, fan of Dr. Sam's radio program. Yeah, he was a sick bastard all right.

And now he was back.

From the looks of it vandals had found the cabin. Luminescent paint had been scrawled over the remaining boards, a sleeping bag with its stuffing spilling out hung over what was left of the railing near the stairs, and beer cans and wrappers were visible. A wasp's nest hung from a low branch, slim black insects crawling on its papery shell. Mosquitoes and dragonflies buzzed near the water craft.

Montoya gave a wasp a swat as it hovered near his head. "Jesus, I *hate* the swamp."

"Bayou," Calloway corrected.

"All the same." Montoya swore, slapping at his neck. "Shit, that fucker nailed me." Sure enough, a red welt showed just above his collar. "God *damn* it!"

Over the idling of the boat, Calloway said, "Should never swat at 'em."

"Yeah, right." Montoya's lips were pressed tight.

"I think we've seen enough," Bentz said.

"Not much to see." Giving out a raspy chuckle, Calloway jammed a cigarette into the corner of his mouth and circled his small craft around the cabin. He didn't bother lighting his Pall Mall, but headed to the opposite shore where Montoya's Mustang was waiting.

Bentz was sweating heavily as he climbed out of the boat one step behind his partner. He paused on the dock. "Thanks," he said to Calloway.

"Any time." The ex-cop flicked his lighter to the end of his cigarette. "Seriously, Bentz, you should come back. And next time, not on business. Spend the day out here. You could catch yourself and the missus a mess o' catfish."

"She'd love that," Bentz said with more than a trace of irony as he pictured Olivia cleaning a bunch of fat fish at the kitchen sink. She'd done it all her life, of course, growing up with Granny Gin, but still she wasn't fond of gutting and filleting the whiskered bottom-feeders.

"I'll bet she would." Chuckling again, Calloway eased his boat into the bayou. Cigarette clamped firmly between his teeth, hand on the tiller, he sped through the murky water to disappear around the bayou's bend.

"Now what?" Montoya asked, rubbing the red mark on his neck as he and Bentz made their way along the overgrown path to the car.

"Haven't figured that out yet," Bentz admitted as he slid into the passenger seat and rolled down the window. "But I will." He'd already pulled the file on Father John from the Cold Case Archives and had made inquiries. It wasn't as if the police department didn't know his identity. Of course, they had a contact list of his friends and family. So far none of those who had known the killer had admitted to seeing the man who disguised himself as a priest and used a rosary as a murder weapon. Every contact had expressed surprise that Bentz was asking questions again; they insisted that Father John had to be dead.

Were they lying?

Time would tell.

"The bastard's taunting us, you know." Montoya fired the engine and hit the A/C, then backed onto the overgrown gravel road.

"Yep."

"Daring us to catch him." He found a wide spot where the grass was mashed down and turned around, the Mustang bouncing on the uneven ground.

"We will."

"Not by doin' what we just did. The boat ride out to the old lair? That's what we professionals in the business call a wild goose chase!"

"I just wanted to get the feel of him again."

Montoya slid him a glance. "Feel of him?"

"Yeah." Bentz couldn't explain it, not even to his partner, but he had a strange connection with the killer.

"I'm tellin' you that sumbitch is evil, that's the *feel*

of him he left me with. Shit." He shot his partner a
glance. "Here's a news flash: Father John wasn't there
at his old cabin. Probably hasn't been there in nearly a
dozen years. So, again, I'm sayin' a bust, and not in the
good, we-got-your-asses prostitution or drug ring bust.
I'm talking a bust like in Vegas when you lose everything and get your ass kicked out of a penthouse suite."

"Sounds like the voice of experience."

"Maybe." Montoya rubbed at the welt on his neck,
his lips tightening as he eased onto a county road and
hit the gas.

"Nothing lost," Bentz said, staring out the windshield.

"Just a couple hours of my life." But Montoya was
settling down, his volatile anger subsiding. "Hell, I
can't believe the psycho's back. Why now? And why
kill a nun?"

"Who was as bad as he is."

"Yeah, well, maybe. It still gets my back up. She was
unarmed, man. Trusting," Montoya said as the car's
wheels hummed over the pavement. "I don't go to mass
anymore, and hardly ever pray, y'know, but hell, I was
raised Catholic and I hate the fact that the twisted son
of a bitch impersonated a priest. What kind of sick bastard does that?"

"He isn't a man of God."

"You got that right. Being a priest, a holy man, takes
years of study and commitment and dedication and
piety and honor, y'know, and a rosary. It's holy. Sa-
cred." His hands tightened over the wheel. "It pisses
me off."

"Me too," Bentz admitted, drumming his fingers
against the passenger door. "Me too."

*   *   *

She would never get the chance to escape again.
Chloe knew it, as surely as she was locked in this win-
dowless basement, alone and naked. At least she was
no longer hog-tied. Instead, he'd bound her wrists in
front of her and left her with a pail to pee in and a night-
light that gave off a weird blue glow from a battery-
powered disk on his work table. He'd been bloody and
covered in dirt, but had found some clothes, a plaid
shirt and old jeans that he'd thrown on.

Then he'd taken off with the final words. "I'll find
her, you know. I'll find that bitch and bring her back
here. And then . . ."

He'd never finished his threat, leaving her to guess
at his sick plans. He had climbed the ladder, hauled it
up after him, and slammed the trapdoor closed behind
him. She had heard his heavy tread cross the floor
above, and then silence.

Chloe figured he hadn't decided what to do with
them now that his original plan had been thwarted. She
didn't know what kind of macabre rite he'd dreamed
up, but it certainly would have involved pain and the
twins' eventual deaths.

So now she needed a plan.

Either he'd return and hurt her, or leave her in this
miserable basement to die. Both scenarios were terrifying, so she had to find a way to free herself. That was
what Zoe would do. She would find some way to either
climb out of here or wait until the whack job returned
and somehow get the drop on him. That would be
harder than ever, now that Zoe had done it once.

And, she told herself, she wasn't Zoe. She wasn't
brave or strong or athletic. She didn't have Zoe's fire

and edge. She'd always been content to let her twin be the leader in their lives, but now, she had no one to rely on but herself.

Worse yet, Zoe was counting on her.

But it was an impossible situation.

She was trapped in this prison.

Blinking back tears, she curled into a fetal position on the cool stone floor and tried to calm her racing thoughts. She needed a plan. Something clever, like the thing Zoe had done. She tugged at the binding on her wrists, which was tighter this time. It was no use. Her twin would have to find a way to save them both.

Brianna paced to a window of the college's admin building and stared out at the pathways cut through well-manicured lawns. The windows in the stone building were small, reminiscent of a medieval monastery, but they allowed her a sweeping view of the campus grounds. How she would have loved to recognize Zoe or Chloe among the handful of students and faculty crossing the campus, heading off to a dorm or summer session classes. Behind her, Selma sat silently. Waiting and waiting to meet with the Dean of Students. After a tough morning spent searching this campus, they were more frustrated than ever.

They had fast-talked and finagled their way into the twins' rooms, appealing to a very annoyed-looking resident assistant who'd been taking advantage of the summer break to catch up with her shows on a laptop at the reception desk. Zoe's room had been unremarkable, with clothes strewn over the twin beds, books scattered, posters of sunsets and pop stars pinned to the

walls. Chloe's room had been more of the same, though
a bit tidier.

Distraught to find another empty room, Selma had
collapsed on Chloe's bed and buried her face in the pillow before Brianna had been able to stop her. "We can't
disturb anything," she'd reminded the twins' mother.
"You know, just in case . . ."

"The police investigate."

"Yes, I just thought we needed to check their rooms,
but . . . let's move on. "

Selma had stiffened. "I told you they weren't hiding
from me or sleeping it off or whatever."

"Right. I know. I'm sorry." Though contrite, Brianna
had known it was no time to deal with Selma's overly
raw emotions. "Come on."

They'd stopped at a McDonald's near campus for
lunch, but Selma had picked at her Big Mac, barely
touching it in favor of a Diet Coke and cigarette. Afterward, they had talked to a few of the girls' friends who
lived nearby and confirmed that their last contact with
Zoe or Chloe had been around nine in the evening.

"I thought they were going to meet us at the Watering Hole," Annie Rolands had told them. "I mean, it's
our place. All the students kick it there." A petite
brunette in frayed denim shorts and a tight sleeveless
T-shirt, Annie had come out on the porch of her apartment, blingy cell phone in hand. "I was, like, 'Come
on, let's go to the Watering Hole now,' and they were,
like, 'No way, we want to party on Bourbon Street,' and
I was, like, 'Whatever.' I thought they'd show up at the
Hole after a bit, but no." She shrugged, checked the
phone's screen. "But they're okay, right?"

"We hope so," Brianna had said, and Annie had

promised to text everyone she could think of to locate the girls.

"Social media, too," Brianna had instructed. "Facebook, or whatever it is you guys connect on."

"Sure." Annie had bobbed her head. "I'm all over it."

Once they were back in the car, Selma had confided: "I don't think I can trust her to find the twins."

"It's a start," Brianna had assured her. "It's good to put the word out with someone tied in to their social network."

Now, at last, the Dean of Students appeared in the reception area, his hands clamped to his chest, as if in prayer.

"I apologize," he said with the barest hint of a brogue hinting at his Irish roots. "Summer is our season of retreats, and that keeps me busy. But come in, come in." A fortysomething priest dressed in black slacks and shirt and a stark white clerical collar, Father Crispin was friendly, though harried, as he guided them up a curved staircase and into an office with tracery windows, coved ceiling, and a carved bookcase filled with well-worn tomes. Checking his watch, he waved Selma and Brianna into side chairs before taking his seat at the massive table serving as his desk.

"Now, then, what can I do for you?"

"It's about my daughters. They're students here. Zoe and Chloe Denning," Selma said. As the priest listened, she explained about the twins' disappearance, her worries for her girls, and her fears that a monster serial killer was at large in Louisiana.

As her story went on, the dean's cocked head rose to alert, and his ruddy face clouded. "Murder?" Caution flared in his eyes. "Here?"

"I . . . I don't know," Selma answered. "All I'm sure of is that my daughters are missing."

"But a serial killer?" Father Crispin glanced at Brianna for verification. "We had a situation—" He caught himself. "There was a time when students were at risk here, but that was years ago. We've had no trouble since then. And your daughters, they probably are just late; you know how kids are when they turn twenty-one."

It was time for Brianna to step in. "Father, we believe they may have been targeted by a killer."

The priest's dark brows drew together as he listened to Brianna's account of 21 and her theory that the killer was still at large. His expression of concern was heartening, until he spoke again. "That's a frightening account, but if this is true, you ladies need to speak with the police. This is a matter beyond our campus."

Brianna's heart sank in disappointment. This was a waste of time.

"Of course, there will be full cooperation on our end," he said, glancing pointedly at his watch. "We'll do everything we can. I assure you, All Saints is a safe haven for all students." Then he stood, indicating the meeting was over. "Please, try not to worry," he suggested while opening the door and effectively ending their discourse. "LA's a long way from here and, as you said, the police think they've got their man. These other . . . *incidents* are disturbing. Unfortunate. But your daughters are adults now, ma'am. It's time to let them make their own choices and hope that they choose wisely. Now, come along, walk with me. The afternoon workshops are about to begin and they're on the other side of campus. Can't keep our guests waiting."

Selma and Brianna kept up with his long strides as he crossed the grassy quad where a few students were sprawled, books open, iPhones in hand. The sky was a silky blue, not a breath of wind, the day filled with the warmth of summer. And yet Brianna felt a chill as cold as all of December. As each hour had passed without a word from Selma's daughters, her own fears had increased.

At a juncture in the paths, Father Crispin stopped and touched Selma lightly on the shoulder. "I'll do what I can," he promised. "God be with you." He turned on his heel toward another cathedral-like building facing the manicured lawns. Taking the steps two at a time, he rose up the stone staircase and disappeared behind a massive door.

"He's not going to do anything," Selma said in a hollow voice. "He thinks I'm a nutcase. An overprotective mother." Her skin was pale, her demeanor laden with weariness.

"He's passing the buck." Brianna slid an arm around the older woman's waist and propelled her toward the student parking lot. "But he was right about one thing. It's time to talk to the police."

"I told you I called them."

"I know," she said, guiding Selma toward her beat-up Honda. "But it's time to see them in person."

At the station, they encountered the same lack of concern they had sifted through all day. They found their way to an officer in the Missing Persons Division, Crecia Brown. A fit, African American woman, Brown gave off waves of self-importance and bureaucratic weariness. In her mid-forties, with clipped hair and a no-nonsense attitude, she listened somewhat impatiently to Selma, who stood with Brianna on the opposite side of a glass-enclosed counter.

"You called earlier." Her lips flexed a frown as she checked her computer.

"That's right."

"I just have a little paperwork for you to fill out." Her chilly demeanor thawed slightly as she found some forms. "But we've already started checking with the necessary agencies. And we put out BOLOs on both girls." Her dark eyes had given Brianna the impression that Officer Brown had seen it all and, right now, she was simply going through the motions.

Selma, though, seemed heartened. Maybe it felt good to know that the alerts were out, even if no one seemed to be taking them seriously. Selma filled out the forms, providing as much information as she could. By the time they returned to the car, the older woman was beat. She slid into the Honda's warm interior and closed her eyes. "I feel like I could sleep for a hundred years, and yet I'm so keyed up and worried . . . oh hell." She checked her phone for what had to be the hundredth time as Brianna started the engine. "We may as well go home." There was sadness in the deep lines on her face as she cleared her throat and stared out the window. "Thanks for all you've done."

Nothing. I've done nothing but drive you here and help you file an official Missing Persons Report. It's not enough.

Brianna eased her little car into traffic that was heavier now. She'd started out the morning trying to convince Selma the girls would return, but as the day had worn on with no news from the twins, Brianna had begun to believe the horrifying possibility. Her hope was waning, her anger at the people who had put the wrong man behind bars increasing. She knew Donovan Caldwell was imprisoned falsely, and that meant the real killer, the maniac who targeted twins, was still at large.

Worse yet, she suspected he was hunting again, his killing ground having expanded from Southern California, heading east, if her theory was correct. And then there was the fact that Rick Bentz was now a working detective in New Orleans, where Zoe and Chloe had gone missing.

Her stomach twisted and her fingers tightened over the wheel as she fought her fears.

Where the hell were Zoe and Chloe?

CHAPTER 8

"I don't have any comment," Bentz said. He finished the last swallow of cold coffee and glanced at the clock mounted on the wall of his office: 4:57. Time to be thinking about heading home, and here he was cornered by Jase Bridges, a reporter pounding the crime beat for a local paper.

Bridges was all over the Father John case.

"You know the identity of the killer," Bridges pointed out. Seated in a chair at Bentz's desk, the reporter stared at Bentz as if watching for weakness, looking for a crack in Bentz's responses.

Bentz nodded. "It's just a matter of finding him. That's all I have. Hopefully that will change soon. The Public Information Officer will release a statement with any new developments." He held the younger man's gaze. They both knew the current PIO was stepping down. Jase Bridges was one of the few candidates for the job.

The reporter hesitated, then appeared to realize that he wasn't going to get anything more from Bentz. "Good.

Keep me posted." Bridges placed a business card on Bentz's desk, nodded, then ducked out the door.

Bentz swept the card into the trash. He knew Bridges by reputation—a wild, tough-ass kid who had somehow turned himself around and landed the crime beat for the *Observer,* a local paper still hanging on despite the downturn in the print newspaper industry.

Bentz had never had much use for the press. Sure, fine, the public needed to be informed or when the department needed the public's awareness and assistance. But as for the reporters who made something out of nothing, creating a story when there was none, Bentz wasn't interested. Was Jase Bridges one of those, so hungry for drama that he blended truth and fiction, or a real hard-nosed, truth-seeking reporter?

The jury was still out.

And the thought that Bridges might end up working for the department didn't sit well with Bentz. His innate distrust of reporters had been honed years ago when he'd been working for the LAPD. Bentz had made the tragic mistake of shooting a kid who had a gun aimed at his partner. Turned out the gun had been a toy, and the press had ripped into Bentz.

"I'm looking for Detective Rick Bentz." A woman's voice out in the hall caught Bentz's attention.

"Just a minute. Do you have an appointment?" demanded the higher-pitched voice of Nellie Vaccarro, a recent hire in the department. "Hey! Wait! What do you think you're doing?" Petite and bristly, Nellie was the secretary and receptionist for the department, and she took her duty of guarding the gates to the inner sanctum to heart. "Did you hear me? Detective Bentz is—"

"In?" the other woman guessed, footsteps now rapidly approaching.

Bentz rolled his chair away from the desk and stood just as a thirtyish brunette stepped into his office.

"You're Bentz," she guessed without any preamble. "Right?" She wore faded jeans and a gray T-shirt, the strap of an oversized bag slung over one shoulder. The woman was slim, around five eight or nine, and serious as hell. No humor sparked in her eyes, no smile tugged the corners of her mouth.

"That's right."

"I need to talk to you."

Nellie, barely visible in the doorway behind the newcomer, lifted her hands, then dropped them in frustration before wedging her body past the visitor. "I'm sorry, Detective," she said, glossy lips pursed into a frown. In a short dress, heels, her straight blond hair framing her heart-shaped face, Nellie always appeared ready for a surprise photo shoot. "I tried to stop her, but—"

"You checked my bag and practically frisked me," the woman cut in, sending Nellie a withering glare. "I just need to talk to Detective Bentz."

Spine stiffening, Nellie wasn't about to be dismissed. "But—"

"It's fine, Nellie," Bentz said, raising a hand. "I've got this."

She hesitated.

"Really," Bentz nodded.

Her suspicious gaze skated from Bentz to the intruder, then back. Obviously unhappy, she said, "If you say so, Detective." Not pleased in the least, she let out her breath and walked away, high heels clicking curtly down the hallway.

"I think you ticked her off," Bentz said.

"Probably." The woman stared at him. Her hair was piled loosely on her head, and if she was wearing make-up, it was invisible. "But I need to talk to you."

"Okay. What about, Ms.—?"

"I'm Brianna Hayward."

He turned her name over in his mind. It rang distant bells.

"Two girls are missing," she said, her face etched in worry. "Zoe and Chloe Denning. They just turned twenty-one today, and no one's heard from them since before midnight." Before he could ask, she said, "We filed a Missing Persons Report in Baton Rouge, where they live, but they were last seen celebrating in New Orleans." She slid a page across his desk. On it were three pictures. Two were head shots of nearly identical women, each with a big smiles and streaked blond hair. One was marked Zoe, the other Chloe.

"Twins?" He felt his stomach tighten. "Just turning twenty-one?" Memories of other cases came to mind, double homicide cases of twin sisters who had been rit-ualistically murdered the moment each became a legal adult.

"Yeah." She didn't mince words, but met his gaze and he felt a cold knot of dread tighten in his gut. Not that there was any connection. There couldn't be. He turned his attention to the photographs.

The third photo showed the two young women dressed in short dresses and tall high heels. It was a glamour shot, their streaked hair pulled away from their identical faces to fall in loose curls down their backs as they hugged each other.

"Where'd you get these?" he asked, pointing at the images.

"Internet. The photo of the girls together is the last picture they posted, taken last evening. From the daylight in the shot, I'm guessing it was probably taken around eight last night, an hour before all communication was lost. And from the landmarks, it looks like they were on Bourbon Street, near Toulouse."

He agreed. "I guess I don't understand why you wanted to talk to me."

"Because I'm . . . I'm afraid this isn't just a matter of girls going missing," she admitted and again her gaze held his. "I think it's probably worse."

"You think they met with foul play? Were abducted?"

The fear in her eyes said it all and that knot in his stomach twisted painfully.

"You worked on a couple of cases years ago, where twins were abducted and killed on their twenty-first birthdays."

Bingo. No reason to beat around the bush.

"You think the 21 Killer is behind this?"

"God, I hope not," she said fervently. She bit her lip before adding, "But, yeah. I think so."

"He's in prison."

"Donovan Caldwell isn't the 21 Killer," she said, shaking her head. "The LAPD sent the wrong man to prison."

"Really?" Bentz squinted at her and told himself not to leap to conclusions. "Why don't you slow down and start over?" he suggested.

After a moment's hesitation, she dropped into one of the side chairs and launched into a tale that only caused the knot in his gut to twist. As if she'd been practicing her spiel, she delivered an explanation of Caldwell's innocence, claiming that charges against him had been trumped up. The case was circumstantial. Caldwell was snagged in a bad sting operation, but since the LAPD needed to make an arrest on the high-profile case, the charges stuck. "And it didn't help that Bledsoe was the one making the arrest."

Bledsoe, now retired from the police department, had been the arresting officer who had put Donovan Caldwell behind bars for the murders of his twin sisters. A thorn in Bentz's side while he'd been with the department, Bledsoe was adequate at best in Bentz's opinion.

"I even went to LA to talk to the police there," she went on, "but no one was interested. Bledsoe's retired."

"So I heard," Bentz admitted.

"So I ended up with Detective Hayes, your old partner. He worked the case with you, before you left, then with Bledsoe, so I figured he'd want to hear what I had to say." She held Bentz's gaze. "Turned out he didn't. No one in the department, including Hayes, was interested. I was told that the case was closed and was politely but firmly given the brush-off." Her jaw tightened visibly, bone showing through her skin.

"They've got their convicted killer," Bentz pointed out. "The murders of twins stopped when they locked up Caldwell."

"For a while."

"You think 21 is killing again?"

"I know he is, but I hope to God that he's not behind

the Denning twins' disappearance. Oh, dear God . . ." Some of the starch seemed to leave her.

Was it possible? Was the wrong man imprisoned, leaving 21 still at large? Bentz was skeptical, despite his own gut fears, the similarities to long-ago crimes. He looked back at the photos of the girls. "Tell me what you know about these young women."

Brianna gave him a rundown on the Denning twins' disappearance, how she was involved, what she and the girls' mother, Selma Denning, had learned this morning in Baton Rouge before returning to New Orleans, where Brianna only stopped to print out photos of the missing girls. She explained how unlikely it was that they wouldn't show up for work or respond to phone calls and texts. She told of the lack of concern they'd encountered in Baton Rouge, and why she felt the twin girls were at risk.

"What's your personal interest in the 21 Killer?" he prodded.

She explained that she was a twin herself, as well as a cousin of the Caldwell twins and their brother, Donovan. She'd begun studying the case because of the family connection, and then sort of fell into it. And therein lay the kicker. Not only had she studied the crimes of record; she thought she'd found two more recent incidences of the 21's macabre activity.

Reaching into her beat-up leather bag, she found a sheaf of papers and slid them across his desk. "Zoe and Chloe Denning are . . . or might be the latest of his victims, but they're not the only ones. I couldn't prove that he was still working when I went to LA."

"But you can now?"

Her gaze drilled into his and silently assured him that

she was dead right. At least in her mind. He glanced down at the pages, most of them articles taken from the Internet. Two sets of twins who had gone missing in the past six months, twin brothers in Phoenix, a sister and a brother in Dallas.

"These kids all disappeared not long before their twenty-first birthdays. To my knowledge none of them has been located."

"They're still considered missing, right?" He narrowed his eyes, the knot of dread in his stomach tightening as he scanned the pages of information. "No bodies?"

"Not yet."

He glanced up.

"They're out there, somewhere." She was nodding, as if agreeing with herself. "He's hidden them."

"Just because they can't be located—"

"Twins. Every one of them. Twenty years old. Went missing only weeks or days before they turned twenty-one. Don't you find that strange?"

"Could be unrelated."

"But not necessarily." Her eyes darkened a bit. "Look, Detective," she said. "I wish to God that I believed for even a second that they were still alive. But I don't. And my guess is, when you dig a little deeper into this, you won't either." Her anger washed away into worry. "And now, Zoe and Chloe . . . Jesus, I hope I'm wrong."

It wasn't much, but it was something. Bentz had never been completely convinced that Caldwell had been the killer, but he'd been off the case since he'd moved to New Orleans, long before Donovan was collared.

"LA was his killing ground."

"Was," she repeated. "He's on the move. Heading east."

She held his gaze for a second as he scanned the news articles again.

"Now, he's here because of you."

"Me?" He lifted his head to stare at her. "Why?"

"Because you were one of the first detectives on the case. There was a big gap when he killed, twelve years, right?" When he nodded, she went on. "The first time when you were the lead detective on the case, and then a dozen years later when you went to LA on a different case, something more personal," she said.

The muscles in his back tightened when he remembered that trip and the reasons he'd ended up in LA, a place he'd left years before and a place he'd vowed to never return. He met this serious woman's gaze. So far, she had her facts straight. "That's right."

"And I bet there was some speculation at the time that the reason he'd quit was that he'd moved on, or had been imprisoned or was somehow out of commission. Did anyone suggest that your appearance in Southern California might have spurred the new killings?"

"There was discussion, yeah. Never any real proof."

"So what if that's right? What if you are the impetus for him to start killing again?"

"I've never worked in Phoenix or Dallas."

She waved away the argument. "He was on his way east and opportunity struck."

"21 doesn't leave much to chance."

"Whatever," she said, her gaze level. "My guess is he's taunting you, but really, who knows?"

He wanted to dismiss her, to believe that she was

dead wrong and the killer was locked away forever, but he saw desperation in her eyes. "Okay, so just for the sake of argument, let's say you're right, so 21 does what? Drives to Phoenix to find his next victims?"

"Maybe he didn't choose Phoenix. Maybe he found out via the Internet or mutual acquaintances that there were twins about to turn twenty-one, so he drove there."

Bentz sifted through the papers and found the missing persons report for Garrett and Gavin Reeves, who had disappeared in early February, three days before their twenty-first birthday. "Men?" he said, staring at the photos from the driver's licenses of the two brothers. They appeared identical.

"I know that 21 usually targeted women."

"Only women."

"That you know of," she said, then added, "or until now. Sometimes a killer's MO changes due to outside influences."

Unlikely. The homicides had been ritualistic, the victims left naked, a sexual element to them. And yet . . . Bentz shifted the pages and read the next reports. As he scanned the information, the knot in his gut twisted. According to what was written, Beau January of Dallas, Texas, and his twin sister, Belle, had vanished. Beau, who lived in east Dallas, hadn't shown up for work about a month before his twenty-first birthday. After his family had no luck locating him, his twin sister, Belle, had gone looking for him nearly three weeks later and never returned. "Beau January went missing the middle of April and his twin sister the first week in May?" he said aloud, scanning the reports, then their pictures. "Their twenty-first birthday was May tenth."

"That's right."

His jaw tightened. "And the LAPD knows about these?"

"They do now. I faxed over the information to Detective Hayes last week, once I found out about it."

"Wait. You live here, right?" he asked, and she nodded. "So if you didn't have proof when you went to LA, why did you go?"

Her gaze flickered and he wondered if she was going to lie to him. "I was out there visiting relatives. Including Donovan Caldwell," she admitted. Then quickly added, "The point is, 21 is still at large. He didn't just land in Louisiana, Detective. He came here with the express intent of flaunting the fact that he's smarter than the first detective in the case against him."

"You think you can see inside the mind of a serial killer?" he asked.

"Maybe." She was suddenly defensive, her patience obviously wearing thin.

"Why's that?"

"I'm a psychologist."

Holy Mother Mary. A shrink. Just what he needed. "*Criminal* psychologist?"

"Crime isn't my speciality, but I've taken classes—"

"Perfect." A shrink, but also a *student* of criminal psychology? And related to Donovan Caldwell? This was going nowhere and fast.

As if reading his mind, she said, "My credentials aren't important. If I'm right, it means that the 21 Killer is still out there and he's got Zoe and Chloe Denning and we have to find them. ASAP. I need your help, Detective."

He felt the chill of déjà vu run through his bones.

Hadn't another woman, one he thought might be a lunatic, come raging into this very office years ago? Swearing she could "see" the crimes of a killer, she'd ranted in front of his desk. Hadn't he scoffed at her, written her off as a nut job, and then eventually become swayed that she knew something? That woman, Olivia Benchet, was now his wife.

"Unfortunately, Ms. Hayward, if you're right, those girls are most likely already dead," he said, deciding that there was no way to sugarcoat the truth. "According to you, the exact time each twin turned twenty-one has already past."

She winced as if in pain.

"21 is precise. So let's hope you're wrong."

A knot appeared in her jaw and her fingers stretched and curled on the arms of the chairs. "All the more reason not to waste any time." Frustration yanked her eyebrows together and she appeared to lose what little control she'd had. "The way I see it, Detective Bentz, a homicidal maniac is walking around free because your partner and Bledsoe arrested the wrong man and trumped up their case against him. Not only is the wrong man serving time in a hellhole of a prison, but the real killer is at large." She was angry now, at the end of her rope, and she wasn't holding back. "Any other victims who die at his hand, including Garrett and Gavin Reeves, Beau and Belle January, and now probably Chloe and Zoe Denning, will be dead due to police negligence. I was hoping you would be different from the other detectives I talked to, that you might actually give a damn since you're some sort of hero cop around here."

"I'm no hero—"

"I've read about the cases you've solved, how you've

put your life on the line, nearly got killed a while back. But maybe they've got it all wrong about you here in New Orleans. Maybe that bad shooting, the incident in LA that has been conveniently swept under the rug, is what you're really made of." Her color was high now, her ire palpable. "I was hoping that you would actually give a damn about the 21 Killer, the fact that the wrong man is in prison and that twins have been kidnapped. I thought you would care, Detective, but I guess I was wrong!"

"Hey," Montoya said, suddenly filling the doorway and taking in the scene. "Is there a problem here?"

Bentz scowled as he glanced at his partner. "Nothing I can't handle."

"Then do something!" Brianna said.

"Whoa!" Montoya was inside Bentz's small office in an instant. He was bristling, his shoulder muscles bunching under his shirt.

Bentz lifted a hand to silently calm his partner. "I've got this."

"I hope so, because I expect you"—she jabbed a finger in his direction—"you and every man on the force here and in Baton Rouge to find Zoe and Chloe Denning before it's too late!" She flung a business card onto the desk, hooked the strap of her purse over her shoulder, and then motioned to the papers still in his hands. "Those are your copies." She turned, giving Montoya the once-over as he stepped out of the way. "I've got my own. If you need to get in touch with me, my cell's listed on my card." With that she left, striding out of his office as quickly as she'd stepped inside moments before.

As Olivia had years ago. Olivia, too, had been spouting outrageous ideas as well, theories he'd disputed but had proved true. On first meeting Olivia Benchet, he'd thought her a bona-fide nut job and tried to dismiss her. So, who was to say that Brianna Hayward was wrong? Hell, was it possible the LAPD had made a mistake? That the 21 Killer was still at large? And here, in New Orleans. Nah, that was crazy. Right? The evidence, though circumstantial, had been sufficient to sway a jury to convict the brother of Delta and Diana Caldwell for their murders.

His jaw slid to the side and he didn't like where his thoughts were carrying him.

"What the hell was that all about?" Montoya craned his neck to peer out the doorway and watch her leave.

Bentz reached into the top drawer of his desk and pulled out a near-empty bottle of antacids with his free hand. "Something I've got to look into." He popped the pills, jammed the cap back onto the bottle, and pushed back his chair. As he stood, he stole a glance at his computer screen and noted the leering image of Father John freeze-framed in the security video from the prison.

Great, he thought.

It looked like two of his most difficult cases, both of which he'd thought were closed and nailed shut, had suddenly reopened to converge at this point in time.

What were the chances?

And why had the 21 Killer or a copycat struck right here in Louisiana? "Let's go."

"Where?" Montoya asked.

Bentz grabbed his jacket from the hall tree in the corner. "Probably on our next wild goose chase."

* * *

Zoe opened a bleary eye.

Where was she and why was she so damned wet? *Oh, crap!* She was only partially wet. The other part of her was covered in mud. Half of her body was in the water, half out on the riverbank. Her arms still hugged the branch that had carried her to this spot, where she must have gotten hung up as the tree limb locked with other snags protruding into the river. Water lapped at her legs. The water, along with the dappled shade provided by the tangled tree limbs, had probably saved her skin from burning in the intense sunlight.

She tried to think past the ache in her forehead. She noticed that the sun was lying low and figured that she'd lain here, from the early-morning hours of last night until now when it seemed to be late afternoon. Her thoughts went to Chloe and her heart cracked. Surely she'd gotten away from the madman. Surely she was somewhere safe and alerted the cops. This very minute there were probably hordes of police and volunteers, along with Zoe's own family and friends, looking for her.

Zoe raised her head.

Pain exploded behind her eyes.

"Ouch! Crap!" Slowly lowering her head, she let out her breath. Geez, that hurt. Even staring upward burned her eyes. Her bare skin was red; though painful as it might be, a sunburn was the least of her problems. As far as she knew the sicko was still after her. After them.

Oh, God, she hoped not. She hoped that psycho was dead.

Nonetheless, she couldn't just lie here, exposed to

the elements, waiting for that creep show to appear. If he wasn't dead or incapacitated, he'd be looking for her, and he would realize that she had drifted downstream.

Dear God, he could be nearby for all she knew.

Paddling a canoe. Driving a motorboat or hiking through the swampy forest.

"Damn it all to hell." She watched as several pelicans drifted on the air currents high above, beaks long and wings wide against a sky where clouds moved slowly . . . Or was it her head swimming? She tried to roll over and felt a shaft of pain sear through her ankle. Oh, God, she couldn't move. She was stuck in this muddy shoreline of twisted tree roots and weeds, a veritable haven for alligators and snakes and God knew what other slithery, dangerous creatures.

But the gators and cottonmouths, copperheads and rattlers were far less dangerous than the beast who had captured Chloe and her just hours before midnight. Had it been yesterday? Or the day before? Surely she had only been "out" for less than a day. Right?

Did it matter?

Her stomach rumbled, reminding her it had been forever since she'd eaten, and her bladder suggested she might want to find a place to relieve herself.

"Great," she muttered.

More slowly this time, she lifted her head and closed one eye as she suffered through the throbbing beneath her skull. Trying to ignore the worst headache of her life, she surveyed this bend in the river. Surely there would be fishing boats or pleasure craft passing? Even one of those jet boats that roared up and down the slow-moving river, bayou, and inlets.

She squinted, searching through the brush and trying to determine where she was and how she could get out of these swampy woods and back to civilization. She must've passed the spot where she'd seen lights in the night. Now there was no sign of civilization. She had to get moving, couldn't hang around with the vague hope that someone other than the freak would find her. No, she had to find a road, steal a boat, locate someone in a farmhouse or a cabin, or flag someone fishing from a dock. Anyone who could help her.

As she attempted to move, pain splintered up her ankle. She lifted her head to survey the damage. Sure enough a baseball-sized knot, blue-green and bulging, appeared above her foot. Broken or sprained, it didn't matter. She had to leave this spot. But as the sun lowered even farther to the west, she eased her throbbing head back down and closed her eyes.

Just for a second.

CHAPTER 9

Brianna figured she'd blown it.

Big time.

Lost her cool as well as her perspective. And now, probably any chance for help.

The police department was teeming with people. Uniformed officers, plainclothes detectives, clerical workers, suspects, or people like herself needing assistance jammed the place, inside and out. Conversation buzzed and echoed off the tall ceilings. Cell phones rang and the slightly musty smell of the old building couldn't be hidden by the acrid odors of floor cleansers, perfume, and human sweat.

"Crap!" she whispered as she left Bentz's office and squeezed past a hefty man who was heading in the opposite direction.

Angry with herself, Brianna still held on to the hope that the Denning twins were alive as she made her way through the homicide department. She'd come on too strong, had gotten Bentz's back up, just as she'd warned herself she might. The trouble was, she thought as she hurried down the stairs, the heels of her boots ringing, she was too passionate about this case, too personally involved despite what she'd told Bentz.

Scared to death for Chloe and Zoe, she was heartsick and frustrated and wanted to scream and rail at the heavens. Instead, she'd taken out her anxiety on a detective who hadn't investigated the 21 Killer for years. Still, she was certain 21 was here because of Bentz. Call it a hunch. Or an educated guess. It didn't matter; Brianna was certain she was right. Hence her overreaction.

"Idiot," she whispered under her breath, and was vaguely aware of other footsteps on the old steps behind her.

Telling herself she wasn't going to let her own paranoia get the better of her, she wended her way down the battered old staircase where, suddenly, she was swimming against a tide of officers and visitors moving upward. Crowds had always bothered her, but she fought a surge of panic as she descended to the main floor. There she wended her way through a wide hallway to the front doors.

Outside she felt as if she could breathe again even though the sun was intense, heat still rising from the streets where late-afternoon shadows lengthened. She'd blown it with Bentz. She knew that and mentally kicked herself for the way she'd handled the meeting. Maybe she should have come to him first rather than head to Baton Rouge, but she'd thought she could gain more information at the college and offer it up, maybe set some wheels in motion. She'd thought she could help.

She'd been wrong.

"Fool," she told herself as she walked along the sidewalk. Her meeting with Bentz had been a disaster.

A breath of wind chased through the magnolia trees, rustling the leaves and bringing with it the scent of the river, thick and musty, and reminding her that New Orleans wasn't her native home. She, like so many others here, was a transplant.

She'd been born and raised in Bad Luck, Texas, until middle school, when her father had gotten a job at Tulane University and packed up his wife, twins, and family dog to move to New Orleans. Since that time she'd called Louisiana home. Now, of course, she felt as if she'd lived here forever.

She loved this town. But with each passing hour of not hearing from the Denning girls, Brianna was more and more certain the 21 Killer was right here in her backyard.

Her stomach squeezed at the thought as she jaywalked across the street. She'd found 21 terrifying as well as fascinating from a purely psychological point of view. What was his need to kill twins on their birthdays, the very date they became adults?

She couldn't help but wonder if his journey to New Orleans had something to do with her rather than Bentz. After all, she'd started rattling the cages of the LAPD not long ago, when he was already on the move.

Ridiculous! He knows nothing about you. Nothing. How could he? And why would he be interested? You're far older than twenty-one, your twin sister long dead. You aren't his type.

But she had been stirring up a hornet's nest. He could have easily found out that she was fighting to get

Donovan Caldwell released, that she was determined to see the real killer hunted down.

Even so . . . you don't fit his victim profile. You are not *the reason Zoe and Chloe are missing.*

So she was back to her theory that Rick Bentz was the audience the killer was playing to. But even that theory was a stretch. Why not stay in LA and stick it in the police department's face that he'd gotten away, that they'd imprisoned the wrong man?

After her meeting with Bentz she wondered if she, in her freaked-out, impetuous state, had come to the wrong conclusion. Hopefully. Then there was a chance the Denning girls were alive.

As she rounded a corner, she pulled her phone from the back pocket of her jeans and checked her messages. Nothing. Selma had promised she'd call or text the moment she heard anything, so no news wasn't such good news, contrary to the old saying.

So now what? Deep in thought, she slid her phone into her bag and found her sunglasses. The sun was low in the sky now, afternoon slipping into evening, the glare still bright, so she slipped the pair of retro Ray-Bans over the bridge of her nose. Calmer now, she contemplated her next move as headed toward her car parked one street over.

"Brianna!" a male voice called.

Tensing, she hazarded a quick glance over her shoulder to spy a tall, rangy man striding her way, his hand raised to flag her down. "Brianna! Wait up!" Something about his face was familiar, but she couldn't quite place him. He moved fast, closing the distance. Brown hair, straight and thick. A strong jaw. A jagged scar visible near his right temple.

Oh. Dear. God. In an instant, she recognized him.

Her heart beat a quick double-time and she chided herself for her reaction. The man jaywalking, avoiding traffic, was none other than Jason "Jase" Bridges, her first real high-school crush. Though, of course, she hoped desperately that he didn't know that.

"Jase?" she said, forcing her overactive pulse to slow as a full image of him as a rebellious teenager came to mind. Three years older than her, nearly out of high school when she'd entered, he'd been a hellion her mother had constantly warned her to avoid.

"He's no good, you know," Ellen Hayward had told her twin daughters on more than one occasion. "He's like his father, who, I hate to say, drinks way too much. It's no wonder Edward's wife ran off and left him with the boys." In the kitchen of their home off Royal Street, Mom had carefully cut biscuits from the thick dough she'd flattened over their grandmother's wooden cutting board. Pausing, she'd straightened, the flour-dusted cutter in one hand, poised over the dough. "Oh, my." She'd shaken her head and pursed her lips. "I hate to say it, girls, but those Bridges boys? Big trouble." She set down the cutter and fingered the cross dangling from a gold chain on her neck. "Lord have mercy on their souls."

"'Lord have mercy' is right," Arianna, the bolder of the twins, had said. She'd sent her sister an amused glance as she'd stage whispered, "Jase is hot!" Her eyes, the same golden brown as her sister's, had sparkled with mischief.

"Oh, for the love of Saint Peter," their mother had admonished. "Girls!" She'd raised her eyes to the ceiling, as if seeing past the plaster and molding she could view heaven. "Why did you give me girls?"

The twins had giggled at their mother's discomfiture, because truth be told, what would Ellen Mae Allemande Hayward have done with boys? Dealing with all that energy and testosterone? Oh, sure. Hunting, fishing, boxing, and football were *not* on their mother's top one thousand things to do. Nope, Ellen wasn't exactly the den mother or football mom type. She was lucky she had girls. Brianna's tendency toward being a tomboy was worrisome enough for their mother. As it was, the girls kept her on her knees and praying throughout the week. With boys, she would've had permanent scars on her patellas.

So, of course, Ellen's warnings had gone unheeded and added gasoline to the fire of Brianna's interest. Now, though, she pushed aside thoughts of her mother, their tidy home not far from the university, and her own fascination with the wild teenager who had grown to become this man striding toward her.

"Jase Bridges," she said, feeling her shoulders straighten a tad.

"So you do remember." His smile stretched.

"Yeah, of course." As traffic passed, she hoped that she hid any indication of her fascination with him way back when. The rebellious kid who had flagrantly disrespected authority was almost gone. Almost. From first glance Jase appeared to have straightened up from the tattered, I-don't-give-a-rat's-ass eighteen-year-old. But something told her that the same rebel lurked beneath the façade of slacks and white dress shirt with its sleeves rolled up, a bit of a tattoo showing above the bend of his elbow. A rattler, she recalled, coiled around his biceps.

"I overheard your conversation with Detective Bentz."

"How?"

"I was still hanging around after my interview with him." He flashed that sardonic grin she remembered. "Yours sounded way more interesting than mine."

"And you were there . . . Why?"

"Business."

Huh. Who was this new, older, cleaned-up version of the irreverent kid she once knew? "You eavesdropped?"

A twitch of one corner of those blade-thin lips. "For once I didn't have to." He leaned a hip against the side of her Accord. "You were pretty loud."

"I tend to get that way when I'm passionate about something." She cringed a little, wondering how many others besides Bentz's partner and Jason Bridges had heard her.

Again, the eyebrow. Cocked. Silently sarcastic. And irritating as hell.

"Is there something you wanted?" she asked, extracting her keys from her purse. "I don't think you flagged me down just to catch up for old times' sake or whatever."

"I want to help."

"With?"

"Finding 21."

Her back muscles tightened. Though she'd take any help she could get in tracking down the 21 Killer, this, running into Jase at the station, having him hear her plea to Bentz, seemed off somehow.

"Why?" she asked.

"I'm a reporter."

"Not a cop?"

"Not yet, though I do have my app in for the Public Information Officer job that's coming up."

"So *almost* a cop."

"More like *maybe-if-he-gets-lucky* a cop," he admitted. He crossed his arms over his chest, the seams of his shirt pulling as he glanced back at the police station.

"Jase Bridges, lawman?"

"Yeah, hard to imagine. I know." He snorted at the irony of it all, and she felt the corners of her mouth twitch, her first inclination to smile since she'd found Selma Denning on her porch early this morning.

"But still a reporter."

"Probably always. No matter what the job description reads."

Because she was fast running out of options, unable to galvanize Bentz, or the cops in LA or Baton Rouge into action, she was tempted to agree. Why not use this man who was willing to help?

Because deep down, she didn't trust him. Didn't trust her feelings for him and heard her mother's warnings running through her mind. "He's no good, girls. Not him, not his brother, and certainly not his father."

So when had she ever listened to Ellen?

She unlocked her car but didn't get in. "Then you know about 21."

He gave a curt nod. "It made national news. A bizarre ritual killer usually does. And, of course, I was on the crime beat, so he intrigued me. I was in Savannah at the time, but I kept up."

"He scared the hell out of me."

"He scared a lot of people."

"He still scares me."

"You don't think they"—he hitched his chin toward the police station—"got their man."

"I'm sure of it," she said, and her thoughts turned dark again. "At least ninety-nine percent. You eavesdropped on the conversation, so you know the details."

"I heard part of it. Why don't you fill me in?"

She studied him for a second, decided she had nothing to lose. "The long and the short of it is that I think 21 has come to New Orleans. Why? Probably to show off for Bentz, but who really knows? A couple of girls are missing and we . . . their mother and I, are worried sick that he may have targeted them." Staring into his eyes, she felt the now-familiar lump form in her throat when she considered the fate of the Denning twins. "But I hope not. God, I hope this is all a mistake and that I'm just a paranoid conspiracy theory nut who's got it all wrong."

"But you don't think so."

"No," she admitted. "I don't." Her cell phone rang and she fished it out of her purse to see Tanisha's name and number appear on the screen, along with the time. "Look, I've got to run." She let the call go to voice mail. "I'm late as it is."

"Give me a call." He pressed a business card into her palm before stepping away from her Accord and jogging across the street.

She watched him go, noticing that despite the khakis and pressed shirt, he still had the pace of an athlete, his hips moved fluidly, his stride long. "Get over it."

She slid into the hot interior and fired the engine, then hit the A/C. It was giving her trouble, often times blowing hot air, other times working, but she didn't have the time to deal with it, so she took her chances and today, all day, it had complied. She caught another glimpse of Bridges as he disappeared around the corner of the police station and again felt that accelerated thump of her heartbeat.

"Schoolgirl crush," she reminded herself as she glanced into her side-view mirror and nosed into traffic. She had twenty minutes to get across town where Tanisha would be waiting.

No doubt it would take her thirty.

"You could just call the Baton Rouge PD," Montoya said as he followed Bentz through the station. "Wouldn't that be a helluva lot easier?"

"I will." Bentz skirted a couple of uniformed officers climbing the stairs as he hurried down. "But I'm heading up there anyway. I want to see what they've got on the missing Denning twins. You can come along or not."

"You know, just because some crazy-ass chick comes in and starts rattling your cage doesn't mean she's legit," Montoya pointed out, but kept stride with his partner as they reached the first floor.

"We'll see." Bentz took a hallway leading to the back door and parking lot.

He was heading for his vehicle when Montoya said, "I'll drive. That way you can make your calls on the way and it won't take three hours to get to Baton Rouge."

Bentz wanted to argue, but his partner had a point. Together they crossed the lot to the spot where Montoya's Mustang was parked. Unbuttoning his collar,

Bentz slid into the hot interior. The truth was that Brianna Hayward had hit a nerve, a raw one. He'd never felt a hundred percent certain about Donovan Caldwell as the 21 Killer. Back then the evidence had pointed his way and there'd been no other suspects. The DA had been intent on nailing Caldwell, and Bledsoe had zeroed in on Caldwell as the doer. As Brianna had pointed out, the evidence was highly circumstantial and largely due to Donovan Caldwell's own Internet presence, where he'd hinted that he was instrumental in his sisters' murders. He'd been stupidly bragging to what he'd assumed were like minds but, in reality, had been female cops looking to discover what turned him on.

Caldwell had pretty much buried himself. The jury had found Delta and Diana's brother guilty of their ritualistic murders.

As Montoya sped through the city streets, Bentz dialed Jonas Hayes's cell phone. It was two hours earlier in LA, so Bentz figured Hayes should still be working.

The Mustang's air conditioner kicked on, cool air starting to stream through the vents as Bentz waited. He watched as the buildings of the city passed by, shadows crawling across the storefronts before Montoya angled the Mustang to the freeway, heading northwest.

His call went directly to voice mail.

It figured.

So far today, nothing had come together. He left his name and number.

Maybe he'd get lucky in Baton Rouge.

Then again, maybe he'd strike out.

CHAPTER 10

The meeting hall smelled of age and disrepair. None of the antiseptic, bleach, or pine-scented cleaning supplies used to freshen up the old floors, walls, and counters could hide the fact that Aubrey House was well over 200 years old. As such, the timbers, bricks, and mortar had endured and survived dozens of disasters including hurricanes, floods, and even fire. Located in the French Quarter, Aubrey House had been built as the home of a baroness; over the decades and centuries it had been renovated and remodeled, cut into apartments, and retrofitted to its original glory. Now, it housed a variety of businesses, everything from a CPA to a psychic who read tarot cards and Brianna's own business office, where she met with clients who were more comfortable in an office setting rather than in her home.

The original ballroom was now a meeting area, complete with portable walls that could be moved to accommodate different sized groups. Tonight, the northwest quadrant was home to a twinless twins support group, which Brianna oversaw. Like Brianna, each person who attended the weekly meetings had lost his or her twin. The group provided a community of support to acknowledge feelings of loss over the death or removal of a twin. Discussions ranged beyond grief and separation anxiety to everyday stresses. They talked about jobs and bosses. Another family member, spouse, or significant other. Any topic was fair game, and the information shared here did not leave these walls. The idea was that victims with the shared experience of losing a twin could relate, but sometimes that wasn't the case due to the many diverse personalities involved.

As the organizer and leader, Brianna usually arrived at the room forty minutes before the scheduled meeting. Tonight, running late, she hurried in to find Tanisha busy making coffee and arranging cups and napkins on trays set on the stage, now used by the group as a serving table. An extension cord snaked from the coffeepot to the nearest outlet, and an Air-Pot held hot water. On the other tray sat a container of powdered creamer and two sugar bowls, one with individual packets of different sweeteners, the other with varieties of tea.

"Where have you been?" Tanisha chided as Mr. Coffee gurgled and sputtered. Dressed as always to the nines, her hair scraped back by a glittering headband that held her tightknit curls away from her face, Tanisha sent Brianna a smile meant to convey that she was kidding. "It's not like you to be late." Plucking a packet of sugar from the bowl, she shook the little package while waiting for the coffee to finish brewing.

"Delayed. Sorry." Brianna dumped her purse on the far end of the stage.

"I know what you mean."

Brianna seriously doubted it.

"I tell ya, I couldn't get back to sleep last night," Tanisha went on, her mocha-colored skin looking smooth as silk under the once-upon-a-time ballroom's chandeliers. Suspended from twenty-foot coved ceilings, the lights gave off a warm glow reminiscent of another era. The old-world charm was definitely at odds with the mismatched twentieth century furniture and portable "walls" used to separate the huge space.

"That dream I had?" Tanisha continued. "Whooee. So damned real. Lord!" Her eyebrows drew together as if she were still attempting to figure out the nightmare. "Don't know what it means. But something was off last night. Something big, a separation thing." As if she realized she was talking to herself, she glanced at Brianna. "What about you? You said you had a bad dream, too. Everything okay?"

"No."

"Uh-oh."

"I guess you haven't talked to Selma?"

Tanisha gave a soft snort of disgust. "Why would I?" Tanisha rolled her expressive, mascara-rimmed eyes. She and Selma had never really gotten to know each other. Whereas Selma Denning was in her mid-forties and stuck in a rut where her ex-husband was concerned, Tanisha, at twenty-eight, thought Selma should "kick that son of a bitch's ass to the curb and move the hell on." Ever forthright, Tanisha had said as much in one session. Of course, Tanisha's advice had gone over like the proverbial lead balloon.

"I don't know, I thought she might have called you and . . . and some of the others in the group," Brianna said as the coffeepot gave off a final hiss and the warm scent of java tried valiantly to hide the musty odor of the building.

"Well, she didn't." Tanisha's back was still up. "So what's up? God, that woman's a dishrag. No backbone, y' know."

"Her twins are missing. Both girls."

"Missing?" She still wasn't getting it. Pouring herself a cup of coffee, she frowned. "What do you mean 'missing'? As in adult kids didn't come in or call Mommy?"

"It's more than that."

As Tanisha doctored her coffee with sugar and powdered cream, Brianna gave her a quick rundown, and as the gravity of the situation sunk in, Tanisha's face fell. Compassion replaced belligerence. "Oh, my God, that's awful. You don't think . . . holy shit," she whispered. "The 21 Killer?" She blinked, disbelieving. Though she and Brianna had discussed the fact that Brianna thought the wrong man had been imprisoned, Tanisha had believed, or wanted desperately to believe, that 21 was behind bars.

"We don't know. Yet."

"This is awful." Tanisha set her undrunk cup on the tray holding the Air-Pot and glanced toward the entry as members of the group began to stream in.

Lincoln Robinson, a musician, could rarely scare up a smile despite the fact that he was happily married and the father of a fifteen-year-old scholar who was following in her father's footsteps as a pianist. Still, the weight of losing his brother was a burden Lincoln had trouble shouldering. Survivor's guilt. Both boys had been in an automobile accident nearly twenty years ago; while Lincoln survived, his brother had been pronounced DOA at the hospital. Tall, lean, and African American, Lincoln was a thoughtful member of the group, offering his stories and opinions quietly. He was the opposite of outspoken and direct Tanisha.

Lincoln lifted a hand in greeting and made his way to a chair he favored, positioned near the broad bank of windows running along one side of this third-floor room. "Evenin'," he said with a nod as Milo and Desmond walked in.

Milo, in his usual camouflage gear, grabbed a cup of black coffee and found a seat. He was on the quiet side, his connection being the loss of his twin sister when he was in his early twenties. He rarely spoke up and was vague when asked questions, even concerning his twin's death, but seemed to gain strength just being a part of the group.

Desmond didn't bother with coffee, and as he lumbered in, Brianna felt her insides twist a little. Desmond Underhill had always made her uncomfortable. She thought of him as a lurker. A big man, fortyish, and a carpenter with meat hooks for hands, he never offered much, even when spoken to. All she knew about him was that he'd lost his twin sister, Denise, when she drowned at age seven. That was why he felt out of step with other people. That was why he was here.

However, Desmond had never connected with the group or anyone who attended. It was almost as if he were an obvious voyeur, one who came and listened to everyone else's story without adding much of his own. Tonight, he was wearing his plaid shirt buttoned to his neck, his thin hair pulled into a scraggly ponytail, a few cuts visible on his face, which wasn't unusual. When asked about the abrasions, he'd always shrugged. "Work," he'd say, or "Huntin' in the woods." He beelined for his chair, in this case a faded wingback, pushed into the farthest corner, away from the rest of the group.

In the past Brianna had suggested that he pull in closer and engage in the discussion, but her request had always been met with silent resistance. He maintained his distance, content to watch the others. Despite the weather, he always wore a long-sleeved shirt and a vest with big pockets that often times bulged. She wondered what he was hiding. A bag of jerky? A recorder? A folding knife or gun? Or just his wallet? Her imagination took her to places she'd rather not go.

She told herself not to be so paranoid, recognizing that the situation with the Denning girls had amped her fears upward in the stratosphere.

For the most part, Brianna had given up trying to include Desmond in the ongoing discussion. It was hard enough to get Milo or Elise to participate, especially when Tanisha and Enrique always threatened to take over the meetings. Brianna hoped Desmond would join in when he felt compelled. But she wasn't counting on it.

Others filtered in. Elise Gaylord, the introspective thirty-five-year-old working on her PhD in history who was never without her knitting, was followed by Enrique Vega. Muttering under his breath, Enrique strutted across the room, found a chair, and plopped down with an energy drink he didn't appear to need. He worked out daily at a gym, his biceps huge beneath a tight T-shirt. Brianna believed his constant state of anger had more to do with still living "at home" at thirty than the loss of his twin, who might not even be dead. Juan Vega had disappeared, leaving for San Francisco and never talking to anyone in the family again. Enrique didn't know if his brother was still alive with a new identity, deliberately separated from the family, or the victim of foul play.

More than anything Enrique seemed pissed that his brother had taken off without him. "If Juan had taken me with him," Enrique had said on one occasion, his shaved head shining beneath the overhead lights, "he would be alive today. Okay? See what I mean? But he didn't even tell me he was leaving! What kind of brother does that? And he calls himself a twin! Bah!"

Now, slumping in his chair, his long legs crossed at the ankles, his eyes sparking with anger, Enrique popped open his drink and glowered as he drank and waited for the meeting to begin. Twice he glanced at the clock, then at Brianna. "We doin' this, or what?" he asked impatiently.

"In a minute," Brianna said loudly enough for him to hear. There were still a few others who might attend. Roger, the ex-football player who lived out of town. A big man who rarely spoke, he seemed bottled up and Brianna thought if anyone prodded and poked him too much, he might explode. There was anger beneath the surface of his calm. All Brianna really knew about him was that his twin, Ramona, had died at a campsite and that he blamed himself. Though her fall had been ruled an accident, Roger sensed that everyone, including his parents, thought he should have saved her.

A cell phone rang and Elise jumped, pulled it from her knitting bag, and spying the number on the screen, scuttled out to the hallway to find some privacy as she answered in hushed tones. She glanced furtively over her shoulder, as if she'd been caught in some kind of crime.

That was the thing with Elise. She always acted as if she had something to hide and much of her life was secret, which wasn't unusual in this group. The call was short and she hurried back inside to reclaim her seat. "Sorry," she said. "Ashton."

Tanisha turned her back to the young woman and rolled her eyes. Ashton was, as Elise had said in a moment of candor, the love of her life. But in the few comments Elise had made about him, Ashton seemed obsessive and controlling. Once Elise had received a call from him that prompted her to jump up and leave in the middle of the session. "I'm sorry. I'm so, so sorry. I just . . . I just have to go. Ashton needs some cold medication . . . he's not feeling well . . . I have to go." She'd nearly run from the room.

"That is such bullshit," Tanisha had said.

Brianna had shook her head as there were supposed to be no judgments in the group.

"You know it. I know it. Even *he* knows it," Tanisha had added, hooking a thumb toward Desmond. "That guy she's with, he's a control freak."

Elise had missed the next meeting, but had shown up ever since, never saying a word about her abrupt departure. She simply acted as if nothing out of the ordinary had happened. However, one time when Tanisha had asked how Ashton was, Elise had flinched. Her knitting needles lost their rhythm. "What do you mean? He's fine."

"Got over that cold or flu, did he?" Tanisha had asked as if she were truly interested, all the time ignoring Brianna's stern glance.

"The flu?" Elise seemed perplexed, then got it. "Oh. Sorry. No. He didn't have the flu or . . . or a cold. No. It was . . . was a rash. He just needed some . . . some cream. We were out." She'd smiled quickly, an embarrassed grin that hadn't touched her eyes and faded quickly at her obvious lie.

Now, Enrique scowled and cocked his left wrist, then tapped it repeatedly, even though he didn't wear a watch. His eyebrows arched as he tried to silently encourage Brianna to get on with it.

Brianna didn't understand what Enrique expected from the group, but she told herself if he didn't need the support, he wouldn't show up each week, which he did, faithfully. As he waited for his turn to speak, his leg bounced nervously, and he stayed attentive, like a racehorse ready to explode through the gate at the starting bell. Some of the members kept to themselves, but not Enrique. Nor, for that matter, did Tanisha, who was ready to tell the entire group about the failings of her family and current boyfriend. Tanisha and Enrique were definitely the firecrackers in the group.

Brianna was about to begin when Jenkins Olander strode into the room. Jenkins was a breath of fresh air. Unlike the other members, he offered a broad grin and lifted a hand in greeting as he made his way to the coffee machine. "How are you?" he asked Brianna, and gave a hug.

"Been better," she said as he broke off the quick embrace.

"Seriously? Ouch. I'm sorry." Jenkins pulled a face. "I hope it's not bad news." In his mid-twenties, Jenkins was blond, with a trimmed beard and quick sense of humor. Gay and in a long-term relationship, he had a job he liked and a supportive family. Still, he couldn't put behind him the fact that his twin brother had died from a rare form of cancer that even a bone marrow transfer from his identical twin hadn't been able to destroy.

Before Brianna could explain, Selma appeared, dressed in the same clothes she'd been wearing earlier in the day, her face devoid of makeup. Her hair hung limp in the ponytail, strands falling around her face and behind her glasses. Her eyes seemed to have sunken into her skull.

Obviously her daughters were still missing.

"Selma," Brianna said, walking to the doorway to greet her.

"You talked with the detective?" Selma asked.

"Yes, I did." Somehow Brianna had to put a positive spin on her meeting with Bentz. "I hope I lit a fire under him."

"But you don't know."

"I'll talk to him tomorrow. For sure."

Selma looked about to fall down. "I don't know what I'm doing here," she admitted. "I should be home, in case Zoe or Chloe show up. They might come for their car. . . ."

"You have your cell. Come on. How about a cup of coffee?"

Tanisha, who had overhead the conversation, was on it, reaching for a cup. "Regular?" she asked.

"I don't care."

Brianna met Tanisha's gaze. "Let's go with decaf, and then I think we'd better get started."

"About time," Enrique remarked with a pissy expression as he glared at the clock mounted to one side of the stage.

"*Some*one woke up on the wrong side of bed this morning." Jenkins lifted an eyebrow and gave Enrique a stare as he stirred Equal into his coffee.

Brianna hated to defend him, but said, "Enrique's right. We should get started." The fact that Roger and Latrice hadn't shown wasn't that much of a surprise. Neither of them was all that tight with the group. "I guess if anyone else comes, they'll catch up."

"Shit, man, are you waiting for Roger?" Enrique snorted his disgust. "You can't count on that dude. He's whacked!"

"Well, aren't we all, to some degree?" Jenkins threw back at him. "Wow. Way to be judgmental, Rico."

"It's Enrique."

"Whatever." Jenkins' smile stretched a bit. He loved toying with the hothead.

Brianna warned, "Play nice."

"Oh, ouch. *I'm* not the touchy one." Jenkins took a sip from his cup, made a face, and said, "You know, we really outta get some real cream here. This chemical garbage doesn't cut it."

"Organic?" Lincoln joked, trying to lighten the mood.

Tanisha wasn't amused. She glared at Jenkins. "Fine. From now on, the cream and sugar and whatever anyone wants, that's *your* job." She pointed a glossy-tipped finger at the middle of Jenkins's chest. "And while you're at it, maybe some of that foo-foo flavoring. Hazelnut, or vanilla, or whatever other crap you all are into."

"Wow. Seems to be an epidemic of irritation around here."

"Excuse me?" Tanisha demanded hotly, but Jenkins backed off and found his seat.

"Take it down a notch," Brianna suggested to Tanisha, and patted the air in a "calm down" motion. "This is supposed to be a support group."

"Humph. With numb nuts?" Tanisha's eyes narrowed on Jenkins.

"Hey!" Brianna shook her head. This could escalate no further. "We're not in second grade. Okay?"

With an effort Tanisha tamped down her temper. "Yeah, I know. I'm just edgy. Lack of sleep."

Reining things in, Brianna focused on Selma. "Are you sure you're up for this?"

"No, but . . . why not? I can't just sit in the apartment."

"Okay, then maybe you should be first tonight. Come on." She guided Selma into a chair and took the seat next to her.

Although Tanisha left the steaming cup of decaf on a small table beside her, Selma didn't seem to notice. She clasped her hands between her knees and hung her head for a few seconds. Then when she finally pulled herself together enough so that she could talk, she took a deep breath. "This isn't about Sandra," she said, mentioning the twin sister she'd lost fourteen years earlier. "It's about my daughters, Zoe and Chloe." Her voice cracked on their names. "They're missing."

CHAPTER 11

"I don't need much," Edward said from somewhere on the other end of the phone connection, most likely the Texas hill country, where he'd been born and raised and had brought up his sons until moving to the farm outside of New Orleans.

Jase imagined his father, thin as a rail, lines marring his face, the scents of smoke and stale whiskey clinging to a graying beard that needed to be trimmed and jeans that hadn't seen the inside of a washing machine for several weeks. Once a lean, tough ranch hand whose craggy face and sexy smile had caused more than his share of female hearts to skip a beat, Edward Bridges was now a ghost of his former Marlboro Man self. "You know, I just could use enough to get me through to the first of the month when I get my check." Ed's words were slurred as he wheedled his way through the pitch, which was always the case when he called to ask his son for money.

"Dad," Jase said, leaning against the wall of his apartment and glancing to the living room where the slider door was cracked a bit, the night air slipping inside. "We've been through this all before."

"I know, I know, but just hear me out. It's been rough around here for the past couple o' weeks. Landlord's threatening to throw me on the street." Ed laughed then, the chuckle rolling into a cough aggravated by forty years of cigarettes. "I'm just talkin' a couple o' hundred. Maybe three. You know I'll pay ya back."

That, Jase didn't know. He had no idea how much he'd loaned his old man over the years. But in a way, it was payback to a father who had, in his dysfunctional manner, stood by his two sons when their mother had taken off after the loss of a third child, the brother Jase had never known.

Prescott had given up on the man who, as far as he was concerned, had done such a piss-poor job of single parenting. As for their mother, Marian Selby Bridges, child-bride and runaway wife? Neither Jase nor Prescott had ever heard from her. Neither man knew if she was dead or alive, and neither cared. At least she wasn't calling and begging for money.

At that thought, Jase cringed.

"The old man's playing you for a patsy," Prescott had advised a few years back. Prescott had never bought into their father's "poor me" act, and Edward Bridges's series of girlfriends who called themselves "Auntie Maureen" or "Auntie Raydeen" or "Auntie Lou" to Edward's sons had left a sour taste in both boys' mouths. It wasn't much of a wonder that Prescott had moved out and married Lena Hendrix, a woman with a firm set of values and a commitment to God, country, and, once she was wed, her husband.

Prescott had offered advice about handling their dad over the years. "You're enabling him, bro," Prescott had said during one memorable phone call. Jase had been in his truck, having just met with his father and, yes, "loaning" the old man a couple of hundred bucks. Again. Prescott had called as Jase was driving through the slanting rain to his apartment. At a red light, Jase waited while a man walking a huge dog crossed the street. His cell had been jammed against his ear listening to his brother. Prescott had said, "Stop. Okay?" Jase didn't respond as the wipers slapped off the fat drops and the streetlight shimmered scarlet against the pavement. "Just don't give him the cash. He'll quit calling. Trust me. That's what I did and he finally took the hint. Hell, I can't take care of a wife and two kids *and* Dad, too."

Jase hadn't argued. He'd known his brother was right, but he'd never had the heart to completely write off his father. Not then. Not now. Not when he felt responsible to the father who'd raised him.

Times had been hard. Jase had grown up rough and tumble as his father had followed the work, moving from town to town, ranch to ranch until Edward with his affinity for the bottle and dragging two trouble-making boys had worn out their welcome. Along the way Jase had learned how to build a fence, round up strays, and buck hay, all the while attending three different elementary schools. He'd also discovered how to fight and when to run. Eventually, with a little luck, a lot of work, and an inheritance from his grandmother, he'd been able to make his way through college and law school. Scholarships and a federal loan or two had helped. He'd also found out that sitting in an office twelve hours a day doing legal research wasn't in his DNA. A year after he'd taken a job with DeWitt, Montgomery and Horowitz, he'd quit and pursued freelance journalism, which had been his minor as an undergrad.

Ridiculously, because of his father's own struggles Jase felt more than a little guilty about his accomplishments, something Edward had sensed and preyed upon.

As he was now.

"The way I figure it," his father was saying, "I took care of you and your brother for all those years after your mother took off. And then you two kids inherit a shitload of money from your grandma, enough so you can get yourself through school and Prescott can pay for a goddamned BMW, a fuckin' engagement ring with a rock the size of Gibraltar, and a damned wedding in the Bahamas. Talk about pissin' it away!" He snorted in disgust. "You two kids ended up with the house and ranch, too." Now he sounded bitter. He'd inherited his mother's twenty-year-old Cadillac and a few thousand dollars, a hand slap from the grave. "So now, son, you and your brother?" Ed said. "You owe me."

"That's not the way it works," Jase said, though he did get it. Their father's portion of the inheritance had been small, and Ed had blown through it within a year.

"Look, Jase, I'm in a bind here. You know I hate to ask, but I got no choice. My back's in a corner."

"Okay, so I send you the money. What happens next month?"

"Hell, next month won't be a problem. I got a side job that'll pay out and by then my checks from the government will be comin' steady-like, so I'll be good."

He shouldn't do it. Jase knew he should stay strong. But suddenly he remembered his old man with a shovel,

Edward's hands so dirty you couldn't see his nails as he stood beneath the spreading branches of that single tree visible from the living room of the house where Jase and Prescott had grown up, the house that it seemed he might soon own.

"I'll pay ya back, son, I promise." A pause. Heavy with portent. "I know things," he said around a cough.

Now it was Jase's turn to be silent, but his fingers clenched tightly over his phone and his shoulder muscles tightened.

He heard a lighter click and then a long intake of breath. "I'd hate to tell the family's dirty little secret, but . . ." A long sigh. "A man's got to do what a man's got to do."

Jase thought about his own reputation, how he'd battled to lose the stink of the poor, tough kid who'd been at odds with the law, maybe even society when he thought about it. His jaw slid to one side as he considered Prescott, now playing the part of a religious man, a pillar in his church, a husband and father.

Trinity and Caleb's innocent faces came to mind.

They didn't deserve this. Jase had lived with the threat of his whole life unraveling, but he couldn't face his niece and nephew carrying that burden with them. They knew nothing of their family's secrets and shadowy past. It was best to keep it that way.

"You're resorting to blackmail now?" Jase said, and heard his father take another deep intake of breath, remembered how the tip of Edward's Marlboro glowed fiery red as he'd stood in the doorway of the farmhouse, staring into the night while rain had peppered the tin roof of the porch and gurgled down the gutters.

His father replied, "As I said, 'A man's got to do what a man's got to do.'"

"Bullshit, Dad."

Another pause. Another drag on the cigarette. Would Jase's old man really do it? Actually go to the authorities, bring up a decades' old crime? Or was Ed just blowing smoke? That was the problem with the past, it never really was over and gone. Long-dead misdeeds, buried and forgotten, had a tendency to rise up and sting you.

"I ain't kiddin', son."

Jase felt as if he were being squeezed in his grandfather's old vise, the one in the barn. Slowly and deliberately his father was turning the handle, making the jaws dig farther and farther into his flesh.

He caved.

Hated himself for it.

"Fine, Dad," he said through clenched teeth. "I'll send the check." God, he was weak. He should have called the old man's bluff. "It'll go out tomorrow, but it's the last time."

"'Course it is, but I was hopin' you might be able to wire it, y'know. Through Western Union. It's faster. Or I'll come get it."

"I'm sending a check. That's it." He hesitated, then added, "And I've recorded this conversation. I've got an app that does that. So, when you call next month, I'm going to play it back to you."

"What? For the love of Christ! I swear it. Aren't you listening? You won't need to, Jase," Edward insisted. "And you'll get your money back, you'll see." Ed hung up then. Mission accomplished.

Jase clicked his phone off and closed his eyes. He leaned his head against the wall and then banged it a couple of times, groaning. The problem was unending. His father had a love affair with the bottle; that was the long and short of it. And though he'd get sober and stay that way for months at a time, even landing jobs, Ed always broke down. Something or someone set him off, and he was soon cozying up to Jack Daniels or Jim Beam all over again.

Never once had he considered rehab. Jase had tried to get him into treatment, but after Ed's flat-out refusals to enter any kind of program, Jase had eventually given up. His grandmother's old adage came to mind: "You can lead a horse to water, but you can't make it drink. Especially if it's a stubborn old mule!"

Edward Bridges had the stubborn part down pat.

And so Jase enabled him, a bit at a time. Sporadically his father called, always about something else, but the bottom line was that Ed ended up pleading for money and making Jase feel like a heel for putting the old man through it.

Jase glanced outside to his deck that ran the length of his one-bedroom unit situated three stories above the street. A moth was beating itself up near the window where, on the inside, a lamp was glowing. "I feel ya, pal," he said. His whole damned family needed counseling, but it wasn't going to happen. At least not tonight.

Ignoring his own sudden need for a beer, he pushed himself away from the wall and walked into the living room, where he flopped onto the couch with his laptop. His flat-screen mounted over the fireplace showed highlights of the week's sports events on ESPN, the sound muted. He clicked onto the Internet through the newspaper's server and started his search for information on the 21 Killer.

He'd heard more of Brianna's conversation with Bentz than he'd admitted and now was on the track of the missing twins she'd mentioned. It didn't take long. After logging in through the *Observer's* Web site, he located information on the Reeves twins who'd gone missing from Phoenix, and Beau and Belle January from Dallas. They, too, had vanished, one after the other.

Victims of the 21 Killer?

Or just a coincidence?

Identical twins in the first case, but male.

Fraternal twins in the second, a man and a woman.

Not 21's MO.

After printing out the information on each of the missing sets of twins, Jase added his own notes, including what he'd overheard about Zoe and Chloe Denning. The Denning girls fit the profile of 21's victims much more closely than the other two sets. Was it possible that the killer had expanded from only female victims? The fact that they were killed as they turned twenty-one, of legal age, had to be significant. The killer was obviously making a statement about reaching adulthood, coming of age. Or was that just psychological crap and the guy was just a freak who had a fascination with twenty-first birthdays?

If they are victims of 21. Remember, the police and the criminal justice system think they got their man. There's a chance this is all just Brianna Hayward's half-baked theory.

He chewed on that; he didn't think Brianna was the

type to go off half-cocked, even if she was motivated by the desire to get her cousin Caldwell out of jail.

Then again, what did he really know about her? She'd been just a kid when he'd last seen her.

Still searching, Jase pulled up everything he could find about Donovan Caldwell, including the abduction and murders of his sisters, Delta and Diana. The abduction and ritualistic murders of Caldwell's siblings mirrored those of Lucy and Laney Springer, two more of the 21 Killer's victims.

Either the identical double homicides were committed by the same nut job, his apprentice, or a copycat who had inside information. From what source? The killer himself? An accomplice? A leak in the LAPD who would have information not given to the press or public?

Again, he made notes to himself. He had a buddy who'd worked at the *LA Times* for years, had some connections with the LAPD. Jase phoned, but his friend didn't pick up, so he left a voice mail, then a quick text. As he read on, one of the most glaring facts that came out of his research was that there had been a gap of twelve years, a long span between the killings of the Caldwell twins and the Springer girls.

Had Donovan Caldwell suppressed his urges for a dozen years?

Unlikely.

Had the killer moved to another territory for a while, then returned to kill the Springer twins? If so, there were no records of Donovan Caldwell moving between the two double homicides, a fact his lawyer hammered home during the trial.

Jase poured over the data.

What, if any, was the link between the two sets of twins?

Leaning back on the couch, one heel propped on the coffee table, he stared at the television mounted over the grate, but he didn't pay attention to the highlights of a recent baseball game. His thoughts were turned inward. The time gap between the murders bothered him. Could the second set of murders have been at the hands of a copycat? If so, had that killer traveled to New Orleans from LA?

The LAPD hadn't prosecuted Donovan Caldwell for the Springer twins' murders. The prosecutors obviously hadn't found enough evidence to link Caldwell to the second set of homicides and had to settle for prosecuting him for the ritualistic killings of his sisters.

Caldwell had admitted to disliking his siblings, even resenting them, and he'd been an odd duck, a person who could make others uncomfortable or wary. But had he been capable of this macabre murder of his sisters, stripping them and hog-tying them and killing them as they turned of age?

The jury had said yes, and he was now serving time for the murders. He'd screamed in the courtroom that he was innocent and he'd been insisting ever since that he didn't kill his sisters. But that was par for the course for convicts. Many claimed their innocence.

Jase raked his fingers through his hair.

He stared at a picture of Donovan Caldwell, a man who blended in with the crowd. While his sisters had been gorgeous and outgoing, popular and, by all accounts, well-rounded, fun individuals, Caldwell had been a loner, a plain-looking man who had trouble holding down a job or forming any relationship. He'd taken the stand and to his attorney's dismay referred to Delta and Diana as "the twins," hooking air quotes. During his testimony he'd been unable to hide his disdain for them.

Probably sealed his fate.

Then there was the question of the murder case that occurred twelve years later. Was Caldwell also responsible for that? Lucy and Laney Springer's murders had brought the unsolved Caldwell twins' homicides to the fore, and somehow the new evidence or technology had been enough to convict Donovan for the older killings of his sisters. Not so for the Springer girls.

Did Donovan Caldwell actually wait twelve years to repeat his crimes, to relive taking his sisters' lives? Or were there other victims scattered around the country, dual corpses of twins who'd disappeared and had never been located?

Far-fetched.

But even the most unbelievable homicides happened. Bizarre murders were rare, but certainly existed. Jase had only to think of the stories he'd covered or look at the true crime books stacked haphazardly on his bookcase near the fireplace to confirm that truth was stranger than fiction. People were capable of monstrous, heinous, and bizarre actions. Some targeted family members, others randomly picked strangers.

Father John was an example of a killer who targeted strangers for the most part. Posing as a priest, he'd killed prostitutes in the city, though his ultimate target had been someone he'd known.

"All kinds of psychos," Jase told himself, cracking his neck to relieve some tension before turning to his computer for more digging. He scoured the Internet for

information on Donovan Caldwell, finding old newspaper reports, court records, and interviews with the
arresting officer. Throughout the arrest, arraignment,
trial, and conviction, Caldwell had screamed his innocence, but was hauled off to jail. To this day he swore
that he'd been railroaded by police and prosecutors,
who felt pushed by public pressure to get the 21 Killer
off the streets. The prosecution had asserted that as the
oldest and only son of a man's man who wanted his
male heir to succeed, Caldwell had been unable to meet
his father's expectations. Told he was a failure, Caldwell had hidden his simmering resentment for years
and plotted his revenge to take away his father's fa-
vorites. He had reveled in his domination and control
of their last seconds of life, ensuring they would never
reach adulthood.

Case closed.

Until now . . . Combing through the data on the missing twins in Arizona and Texas, he wasn't convinced that
the 21 Killer was behind their disappearances. Everything was off about them. But, unfortunately, the Denning girls were a different matter altogether.

Jase set his laptop aside and walked to the kitchen.
Was it possible? Had the cops arrested the wrong man?
Had the jury jumped to the wrong conclusions? Was
Donovan Caldwell serving time for crimes he hadn't
committed? And if so, was the real killer now stalking
the streets of New Orleans?

Why would 21 come here? he wondered. To prove a
point and goad Rick Bentz, as Brianna had asserted?
That theory seemed thin, but Jase wasn't going to dismiss anything at this point.

Opening his refrigerator, he frowned at its meager

contents, which consisted of a cardboard slice of pizza from a week ago, a bottle of ketchup, and three lonely beers. "Pathetic." He grabbed a long-necked bottle from the shelf and cracked it open before heading outside and standing on the deck. Three stories, traffic moved slowly, headlights visible through the leaves and dripping Spanish moss dangling from the branches of live oaks planted along the street.

Taking a long pull on the bottle, he felt the cold beer slide down his throat and hit his stomach.

Mosquitos buzzed near his head. Somewhere in the distance someone was playing a saxophone, the melancholy notes of a bluesy song rising upward from the street. He relaxed a bit. Cleared his thoughts. Until, in his mind's eye, he saw Brianna's face. Damn she looked like her twin.

Arianna Hayward.

Oh, hell.

Leaning over the railing, holding his bottle in both hands, he silently cursed the gods who had gotten him tangled up with Arianna.

His jaw clenched so hard it ached. Though Jase hadn't known Brianna in high school, he'd met Arianna. More than once. A lot more. Dark thoughts came to mind, disturbing images he'd rather forget.

Rolling his bottle in his hands, he told himself not to go there.

But that might prove impossible since Brianna had been on his mind since the moment he'd heard from his brother that she lived nearby. She was trouble, he knew that, and she was the one woman in the world he should avoid at all costs, a woman who was dangerous to him, one who could ruin him if she ever guessed the truth.

And his connection to 21.

A story he couldn't let go.

The 21 Killer was intriguing, if appalling at the same time. "21" would hold the public's interest. Would sell papers. Above that, finding more about him, linking him to the current case of the missing girls, proving that the police in LA were wrong, might give Jase more cred not only as a crime reporter but as an investigative journalist. Someone who could dig deep, uncover the truth.

But if Brianna were right, the LAPD would end up with a black eye. And if Jase was involved in unraveling the story, how would that play here with the New Orleans department? It was a quick way to slam doors in his own face. Bentz wouldn't care; he'd left LA on bad terms, but the brass at NOPD might see him as a rogue.

Well, hell, who really cared?

The story was the story, the truth was the truth, and the public had a right to know. Jase was more than willing to offer it up. Even if there was a personal price to pay.

The prospect that 21 may have resurfaced or that a copycat killer may have stepped into the murderer's bloody shoes made a helluva story, one he wanted to pursue. If it was true. His conscience nagged a bit. Deep down, he hoped to hell Brianna Hayward's theory proved wrong. For the Denning sisters' sake. And for any other set of twins about to become adults and catch the killer's attention.

But if the maniac existed, he needed to be exposed and taken down.

Jase was the man for the job.

Even if it means dealing with Brianna Hayward? Think of the consequences of getting close to her.

Personally, the smartest thing he could do was back away from her and this entire mess.

Then again, he thought as he drained his beer, he'd never been smart where women were concerned.

CHAPTER 12

Jase was waiting for her. Big as life, long legs stretched in front of him, he leaned against the hood of her car as she exited the restaurant two doors down from Aubrey House where she and Tanisha had coaxed Selma to eat some dinner. They'd also drunk a glass of wine and had lingered over dessert while talking for hours.

Jase started to push himself upright, but she held up a finger to keep him at bay, silently asking for a little time. He got the message.

"So you'll be all right?" she asked Selma.

"Of course not, but . . . yeah . . . no . . . Oh, God! I don't think I'll ever be 'all right' again." Pale and shaky, Selma scrabbled in her purse, no doubt searching for her cigarettes.

As Selma found a half-empty pack and lit up a filter tip, Tanisha's dark gaze met Brianna's. The silent message she conveyed wasn't good. They both were worried sick about Selma and her daughters.

It had been Brianna's idea to grab a bite at the pub. She knew it had been an exhausting day for Selma, who had poured her heart out in the meeting. It had been difficult for Selma to let the members of the group witness her anguish. Thankfully everyone had let her speak, the sparse comments confined to condolences and words of encouragement.

The tone of the meeting had been somber, almost bleak. As twins, everyone had heard of the 21 Killer, and Brianna suspected some held a macabre fascination for the killer who targeted twin siblings. The group had been thankful that the murderer had been caught, tried, and convicted . . . until Selma's worries had opened the door to a terrible new possibility that 21 was still at large.

Even usually talkative and smiling Jenkins had been somber. Enrique had put aside his hostility and Elise, though constantly knitting, hadn't turned the discussion back to her problems. Milo had remained silent, and Jenkins had sadly shaken his head throughout Selma's story. Tanisha, who'd always been hard on Selma, had shown a kinder side and insisted on joining them for dinner where not only did she allow Selma to fall apart, but showed true empathy and understanding.

"You sure you want to go home?" Tanisha asked as the three women walked to the spot where Selma's little Chevy was parked.

"Yes, of course. I'll be fine." Selma drew deeply on her cigarette. "I mean as fine as I can be."

Brianna didn't like the idea of Selma being alone. "You could stay at my house," she offered.

"No, no. The girls could come home or call the house phone. Oh, please God!" She took a calming drag from her Salem Light, and added, "No, I really need to go home."

"Then I could come over," Brianna said.

"Or me," Tanisha offered. "I got nothing goin' at home." She slid a meaningful glance toward Brianna's Honda and the man leaning against the passenger side before her gaze met Brianna's.

"No, please . . . it's been a long day and a long night before that. I just need some time to think and—" Her phone jangled and she jumped. Juggling her cigarette, she anxiously pulled the cell from her bag. "Carson," she said, her frown deepening. "Look . . . I'd better take this. He might know something." She answered with so much hope in her voice that Brianna's heart twisted.

She slid a glance at Jase, ever-patient, it seemed, as if he didn't have anything better to do than wait there beneath a tree. Lingering in the lamplight, his hands in his pockets, he appeared cool and at ease, which she doubted.

"Damn," Selma said on a breath that drew Brianna's attention back to her. "Okay. Fine." The droop of her thin shoulders and disappointment in her short answers suggested that her ex-husband wasn't offering any support. "But don't blame me . . . no, don't. Carson, just don't! No excuses . . . For the love of God, we're in a crisis here." A pause. She took another drag, then dropped her cigarette onto the curb and crushed it beneath one sandaled foot. "Oh . . . Jesus, please, just call me if you hear anything and I'll do the same." She clicked off the phone and quickly fumbled in her purse again, found a fresh cigarette, and lit up. "Such a bastard," she hissed in a cloud of smoke. "Such a damned bastard." As if suddenly remembering she wasn't alone, she fought a fresh onslaught of tears and forced a tremulous grin. "I'd better go. Maybe the girls will show up at my place. . . ." But her brave smile faltered and she swallowed hard.

"I'll follow you," Tanisha said. Before Selma could argue, Tanisha sent Brianna an I've-got-this glance, then hurried to her own vehicle, a muscle car one of her exes had suggested she buy. The Dodge was parked half a block up the street.

Brianna watched her wend her way past a couple locked in an embrace. Tanisha sent them a dark glare as she strode past them.

"Look, Selma," Brianna offered, "I'd be glad to come over to—"

"No! Go. Talk to Bentz or the police or anyone else who might help. Work on it from that end. Please. I . . . I just can't deal with the cops or any more questions right now, but we have to get the word out, have to find the girls . . ."

"I will," Brianna promised as she hugged her friend and felt the smaller woman nearly crumple in her arms. "Call me if you hear anything. And when you have time, send me that list."

"List? Oh, yes. Right."

"And the timeline," Brianna reminded her. Over dinner they'd discussed putting together a timeline and a record of the events as they knew them, as well as a complete list of everyone the girls knew, or may have come in contact with last night. Although Selma had filled out a report at the Baton Rouge PD, she'd been upset at the time, well, more like totally freaked out, so Brianna had suggested she write down everything she could think of: friends, enemies, teachers, employers, arguments the twins had been involved in, boyfriends they'd broken up with, out-of-town friends or relatives, e-mail addresses, social media platforms, and phone numbers. Anything that might lead to finding the girls. Brianna wanted to wade through the information and pass it on to both police departments.

"I will," Selma promised. She settled behind the wheel of her Chevy and rolled down the window.

"Take care," Brianna said.

Selma placed her cigarette in the car's ashtray. "Thanks." As Brianna stepped away from the curb, Selma pulled into traffic, narrowly missing a motorcycle that came roaring down the street. Up the street, brake lights flashed in Tanisha's Charger, and as soon as the Chevy passed, Tanisha's car moved into the street behind her.

Brianna turned.

Jase had straightened, his hands in his pockets, his athletic silhouette backlit by headlights as a truck rumbled past. His gaze found hers, and for the briefest of seconds the back of her throat turned to dust and she was a schoolgirl again, harboring a secret crush.

Damn.

No matter how it all played out, she figured, this was gonna get messy.

Zoe's ankle throbbed and her skin was burned, hot to the touch. Add to that, she was hungry and thirsty. Yeah, the river was right there, a few feet away, but so far, she hadn't drunk from it. Well, as long as you didn't count the kabillion gallons of water she'd swallowed during her swim the night before. She couldn't just lie here of course. If she did, she was a sitting duck. Besides, no one would find her in the dark.

Once again she thought of the creatures of the night.

As frightening as snakes and gators were, they were nothing compared to the psycho who'd abducted her and planned her torturous demise.

Setting her jaw, she pushed herself upright and ignored the headache pounding behind her eyes and the pain splintering up her leg from an ankle that felt as big as a cantaloupe. Her stomach grumbled, but that was to be expected. Slowly, painfully, she pushed her way up the bank and felt the ground. She thought she'd seen a stick she could use as a crutch, something to lean on, but her progress would be slow. Her plan, if she had one, was to walk as far as she could into the forest and then, come first light, head farther down river.

She had searched for signs of civilization, a light shining on either side of the river, but here, in the middle of nowhere, the darkness offered no beacon of hope. Even if she caught sight of a flashlight's beam, she would have to hold her tongue for fear that is was the freak on her trail. Although there were night fishermen and poachers and alligator hunters—all of whom would use a flashlight to find and kill prey—she wouldn't know whether the light was generated by an outdoorsman or the douchebag himself.

Slowly she inched her way up the bank, her skin raw and muddy, her thoughts returning to Chloe. God, where was her twin? Hopefully, Zoe prayed, at a police station telling the cops what had happened, or somewhere using a telephone and calling Dad. He would know what to do. Not Mom. Not first. She would just fall apart or scold before she pulled herself together and called the authorities.

Zoe's heart grew heavier when she thought of her mother. No doubt Selma was going out of her mind with worry, having no idea of the terrifying circumstances her daughters had fallen into. She might even be pissed, thinking Zoe and Chloe were hungover somewhere and sleeping it off.

If only.

Her hand slid along a sharp blade of some kind of grass, which sliced into her skin.

"Crap!" Zoe whispered, jerking her arm back. "Shit!"

Craaack!

A twig snapped nearby.

Zoe froze.

Heart beating a wild tattoo, she strained to determine the source of the noise. All the while she braced herself, certain that the monster would leap out of the darkness, a machete raised, his eyes and teeth gleaming hideously in the barest light from the weak crescent moon.

Her skin crawled and she slid her fingers through the darkness, across weeds and grime, searching for a rock or stick, any kind of weapon.

Ssssh.

A rustle in the brush. Movement in the cattails and nettles.

God, have mercy.

Her fingertips scraped across a stone buried deep in the mud. She dug around the edges, forcing her nails and fingers to clutch the golf-ball-sized rock and jerk it upward. A sucking sound ensued.

Okay, Freak, I'm ready for you—

The grass beside her shifted.

Zoe jumped backward and pain streaked up her leg. Her pulse pounded like crazy.

Hoisting the rock into the air, she spied two shiny objects in the scant moonlight. A pair of eyes, small and beady, poised only a few inches from the ground. The creature glared at her.

Hiissss.

A jagged smile of white teeth glistened.

Her heart nearly stopped.

She raised her hand. Aimed.

The creature uttered another sibilant hiss just as Zoe recognized it as a possum.

Letting out her breath, she watched as the shaggy marsupial bared its needle-sharp teeth again, then waddled away into the darkness, leaving Zoe, arm still raised to hurl the rock, gasping and inwardly calling herself a fool.

A possum?

All that panic for a possum?

"Grow some balls," she whispered to herself. Rather than take the encounter as a warning, she decided instead to think of the meeting with the possum as impetus to find her way to the nearest farmhouse or cabin.

If the damned possum could wander safely around in the dark, she decided, her chances weren't as bad as she'd imagined.

You could take to the water again, float downstream, save your ankle from bearing weight.

But she was too exhausted to consider swimming right now. Too easily she could get caught in the current and drown. Besides, she'd rather take her chances with the creatures on land than find herself wrestling with an alligator or water snake.

There are plenty of snakes in the wetlands. Alligators, too. Maybe even a bear or boar as well.

"Awesome," she said under her breath. Still, she was determined to get as far from the river as possible. It would be easy for her hunter to spot her on the open water. She was certain of it.

Time to move on.

Regardless of how excruciating the pain.

"How's she doing?" Jase notched his chin toward the street where Selma's car was rounding the corner. He'd obviously guessed that the fragile woman Brianna had walked to her car was the mother of the Denning twins.

"I'd like to say 'hanging in there,' but it would be a lie." Brianna only hoped that her friend would get some rest and take the time to make that list. It might provide crucial information to track the girls down. Keys in hand, she hit the button on her remote. The car made a sharp noise and the locks clicked in response. "But I can't blame Selma for being frantic. How would any mom hold up under these circumstances?"

"Point taken."

"I assume you're waiting for me."

"See? You do have detective skills." A hint of a smile slashed across his beard-shadowed jaw.

She wasn't in the mood for jokes. Nor would she allow herself to be charmed by this old high-school crush, even if he was damned handsome in the warm summer night. She stepped into the watery glow of the streetlamp and tried to tamp down her awareness of him: his shoulders wide, his lips blade thin, his eyes deep-set and intense. And then there was that scar. He appeared as rugged and sexy as she remembered from high school. Maybe even a little dangerous.

Ridiculous!

Years ago she would have killed to have him stare at her as intently as he was now, but tonight she wasn't about to get lost in his gaze. "How'd you find me?"

"I'm a wiz on the Internet."

"Humble."

"Hey, it's what I do." He flashed a self-deprecating grin. "And it wasn't that tough. You were written up a few months back, in the *Observer* no less, about the twinless twin thing."

She remembered. It had been a small, obscure human interest story, a few column inches, the interview done over the phone by a female reporter.

"I put two and two together," he said. Again the barest of smiles, almost self-deprecating.

Was it possible? Jase Bridges could actually not take himself seriously?

No way.

"So, okay. You must want something."

One eyebrow lifted. "Direct, aren't you?"

"I'm not big on beating around the bush. Besides, I'm tired. It's been a long day." And it had been. She felt as if she'd been spinning her wheels for hours, getting nowhere, slamming her head against a brick wall, making zero progress. And all the while there was so much at stake; the twins were missing. "Last night wasn't much better," she admitted, thinking of her dream and Tanisha's phone call. Trouble sleeping. Again. "Is there a reason you're here?"

"I've been doing some checking. I think you might be on to something."

Finally, someone who believed her. Someone with intense hazel eyes that, she suspected, didn't miss much.

"But I'm not sure you've got it all right," he said as a horse-drawn carriage rounded the corner. "I don't see that the twins who are missing in Phoenix and Dallas play into it."

"You did eavesdrop."

He didn't deny it. "Yeah, and then I checked into the missing persons cases you described. Tell ya what, why don't you let me buy you a drink and we'll discuss?"

She was about to argue, but he said, "I know. I get it. You're tired. Been through an emotional wringer with your friend, whom, I assume, is close to you."

"Pretty close." The carriage rolled by, the clop of steel hooves ringing as the dappled horse plodded past.

"So, this won't take long," he said, his eyes following the carriage's progress. He turned his gaze to her again. "Promise. One drink. Let's just go over your theory that Donovan Caldwell was wrongly convicted and that 21 has started up again."

She shouldn't. She knew it was a mistake. But, in truth, a drink sounded like heaven. And she still had a fascination with Jase Bridges, stupid as that was. Besides, she could use an ally, any ally, and one in the press, especially one with ties to the police department. Deciding to hear what he had to say, she gave a quick nod. "Fine." She remotely locked her car again and heard it chirp a response. "You're on, Bridges. But you're buying."

His lips found that same irreverent smile she'd remembered from high school. "Wouldn't have it any other way." He hitched his chin to indicate the other side of the street where a pub with a wide, paned window and glowing neon lights was wedged between a retro boutique and a sandwich shop offering tarot readings along with a soup of the day. "We can talk in there."

CHAPTER 13

A slice of moon was barely visible from the clouds scudding across the night sky. Inside the Mustang, Bentz stared at the stream of northbound traffic, headlights bright, while Montoya drove steadily back toward New Orleans. Bentz undid the top button of his shirt. He was sweating, the interior of the car muggy, despite the efforts of the Mustang's air-conditioning system.

Regardless of the heat and humidity, Montoya was still wearing his leather jacket, the diamond stud winking in the half-light. Montoya was always as cool, it seemed, as the proverbial cucumber. He had, though, ditched his shades. Sometimes one had to be practical.

"So, we're battin' a thousand," Montoya said sarcastically as he pressed on the accelerator to pass a white Buick LeSabre whose driver, wearing a driving cap, kept his vehicle five miles under the speed limit.

"I guess."

The trip to Baton Rouge had proved uneventful and brought back a slew of memories, not many of them good, to a time when Bentz's daughter Kristi had at-

tended school at All Saints. As the sun had lowered and
shadows lengthened over the campus, Bentz had walked
across the quad, past the library, and in front of Wagner
House with its elegant façade and dark, hidden tunnels
below. A feeling of déjà vu had chilled his soul and
fear had slid down his spine when he'd remembered the
terror of nearly losing his daughter a few years back,
here at the small school still run by the Catholic Church.

At the time Kristi had left for college, Bentz had
thought All Saints would be a haven for her. With its
fine academic reputation, purported easy access to
one-on-ones with teachers, and a small student body,
the school had seemed perfect. The campus itself was
bucolic in appearance. Red brick buildings, stately
trees, lush grass and winding paths seemed serene, and
in the brochures that Bentz had poured over, he'd seen
pictures of students and teachers in state-of-the-art
classrooms, kids in lounges with guitars or in the library
studying or in the quad gathered on blankets. Some of
the photos had shown off the stately and dominant
cathedral, the center of the complex, or a chemistry lab
with a serious student studying the contents of a test
tube. Later he'd found out that the studious serenity
had been a façade for a growing evil that had pulsed
beneath the academic surface. But none of that had
surfaced until after Kristi had enrolled.

His jaw tightened at the memory, and he absently
rubbed his hip, where he still bore a scar from the horrifying experience. While desperately trying to save his
daughter from a killer terrorizing the college, he'd almost lost his own life. The pain lingering in his leg reminded him how much he despised All Saints. It hadn't
helped that today the Dean of Students had been less

than cooperative. Not that Father Crispin wasn't concerned; he just appeared to be more interested in protocol and the reputation of the campus than in finding the Denning twins. Oh, his brow had furrowed and he'd taken a few notes, but his interest had seemed polite. The dean obviously thought Bentz was jumping the gun.

Then again, hadn't Bentz believed the same of Brianna Hayward when she'd pled her case in his office earlier in the day?

Drumming his fingers on the passenger door, he replayed the scene with the Missing Persons Officer at the Baton Rouge Police Department. Bentz had certainly held more sway there than he had with Father Crispin, but really, things hadn't been all that much better. The officer had pointed out that so far no known crime had been committed, which, of course, Bentz already knew. But the officer had insisted the wheels were in motion. Baton Rouge detectives had gained access to the dorm where the girls lived and, it seemed, from the state of things, had intended to return. No cell phones were found, nor iPads or other electronic tablets. No purses or keys.

Still, he was bothered. Big time.

"You think it's 21?" Montoya eased up on the speed a bit.

"Hope not."

"You and me both. What're the chances that 21 would show up around the same time Father John reappears?"

"Coincidence."

Montoya sent him a look. "Thought you were the dude who didn't believe in coincidences."

"Yeah, I know. This time . . ." He rubbed the back of his neck and thought about a beer, then quickly shut his mind to the idea. Booze and he had separated years ago, and except for an occasional slippage, he kept it that way. Last night had been a mistake; one he wasn't going to make again. At least not today. He cracked his window, let the warm summer air rush into the Mustang's interior.

Truth to tell, Bentz was worried. At least about the Denning twins. The others who Brianna Hayward had mentioned were indeed missing, but the fact that they weren't twin females wasn't consistent with 21's MO. His phone buzzed, and he saw that the caller was Jonas Hayes.

"Hey," he said, putting his cell on speaker so that Montoya could hear. "How are ya?"

"Okay," Hayes said, "I got your message about the woman who thinks Caldwell isn't 21. She was in LA and I did talk to her on the phone, but never met with her. I figure she's another nut, a relative no less, who thinks justice wasn't served. But the killings stopped."

"I know, but we got a new situation," Bentz said as Montoya closed in on a pair of red taillights. "A couple of college girls. Twins who disappeared."

His ex-partner waited.

"On the night before they were about to turn twenty-one. Last night, as a matter of fact."

"Where?"

"New Orleans."

"What? New Orleans?" Jonas said, and Bentz pictured him, a tall black man with serious eyes and perpetual lines of worry etching his forehead. "You think this is 21? Nah, that's impossible. Donovan Caldwell's still locked up, and 21 stayed in LA."

"Still claiming to be innocent," Bentz pointed out. "Not to ruffle any feathers there, but this case has all the earmarks of 21."

Hayes gave a frustrated growl. "Okay. So why don't you tell me what you've got and . . . hell, I'll pull the case file and see if there's anything that we missed."

"Send it to me. You've got my e-mail," Bentz suggested as the lights of New Orleans appeared on the horizon. And then he brought Hayes up to speed.

The interior of the pub was ten degrees cooler than it had been on the street. The walls were exposed brick, with a glossy wood bar that looked as if it was over a hundred years old. It stretched in front of a mirror that rose to high ceilings, where paddle fans churned lazily. Most of the stools at the bar were occupied. While conversation buzzed over the clink of glasses, two bartenders were busily mixing drinks in front of a display of bottles backlit by hidden lights.

Brianna slid onto the bench of a booth near the back of the establishment, a quieter spot. On the table, menus were propped between salt and pepper shakers and a small candle burned near a dish of peanuts. Here, the distinctive click of billiard balls could be heard. Bridges took the seat opposite her just as a waitress in a short skirt, white shirt, tennis shoes, and bow tie appeared.

"Something to drink?" asked the young woman whose nametag read TAMI. She wore her red hair pulled to the top of her head in a tight band that allowed a spray of curls to escape. Her skin was clear, her smile infectious. Brianna pegged her for twenty-two or twenty-three, not much older than the Denning twins. Her heart twisted a bit.

Bridges ordered a beer and Brianna, forcing her thoughts from the missing girls, opted for a glass of merlot.

"You got it!" Tami said, and hurried off, nearly bouncing. She was so full of life.

As it should be for Zoe and Chloe.

Dragging her gaze away from the waitress, Brianna found Bridges staring at her.

"You okay?"

"Yeah . . . no. God, I don't know. What's 'okay' when a friend's kids are missing?" She squeezed her eyes shut for a second, but that didn't help. Zoe and Chloe's images kept coming to mind. What had happened to them? Where were they? Dear God, she hoped beyond hope that she was wrong about the 21 Killer.

When she opened her eyes again, Jase was still watching her intently. "Sorry," she said. "It's a nightmare. Sometimes . . . sometimes I lose focus."

"I get it."

For a second she believed he did. There was a sudden tenderness to him, a concern in his hazel eyes that she'd never expected to witness, and that glimpse of compassion touched her far too deeply.

"So the deal is I've spent the last couple hours going over the case against Caldwell. It was thin, but enough to convict him." He squinted at the small candle, suddenly cautious. "I know he's your cousin, but the murdered girls were your cousins, too."

"All the more reason to make sure that their real

killer is behind bars. Look, I didn't really know Delta and Diana. But when the news of their murders broke, it was horrible. We were all beside ourselves even though Mom and her sister, Cathy, were never all that tight. I only met the twins a couple of times. We didn't live close and were caught up in our own lives. In the beginning, I read about the case in the newspapers and online, just like everyone else. I didn't have an inside connection."

"But now you do, as the new advocate of Donovan Caldwell. That surprises me. Even you have to admit he's off. A loner. The guy has issues. Serious issues."

"You're describing a good percentage of the American population, Bridges," she pointed out, "not a serial killer." That warm connection she'd felt with him swiftly faded. "You know, people can be odd or 'off,' as you put it. They can even hate their siblings or other family members. That doesn't make them killers."

"Donovan Caldwell had assaulted a woman before."

"A woman who dropped the charges. A domestic abuse case that was never proven, never went to court." Her back was up now. "I don't condone any kind of conduct where one party hits another, man or woman, but in this country, it's still 'innocent until proven guilty.' At least it's supposed to be."

"Right. Okay. Got it." His hands lifted in a gesture of surrender, and he quickly changed his tack. "You're a psychologist."

"Right."

"That's what this support group is about. The one you were at tonight."

"It's part of my work, yes. But it's a non-profit group, and I volunteer my time. Members come and spend time together, hang out, talk." She was still a little agitated but tried to let her anger go. He now knew where she stood. "I organized the group, and I facilitate the meetings. All participants are twinless twins, people who have lost a twin sibling."

"Like you." Something skittered through his eyes, an emotion that she couldn't name. The expression unsettled her, but it vanished a moment later.

"Yeah, like me." She rarely discussed Arianna's death with anyone outside the group. Even though she'd known Jase for much of her life, she wasn't comfortable talking about the loss that still haunted her.

He began to say something else, but at that moment the waitress returned, placed their drinks on the table, and asked if they'd like to look at a menu. "The manager's extending happy hour, and we've got incredible shrimp poppers and sliders that are to die for! No kidding!" She held up both hands in a motion of trust-me-I-know-of-what-I-speak. When they declined, she shrugged with body language meant to convey "your loss" before she was off again, making her way to a booth where two women were trying to get her attention.

"We were talking about your sister," he said, getting right back to the subject.

Pinching the stem of her wineglass, she wondered why she'd ever agreed to this meeting. What good could come of it?

Chloe found a piece of glass. Small and jagged, it was probably part of the light fixture that had shattered in the struggle when Zoe had escaped. Unnoticed by the brute, the bit of glass had skittered to a dark corner and wedged into a crack in the wall where water seeped through, the very spot where he'd left the bucket that he expected her to use to pee. She had used the plastic pail, of course, because her bladder could only hold so much, but it was gross. Messy. Smelly. And so wrong. She had to escape. Had to.

The entire situation was dire, but she'd bolstered herself, silently prayed that Zoe had gotten away and found civilization, that she'd alerted the police who, any second now, would burst through the door upstairs and find the trap door. She waited, hoping to hear the wail of a siren, the whir of helicopter blades, the rumble of an engine. And then the awesome sound of a locked door being forced open, wood splintering and boots pounding overhead.

Instead she heard nothing but her own breathing, the drip from a leak somewhere and the god-awful ticking of the clock, counting off the remaining seconds of her life. She shuddered knowing it all might end here in this dank underground cell. Unless somehow, she found a way to make this little shard a weapon. Zoe had already sliced the prick's throat. Somehow he'd survived, so obviously she hadn't cut the jugular or carotid or whatever it was that needed to be severed. An artery would be best. The femoral would do.

Only a week ago Chloe had watched a YouTube video about a guy who was killed when his femoral artery was sliced by a beaver that he was filming. The beaver had been lumbering down the roadside; the photographer had seen it, gotten out of his car, and started videoing the beast, never expecting it to attack.

But it had. The beaver had gotten spooked or irritated or scared or whatever and had lunged at the photographer with long teeth that were meant to chew through wood. Those teeth had ripped skin, muscle, and the artery in the guy's thigh and he'd bled out. His footage was found by a friend and posted on the Internet with an "RIP Brian" footnoted at the end.

Chloe had been sickened, grossed out by the footage, but the information stuck with her, and now it might come in handy. Well, maybe. Actually severing the femoral artery was a long shot. The guy's thighs were thick pillars of muscle. How deep would she have to plunge the glass? Even then, would she hit the right spot?

Maybe she would be better going after his throat again, or aiming for his eyes to blind and disable him.

If she had the guts to do it.

You have to do it. You can't wimp out.

Zoe wouldn't think twice. She'd cut off his balls or blind him. Whatever it took to free herself, to free you, too. So do it, Chloe. You can! If you don't, he'll kill you. That's a fact. He just hasn't yet because he hasn't hunted Zoe down. But he will.

Of course she held out the hope that her twin had gotten away, that even now, Zoe was safe and directing the police to the cabin. But Chloe couldn't count on it. No, she had to fight this monster if he ever came back.

Another fear wiggled snakelike through her brain. What if the freak never returned? What if he just left her here to die, to waste away in this dark, dank prison? What if he got killed and never gave up the location? And maybe Zoe wouldn't recall where this crappy cabin was . . . oh, sweet Jesus. Her insides curdled at the thought.

Don't go there!

But the dingy, moist walls seemed to shrink in on her and she knew that she'd go mad if she had to stay here much longer.

Find a way to escape. You're a smart girl. Plan what you're going to do and then execute. Literally.

Swallowing back her fear, she clutched the ragged fragment from the broken light and prayed she'd have the strength to take the bastard on, to actually kill the freak and find a way out.

Tears welled in her eyes.

Fear twisted her guts.

She wanted to fall back into her own weakness, into her position of being the shy and emotionally frail sister that she'd been for twenty-one years. It was a comfortable role. This new position of taking care of herself to the point of murder just wasn't who she was.

Shut up! Don't be your own worst enemy. You have to take him on, Chloe. Your life depends on it!

She was shaking, trembling at the thought.

Grow some damned balls!

Oh, geez, she nearly peed herself she was so scared.

You cannot rely on anyone but yourself!

"God help me." Closing her eyes, she dug deep. Her inner voice nagging. She had to do whatever it would take to save herself. And she would, damn it, even if it killed her.

CHAPTER 14

"Did you know Arianna?" Brianna asked as a roar went up from the bar, indicating that one of the baseball teams shown on the screens had scored.

"Not really. More like knew of her," he said with a shrug.

Now he seemed uncomfortable.

She let the subject of Arianna drop.

For now.

Brianna picked up her glass. "You know, you're about the last person I ever expected to go into law enforcement."

When he seemed about to argue, she waved a hand. "I know, the Information Officer is probably just the mouthpiece for the department, but still . . ." She studied him more intently. "I always figured you'd end up, I don't know, a cowboy, rodeo rider, maybe an Air Force pilot or something. Navy Seal? But, you know, something a little more dangerous, I guess, and physical. Certainly not a desk job."

He tapped the tip of his bottle against her glass, then took a long pull. "Sorry to disappoint."

"Just an observation." She took a sip of wine, felt it slide easily down her throat, leaving a hint of cherries. Yeah, this was a good idea. Maybe. She held the stem in her fingers, watched the wine's "legs" appear on the bowl of her glass. "I guess I just never thought of you as the buttoned-down type."

"Buttoned down?"

"In high school, you were a little . . ."

"Edgy?" He took another swig of beer and she watched his Adam's apple move just above his open collar. "One of those dark, sexy rebel types?"

"Oh, right." Good God, was he flirting? Teasing? "Well, okay maybe." Then she grinned and took another swallow. "Or maybe not."

"Mrs. Gillespie would probably die if she heard that Jase Bridges was a reporter," he said. "Or, God forbid, hoping to join the police department."

"Too late. I think she's already dead," she said, remembering the woman she'd considered ancient at the time, though Edna Gillespie had probably only been in her early sixties when Brianna had attended high school. Not exactly ready for the grave, but back then, anyone over thirty had seemed really old. Mrs. Gillespie had been sharp and demanding, a no-nonsense teacher. Brianna had dreaded her class.

His lips twisted into a sardonic smile. "She always told me that if I didn't, oh, wait, what was it?" He paused, the beer halfway to his mouth, his brows arched for a second, then he snapped the fingers of his free hand. "I got it. If I didn't 'mind my p's and q's', whatever the hell they are, I'd end up in prison or worse. Yeah, that was it. The dire warning."

"Guess she was wrong."

"Shhh." He leaned closer. "Don't let her hear you."

She felt her heart warm to him and blamed it on the wine that was going down much too easily, her glass nearly empty. Nonetheless, she wasn't going to let her thoughts be muddled by the semidark ambiance of the bar, or a glass of wine, or the fact that she'd always found this man intriguing.

"She didn't much like me."

"Always nice when a teacher is so supportive."

"Well, I did give her hell," he admitted, not appearing the least bit sorry. "It really pissed her off that I could cut class all week and still manage to pass her tests in Senior English." Another swallow. "Come to think of it, I was a shit."

"We all were, but," she admitted, the wine making her bold, "my mother did warn us, me and my sister, about you Bridges boys. She claimed you were trouble."

"She was right. Probably best to avoid." There was something heavy in his words and he looked away.

"You knew Arianna, right? She said she'd hung out with you a couple of times."

A slight hesitation. "I'd met her. In a group. With my brother."

"Mom would have grounded her for life if she'd found out."

"We were that bad?"

"All boys were bad. You two?" She held up a hand and tilted it up and down. Maybe yes, maybe no. "Probably the worst of the lot."

He laughed a bit, but it sounded hollow and the humor didn't find his eyes.

"And it obviously didn't work if Arianna met you

way back when and I'm here now." As soon as the words were out, she regretted them. What was she, a teen on a first date? Here she was, letting the worries and stress of the last couple of days melt away because an old high-school crush had invited her for a drink, probably to get information from her for a story he smelled. All this while Selma's daughters were missing, their fate unknown, perhaps even now in the clutches of a deranged killer. Or worse, already dead.

The warm ambiance drained away.

"Again, don't tell them about me," he advised.

"No worries. Mom and Dad are gone," she said. "She got cancer and he . . . even though he wasn't all that old, just kind of wasted away and had a stroke." She frowned at her glass. "I can't help thinking the stress, you know, of losing a child, cost them years."

He looked away for a moment, as if considering something, then said, "You know, since we're talking about high school and all, I remember you."

That surprised her. "I look a lot like Arianna. I mean, I looked like her back then."

He shook his head. "Not identical."

"No, but close."

"I could tell the difference."

"Could you?"

"Mmm." Nodding, he added, "I always figured you'd marry a rich man and sip mint juleps on the back porch of a huge mansion that overlooked a pool or a lake or whatever." Another swig. "Something like that."

"But you didn't even know me."

"Everyone knew you, Brianna. You had a rep before you stepped across the threshold of Monroe High." He said it matter-of-factly, as if he were stating a truism anyone would understand. "You were a rich kid. All the privileges. Your dad was a professor at Tulane, right?" He popped a peanut into his mouth.

She nodded, though his account was a slight misconception. The meager wealth in their family had come from her mother's inheritance.

"So, I figured you'd go to college, find Mr. Right at a sorority dance or something. He'd end up being a lawyer or a doctor or maybe even a politician, and you'd settle down and have a passel of kids."

"As I said, you didn't know me."

"I paid attention."

"To a freshman girl?"

Again, the crooked smile.

Again, the stupid racing of her heart. Oh, God, she hoped to high heaven she wasn't blushing.

"I paid attention to all freshman girls." He hesitated, thought a second. "Really, come to think of it, to all girls. It's a guy thing. Isn't that what women say?"

"Sometimes," she admitted, and even chuckled a little. She was surprised that he'd noticed her; hadn't dared believed he'd even registered that she'd walked the same overly polished halls of the same school he barely attended.

"You ever marry?"

The question surprised her, but it probably shouldn't have. Shaking her head, she studied the dark depths of her wineglass. "I got close once," she said. "I was engaged." *Briefly. Like for ten seconds!*

"What happened?"

"Didn't work out. I got cold feet."

More like ice-cold frigid-as-hell feet.

"Runaway bride?"

"More like never-made-it-near-the-altar bride," she said. Then, refusing to think about that time in her life, she threw it back at him. "You?"

"No, never even got close." He scratched the back of his neck. "There were a couple of girls, well, women who might've worked out, but I don't know . . ." He paused, leaning against the back of the booth, and she guessed that he did know but was equivocating to avoid discussing a subject that bothered him. "I guess I didn't have much of a role model for a relationship. My old man raised me. Never knew my mother, and my grandparents . . ." He shrugged. "They were just old, you know? Then again"—he reached for his bottle—"maybe I just never found the right woman."

"Oh, I smell a cop-out," she said, hiding the fact that her pulse leaped whenever their eyes met. She buried her nose in her glass.

"Probably." He cocked an eyebrow. "So you're single?"

Very. "Yeah. Sorry, no rich husband is at home in some grand antebellum home with a pitcher of martinis. No, wait, you said mint juleps, right? Well, he's not there with those either. And by the way, that grand Southern mansion? It's a little two-bedroom cottage." She set her glass on the table. "Guess you were wrong about me."

"Then that makes two of is, doesn't it?" he said with an ever-widening grin that told her he'd been lying to her about his supposed fantasy of her life. He hadn't really cared about her life, but wanted her to realize her preconceived notions of him were as false as his might be. The fact that he wasn't all that interested stung more than it should have, but the truth was he just hadn't liked her calling him out on his high-school bad rep crap. Fair enough.

"Okay, I get it. Sorry. You're a reporter. On the straight and narrow. My bad."

He laughed a little, a deep chuckle she remembered from her youth. "Just not too straight," he said with a wink that caused her silly heart to leap. "So, are you gonna let me help you with the missing Denning girls?"

"So that you can whitewash Bentz and keep track of me? Isn't that what this is all about? Damage control. So you can look good for the cops and land that job with the department."

He let out a sigh. "What do you think?"

She met his gaze and was reminded again of the boy he'd once been, a teenager who had never let anyone control him. "I don't know."

"I told you, I want to work with you."

"For an exclusive?"

One corner of his mouth lifted. "That wouldn't hurt," he admitted. "Sure. But I do really want to find out what happened to your friend's daughters. And didn't Selma Denning say something about you reaching out, getting the word out?"

"She did." She nodded. "But there's a difference between information and exploitation."

"A fine line, but I'm willing to walk it to help those girls," he said as if he meant it. "So, to answer your question, it's not just about me reporting the story."

"Good." She hoped he wasn't lying, but couldn't quite believe him. Besides, maybe it didn't matter. Maybe it was a good thing. His story, through the print newspaper and online services of the *Observer,* would notify the public. It would help spread the word, hopefully catch the eye of someone who'd seen Zoe or Chloe Denning. The more she thought about it, the more collaboration with Jase Bridges seemed a good thing.

"What about the girls' father?" he asked.

"Still around. Divorced from the mom. He's remarried with kids. A new family. Well, sort of. He married Selma's niece."

"Ouch."

"Yeah, major ouch. Anyway, I'm sure Carson's concerned about his daughters, but not much support to Selma."

Jase nodded, taking it all in.

Brianna sat back and let her tired eyes go fuzzy for a minute as she studied his dark silhouette in the muted light. Could she trust him? Lord knew she needed someone with some connections to try and find the twins. So far, the police hadn't been much help, Selma was a wreck and Brianna was fast running out of options. Someone had to do something. But it was hard to believe that the someone she was hoping for would end up being Jase Bridges.

The waitress returned with the check and when she reached for her purse, he reminded her that she'd insisted he buy. After a brief protest, she let Jase pay the bill.

"This way you owe me," he said. He dropped a few bills on the table, then found a business card in his wallet. "Here. You can call me on my cell. Any time." He slid the card across the table.

"Any time?"

"Day or night."

"Three a.m.?"

Again the flash of a smile, a quick spark of humor flashing in his eyes. "Try me."

"Promise you won't bite my head off?"

"Never."

"We'll see." She fished in her purse, found her keys, and made her way to the door.

Outside the air was heavy, rain threatening, though the temperature was still hovering near seventy. Cars and trucks rumbled down the street.

"I'll talk to Selma."

"You know where to find me," he said as they crossed to her car.

"Yeah." She unlocked the Honda with her keyless remote, then slid inside to leave him wedged in the open space with one hand on the top of her door and the other on the roof, preventing her from yanking her door shut.

"Then call. I'm available."

From inside her car, she glanced up at him quickly, expecting a grin to indicate the double entendre, but his face held a guileless expression that she couldn't read. For a second she got lost in his gaze.

"Okay," she said, noting that she sounded a little breathless. God, she was an idiot. "Got it."

He tapped twice on the roof, stepped away, and she, all the time trying to get her stupid racing pulse under control, tugged the door firmly shut.

She flipped on the A/C even though it would take several minutes to blow cool air, then went about trying to pull out without nicking either of the two monster pickups that had wedged her in. After several attempts, inching backward and forward, she was able to finally pull away from the curb just as her cell phone went off. Ignoring the call, she checked her rearview and saw Jase Bridges standing where she'd left him, his hands in his pockets as he stared after her.

What was his deal? she wondered.

Why did she feel that he wasn't being completely honest with her, wasn't entirely on the up-and-up?

"Because he's one of the Bridges boys," she told herself as cool air began to blow from the car's vents. Then, silently, she added, *And you're paranoid, anyway, Brianna. You don't trust anyone. Least of all a boy, no, make that a man, who might have the ability to turn you inside out.*

Still, there was something about Jase Bridges that caused her to think he knew more than what he was saying, that he had his own agenda. Something hidden. Something she couldn't put her finger on and certainly didn't trust.

So don't call him.

"I won't," she promised herself. But even as she made the vow, she knew she was lying to herself.

CHAPTER 15

"**Y**ou're an idiot!" Myra's voice echoed through his brain as he drove to the cabin. The van bounced over a pothole, warm night air whistling inside through the broken window. His arm still hurt from where he'd smashed the glass. Oh, hell, he hurt all over from Zoe's sneak attack. Little bitch!

Of course he had to report what had happened and now with his cell phone rammed against one ear he was taking the brunt of Myra's wrath. He had known Myra would be angry, and he'd considered not telling her, but he'd let the truth slip and now she was furious with him.

"I'll find her." He made the promise aloud though Myra seemed to be seething and didn't immediately answer. He almost thought the wireless connection had been lost. Again. That was the trouble with Myra; she'd often ice him out, not answer, make him think she wasn't listening or worse yet, wasn't there.

Finally, he heard her. "You bet you will. If you don't, what do you think will happen?" She was nearly screeching now, her rage propelled by her own fear, her anger bouncing through his brain. "The police will come, you know. And you won't get away."

"I'll handle it."

"I wish I could believe that."

He imagined her lips, full and red, the color of Christmas ribbons, pulled down at the corners, her sharp white teeth flashing between them.

"I'll use the dog," he said. "I've got her clothes. Old Red, he'll catch the scent."

"You hope! For all you know, she could be miles away by now. What did you say? She floated down river? For the love of Christ, how do you know she hasn't been found? She might be at the police station even now."

"She's hurt."

"Hurt?"

"Something was wrong with her leg."

"But she got away," Myra pointed out, and he nodded, as if she could see him, then nearly missed the turnoff from this backwoods road to the cabin. Wrenching on the wheel, he swore under his breath and nearly dropped the damned phone. His van skidded, narrowly missing a fence post.

"Look, I gotta go," he said.

"Find her."

"I will."

"And don't kill the other one until you have the first," she reminded him, disgust evident in her dulcet voice. In his mind's eye he saw those ruby-colored lips curled in repulsion. "There has to be order."

"I know. Don't worry. I'll fix things."

"You'd better," she said, and it was nearly a threat. He felt his blood begin to boil, the way it always did when she pushed him too hard. "You don't have a choice." And then she was silent. As she was so often.

"Bitch," he whispered, not caring that he hadn't actually heard her click off. Tossing the phone onto the seat, he felt the familiar storm roil within. This is how it had always been with Myra, for as long as he could remember, and yet he loved her, had always loved her. That was the sick thing about their relationship. She took him and his love for granted. If he were smart, he'd get rid of her, too. She knew far too much, pulled his strings much too tightly.

He slowed, left the van idling in Park, and climbed out. The scent of the river and forest was strong here, climbing up his nostrils, burrowing deep in his chest. Pausing for a moment to look for stars and spying only a few, he took a couple of deep breaths, shook off Myra's tirade, and unlocked the twisted gate. He'd have to fix it. Before Myra got a peek at the nearly ruined bars.

It took a little effort to force the bent latch into place, but he managed, locking himself in and climbing behind the wheel again.

Myra's words still stung, hot as a bald-headed hornet's bite. Jesus, he should just off her. She made him crazy. Even now, driving along the ruts leading to the cabin, the dry grass bending and scraping the undercarriage of his van, he felt sweat collect on his hands. With an effort, he tried to turn his thoughts from Myra. He couldn't let her get under his skin, not when he had so much work to do.

Not only did he have to find that fucking Zoe and deal with her sister, but he also had to fix the window on his van before anyone started asking questions. He hadn't been completely honest with Myra. The truth was, he was worried about Zoe. That little twit had tricked him. He'd spent a good part of the day searching for Zoe. Of course, he'd taken the dog, who had followed Zoe's trail to the river. But from that point on, his hound could find nothing other than a couple of squirrels and a nasty raccoon that had bared its teeth, dark eyes glaring from the lower branches of a tupelo tree.

He and the dog had walked more than two miles downstream, searching the banks on this side, but the truth was that bitch might have floated to the next town. If that happened, it was all over. She'd seen him. Could ID him to the damned cops. And then it wouldn't be long before they'd find him.

"Son of a bitch."

Or she could be dead. Drowned. Killed by an alligator or snake or a damned bear. Anything is possible.

He told himself that her demise would be a good thing; she wouldn't be able to identify him. But that would leave him with the mess of the other one. Should he kill her? Assume the older twin was already dead and end the younger one's life? It would disrupt his routine. Not good. Even now, just thinking about the order being upset caused his chest to tighten and his scalp to itch with anxiety. That wasn't the way it was supposed to happen.

He knew it.

And so did Myra.

She was just pissed, that was all, and she'd get over it. Maybe. If he could rectify the situation and find that damned Zoe. He'd made a big mistake the night before. He should have taken the time to release the dog, put

Red on the scent right away, but he'd been running blind, fueled by pain, adrenaline, and outrage. And he hadn't had his night-vision goggles with him. Another mistake.

That was what happened when you allowed things to spin out of control.

That was why there needed to be order and precision.

As he rounded a final corner, the right front tire hit a pothole. The entire van shimmied, agitating him further.

There are others. You have to finish this business and go after the others. You cannot be distracted.

He was sweating profusely now, and as the beams of his headlights played over the peeling paint of the small cabin, he tried to calm himself. He slowed and guided the van to the far side of the structure. Though the cabin was settled deep in these woods and it was highly unlikely that anyone would spot his vehicle, he took every precaution.

You couldn't be too careful, he decided as he cut the engine. There were always hunters and poachers in these woods, nosy types who might catch a glimpse of something out of the ordinary. Then there were the squatters, people who came in and made old shacks and cabins their homes until they were rousted out. All the warning signs in the world wouldn't keep the squatters at bay. He'd posted NO TRESPASSING, PRIVATE PROPERTY, KEEP OUT, and even BEWARE OF DOG signs all along the perimeter of this scrap of land, but did everyone abide by them? No fuckin' way. There was always someone willing to break the damned rules.

And that was the problem.

No order.

"Fuckers," he growled under his breath. Hopefully now, with the dog, people would stay away.

In life, there were rules.

You had to play by them, he thought as he reached into the glove box and grabbed his flashlight.

That's why he couldn't kill that whimpering, whiney Chloe first.

Angry, he climbed out of the cab, kicked at a clod of dirt, took two steps toward the building, then stopped. He returned to his vehicle, reached inside, and yanked the keys from the van's ignition. That's where he'd made his mistake yesterday. Well, *one* of his mistakes. Leaving the keys in the damned van. Yesterday's plan had turned into a major clusterfuck of errors.

Today would be different. He slid the automotive keys into a front pocket of his jeans, then whistled loudly just as he opened the gate to the dog run and spied Red bounding from his shed. Smiling, he stopped to pet the bloodhound with his notched ear, the result of a tussle with a raccoon or worse, then followed the dog back inside. "Ya hungry?" He took down a plastic tub of dog food, measured out two cups, and checked to see that the water was fresh. It wasn't, so he pumped a bucket from the long sink on the back porch, then returned to fill several bowls, not that the dog couldn't make his way down to the river if he really had to.

"There ya go," he said, once Red had buried his nose into the dry food. A stray, Red had landed here and stayed.

It had worked out.

"All good here?" he asked. "No trouble, eh, boy?" He rubbed the scruff of the hound's neck. "Good. You stay out here and guard the place, y'hear?" Straightening, he pulled a second small key ring from his pocket and crossed the open space to the rotting back porch. Bullfrogs were croaking, insects were humming, and the warm Louisiana summer night smelled of the bayou. The kind of night he loved. If he didn't have so damned much to do, he would have loved to sit on the ancient bench with the dog, crack open a cold beer, let the country air soak into his skin, and find himself some peace of mind.

But he couldn't.

Not yet.

Unlocking the door of the cabin, he felt the heat of the small interior. With the windows closed and boarded up and no insulation in the old pine walls, the cabin was an oven. Evidence of insects, wasps, and mice was visible on the floorboards.

All the better for the place to seem unoccupied, he supposed, and flicked on his flashlight to better survey the place. Boots creaking on the ancient dusty floor, he walked to the trap door and smiled when he noticed it hadn't been disturbed, the lock in place. The only time the latch was open was when he was inside, doing his work, making certain everything was perfect. And it had cost him one twin.

But he still had the other. The weaker one who had proved a little more gutsy than he'd expected. He'd thought he could control her easily, but she'd proved to have a little fight in her, like her wilder sister, Zoe. He had known Zoe would be difficult. One always was.

They both needed to die, of course. Their birth times had passed, but he could still re-create the ritual. First, he would have to find that fucking Zoe and bring her back here. Then he and Myra would pick the appropriate date. That part was easy. And then he would wait for the exact time of her birth and kill her and her sister in the same manner as he had the others.

Dealing with the twins was a spiritual rite for him, almost religious in nature, though he didn't consider himself a God-fearing man.

He unbolted the trap door, slipped the ladder down to rest against the floor, and braced the top rails against the edge of the opening. He tested the ladder with his weight and squeezed through the tight opening. As he descended, his body ached a bit where he'd been wounded. Carefully, he made his way down, rung by rung, as cool, earthy air hit his nostrils and the sound of quiet sobs greeted his ears.

She was scared.

Good.

He actually smiled, though his skin was so raw it was probably a grimace.

Maybe if she was frightened enough, she wouldn't give him any more trouble. She'd be good and compliant.

As he swung his flashlight's beam across the cracked floor, he found her cowering in a corner, looking scared enough to piss herself.

Perfect!

The room was as he'd left it, but the disarray and blood, the untidiness of it all bothered him. He, himself, was neat. Precise. Even though this underground room was just a work space and a prison, he kept it well-ordered. But now he didn't like the broken light giving off its weird illumination, or the way his work had been strewn over the workbench in his struggles to dislodge Zoe as she'd attacked him.

No, the prison wasn't right. Wouldn't do.

Frowning, he glanced at Chloe in the corner. She'd been staring at him, he'd felt it, but now she shrank away, tried in vain to cover her body and avoid eye contact.

Weakling.

At least she wouldn't give him any trouble, he decided, as he slowly removed his clothes, hanging his jeans and shirt on hooks in the wall, stripping bare before putting on his apron. It unnerved her to see him naked, to be without any shred of clothing herself in his presence. He sensed it, but that was a good thing. For him. Realizing that she was on edge was comforting. Calming. He'd let her watch him work, see that he was righting the small room, creating the perfect space for his ritual.

Taking care, he refolded Chloe's clothes and felt a tightening in his gut as he did the same with her sister's. The short dresses were so soft, a clingy material that felt like satin in his fingers. He couldn't help but fantasize when he considered the smooth fabric stretched over their bodies, molding as it had to their skin. His cock twitched a bit as he imagined how the silken material stretched over their breasts, how it would feel to his touch, a bit of resistance between his palms and their nipples. He stole a glance at Chloe, at her boobs, so white, with blue veins visible and tiny, hard nipples that looked like buttons. Sexy buttons. A tingle invaded his crotch. He licked the edges of his teeth. Turning a bit, he gave her a gift, a quick glimpse of his cock, thickening with thoughts of sex with the two of them, their long, streaked hair falling over him, their mouths painted red, bright red, and ready to open to him. He let out a groan when he thought of those slick, scarlet lips and the joy they could bring.

Stop it.

He heard Myra's voice as clearly as if she were in the room with him, his conscience sounding as shrewish as her cloying reminders.

You have work to do! The nagging voice never let up.

His dick started to shrivel.

Chloe recoiled farther into the corner.

With clenched jaw, he turned away from his prisoner and tied on his apron. There was no time for sexual fantasies. None. He had to feed her, just so she would stay alive. He had a straw, several water bottles, and a can of a protein shake that he'd seen the caretakers give his mother when she'd been living in a memory care unit in the nursing home.

A bitter woman to start with, Mother had only gotten worse as her decline into dementia had made her more nasty and critical than ever. Even when she'd no longer recognized him as her son, he had visited, watched her rot in that twin bed with its beige sheets, an afghan at her feet. Her scraggly hair had been tied away from her face in a thin ponytail and she'd squinted through thick glasses, trying to place him.

"You," she'd finally said, nearly spitting as her roommate's television blared from behind a striped curtain that rattled on metal hooks whenever an attendant whipped into the room and pushed the drapery aside to check on the residents. "You're the bad one."

"No, Mother." He had shaken his head as he looked

down at her, shriveled into half the woman he remembered. "I'm good. Your boy. Remember? I only do what's right."

Her eyes had narrowed suspiciously. "Are you my husband?" she'd asked.

"No, I'm not him."

"Well, that's what he said, too. That he did what was right. Oh, sure. Lyin', cheatin' son of bitch."

"I'm not my father. I'm your son."

Her laugh had been a brittle, cold wind escaping in a hack from her lungs. "Son?" Her thin nostrils had flared, her pale face infusing with the color of the ribbon tying her hair. "I have no son." With that, she'd turned away, closing her eyes and refusing to speak or look at him again. The ribbon had loosened over her wisp of graying hair, resembling a twisting rivulet of blood upon the institutional beige of her pillow.

He'd left her then. Never returned. Didn't attend her damned funeral. For if she had no son, then he had no mother.

Now, in this basement with its bluish light, the girl looking nearly catatonic, her hands clutched together as if in prayer, he opened the can of Ensure, slid in a straw, and carried it to her. Eyes round and staring straight ahead, she shivered against the cracked cement wall, huddled close to the corner.

"Drink," he ordered when she turned her big eyes up to him. They shined in the half-light, shimmering with tears.

She was scared shitless.

Excellent.

When she didn't reach for the can, he placed it on the floor close enough that she could grab it, and he noticed something else about her, a kind of zombie-like expression. Shit, she was a basket case.

"Suit yourself." He turned back to his table, carefully returning his tools, the ribbon, and the folded clothes, relegating each to its assigned spots.

Once he'd restored some order, he felt a little less tense.

He thought about Zoe, how he intended to track her down at dawn's first light. The dog hadn't had any luck on this side of the river, so he would canoe over to the far bank and start over again. His bloodhound was a tracker. Old Red would find Zoe if she was anywhere in the area, and he'd wager that if she was still alive, she hadn't gotten far.

He would find her. Come the morning. That was what would happen, and he wouldn't even consider that he might not catch her. If the day lengthened into darkness, he'd use his night goggles. She wouldn't get away.

Hadn't he promised Myra that he would fix things? He couldn't fail.

CHAPTER 16

W hy not trust Jase? Brianna asked herself as she showered in her bathroom.

He was a reporter, and that could work in their favor. Let him write his story, spread the word, maybe get coverage on television and radio as well, get people looking for Selma's daughters. Why wait for the damned police to take her seriously?

Her thoughts played out as she scrubbed, washing her hair and body, rinsing off the long hours, sweat, and frustration of the day in her claw-footed tub that had been retrofitted with a shower kit.

After all, Jase Bridges had resources. What did it matter if she'd had a stupid schoolgirl crush on him half a lifetime ago? And just because as a kid he'd been only half a step out of juvie way back when didn't mean he couldn't be trusted now. In fact, it might help that he had some street smarts. He'd already started gathering facts on the story. She realized he might be trying to get close to her only to get a leg up on the case. And maybe he was motivated more by the lust for a story to boost his career rather than any real empathy for Selma and her daughters. So what?

And hadn't Brianna witnessed flashes of compassion in his eyes when they'd discussed the situation? She rotated under the spray, letting the lather and warm water slide off her body. She wondered what it would be like to have Jase here in the shower with her, his hands sliding over her slick skin, his lips trailing along the length of her neck, his legs pressed against hers. . . .

"Oh, for the love of God!" Angrily she twisted off the spray, reached past the curtain, and pulled her towel from a decorative hook. What the hell was she doing, thinking about a steamy sexual encounter, a fantasy? Now? With all that was going on? But wasn't that always the way it was in times of stress, she thought, drying first her body, then her hair. People sought physical and emotional release, whether it be running the city streets, swimming miles, maniacally cleaning house, or, yes, having wild, passionate, stress-relieving sex.

Not that she would know personally.

Lately her love life had been nil.

Angry with herself, she threw back the curtain to find St. Ives seated on the small counter next to the sink. His tail was flicking dangerously close to her can of hair spray and her toothbrush holder. "Pervert," she accused as he stared at her, and she wrapped the towel around her torso. "What're you looking at?"

He stared at her with unblinking eyes.

"Down!"

Ignoring her, he set about washing himself.

"Fine. Suit yourself," she said, but petted his head.

He paid no attention.

Using a washcloth, she tried to wipe away the condensation that had collected on her mirror. When that didn't work, she opened the window over the tub. As she did, she peered outside to the darkness and told herself there was no one lurking outside. She forced herself to remain calm, just as she had earlier on her drive home when she'd thought for a few anxious minutes that someone was following her.

Of course the delivery truck had turned off.

"Silly," she said as she padded to the bedroom. Discovering her robe at the foot of her unmade bed, she let the towel fall to the floor and shrugged into the soft terry wrap. Back in the bathroom she stood in front of the mirror and tried to untangle her wet hair. As usual, her curls fought her, but when the mirror slowly defogged, she was able to drag her comb through her wet hair.

Again, she thought of Jase. Of course. Despite all her worries about the Denning girls, his image had chased her home. She'd replayed their conversation and tried to convince herself that her only interest in him was as a partner, someone who would help her find Selma's daughters. She wouldn't even go as far as saying she thought of him as a "friend," because she didn't really know him. She hadn't befriended him when she was in her teens, and now she knew little about him aside from what he'd divulged.

Who knew how much of that information was true and how much was, if not fiction, an edited version of his life, a whitewashed story molded to gain her trust?

And that was a big part of the problem.

Her inability to trust.

Although she hated to blame every bad emotion that

slipped through her on the loss of her twin, losing Arianna had helped erode her ability to have faith in others. But it was time she stopped using her sister's death as a crutch. She had to own up to her wariness and deal with her feelings and problems. "It's simple as that," she said to St. Ives. She flipped on the hair dryer and he took off like a shot, jumping off the counter and streaking into the bedroom.

"Chicken!" she called over the roar of the dryer. God, she loved that cat. Sometimes she thought she should adopt a dog, one that would bark wildly if anyone came near the house and stay by her side when she went out for a run, but St. Ives would never stand for it.

Once her hair was dry and semi-manageable again, she turned off the dryer and put it away only to find the cat back in the doorway. "Yeah, a whole lot of protection you are," she said, and scooped him up, holding him close, listening to him purr. She'd adopted him as a kitten after the loss of the tuxedo tom she'd had since high school, a pet she'd shared with Arianna. When Jeeves had died at twenty, Brianna had doubted any animal would ever fill the void in her heart. But months later, she'd visited the local animal shelter and found the love of her life in a saucy little orange kitten. "Must've been the way you bit my hand when I picked you up," she said, reflecting on the day she'd brought him home.

Funny how she could commit to a fluffy little animal when she'd failed at every serious relationship with a man, even Max Strahan, the one man she'd thought she might marry. Max, too, had lost a twin. She'd met him at a meeting; they'd hit it off and since he wasn't her client, she'd agreed to date him. After a few months, when he'd proposed, she'd been surprised and flattered. Although she'd had a few doubts, she'd thrown caution to the wind and accepted. A mistake. After wearing the diamond for a week, she realized that the engagement didn't feel right; she sensed that their relationship was based on mutual needs and mutual losses, and they were trying to fill a void with each other, rather than truly being in love.

When she'd explained as much to Max, he'd not been heartbroken as she'd expected, but furious. He'd accused her of "leading him on" and "playing with his heart." Worse yet, red-faced, the veins throbbing in his neck, he'd taken the ring she'd returned and sworn he was going to throw it in the river.

Whether he did or not, she never knew.

From that day forward Max had not attended any of the group meetings—a relief—though for a few months after the breakup she had felt her insides churn before each session. Just the thought that he might appear had made her suffer from a cold sweat. What would she say to him? How awkward would it be? But thankfully, he'd never shown his face again. If he'd contacted any of the other members of the group, they'd kept it to themselves, though, of course, Tanisha wouldn't have been able to keep the secret.

It seemed as if he'd moved on.

"You're my guy now," she said to the cat, and buried her nose in his soft fur. His head was lolling beside the base of her neck, his purring vibrating against her skin. She smiled to herself just as she felt him stiffen, his gentle little motor stopping suddenly.

"What?"

Agilely flipping in her arms, his claws digging into her robe, he stared over her shoulder.

"Hey, what's the—"

"Sssss!" he hissed, showing his teeth, his eyes focused behind her on the bathroom window. She glanced in the mirror. In the reflection she saw her own worried face and the cat's tense body. And something else. Movement? Oh, God. A face in the window beyond the screen?

For a second she froze, her eyes meeting another's in the glass. Then she whirled around. St. Ives's claws dug deeper. He launched himself to the floor and scrambled into the hallway.

She hit the light switch.

The bathroom went dark, the only slice of illumination through the open doorway from a lamp in the living area.

Pulse pounding in her throat, Brianna stared at the window.

She saw nothing in the shifting darkness.

The window was a black box.

Empty.

No menacing face appeared.

No eyes reflected the tiniest gleam of incandescence.

All your imagination.

Then what about the cat?

What had caused his reaction?

Even now, from the safety and shadows of the hallway, he was growling low in his throat, a warning.

Yet she saw no one. Nothing.

Just your imagination, brought on by St. Ives's paranoia. He's a cat. He might have sensed a raccoon scour-

ing the garbage cans. Or a bat flying close to the window. Or nothing.

She let out her breath, half-convinced she was imagining things. It wasn't as if the cat wasn't skittish.

Her nerves still on edge, she closed the window and snapped the blinds shut. Then she walked through each room in the house, double-checking that every window was latched, every blind or curtain closed, every door locked and dead-bolted.

You're acting like a crazy person.

"Too bad," she said to herself, and quickly donned pajamas. After drinking a glass of water, she made a pot of herbal tea, then settled into bed with a cup of chamomile and her laptop.

Her jangled nerves finally calmed and she convinced herself that she had *not* met the gaze of some pervert in her open bathroom window.

Logging into her e-mail, Brianna found that Selma had sent her the information she'd requested. There was a list of people Selma had called or contacted, along with their responses. There were profiles of the girls that included cell phone and credit card numbers, previous addresses, places of employment, volunteer history, and social media accounts. She'd included some contacts she hadn't reached, as well as past boyfriends and a handful of people either girl hadn't gotten along with. Extended family members were included. The information was much more complete than the sketchy data she'd left with the police departments earlier.

It was a start.

And, from the looks of it, Selma had e-mailed the police departments directly, which was good. She was starting to be more proactive.

Brianna thought about sending the info to Jase, but stopped herself. She'd have to weed through it first, and she still wasn't sure about Jase. But with time running out, she knew she had to do something, and soon. She caught sight of the most recent photo of Zoe and Chloe, both girls all dressed up, their smiles huge, each with an arm around the other, the lights of Bourbon Street visible behind them. Their last picture. *So far,* she corrected herself. There would be future photo ops. There had to be.

But her mind wandered to morbid images of those who had died at the hands of the 21 Killer.

Her throat grew thick. "Where are you?" she wondered aloud and bit her lip. Two beautiful girls out on the town, feeling safe with each other, their lives stretching out in front of them.

Were they alive? Just unable to communicate for some reason?

Or had they come to some horrid fate, possibly at the hands of the 21 Killer?

She glanced at the clock and felt a chill run through her.

With each passing hour, she knew the chances of finding them alive slowly dwindled.

Chloe could barely breathe.

Wincing against the smell of dirt and foul water, she watched as he went through the musty basement, straightening, sweeping, and then neatly refolding their clothes, as if he were in the military and getting ready for an inspection. Dresses were first, then underpants, her red thong and Zoe's black one, which he held up to the light, then actually brought to his nose and sniffed.

Ick! She shivered, watching him.

He wasn't as calm as he had been before Zoe attacked him. No, he was more agitated and antsy; whatever was left of his serenity was forced. A tic had developed under his eye, and a muscle clenched and relaxed in his jaw. She hoped his agitation meant that he hadn't found Zoe.

He was naked again except for his apron, and she didn't want to think about what the undressing was all about. But from the way he had barely acknowledged her, she knew he wouldn't let her survive. No way. Not after she'd seen his face. The same went for Zoe. They would be able to give the police a very detailed description of him, from the nose that appeared to have been broken at least once, to his tall, muscular build, and the weird tattoo of a mountain and a bleeding heart on one shoulder. He also had a mole on the cheek of his right buttock. She had memorized these features, vowing to remember every detail of the dickwad's face and body, just in case she ever got the chance to identify him for the police.

Oh, God, would that ever happen?

Much as she hated to admit it, he was an okay-looking dude. Although she considered him repulsive as hell, some might find him attractive. Fit and strong and cold as ice.

It was his eyes that really changed his appearance. Deep-set beneath heavy brows, they were flat and nearly colorless. Like a reptile's eyes.

Now, of course, he had some scratches on his throat, compliments of Zoe.

He wasn't quiet, but at least he no longer sang the birthday song, a tune she used to love and now would hate for the rest of her life—however long that was going to be. He kept rambling about someone named Myra. His wife? Girlfriend? Who would be involved with such an effin' freak? Whoever this Myra person was, she really pissed him off. His muttering was so disjointed that Chloe suspected he didn't even know he was talking.

The lunatic was just weird, weird, weird.

Even more so, as he snapped up the phone and said, "Yeah?" as if he'd heard it ring when she hadn't heard anything, not even the tell-tale rattle of a phone on mute humming across the table. What the hell? God, maybe the guy was psychic as well as psychotic or maybe he was just plain nuts. "I know," he said sounding almost disgusted. "I just need a little more time . . . I already told you. I'll get her."

Chloe strained to hear, but the other end of the conversation was muted as the phone was pressed tightly to his ear. She couldn't catch even the tiniest sound to indicate what the person on the other end of the phone sounded like.

"Myra, give it a rest. Will you? Have a little faith."

Myra. The only one who ever communicated with him.

Again he paused and this time when he hung up, he tossed the phone aside and muttered, "Bitch!" Geez, the guy was off the rails, worse than she'd first thought.

She swallowed back her fear. She was certain she had to be doubly careful because, now that his sick twin birthday was off, there wasn't anything preventing him from killing her on the spot. Right? With their birthdays over, would he wait for Zoe? Who knew? He was such a freak, anything might set him off. She decided not provoke him. Not to utter a single word that might make him go ballistic. Better to lull him into thinking she was a complete rag doll and wimp.

Then, she would attack.

With her pathetic shard of glass.

She prayed she could find the guts to kill him.

Surprisingly, she had come to realize that she wasn't the total coward he believed her to be. Now, with her situation so dire and with the realization that she couldn't rely on Zoe or anyone else, she realized she could do it. She could attack.

If he came close and faced her, she'd give him a sharp, hard knee to the groin; she knew she could drive her leg upward with tremendous force.

Chloe, like her twin, had been a soccer player for years in junior high and high school. Hence, she'd developed thighs of steel. On the playing field she'd been much more aggressive than in day-to-day life, so she knew she had it in her. Hell, she would summon all her aggression and fear, and rocket his balls into the back of his brain. Bam!

Just give me the chance.

Guts grinding, nerves tight, so scared she wanted to fall into a million pieces, she clutched her bit of glass and decided after kicking him hard in the nuts, she'd find a way to gouge his eyes.

Oh, Jesus, she thought she might throw up as she watched him work.

After he'd tidied up, if that's what it was, he began to fuss with their clothes again, patting and primping the items on his workbench. With an almost religious zeal he placed the thongs on the dresses, carefully making certain he'd placed hers on her red dress, then Zoe's on the black one. The bras were next, hooked, lacy push-up cups pointing toward the grimy ceiling. He eyed her bra and clucked his tongue a bit before gently placing it over her thong. "Naughty girls," he said.

Oh, yeah, wearing sexy underwear was "naughty," but kidnapping, hog-tying, and probably murdering a person in some sick ritual was okay? What kind of fucked-up thinking was that?

Anger sizzled through her blood.

Who was this guy?

Why did he think he had the right to do this to her? To torture her? To keep her captive? Expect her to pee in his awful pail and drink his goddamned protein drink and be grateful that he was keeping her alive for a few more hours or days in this damp, smelly, filthy dungeon? What kind of a neat freak was he? Folding clothes gently, sniffing crotches of panties, and keeping her captive in this sty?

She clutched the bit of glass.

Oh, hell, he was getting ready to leave! He'd straightened this prison cell as best he could and seemed agitated, angry. Muttering to himself, he patted his pockets and found a cell phone.

A cell phone!

Her heart leaped as he dragged the ladder into place and wedged the rails into the trap door above. Could she somehow get away and maybe steal his phone from him in the process?

Get the drop on him and call 911?

She couldn't believe her good luck. Now, if she only had the nerve . . . *God, help me.* Her mouth grew dry, not a drop of spit in it.

She had to try. Before he left. It was her only hope.

Did his damned phone work underground? Where the hell would the nearest cell tower be?

Shit, shit, shit!

She amped herself up.

"I told you," he was saying. "I'll get her in the morning, yeah, yeah, with the damned dog . . . what? The other one? She's here. Got her." He glanced at Chloe over his shoulder. "Trust me, she's no problem. It's the other one. Zoe. That little cu—er, bitch that got free, but no worries. I'll get her. First light."

So he hadn't caught Zoe. There was hope. . . .

He fell quiet for a moment, then went on. "Yeah, I know, I know. For Christ's sake I get it. *She's* first . . ." Another pause. "No, no. This one will wait. Uh-huh. Second-born. Always weaker." Then a merciless laugh. "Yeah, that's right. Like the runt of the litter." Another ugly chuckle.

He paced, listening, and Chloe quietly gathered her legs under her. If she could just catch him unaware, while he was on the phone, one hand busy holding the cell to his ear . . .

Do it. Do it now. Before he hangs up!

"Look, just have some faith, Myra. I'm on it," he was saying as he turned his back to his captive.

Holding the shard in her palm, Chloe perched on her feet, still huddled down, and took a deep breath.

NOW!

Without another thought, she sprang.

CHAPTER 17

"**O**wwwwrrrrr!"
    Son of a bitch!

The pathetic little bitch had blindsided him!

Launching herself at his back from the dark corner of the cell, she'd wrapped her legs around his torso and clamped herself on. Holding on with her legs, she'd reached over his shoulder and, using both hands, rammed something sharp and hard into his cheek.

He roared and bucked, his cell phone flying from his hand.

Pain shot through his cheek and she thrust upward, slicing through skin and muscle, scraping against bone.

Jesus effin' Christ, she was trying to put the knife or scissors or whatever it was into his eye, drag the blade into his orbital socket with the intent to blind him.

Goddammit, how had this happened?

"You little shit!" he screamed, grabbing hold of her hand, forcing it away from his face as blood poured from the wound.

"Die, die, die!" she shrieked, frantic.

Twisting in the air, he forced her arm backward and

heard a sucking sound as her weapon was forced from his flesh. The pain! It felt like his face was ripped open. He bucked again. This time her legs lost their hold.

Squealing, she went flying across the room.

Thud!

Her body hit the concrete wall, probably rattling her bones, possibly cracking her skull as she slid limply to the floor.

"What the hell was that?" he demanded. He lunged at her, hot, sticky blood dripping from his chin. For the love of Christ, what was wrong with her? Didn't she know he could snuff her life out in an instant? He could've killed her at any moment, but instead he'd kept her alive.

Because you have to. This one, she has to die second as she was born second. Besides, she's bait for the other one.

Bleeding like a stuck pig, he reached down, intent on subduing her. But there was no need. She'd obviously been knocked senseless. But he could take no chances. This time he wouldn't be so foolish. He would tie her as he had originally, feet and hands bound together behind her back. Fuck her need for food and water. So she had to piss or shit? Who cared? She could foul herself. No more Mr. Nice Guy.

He grabbed for her arms, intent on hauling her to her feet so he could adjust her manacles.

One leg shot upward. *Bang!* Her knee connected with his groin. "Owwwww!" he roared, fury and pain ripping through him, his crotch on fire. Immobilized, he doubled over. Held himself. Crumpled from the sheer agony radiating from the juncture of his legs.

"Bastard," she hissed, and scrambled quickly away.

From the corner of his eye he saw her scuttle to the spot where his phone had landed.

No!

Through a veil of raw pain he saw her snag the cell, then clamber ungainly up the damned ladder.

For the love of Christ, why had he left it down? Holding his nuts and willing the pain to lessen, he could only ride the wave of pain and watch her flee. God, it hurt. It hurt so damned bad. But he couldn't let her get away.

Sucking his breath through his teeth, he rolled to his knees and made the laborious crawl to the base of the ladder. But she was already up and out. Fuck! He nearly passed out again, and paused to drag in deep breaths.

He was trying to breathe through the searing pain when the ladder moved.

What?

The ends of the rails scraped against the floor and then slowly, the ladder started to lift. No! That little bitch was going to take away his only means of escape from this place? Leave him in here to wait to rot? All of a sudden his private sanctuary, where he'd always felt safe from the world, began to close in around him like a tomb. A dark, wet, hopeless dungeon.

Hell, no!

The end of the ladder was moving upward, inching its way through the opening. Christ Almighty!

Forcing himself to his feet, he took a swing at the bottom rung.

Missed.

Up it went a bit farther.

"NO!"

Another swipe.

Another miss!

God, his balls ached. Shit! His heart was thudding, a new fear sweeping through him as the idea that he was going to be trapped like a rat became more of a reality. His groin throbbed as the ladder moved steadily upward.

He coiled, released, and jumped. This time, the fingers of one hand curled around the lowest rung. The ladder stopped—his weight was too much for her—but just then she gave it a shake and his hand started to slip.

No damned way.

With all his strength he grabbed hold with his free hand and then gave a loud, sharp whistle. A second later he heard a responsive bark and knew old Red had heard him.

The dog would come running. She would let the ladder slip through her fingers and—

Swish!

His fingers had slid from the ladder and he was falling backward. His feet slipped out from under him as he went down, hard.

Craaack! He landed hard on his back. His head slammed against the cement floor. For a second, blackness swirled around him. He blinked just as the ladder, a massive projectile, shot downward, straight at him.

Reflexively, his arms flew up.

Too late! The wooden missile twisted, the bottom of the side rail, ramming his throat. Pain exploded in his neck. For a split second he thought his Adam's apple and larynx had been crushed.

The room went dark and he fought to stay conscious. Struggled to breathe.

Overhead he heard the dog's warning growl.

Old Red had come to save the day. If only it wasn't too late. Over the throbbing in his body, he felt a moment's relief. If he could just pull himself to his feet, ignore the pain radiating from his skull, throat, and groin, then he might be able to set the ladder up and—

"Good boy, it's all right," Chloe was saying, actually trying to talk to the dog.

No!

"Red, attack! Sic 'em!" He tried to call out to the dog, but his voice failed him, and all that came was a whistle of air from his lungs. Damn! He tried again. "Red! Attack!" But once more all that he was able to do was a whistle.

He hoped the dog would understand and detain her. Even if she managed to get away, Red would track her down. The dog had been trained that way. He found the ladder and started to right it when he heard the dog bark an alarm. Good. Probably had the bitch pinned down.

In the next moment a banging sound startled him as the trap door overhead dropped into place.

Wait! She couldn't . . . wouldn't . . .

Over Red's now-muted but furious barking, he heard the trap door shut with a heavy thunk. Then, the distinctive click of a lock snapping shut.

Shit!

That fuckin' little bitch, the girl he thought was a complete wimp, an absolute coward, had not only duped him. She'd locked him in his own damned dungeon.

Worse yet, she had his cell phone.

* * *

True to his word, Jonas Hayes had sent over the 21 Killer file via the Internet. For the second night in a row, Bentz sat at his computer, but instead of drinking beer, he was letting a cup of coffee go cold on a side table. Also, tonight he wasn't staring at footage of Father John exiting the prison where he'd left his last victim, but was skimming the reports and notes on the Diana and Delta Caldwell murders. Trial testimony was included, as well as interviews with Donovan Caldwell, who repeatedly maintained his innocence.

Hayes had also sent information on Lucy and Laney Springer, twenty-one-year-old twins who had been killed more recently in the same ritualistic manner as the Caldwell sisters. Although the DA did not have a strong enough case to indict Donovan Caldwell for the Springer twins' homicides, it had been generally assumed that Caldwell was the murderer. Evidence at the Springer crime scene and the circumstances of the killing followed the patterns of the Caldwell homicides.

Not only were both the crime scenes in the Caldwell and Springer homicides nearly identical, down to the way the victims were found hog-tied and naked near their neatly stacked clothes, but the same kind of heavy-duty Christmas ribbon had been found at each scene. The ribbon of choice was red, with wires running through it. This detail had been hidden from the press and public until Donovan Caldwell's trial, of course, when all of the evidence had been presented. The differences in the ribbon, Bentz figured, was one of the reasons that the prosecution did not try Caldwell for both sets of murders at the same time, as it wasn't an exact match. Very close, but not from the same "batch." And the DA hadn't wanted to give the defense any discrepancies that might weaken the charges against Caldwell. They only needed the killer to be found guilty of one set of murders to get him off the streets.

Bentz's chair groaned in protest as he leaned back and sorted through some of the images on file, stopping at a series of photos of the victims, their naked bodies bruised with ligature marks that indicated how they'd been held captive before they died.

"Sick son of a bitch," he said, and felt his stomach turn just as it did when he first visited a crime scene and saw the victims. It was literally a gut reaction, one he couldn't control, and had been the cause of many a sneering joke from Brinkman.

"What's wrong, Bentz? Can't keep your cornflakes down this morning?" Brinkman had asked at one scene where the victim's head was nearly severed and Bentz's stomach had roiled. Watching Bentz turn green, Brinkman had smirked and smoked a cigarette. At another gruesome crime scene where a domestic dispute had turned deadly and both husband and wife lay dead in their blood-soaked bed, their flesh turning fetid from the days of summer heat, their bodies bloated, Bentz had fought to keep the contents of his stomach down. But Brinkman had waltzed in, noticed that Bentz was struggling, and said, "Smells great in here, doesn't it? Makes me want a ham sandwich. How 'bout you, Bentz? Or is your system too delicate for it?"

"Jerk," Bentz said to himself. He studied the bodies and listened with half an ear to *Midnight Confessions* as once more Dr. Sam gave out advice over the airwaves. Somewhere, Bentz was certain, Father John was also listening intently. Bentz was so caught up in his thoughts, he didn't notice his wife step into the room.

"Rick?"

He glanced up.

Olivia was standing on the other side of the desk. In her arms was their daughter, Ginny, all of eight months, with what little hair she had sticking up as if she'd just put her finger in a light socket.

His heart melted at the sight of his sleeping child, tiny head resting on her mother's breast.

"Hey." He met his wife's sleepy eyes. "What about our vow to let sleeping kids lie?"

Dressed in oversized pajamas, her own hair a crown of wild curls, Olivia didn't crack a smile. "I took that oath when I thought there was a chance our daughter might actually get to see her father once in a while."

"Oooh. Low blow."

"Not low enough," she muttered, and rounded the desk to perch on the extension that had once housed a typewriter. With a glance at the computer screen and a view of the photo of Laney Springer's corpse, Olivia scowled.

"Nice," she said. "Healthy environment for our daughter to grow up in, don't you think?"

He clicked off the monitor. "You knew I was a homicide cop," he said, touching her knee. "If you don't remember, that's how we met."

"Oh, I remember." A little smile toyed at her lips and she met his gaze with the gorgeous round eyes that had seen into a killer's mind. "Like it was yesterday." She handed the baby off to him. "And it's not a good thing."

"Our meeting?"

"The circumstances of it." Cradling his child against him, he felt the ruffle of Ginny's downy hair against his neck, smelled her clean baby scent, watched in fascination as rosebud lips let out a sigh.

"I know it bothers you—"

"A lot," she responded quickly.

"Okay, I get it. Really. But this is my job for now. And I can't just turn my back on my cases. You know that. And come on, how would you have felt if I'd ignored you when you came storming into my office, ranting and raving about seeing women as they were being murdered?"

She winced at the memory. "I know."

"Look, if I hadn't followed my gut, if I hadn't believed in you and tried to help you, a murderer might still be stalking the streets of New Orleans."

"Another murderer," she corrected.

"Yeah, another one."

"I know your job's important. Don't get me wrong. But you've done it a long time." She let out a sigh through her nose. "Let someone else do it. There are other cops at the department. Younger cops."

"They have families, too." His daughter nestled closer to him, and he felt her soft breath against the base of his neck.

"Are you going to try and make me feel guilty for wanting you to be around to watch your daughter grow up?" Olivia cocked her head to look at him more closely. "Is that what you're trying to do? Because it won't work."

"It's my—"

"Yeah, I know. You've already said. But think about it. You've got enough years in. You could retire."

He thought for a second. The same old arguments played through his head. "I'm not even fifty."

"I'm not saying quit working, I'm just saying change jobs. Do consulting. Become a PI. Go back to school. Teach. Whatever." She threw up a hand. "Just something less dangerous. Okay?" Little worry lines appeared between her eyebrows. "I'd like you to see Ginny graduate from college and become the greatest nuclear physicist, or a senator, or the researcher who cures cancer."

"Not the first female president of the United States?"

"Hopefully by then, the second or third woman who's been elected, but, sure, Ginny could handle that in her spare time."

He chuckled and the baby reacted, startled a bit, but didn't wake. "Lofty aspirations, Mom." He pressed his lips to Ginny's head.

"Don't be obtuse. You know what I mean. Your job is dangerous. Dear God, I almost lost you a few years back."

"True." Didn't his leg still bother him, a constant reminder? He was suddenly stone-cold serious. "And I've nearly lost both you and Kristi." A muscle worked in his jaw as he replayed the horror he'd felt knowing those who were dearest to him were at the mercy of monsters, psychos seeking revenge. "More than once."

They stared at each other. Silently. Didn't state the obvious, what they were both thinking: Bentz's profession could potentially put their precious, innocent daughter at risk. His mouth went dry at the thought. He replayed his fears when both Olivia and Kristi had been kidnapped, each of them more than once, each of them nearly losing her life at the hands of a homicidal maniac, a killer Bentz had been chasing.

Bentz hunted the monsters.

And he attracted them.

Involuntarily his arms tightened around his daughter, and Ginny let out a soft little sigh. No, he thought as he breathed in the sweet smell of baby lotion, he could never put her at risk.

"Let Montoya handle the cases. He can partner up with . . . Lynn Zaroster or . . . or Brinkman or whoever.

In his mind's eye Bentz thought about the younger junior detective. Zaroster was a little green, but eager and smart. Then there was Brinkman, past middle age and repellant. A decent-enough cop, Brinkman got the job done, but was a foulmouthed misogynist whose off-color jokes and offensive remarks cost him several wives and brought him few friends, rebukes from the brass, and disdain from his colleagues.

"If he ended up with Brinkman, Montoya would cut my retirement short by personally shooting me."

"See what I mean? All this violence!"

"I was just kidding."

"But that"—she pointed at the now-blank monitor—"that's no joke."

"No, it's not," he admitted. "But this is someone I need to put away."

"You mean 21?"

He nodded.

"And the other one? The reason why you're listening to psycho-babble in the middle of the night? Father John. I suppose he's another one you need to lock up."

"Yes, two of the worst I've dealt with. It's a personal thing with me. Both slipped through my fingers. Well, I thought 21 was behind bars, but I have to be sure.

These guys, they're bad men, and I want to make certain *both* of them are locked away forever."

"It's your personal mission?"

"I guess so. Yeah."

She rolled her eyes and shook her head, blond curls dancing around her face. "When will it ever end? No, don't answer that because you don't know. No one does. And that end I'm asking about? It could be bad, Rick. For all of us."

In his arms the baby stretched, her nearly nonexistent neck straightening, her little chin pointing upward for a second before she burrowed against him again. He knew Olivia was right. He could never do anything to put this precious child in danger. Nothing was worth that.

Not even his damned job.

CHAPTER 18

Sitting on the edge of the bed in her one-room apartment, Tiffany Elite waited. She checked her watch. He was late.

Great.

Face it, he might not show.

That would really piss her off.

She crossed to the front window, pushed aside the curtain, and looked past the bars. Her apartment was located half a block from Chartres and just enough outside the French Quarter to be affordable, but easy enough for her clients to locate. The place was a bit of a dive, but the good thing about it was the manager turned a blind eye to the happenings within the old building. In return, the occupants didn't complain too much about dripping faucets or a rat or two that scurried around the corners of the crumbling brick and mortar apartment house. Well, except for Mrs. Kowalski. That old hag bitched about everything from her high electric bill, to the street noise, to a toilet that wouldn't quit running. Tiffany wanted to say, "Hey, lady, you live in New Orleans in an apartment that's older than you. Get used to it!" But she'd always just smiled, afraid to rattle the older woman who might suddenly take offense to her nocturnal visitors and call the cops. Nosy busybody.

Her A/C was on the blink again, and the first-floor unit got a little stuffy. She opened the window over the sink in the area that was the designated kitchen, barely more than a closet with a hot plate and microwave sufficing as the stove, and a refrigerator that couldn't hold much more than a quart of milk. Not that she cooked much anyway. In Tiffany's opinion, culinary skills were highly overrated.

Sounds of the night filtered in, though it was late enough that there was little traffic. There was the occasional hum of wheels on the city streets, or an engine purring as it passed, but at least there were no horns honking, no damned sirens screaming. A peaceful time in the city.

From this window she had a direct view of the apartment building just beyond the alley, but the unit across the small space was dark. Its occupants had probably gone to bed already. The elderly couple who occupied it kept opposite hours from Tiffany. The Sorensons were just getting up and shuffling around about the time that Tiffany turned out the lights. Once in a while Tiffany would peer through the window and catch the old lady in her bathrobe and hairnet, studiously making coffee while Tiffany was downing her last shot of vodka for the night.

"Different strokes," she murmured, and felt a breath of night air against her skin. Was that the scent of magnolia on the breeze, or her imagination?

Again, she glanced at the clock.

Ten more minutes had passed. If he ever had the balls to show up, she'd charge him extra. With each passing minute, she became a little more agitated. She figured the john could at least be prompt. She was a working girl, had to stagger appointments. Fortunately this guy, not one of her regulars, was her last client of the night. A good thing, 'cause she was beat. Besides this gig, which she considered her side job, she worked part-time as a waitress at a restaurant in the brewery-turned-shopping mall on Decatur. Usually she covered the lunch shift, but sometimes dinner as well. For all her work at Sylvia Black's, she collected a few piddly tips for umpteen orders of po'boys, gumbo, and crawfish étouffée. So she supplemented.

"Come on, come on, I ain't got all night," she said, catching a glimpse of herself in the mirror. So far there was no sign of gray in the springy black curls that she'd highlighted with a few thin gold streaks. She told herself the lines on her face just added a little character, and there weren't many. Not yet. Her eyes were still clear, a light brown with flecks of green. Tonight, they were sultry, rimmed in glittery shadow and thick mascara.

Unbuttoned to her navel, her oversized blouse was sheer and showed off her figure as well as offering a peek-a-boo glimpse of her breasts, still firm and high despite having a child and pushing thirty. She'd compressed them into a leopard print bra with cups at least one size too small so that she appeared to be spilling out of it.

She was fit. Trim. Waitress work kept her in shape and she'd given up her pack-a-day habit. Well, not entirely, but at least she could make her pack stretch for three or four days. An improvement, right? Wasn't that what life was all about? She'd kicked the meth and most of the booze, now the cigs. Well, almost. By the time she was forty she'd be so damned healthy she wouldn't be able to stand herself, and then maybe she'd get joint custody of Logan back. Her heart turned a little cold at the thought of her son. He was nine already. Nine? Oh, man, she'd already missed so much and by the time she turned forty he would be . . . oh, sweet Jesus, he'd be twenty, the age she was when she bore him. No, no, no. It was going too fast! She couldn't wait that long. She needed her baby boy back now. Somehow she'd have to clean up her act and—

Rap. Rap. Rap.

Finally, knuckles knocked sharply on her door.

She straightened her short skirt, made sure it was snug and even across her buttocks, tossed her hair over her shoulders, licked her lips, and stepped into her heels before crossing to the door. Placing a hand over the top lock, she said, "Who is it?"

"John."

That was what he'd said his name was. Really? Some of her first-timers used it as an alias, thinking it was funny, but that was just fine. As long as they paid. She unlocked the first deadbolt, then the second, opened the door a crack, and peered through to the outside.

He stood beneath the porch light. A tall man dressed in black, with thick, coffee-colored hair, this one was leaner and fitter than her average customer. A pair of Ray-Bans covered his eyes as if he were hiding his identity. No surprise there.

He smiled. A disarming grin showed a flash of white teeth. "I have an appointment." he said. "You're Tiffany?"

"That's right," she said in a cool tone. At night she was definitely Tiffany Elite, not Teri Gaines, the waitress who hopped from table to table, mopping up spilled soda and beer while smiling at her customer's stupid jokes in order to catch a fatter tip. No, tonight Tiffany was definitely in the house. She unlocked the chain and held the door for him. "Come on in." As he stepped through, she felt a little tingle of warning run up the back of her neck. What was it?

No worries. He was already reaching for his wallet and placing a bill on the table, a hundred-dollar bill from the looks of it, though it was marred. "Let's take care of business first," he said, leaving the C-note faceup.

Dear God, were Ben Franklin's eyes actually blackened?

Weird.

But it would spend.

"So," she said with a coy smile. "What can I do for you? That"—she pointed at the bill on the table—"will get you started, but you won't go far."

"Let's see how far we can go," he said. "Why don't you start by stripping?"

She lifted an eyebrow, as if she found his request fascinating when really, wasn't it the normal routine?

"All right," she said, "but I don't like to party alone." Bending over, offering him more than a little glimpse of her cleavage, she slid off one red heel, then slowly, the other. If he wanted a strip tease, she was going to make it was worth his while. She probably should leave the shoes on—guys liked her in nothing but garters and stockings and mile-high heels—but she wasn't going to make the mistake of wobbling while she undressed like she did last week when she fell. That john had laughed at her discomfiture, damn him. As for nylons and garters, she wasn't into that unless a client specifically requested an outfit; then, of course, she'd accommodate him. And charge accordingly.

This one hadn't asked for anything. Just an appointment.

She kicked off the heels and suddenly lost four inches so that now she was a good foot shorter than he. To be expected. Looking up at him, she noticed that he wasn't just fit, but muscular as well. Strong. His black shirt, buttoned to his neck, seemed off somehow. Something odd about it. But it didn't really matter.

Watching him, she slid out of the sheer blouse, let it fall to the floor, and then slowly wiggled out of the tiny skirt.

Was he getting off?

She couldn't tell.

No bulge appeared in his black jeans, but whatever. He wasn't complaining.

"Want to help?" she asked, fingering her bra.

"You do it."

"Whatever you want." She tamped down her boredom and tried to sound breathless, as if she were turning herself on. Though it was all an act, a routine she'd gone through a thousand times. "Why don't you take off some of your clothes?"

One side of his mouth lifted. "Why don't you help me?" he said.

That was more like it.

She looked up at him and offered a sexy smile along with what she hoped was a sparkle of excitement in her eyes. "Sure, baby," she said, and sauntered closer to him. "Let's start with these." Reaching up, she tried to remove his glasses, but he caught her hand.

"They stay." Firm. Almost angry. He jerked his head back.

"Sure . . . sure. Whatever you say."

He let go of her arm and she tried to recover. The guy was a little freaky . . . quick to ignite. Best to do him and get it over with; escort him out the door and turn the lock behind him. She didn't like the edgy ones, but she needed the money.

"How 'bout we start here?" she suggested, and slid her fingers down the waistband of his pants.

"How 'bout?" he agreed, and lifted one hand to tangle his fingers in her hair.

She slipped the button out of its hole, then slid his zipper down slowly and noticed that he wasn't even starting to get hard, no evidence of any erection whatsoever. Damn, this was going to take more work than she'd planned. Big, healthy man, in the prime of his life, and not turned on by her?

Her fingers touched his skin and he flinched, reached into his pocket, and pulled out a chain.

She paused.

What the hell?

No, not a chain, a necklace.

Really? Some kind of kinky thing?

No, not a necklace. A rosary! Oh, God, was he some kind of religious nut, here to try and save her or himself?

"Hey, what's up?" she asked, trying not to frown as

she looked up and saw that his jaw had hardened. "What's going on with—"

He struck quickly, looping the rosary over her head and neck.

"Hey! Wait!" she yelled as the linked beads tightened. She tried to scream, but the air was caught in her lungs. What the fuck was he doing? Trying to scare her? Asphyxiate her?

Tighter and tighter, the holy noose was twisted, closing her throat, her airways, her lifeline.

This was no sex game. No way! She started hitting at him. Kicking. Her lungs were burning. Her eyes felt as if they were beginning to bulge.

No, please God, no!

No amount of kicking could stop him, and her arms flailed uselessly. She grabbed at the links of beads, hoping to get her fingers beneath the string, hoping to break the damned thing, but she couldn't get a grip on it. The beads were sharp, the wire holding it together strong.

He lifted the chord and raised her off the floor. The world started to spin as she struggled, her legs kicking wildly, her lungs ready to explode. She couldn't die . . . she wouldn't die. Not like this. Not without seeing her son . . .

With a grunt he jerked hard.

Her head snapped back, and she caught a glimpse of her distorted image in his dark glasses.

Then nothing.

"Stay!" Chloe ordered the dog as she slammed the padlock shut and rose to her feet. Though totally freaked out, she glared at the dog and tried like hell to seem calm, in charge. She'd heard the monster down in the dungeon whistle to the hound, who appeared more confused than anything else. "Good dog," she said as she edged back. She had to be firm . . . steady. "You just stay there." Backing away, she made her way to the door as the dog stared at the shut trap door and whined. "He'll be fine," she assured the dog, though she hoped the son of a bitch rotted in hell for all eternity and then some.

At last, she stepped outside, but the damn dog was following. She grabbed the door to fling it shut behind her, then hesitated. Should she close the dog up in the house? Locked away from water? Trapped in the heat? Crap! She left the door open behind her and kept one eye on the doorway. The dog seemed disinterested, whining and pacing in and out of the house.

Fine.

She had her own problems. But at least she could breathe gain. Outside the night was thick, the air heavy and sultry, the sound of crickets competing with a chorus of frogs. The stars were out, shining behind high clouds, and a bit of moon cast silver shadows. A plane flew high overhead, lights winking.

She tried to get her bearings as she stood there shaking. She wanted nothing more than to put some distance between her and this god-awful place. But first . . . with trembling fingers she punched 9-1-1 onto the face of the phone.

Nothing.

What? No!

Wait. The screen was dark. *Think, Chloe, think.* She switched the cell on, but no lights began to glow, no numbers lit. She tried again to make the call. The freak had just been talking on the damned thing to that Myra nutcase, and . . .

Again, she only heard dead air.

"What the hell?" Disbelieving, she turned her head to the sky. "Why?" How could the phone be dead? The device wasn't searching for a cell phone tower, and there was no indication of low signal strength. No. The phone was dead. She wanted to throw the useless piece of shit as far as she could, but she restrained herself. The phone was evidence and could link the bastard to Myra, the freakin' mastermind. Holy crap, what kind of mess had she and Zoe stepped into?

Zoe!

Her throat closed. Where was her sister? Why hadn't she returned with the police and guns blazing? Chloe bit her lip. For the first time since escaping from the dungeon, now that her adrenaline rush had worn off, she felt the pain of her injuries. Every muscle in her body hurt, and exhaustion tugged at her. But she couldn't give up. Not yet.

Ignoring the pain racking her muscles, she picked her way over sparse gravel and made her way to the van. It was locked, no keys in the ignition, but the passenger door was still shattered so she was able to reach inside and open the door, then scrounge around the interior. She hoped for a set of keys, but found none. She prayed for a weapon, but guessed if he had any, they were locked in one of the metal boxes bolted to the floor in the back of the van. She found nothing that could help her but an unopened package of cookies, a flashlight, and an old T-shirt. She tested the flashlight. It worked. Thank God! Her stomach rumbled for the food, but there was no time for that now. She had to get moving. He was locked up tight, but who knew if that stupid Myra would show up.

Her insides curdled at the thought of wearing anything that had touched his body, but she couldn't be picky. Swallowing back revulsion, she threw on the dirty shirt and only took the time to shine her flashlight's beam on the license plate. She memorized the numbers, saw the vehicle was some kind of Dodge, and then decided to head for the main road. Zoe had been forced to run through the woods, but no way would Chloe be able to find her at this point. No, the road was better. Find a house and call the damned police.

Again she tried the stupid cell. Just in case.

Nothing, of course. Dead.

"Fine." Carrying the flashlight in one hand and the cookies and useless cell in the other, she followed the flashlight's weak, wobbling beam and started jogging along the dirt ruts, where thankfully there were only bits of gravel to dig into her feet. Still, she'd kill for a pair of running shoes. Hell, no, she'd kill for a car that worked—anything to get her away from that damned cabin of death.

She thought of the monster she'd trapped in the dungeon and hoped he died a horrible death. Prick! What a sicko!

Don't think about him, just keep running!

That part was natural. She'd run all of her life. On the soccer field. For pleasure. With friends in 5K or 10K races, even a half marathon just last year. And now the pain of the injuries she'd sustained while being held by the freak were giving way to an adrenaline rush that surged when she worried that somehow, some damned way, the freak could escape.

Run, run, run!

One foot in front of the other. Around the bend and . . . ahead she saw the gate, battered and shut. She raced toward it and felt a sliver of hope. If she could just get to the main road, find someone . . . oh, please. Reaching the gate, she tried the sliding bolt, but it was jammed, then decided to just climb the sucker and get to the other side. She placed the pack of cookies in her mouth, held both cell phone and flashlight in one hand, and scrambled over. As she landed on her feet, she noticed the dog, who had obviously followed her. He stood inside the gate, panting.

"Go home!" she yelled, turning the flashlight on him.

Another bark.

A good thing? Or bad? Maybe someone would come to her aid. But what if the freak's boss, Myra, was nearby? Or what if the monster had escaped and was making his way to the damned van. If he heard the dog here at the gate, he would know that this was the route she had taken.

"Go away!" she cried. But the hound held his ground and started to bay, sending her into a new panic. "Oh, for the love of God!" She hurled the pack of cookies over the fence. Maybe that would deter him. She didn't pause to look, but took off again.

Soon she'd reach a main road.

Soon she'd get help.

Soon she'd find Zoe.

CHAPTER 19

From the couch in his apartment, Jase hit the Send button on his laptop, then set the computer aside and rubbed his eyes with the heels of his hands. It was late, after two in the damned morning, but he knew he couldn't sleep. He was still too hyped up.

He'd missed his deadline for the morning edition, but his story, a piece about Donovan Caldwell, would run the following day. He hoped by then to have a companion piece about the Denning twins, but he needed to interview their parents, and that would happen in the morning. He'd called and left messages for Selma and Carson independently. Selma hadn't wanted to talk on the phone, but had agreed to speak with him in person at eight in the morning. She wanted the word spread about her daughters, but she insisted on talking with him face-to-face. Probably to make sure he was legit.

Carson hadn't wanted to talk to him and had said so when Jase had finally connected with the guy on the fourth try. "I'm not interested," he'd said flatly. "If the girls are really missing, I want the police to handle it."

No arguments had changed his mind. He wasn't

buying into the fact that the paper with its print circulation, online subscribers, and connection to other news sources could broaden the search for his daughters.

"Look, thanks. I know you have a job to do, but I'm not certain that the girls are missing. Not yet. This is just the kind of stunt they'd pull."

"Stunt?"

"Well, prank, I guess."

Jase had thought of Selma, the way her frail body had seemed on the verge of collapse in Brianna's arms.

"They would do this?" Jase had probed. "Put everyone who cares about them through an emotional wringer?"

"They're kids," Carson had responded. "And sure, now they're supposedly legal adults. You know. Twenty-one. But we all know that twenty-one is the new seventeen. They're all about themselves, still."

Jase had checked his notes. Both girls had been good students and athletes, no arrest records, no real sign of trouble. Chloe worked at a coffee shop near campus. Jase had already spoken with the owner, who'd sung her praises. Chloe had never missed a day of work, and aside from one time when she'd been late due to her car not starting, she'd been on time, a stellar employee. Zoe, who was employed by an accounting firm, had gotten a similar review from her boss. "Tons of energy, always a smile," Peggy Tavernaro had said. "Always eager. Never complains. At least not to me. To tell you the truth, I wish I had three more Zoe Dennings on my staff. I'd love to replace a few slackers."

Both the coffee shop owner and Ms. Tavernaro had expressed concern that the girls hadn't shown up and had asked Jase for reassurance that they were "all right."

"I don't know," he'd admitted, and said he'd hoped so.

But Peggy Tavernaro hadn't been put off. "If someone from the *Observer* is calling," she'd pointed out, "this can't be good news. What's happened to Zoe?"

"I don't know," he'd admitted honestly.

"Well, please, have someone keep me in the loop." She'd sounded worried, and he hadn't blamed her.

Considering everything Jase had learned about the girls, he had been pissed by the flat response of the twins' father. Did Carson Denning really think his twins would "pull a stunt" and thoughtlessly put their mother, and presumably him, through hell? Did he really think they would disappear for a few days as some kind of twisted joke?

No. He didn't think so.

Nonetheless, Jase hadn't been able to convince Carson to grant him an interview.

Yet.

"All in good time," he said, though patience definitely wasn't a virtue that could be attributed to him. Eager. Pushy. Anxious. Now, those were his character traits, and they had served him well in his profession. Just not in his private life. Especially not with women. And so he staved off his new feelings for Brianna. These were emotions best left alone, considering the mess with her sister. Jase cringed a little when he thought of Arianna Hayward.

Of what he knew about her death.

About how he was involved.

"Son of a bitch," he muttered, and squeezed his eyes

shut. His last view of Arianna, in one of his recurring but ever-changing dreams had been at night, through the shimmer of clear water. Hair floating around her face like a feather cloud, strands caught in the current. Skin that was a white, unworldly hue. Eyes open, as if staring upward, reflecting the silvery shafts of moon-light that had pierced the surrounding trees.

Jesus God.

That face had haunted him for over a decade. He was reminded of Arianna's pale countenance several times when he'd caught Brianna staring at him. Brianna's eyes, that same golden hue, and her features, carved so similarly to her twin's, had brought back the anxiety, the anger, the out-and-out fury that he'd experienced the last time he'd seen Arianna. Yes, there were differences in the two women, but when he'd been with Brianna earlier tonight, twice he'd gotten that same hit, that eerie sizzle of déjà vu, and the sensation that he was looking into the eyes of a ghost.

Guilt nagged at him. From what he'd learned about siblings who'd been conceived and grown in the womb together, there was always an invisible cord linking them. If that connection was severed, the remaining twin often felt inconsolable grief. Wasn't it true for Brianna? Hadn't the reason she'd organized the twin-less twin meetings been because of her anguish at losing her sister?

His gut clenched and he walked into the kitchen, opened the refrigerator, and dragged out the last beer from the six-pack he'd bought earlier in the week. After twisting off the cap and taking a long swallow, he discarded the cardboard pack and headed back to the living room, where he flopped onto the couch and stared at the cold grate.

Maybe it was time to unburden himself.

And what? Face murder charges? How would that help anything?

Another long pull on the bottle. More staring at the blackened firebox.

But still no answers.

He couldn't let her get away with it.

If he didn't find a way out of this trap, everything would be ruined. Everything! He couldn't let that happen. With difficulty he dragged in several deep breaths. Then, assured that his windpipe was intact, he grabbed hold of the edge of the workbench and hauled himself to his feet.

He had tools, lots of them. Crowbars and scissors and wire cutters. And screwdrivers that would fit into the screws holding the hinges of the trap door in place.

But getting up to reach it was another problem. The ladder was useless, as there was no opening to rest the rails on. But maybe if he dragged his workbench to the spot below the opening . . . If he stood on the bench, he was tall enough that he shouldn't have any trouble reaching the hinges and unscrewing them.

The hard part would come when he had to force the door open on the hinged side when the locked side wouldn't budge.

But what had his miserable mother told him over and over again? "Where there's a will, there's a way, boy. Don't you forget it."

God, he was glad she died young. Early-onset dementia and some kind of paralysis in her lower extremities had sent her to the nursing facility long before her time.

Served her right.

He rolled to his side and winced. Shit, his face ached, his throat was on fire, and his crotch was still throbbing. God*damn* that Chloe! He pounded one fist against the stained concrete floor, then told himself to rein in his rage.

For now.

Until he caught up with her. With *them.* Zoe was out there, too. His back teeth clenched as he thought of how he'd been duped. By each of them. He'd underestimated both girls.

Myra would be beyond pissed.

Reaching up to the corner of the work table, he struggled to his feet. The longer he lay down here, the farther the damned twins would get. He grabbed both sides of the workbench and, putting his back into it, dragged the heavy table inch by inch, scraping over the concrete.

Ignoring the sting of his own salty perspiration seeping into the cuts on his face, he managed to place the table beneath the opening. Then he found several screwdrivers, slipped them into the pockets of his apron, and climbed atop the heavy structure. He had to hunch a little, but after testing the first screwdriver, he dropped it onto the floor and used a second, a Phillips, which slipped perfectly into the grooves on the first screw.

A slow, determined smile spread across his jaw as he worked. Now the element of surprise would be on his side. Chloe, though spurred to get away, would think she was safe, and that was his advantage.

It wasn't much, he thought as the first screw fell into his hand and he dropped it into the apron's pocket, but it was something. And, by God, he'd use it for all it was worth.

Lying flat on his back, Donovan Caldwell stared at the empty upper bunk and counted his heartbeats. The prison was quiet now; a few men snored, others rustled in their cells, and the guy two doors down tapped the wall rhythmically, maintaining that maddening clicking noise. Donovan had thought it was some kind of code—maybe the inmate, Claude, was punching out some secret message to another con—but the truth of it was that Claude was just tapping out a drumbeat, the tempo of a song that ran through his head constantly.

At first, when Claude had been brought in and the sounds interrupted the inmates' sleep, Donovan had been irritated. But over time he'd gotten used to the ticking. Now he almost found it comforting, which was saying something for this hellhole.

The smells in the cell block were the same as they had been that fateful, god-awful day Caldwell had been locked inside. Some kind of acrid cleaning solution used to wipe away the odors of sweat, testosterone, and yeah, fear. At first the collective smell of confined men had burned his nostrils, but like the clicking from Claude's cage, Donovan had gotten used to the sharp ammonia smell of disinfectant mixed with the aroma of despair that clung forever to the walls of these cubicles.

Though it was long past "Lights Out," a bluish gray illumination slid through the hallways, a perpetual reminder that there was always someone watching.

He'd never gotten used to the half-light. Maybe no one did. He knew that some inmates tossed and turned on their bunks, though a few of the convicts, more than he would have thought, slept like babies through the night.

His head pounded, his heartbeat thudding with adrenaline as it raged through his body. Tonight was to be his last in this godforsaken place.

He thought of his sisters. Diana and Delta, gone for over a decade. Although the girls had been the light of his parents' lives, Donovan felt nothing for the twins.

No grief.

No regret.

No anger.

His emotions for them were as hollow and empty as the polished floors of this prison. His sisters had deserved to die, even if they had died young. He'd never questioned that, but he'd never expected to be blamed.

In the next cell over, Henry was snoring like a buzz saw just as he did every night. The guy slept as if he hadn't a care in the world, as if the void of prison life didn't bother him, as if he weren't going to live the rest of his pathetic years in a tiny box, cut off from civilization, forced to reside in a community of robbers, thieves, rapists, and murdering SOBs. Then again, what did Henry care? He was in for taking an ax to his wife and her lover, a premeditated double homicide that had caught him two successive life sentences.

And yet the bastard slept.

Like a damned baby.

Donovan couldn't remember the last time he'd had a full night's rest. Or even four hours in a row. Since the time he'd landed here, he'd felt out of step and uneasy, swearing his innocence to anyone who would listen, disbelieving that he wouldn't be a free man come the morning light.

It was the dreams that kept alive the nugget of hope burrowed deep in his chest. Dreams of being free, of fishing mountain streams, of running on a beach, the frothy warm Pacific tide spraying against his ankles. Dreams of making love to a woman, usually faceless, but with big tits and a juicy pussy. That was the worst. Waking up to the wet spot on his cot and knowing what he'd thought real had only been a dream, that his chances of ever screwing again were nil.

His head began to pound as he thought about it.

There was a reason coming unhinged was called stir-crazy.

No more.

Silently he pulled his tiny weapon from the inside of his shoe. He'd swiped the bolt from a metal cart in the laundry, where he'd worked for a while. He'd whittled on it as best he could, made certain that it was sharp enough to cut through skin and veins.

Barely an inch long, this tiny bit of metal was his salvation.

If there was a God.

He wasn't so sure about that.

He bit down on his lower lip and held the blade between the fingers of his right hand.

It's now or never. Make your move.

Clearing his throat, he went to work and attempted to slice downward from the base of his palm and across his wrist lengthwise as he'd learned. But the tender skin refused to break despite it being so thin he could see the webbing of blue veins just under the surface, even in this half-light.

Damn. Why wasn't he able to saw through?

Because you're weak, numb nuts. Try again.

Clenching his teeth, he gave it another go. This time he pressed harder, and as he scraped his skin, a hot pain seared up the inside of his arm.

Perfect!

At least he was scratching the surface.

In the dim light he saw the first red drop well.

It ran.

A second glistening globule appeared to chase after the first.

Now, he had only to rip a little more, make a deeper, longer cut, and then maybe a few more. Whatever it took. He needed a lot of blood to flow to get it done.

He felt a grim satisfaction at his accomplishment. Hovering somewhere between euphoria and terror, he pressed the sharpened edge to his skin again and decided to take his time.

He wasn't in that big of a hurry.

He had the whole damned night.

CHAPTER 20

It didn't take as long as he'd expected.

The screws had come out easily, but the trap door was heavy, the lock holding it in place unforgiving. He'd worked feverishly, using brute strength to push against the inside of the hatch. Over and over again he thrust his palms against the trapdoor, shoving his weight and all his force upward. But the door would only wiggle a bit, push up an inch or two, then fall back into place. The long plate holding the lock didn't budge.

Not good enough.

But there was movement. Progress.

He stopped to throw on his jeans, shirt, and boots, which gave him protection and extra height. Dressed, he'd be able to chase down that stupid Chloe. If he could find a way to escape!

Every time he thought of how she'd duped him, he saw red and felt the pain still throbbing in his crotch and face. Revenge burned bright in his soul as he scowled and paced the room, noticing the crowbar mounted on the wall. Would it work? Only one way to find out. He yanked it from its hooks and climbed on the table again. Wedging the curved part through the opening, he put all of his weight on the handle and shoved, hard.

Crreaaak. The wood and metal resisted, but started to give.

He tried harder. Pushing. Prying. Forcing the bar to move the door. And sweating. Oh, man was he sweating. In the dank cement room, one of the few basements in this area, the air was still and warm. Salty perspiration ran down his face, irritating his wounds.

But he didn't stop.

With each straining thrust of the metal rod he thought of the Denning twins, how they'd outwitted him, played him for a fool.

That thought burned in his gut and inspired him.

Harder he pushed, screaming with the effort.

He'd become complacent, felt as if he could control the situation, and he'd been lulled into a sense of security, of his own infallibility. Stupid. Stupid. Fucking stupid! Was it possible that his bitch of a mother and Myra, sweet know-it-all Myra, were right about him? "No way!" he yelled through gritted teeth.

Again he threw his weight on the bar.

Metal groaned, bending.

Good.

He figured the screws holding the plate with the lock, or maybe the plate itself was giving way.

Once more!

All his force!

Hard on the damned crowbar!

Clenching his teeth, he drove all his weight against the crowbar. His muscles screamed, sweat poured down his face and, inside his gloves, his fingers clutched so hard he was sure the bones were showing through his skin.

Again the door moved, metal twisting.

His entire body was trembling with the effort, pain rocketing through his muscles. His legs shook, but he resisted the urge to give up. No, damn it, no!

Another eerie moan of twisting steel.

"Come on, you fucker! Open up!" With a final wrench, wood splintered and the door quit resisting; he almost fell forward but caught himself before he shot off the table.

"Son of a bitch." Dropping the bar, he stood straight, pushed hard on the door and felt it give.

Three seconds later, he'd moved the table, set the ladder, and climbed to freedom.

Barely catching his breath, he found his keys in his jeans and raced outside. The blast of night air was a relief, and he doubled over, hands on his knees, and took the time to fill his lungs with fresh air. He had to clear his head.

Chloe had gotten a head start, yeah, but she was barefoot and naked, didn't know the area. He had a vehicle and weapons, as well as his night goggles locked in a metal box in the van. He would use technology, knives, and guns to prod her back to submission. This time he'd make sure she was submissive. And then he'd go hunt down Zoe.

Tricky little bitches.

Straightening, he listened for sounds of Chloe over the rasp of air going in and out of his wounded throat, but there was only the hum of insects and the whir of bat wings overhead. His eyes skimmed the night-draped property to the trees just visible in the starlight, to the sheds that surrounded the old house listed under Myra's name. It had become the perfect hiding spot.

Until those damned twins had outfoxed him.

Eyeing his property, he wondered which way she went. Would she take off through the fields and woods, head toward the river in search of Zoe? Tough as she'd turned out to be, he didn't see that happening. It was too tricky and unlikely she'd connect with her sister. The opposite direction would take her to a band of saplings that led to open fields. But she didn't know the lay of the land or what was behind the brush and trees.

He figured she would try to get as far away from here as fast as she could, get to civilization and call the authorities, if she already hadn't with his damned phone.

Hell.

He had to get moving!

He swung toward his van and frowned at its shattered passenger side window. He knew the damage would attract notice. He could fix it himself, given enough time, but he had to get going now.

"Woof!"

Looking up, he spied old Red loping down the lane from the direction of the main road. He'd bet his last dollar that Red had chased after Chloe, followed her right to the gate. Red knew her smell. The dog would be able to track her down! He whistled to the dog, pulled out the keys to his van, and felt that maybe, just maybe, his luck had turned.

Chloe finally reached the road. It seemed to have taken forever, but at last she'd come to this isolated ribbon of country asphalt. Which way? She'd searched for lights, any sign of illumination, but if there was another farmhouse nearby, they were in bed for the night. No distant squares of light glowed from windows, no security lamps burned as beacons in the darkness.

Damn it all to hell.

Her euphoria at having escaped had withered as the night closed in on her. Alone and naked except for the lousy T-shirt, she was once again aware of her aching bones and her raw feet, now scraped and bleeding. The road was eerily still, with no sign of a car or human in sight. She imagined what lurked in the Louisiana forest surrounding her. Night predators came to mind, and she shivered, only to remind herself that she'd just escaped the worst predator on the planet, so she should count herself lucky.

But were there wolves? Or bobcats? Maybe cougars? She wasn't sure. But there *were* alligators and snakes. That much she was sure of. She'd better stick to the road and hope to high heaven that someone would come along and save her.

Again, her thoughts turned to Zoe.

Was she alive?

Or injured somewhere?

Or . . . could she have suffered and died?

No, don't go there. She's alive, you know it. You would know if she were dead. You would feel it because of that special twin connection, the link would be broken and you would sense it, so just keep moving and quit moping. You're safe. The freak's locked up. It's just a matter of time. Keep moving and don't give up.

Sometimes her internal monologue made her crazy.

God, she missed Zoe. At least their conversations,

jokes, and even fights were out loud. None of this internal voice, head-games crap she'd been playing with herself ever since Zoe had escaped.

Please keep her safe. And me, too, she silently prayed as she kept moving.

Far in the distance, she heard the sound of an engine. Her heart leaped. Was it coming this way? Was it? She turned, searched for headlights, and thought she saw the misting illumination of dual beams.

Finally!

Now what? How to get their attention?

The car, or whatever it was, seemed to be coming fast, the engine whining. She realized she needed a weapon, just in case the driver wasn't friendly. It was late at night. Very late. Who would be out?

Doesn't matter. You need help.

She reached to the ground, found a handful of gravel and waited on the side of the road, afraid if she stood in the middle the car would hit her. Geez, it was going fast. Roaring toward her, the headlights, twin beams, rounding a corner and bearing down on her. Like the eyes of some growing, looming beast.

Heart pounding a hundred times a minute, she started waving from the side of the road, the flashlight in one hand making arcs across the sky. Frantically she swung her arms and hoped the T-shirt was long enough to cover her buttocks.

The vehicle bore down on her.

Faster and faster, as if the driver were flooring it.

"Hey!" she screamed. Did he intend to run her down? Couldn't he see her?

God, the guy must be going seventy on this narrow road.

"Stop!" she yelled. "Please, stop! Help me!" But as the car or truck or whatever approached, she heard the sound of laughter and the thrum of bass throbbing through the night. The music was so loud, it nearly drowned out the whine of the engine and the staccato of her racing heart. "Stop!"

She screamed until her voice was hoarse, but the car, a dark sports model of some kind, streaked by. As it passed the sounds of laughter and hip-hop music and the smell of smoke, cigarette mingling with weed, escaped through the open windows.

"No! Help!" she cried, and saw the car swerve wildly and hit the shoulder. Gravel sprayed, the wheels slid and for a second she was certain the vehicle would crash. But the driver managed to get control and skid back onto the road. Someone threw something from the passenger window. Glass shattered, shards spraying on the asphalt.

Chloe backed up. Damn, she couldn't take a chance on stepping on the broken pieces. She shined the flashlight toward the road where bits of glass glimmered and caught the light.

"Idiots!" she murmured, her spirits sinking as the glass sparkled brightly.

Too brightly.

What?

And then she heard it. Aside from the fading noise of the disappearing sports car, there was a deeper rumble, fast and ominous, approaching from behind her. From the way she'd just come.

Another car!

Another chance?

Whirling, she was caught in the headlights of the larger vehicle, a pickup or . . . or . . . Oh, sweet Jesus, it couldn't be! Not the monster who'd abducted her! He was locked up. In his own damned prison. She'd clicked the padlock closed herself. No way could he have . . .

Her heart took a nosedive as she recognized the van with the broken window as it bore down on her.

She couldn't let him catch her again. She wouldn't! Spinning, she started running as fast as she could, breathing deeply and trying not to freak out. She ran through the glass and gravel, feeling as if a target was drawn on her back. She was directly in the path of the headlights, her silhouette captured in the smoky light.

She veered quickly to the right, shined her flashlight over the terrain. She could vault the ditch, climb over the fence, and . . . Crap! The fence was wire, thorny strands of twisted barbed wire held up by skinny metal posts. She'd have to roll under it or bend the wires and step through.

Fine.

Whatever.

Brakes squealed as the Dodge skidded to a stop.

Over the idling of the engine, she heard a door fly open.

Pulse hammering in her ears, she kept moving. Fast! Fast! Fast!

Blam!

The crack of a rifle thundered through the night.

Holy Christ! A gun? The freak had a gun?

He won't kill you. If he was going to, he would have already. You heard him; he's not going to murder you until he has Zoe. But that was all before she'd locked him up. Before she'd nearly taken his life. How, for the love of God, did he escape? *Who cares? He's here and shooting at you! Keep moving. Get out of his line of fire. For God's sake, Chloe, RUN!*

Heart in her throat, she threw herself over the ditch, her body sailing through the darkness to land hard.

"Ooof!" All of the air came out of her lungs. As she hit, both phone and flashlight fell from her hands. And she could hear him getting closer, nearly upon her. The horrifying crunch of heavy boots on gravel, the crackle of glass smashing under his weight—all the sounds of his hulking body moving through the night sent alarm shrieking through her.

Move, Chloe. Now!

Fast as she could, hugging the ground, she crawled. Mud caked her fingertips as she scuttled toward the fence only to hit it full on, rusted barbs piercing her skin, a sharp post scraping her shoulder.

"Ow," she cried, then bit her tongue.

His boot steps sounded closer and he was running, but at least he wasn't shooting again. Obviously the shotgun blast had been intended to scare her.

It did.

Then the thud of boots stopped and he was airborne, jumping into the ravine. His flashlight's beam bounced over her. She cringed and tried to get away, tried to slide beneath the lowest strand of wire.

She just needed a few more seconds. With her body flat against the ground, she slid, trying desperately to reach the other side, praying she would make it, pulling herself, inch by inch . . .

Until the horrid T-shirt caught on one of the sharp barbs, yanking her back.

She lunged herself forward, heard the T-shirt rip with a sickening hiss just as a huge hand clamped around her ankle. "No, you don't," he wheezed, his voice a harsh whisper. "You're not going anywhere."

CHAPTER 21

The water was cool, refreshing, running over his bare skin like smooth fingers. Overhead the night sky was a blanket of stars, while below, on the river's surface, the moon painted a ribbon of light.

Stroke, stroke, stroke.

He swam easily with the current of the river, the smell of the water filling his nostrils. God, why didn't he do this more often? Steal away at night; get away from Prescott and their old man. Jase didn't want to think of them, they were murky images while the water was clear and cool and touching him in the most intimate of places.

God, was he going to get a hard-on right here, alone in the damned water? How in the world was that happening? But the water was like velvet, soft and caressing. He blinked and realized he wasn't alone; someone else was in the river, a gorgeous woman swimming around him in circles, her hair fanning around her beautiful features. Her lips were pink, her eyes somewhere between green and gold. Wide and wonderful, they seemed to stare into his soul.

"I'm a mermaid," she said from under the water, air bubbles floating around her, a sexy smile teasing her lips.

He recognized her. Arianna Hayward, in the flesh. And swimming naked beside him, sensual as a siren and oh, so tempting.

"If you're a mermaid, what am I? A merman?"

"Oh, no . . . more like a mere man." She laughed at her own joke, then trailed her fingers over his wet skin. Her fingertips traced the muscles of his shoulders, then slid over his chest, causing him to gasp. Arching an impish eyebrow, she let her hand dip even lower, to dance around his erection. "Uh-oh," she breathed, her eyes gleaming with an interested, amused light as she discovered he was hard. "A naughty mere man," she said. Her touch was like magic as her fingers stroked. Or was it the water? He couldn't be certain; he didn't really care. The sensation of euphoria that came with her silken stroke was incredible, mind-blowing.

He groaned in the water, sure he would come.

"You like?" she whispered, the air coming out of her mouth and nose rising upward, bubbles tickling him, her long hair feathering around her features and disguising her to the point he wondered if this sexy creature were Arianna or her twin, Brianna.

Oh, I like, he tried to say, but the words were trapped in his throat and he closed his eyes, concentrating on the warmth radiating from the juncture of his legs. Don't ever stop.

But she did.

In an instant.

Either Arianna or the river quit moving, quit teasing,

and when he opened his eyes, it was darker. Clouds scudded across the moon, stars winked out, and the effervescent bubbles no longer rose around him.

She'd vanished as quickly as she'd come.

Arianna? *He tried to call through his muted lips. Arianna, where are you?*

"I was wrong about you, Jase. I thought you were a good guy."

He turned in the river, fighting the current. Where was she? Where had the voice come from?

Fear closed around him as he treaded water, searching the darkness. He couldn't see her. Arms flailing, he thrashed through the water. Arianna? Where are you? Arianna!

She didn't respond.

He swam again, searching the black night.

In a panic.

Sweating in the cool water.

Where the hell had she gone?

One second she was close, stroking him, laughing with him, seducing him, and then a moment later, she disappeared.

He rotated in the water, tried to yell for her. Again, no sound. Frustrated and scared, he caught a glimpse of her not far away, just a flash of white skin and dark hair. He swam toward her, cutting through the water with speed as he sensed the river changing around him. The water grew darker, filling with an invisible evil. The flash came and went. He saw her, lost her, and then she appeared again, caught in a whirlpool that spun, wildly, the water churning and frothing.

He tried to swim to her, to rescue her, but she re-

mained just out of reach, her body spinning deeper into the eddy's vortex. Her pale face contorted in fear, only to slacken, her eyes becoming fixed and glazed.

No! Hold on! For the love of God, hold on!

Closing the gap between them, he, too, got caught in the whirling current. Tossed by the swirling pull of the water, he felt the maelstrom of cold dragging him to its center.

Arianna! *He was screaming her name, no sound issuing from his throat as the whirlpool dragged him swiftly into its vortex.* Arianna! *He nearly reached her, his fingers touching the tips of hers, only to slip away as she was spun farther and farther into a dark funnel.*

Oh, God, she was dead. Horrified, he noticed that the pallor of her skin had become gray, the whites of her eyes luminous against the ashen tone of her flesh. Her head lolled to one side at what seemed an impossible angle, but still her unworldly gaze found his.

"You did it, Jase," she said, though her lips didn't move. Once again he caught a glimpse of another woman, of Brianna, being sucked into the bottomless blackness.

No! No! No! *Again he tried to swim to her, to dive deeper to reach her, even though he knew she was already dead.*

"You killed me," she said, the words flowing upward to the rim of the swirling funnel of water, the spot where he was trapped. This time, no bubbles rose with her words, and the flesh of her mouth was starting to fall away, long teeth and bone exposed. "You! You're a murderer, Jase Bridges." Accusations formed in her eerie dead eyes. "A killer."

And the truth hit him hard. Twisted his stomach.

He had killed.

She was only speaking the truth.

Guilt rolled over him in cold, numbing waves. His insides shriveled as she spun farther and farther away from him, now only a tiny figure in the roiling swells of water. One he knew he would never again see.

I'm sorry *chased through his mind, but he couldn't speak, couldn't change the past, couldn't—*

Bam! Bam! Bam!

What?

He looked around. Searching for the noise. Gunshots! Bullets zinging over his head? Or—?

Bam! Bam! Bam! Bam!

Jase flinched and awoke with a start.

He lay in his bed, his eyes opening to the darkness that was his room, the display on his clock radio showing 3:15 in the damned morning. His heart was pounding as the dream receded. He'd barely gotten to sleep and now someone was banging on his apartment door?

Not bothering with his bathrobe, he strode in boxers to the front door and peered through the peephole. His brother, Prescott, scowled into the fish-eye lens.

Jase unlocked the door and threw it open. "What the hell, Pres. Do you know what time it is? My neighbors—" His gaze slid from his seething brother, jaw set in anger, to the man who stumbled to keep his balance beside him.

Edward Bridges, his weathered face more lined than Jase remembered, swayed slightly. A cigarette dangled from his lips as he blinked against the harshness of the porch light.

"Dad?" Hell, what now?

"Hey, son," Ed said, his greeting lopsided, his mouth barely moving as he clamped hard on his Camel straight.

He reeked of booze and smoke, and swayed a little as he stood, his condition far past tipsy.

"What the hell is going on?" Jase asked, his gaze moving to his brother.

Prescott's scowl deepened. "Yeah, that's what I'd like to know. He just showed up at my door an hour ago and Lena hit the roof."

"I bet."

"Drove himself, if you can believe it. Parked his stupid truck almost on the front porch. Really lucky in his condition that he didn't wreck and kill or maim someone! Damn it, Dad, what were you thinking?"

Edward didn't react, just tried to squint through the smoke curling up from his cigarette.

Swiping his hair back in irritation, Prescott said to his brother, "So are you gonna let us inside or what?"

"Yeah, Jase," their father said unsteadily, slurring his words. "You gonna less in or what?" Then he chortled and the laughter turned into a coughing fit. He let the cigarette drop and crushed it out with boots that had seen better days.

Jase swung the door wide open, and Prescott clamped one hand on the old man's arm and dragged him inside to the living area. "This has got to stop!" he said, letting their father fall onto the couch as Jase switched on one of the lamps. "Lena is beyond upset. *Beyond* upset! She doesn't want the kids to see Dad like this."

"Like wha'?" their father asked.

"Falling ass-down drunk, that's what. Caleb might think you're funny, but you're not, and Trinity is at that age where she's impressionable and—oh, hell, why am I even trying to explain? You won't remember, you probably don't care." Prescott wasn't in the mood to pull any punches. He was dressed in jeans and a sweat-shirt that was inside out, evidence that he, too, had been sleeping when Edward had landed on his door-step. "This is not acceptable, Dad. *Not* acceptable." To Jase, he added, "He needs treatment. Now."

Edward tried to struggle to his feet, failed, and sat back down. Hard. "I ain't goin' to any of those rehab places, and you two know it. I jes' need a little cash to get me back on my feet."

"Not happening!" Prescott crossed his arms over his chest. "But there's the matter of money. Rehab isn't cheap, and I'm tapped out with the new house and all." He stared pointedly at Jase. "You're up."

"I thought I was buying you out."

"The farm?" Ed blinked, the sodden wheels in his mind beginning to turn. "You buyin' the farm?"

"We're talking, that's all," Jase said to him. "Sit down, Prescott."

"Hell, no. I'm not sitting down. Lena's already be-yond pissed. Wants to call the preacher for an interven-tion, but what then? How do we swing that? The church has got some sort of program, but—"

"I ain't goin' to no fancy-pants holier-than-thou church camp. It ain't my style."

"Not camp, Dad," Prescott reminded him. "Treat-ment. It has nothing to do with style, but everything to do with addiction."

"Sheeeit. I don't need no treatment. I just need a lit-tle—"

"Cash. Yeah, I know. Jase knows. We all know." Prescott threw up his hands. "God, do we all know. Dad, I've had it." To Jase, he said, "Lena wants nothing to do with this. If we go with the church program, you and I have to sponsor him. Lena's out." He pointed to Jase. "We set it up. Get the preacher and his wife involved, and by the way, that's going to kill Lena to have them know, but . . . whatever. If we do this, Jase, you and Dad set up some kind of payment program. Otherwise he's your problem! Totally. I'm out!"

"Problem?" Edward pulled a face, chewed on that. His head wobbled, a frown pulling down the corners of his mouth. "I ain't nobody's problem, least of all you boys. And you know I don't mean to trouble you boys, but I'm just a little short this month."

Prescott shot Jase a look that said can-you-believe-this?

"You are a problem, Dad. For me. For Lena. For my kids. And for Jase here, who is stupid enough to send you money to feed your addiction."

Ed waved his oldest son off. "I'm just talking about the rent money now."

"Right." Prescott skewered their father with a hate-filled glare.

"So what happened? Why are you here, Dad?" Jase asked. "I told you I was sending a check."

"And I told you I'd pick it up."

"You said maybe. Remember? And that doesn't explain why you'd turn up at Prescott's."

Edward turned a bleary eye up at Jase standing above him. "Got a little turned around. You know, isss dark out there."

There was no use arguing when the old man was in this state; Jase had learned that sorry fact long ago. "Maybe you should just sleep it off, Dad."

"Sounds like a plan," Ed agreed.

But Prescott was having none of it. "No way. He's

'slept it off' too many times, and the problem never goes away; it just gets bigger."

"I told you, I'm not a problem," Ed demanded.

"Yeah, right, Dad." Prescott walked to fireplace, sat down on the hearth, and clasped his hands together, letting them drop between his knees. His breath came out in a groan as he tried to rein in his anger. "This is the end. I can't have you showing up at my place, three sheets to the wind. Lena was still going ballistic when we left. Freaking out about the kids and their grandpa and all kinds of crap." He set an angry scowl on his father. "This is it, Dad. As far as I'm concerned, treatment is your only option. If you don't go with that, you stay the hell out of my life. And my wife's life and my kids' lives. That's it."

"And you?" Ed asked, twisting his neck to look at his younger son.

Jase couldn't back down. "I have to be with Pres on this one, Dad." His voice was a little less stern than Prescott's. "You need help. End of story."

"That's right." Prescott stood. "So you crash here tonight and sleep it off." With a glance at Jase for confirmation, he added, "We'll sort all this out in the morning."

"Nothin' to sort out," Ed insisted.

But as Jase walked Prescott to the door, the old man was already stretching out on the couch.

"This isn't over," Pres said as he stepped outside. "Not by a long shot. I will not have him coming to my home and disrupting my family. And don't give me any guff about him being family, too. This is not okay, Jase. And let's face it, you and I, we have enough problems. I think I told you I ran into Brianna."

"Yeah, I think you even suggested I look her up."

"Well, that was a mistake. A weak moment. Crap, what was I thinking? That it was over?" He met his brother's eyes. "It'll never be over," he added grimly, and Jase felt a river of cold guilt run through his soul. "The smartest thing to do is to avoid her."

His brother was right, of course. But . . . "Too late for that. I might have a business thing going with her."

"Damn!" Prescott let out a long breath. "Just remember that she's a complication we don't need. Especially now that Dad's here. He's a loose cannon, Jase. You never know what he might say, what he could do." His jaw worked as he thought. "Use your head if you see her again. I thought everything was long past us, but I was wrong. The old man? He could mess up everything. Everything." And then he was off, hurrying down the front veranda to the staircase.

"Great," Jase said under his breath. "Perfect."

He locked the door behind his brother and walked back into the living room, stopping at a cupboard to pull out an old blanket and pillow. Dropping both onto the couch where his father was already snoring, he said, "Come on, Dad. Here ya go," and tucked his old man in for the night, even pulling off Ed's dusty cowboy boots, remnants of a more vital life lived long ago.

"Thanks, son," the old man said without opening his eyes.

Jase clicked off the lights and heard, "I knew you was the one to keep. Seen it in your eyes."

What? Jase turned and was about to say something when he heard Ed sawing logs again, his snoring ripping through the apartment. Whatever the old man had muttered, it was probably all muddled anyway. Nothing but the rantings of a wasted drunk. But still, it bothered him.

As Jase lay on his bed, hands stacked under his head, he stared up at the ceiling and wondered about the secrets the old man kept. There was the big one, of course, the one that bound the Bridges men together forever, but were there others?

Of course.

Everyone had secrets; he had only to look inward, at his own skeletons, to know how dark and vile they could be.

So what were Ed Bridges's secrets?

I knew you was the one to keep.

Meaning what?

CHAPTER 22

Brianna awoke to the pressure of cat paws on her chest and the sound of her cell phone ringing as it skittered across the top of her nightstand. Opening a bleary eye, she found St. Ives standing over her, his nose inches from hers, his green eyes staring.

"Morning," she whispered groggily as she reached for the phone. Of course, it was Tanisha. "Hold on a sec," she said to the cat. "I'm sure there's some major drama that needs to be straightened out." She yanked the phone from its charger and placed it against her ear. The digital readout on her clock read 7:15. Her first client of the day, the only one this morning, was scheduled for nine. Plenty of time to get ready.

But she could have used a little more sleep.

"Hello?" she said.

"Morning. Sorry to call so early."

"It's later than the last time." As St. Ives hopped off the bed, Brianna threw off the covers, then crossed the room and drew back the curtain on the French door. She pushed it open a sliver in order to let the cat out.

"What's up?" She hoped it was more important than a nightmare.

"Have you heard from Enrique?"

St. Ives trotted through the open doorway to the sun-dappled garden. Shadows shifted across the flagstones and a squirrel in a high branch scolded.

"Enrique?" Brianna said around a yawn. "No, why?"

"He called me last night and you know he's got a temper."

That much was true. "And he called you, why?" Slowly the cobwebs in her mind were disappearing. She made her way to the kitchen.

"He was really upset about Selma's daughters. Well, everyone was, I think, except maybe Desmond or Milo. Geez, those guys are made of stone. And if Roger had been there, he'd be the same. Trust me, that guy's a piece of work. But then they all are, aren't they? Men!"

Even in her blurry state, Brianna could envision Tanisha pursing her lips and shaking her head.

"So you were talking about Enrique?" In the kitchen, Brianna opened a cupboard, saw that the canister of ground coffee was about empty, and found a half-full bag of beans.

"Yeah, yeah, I'm tellin' you, this really got to him, y' know. Probably because of not ever really knowing what happened to Juan. The disappearance thing really bothers him."

"I think it's getting to all of us."

"Good point. I *know* that's what my dream was all about the night before. Anyway," Tanisha continued as Brianna filled the coffee grinder with fragrant French Roast beans, "Enrique, he called me last night, after I got Selma home, and the guy's all like *Dog the Bounty Hunter* rogue, wanting to get together some of the group and do the vigilante thing. You know, find this guy himself."

"With guns drawn, I suppose."

"He's into that."

Several of the group were. Desmond had admitted he possessed a concealed weapons permit, Roger was big into the NRA, and Milo dressed in camouflage from head to toe. They all were quiet types, who listened more than shared, and Brianna had suspected that, if they didn't open up to the group one of these days, they would probably drop out. More than once she had wondered about those three. She had caught Milo looking at her when he didn't think she could see him. She had seen Roger grow red in the face at something Tanisha had said about women not needing a man. She thought that, if prodded, Roger might explode like a pimple under the skin. As for Desmond, she suspected that he'd been in or was currently in some kind of emotionally abusive relationship. Similar to Elise, who seemed to cower at the mention of her ghost of a domineering boyfriend, Ashton. The signs of victimization were there.

"Give me a sec," she said to Tanisha, then pushed the button on the coffee grinder. It screamed for half a minute as the blades whirled and chewed up the whole beans.

"Holy shit! What's that?"

"My next pot of coffee. I grind my own, you know."

"And wake the whole damned neighborhood in the process. You about blew out my eardrum, girl!"

"Never the one for melodrama," Brianna teased.

Tanisha chuckled.

"How was Selma after she left the restaurant?"

"The same, but kind of disappointed, you know. I think she half-expected the girls to be there at the house. But they weren't, and their car was still parked where they'd left it."

Brianna was not surprised by that.

"I figured Enrique would have phoned you."

"He knows how I feel about any kind of violence."

"Yeah, but he knows how you feel about finding Selma's twins. Huh. And get this, I got another call, too. From Elise. Can you believe that?"

"It is a support group."

"I know, but I haven't exactly been quiet about what I think about that loser of a boyfriend she has. Ashton. Humph."

Tanisha was rarely quiet about anything; she put her opinions out there. And when it came to men who lacked respect for women, she did not hold back. A result of her horrid track record with boyfriends. "But she called," Brianna prodded, filling the coffeepot from the tap, then pouring water into the coffee maker's reservoir.

"Yeah, yeah. Worried, you know. Wanted to help."

"Why didn't she call me or Selma?"

"I don't think she wanted to be too nosy or have Selma think she was intruding. You know, give Selma her space."

"Okay. And me?"

"I think she finds you intimidating."

"Me?" Brianna turned on the coffeemaker as St. Ives returned and threaded his way in figure eights between her legs. "What about you?"

"Hey! I'm a friend to all women! Besides, I think she

wanted to tell me how sweet Ashton was being, which made my bullshit meter soar into the red zone. But I let it pass. Bigger fish to fry, y'know. I don't suppose you've heard from Selma yet?"

"Today?" As the coffeepot filled and gurgled, Brianna glanced at the clock on the microwave. Not even eight. "Not yet. It's still early. She e-mailed me late last night. I'll give her a couple of hours, in case she's sleeping."

"Trust me, she ain't gonna sleep. Look, I gotta run if I'm going to get to work on time. I'll talk to ya later!" Tanisha clicked off before Brianna could say good-bye.

Bentz's eyes were gritty from lack of sleep and, so far, no amount of coffee could shake the headache that was beginning to pound behind his eyes. He'd been at his desk in the department since seven and had been vaguely aware of the change of shift, the voices, occasional bursts of laughter and footsteps over the ever-present hum of the air conditioner that, this time of year, worked overtime.

He rubbed his jaw and noticed it wasn't quite ten. In the three hours he'd been at work, he'd already popped four ibuprofen, a handful of Tums, and even downed a bottle of water. Breakfast had been a Snickers bar from a vending machine. He guessed he wouldn't tell Olivia, as she was always getting on him about his eating habits, exercise, and, oh, yeah, the job. That was beginning to be a serious topic of discussion, one he couldn't argue with her; he barely saw Baby Ginny and she was growing fast. Their baby would be one before he knew it, and the years would start flying by. He'd seen that happen with Kristi, his grown daughter, whom he'd raised, for the most part, as a single parent.

He stretched in his desk chair and stifled a yawn. Last night, he hadn't slept much, the argument with Olivia simmering along with his worries about work. Fear that two of the worst criminals he'd ever had to chase down, Father John, the murdering wannabe priest, and 21, the psycho who killed women on their twenty-first birthdays, had bothered him. Women, he reminded himself. The 21 Killer targeted women. Not men.

Or at least so he'd thought.

Yesterday, he'd left messages with the Phoenix and Dallas police, hoping to get further information about the missing twins whom Brianna Hayward had mentioned. He'd spent nearly forty minutes on the phone discussing the case with Detective Crenshaw from Dallas, who didn't buy into his missing twins as being victims of the 21 Killer. As ever, the response had been, "LA got that son of a bitch and he's serving time. And even a copycat wouldn't be interested in a male. Right?" Crenshaw had asked in a heavy Texas drawl. "What I've got here is fraternal twins, one female, the other male, and that's not 21's gig."

"Until now."

"Yeah, well, I talked to someone about this, a concerned citizen or some such crap, and she . . . let's see, where's the note . . . ?" A pause as he either shuffled papers or checked his computer. "Yeah, all right. Here it is. A Ms. Hayward, from your neck of the bayou." Crenshaw had chuckled at his own joke. "She was tryin' like hell to string some kind of theory together that ol' 21, he was at it again, and that the guy in prison, who's her cousin, by the way—I checked—is innocent." He snorted. "That what this is all about? She knockin' on your door now?"

"I've met her."

"Ye-ep, I imagine if you've got a set of twenty-one-year-old twins missin' that you have. Yours are female, you say?"

"That's right."

"Well, I'm not inclined to believe that the January twins are victims of 21. Hell, I believe the LAPD got their man. But yeah, we're doin' some checkin', just in case."

After further discussion, Crenshaw had promised to share the info his department had collected about the missing twins, Belle and Beau January, as well as keep Bentz updated on any new developments in the case. Bentz had hung up and stared at the phone a second or two. A nagging, uncomfortable feeling had crawled through his gut. He was torn.

Crenshaw made sense, he thought.

Yet the Denning twins had disappeared.

As for the missing men in Arizona, the Reeves brothers, the Phoenix PD hadn't yet weighed in. But Bentz doubted that the twins missing in Arizona were the work of 21. As Crenshaw had said, the 21 Killer had stalked only women.

So far.

Bentz wasn't really buying that 21 would take the lives of men as well as women, but then he would never have believed Father John would attack a prisoner in jail, a nun no less. His MO had been prostitutes and, of course, his ultimate target had been Dr. Sam, aka Samantha Wheeler. But he'd changed.

Could 21 have altered his actions, too?

If so, then the wrong man was serving time.

It was still too early to hear from Phoenix, with the time difference. Although he expected a call soon, he didn't think that case would give him new inroads on the Denning case. He'd already checked with the Missing Persons Department here and in the Baton Rouge PD, just to make sure the ball was rolling on the missing Denning girls.

Though Brianna Hayward had already called the local hospitals, the department had reached out to emergency rooms in New Orleans as well as Baton Rouge, verifying that neither twin had been admitted. Credit card companies and cell phone providers were supplying records, and anyone who had contact with the twins was being questioned. A team was going back to the dorm room to go over them with a fine-tooth comb and search for clues leading to the sisters' whereabouts. The friends whom the girls were supposed to meet up with on the night of their birthdays were being interviewed, and social media platforms were being scrutinized.

Bentz had sent officers to the Bourbon Street bars in the area where that last photograph posted on the Internet had been taken.

Now, staring at his computer, he was looking at that photograph on Zoe's Facebook page, where it had been posted about fifteen minutes before their phones had gone dark.

Was the 21 Killer responsible?

Maybe. Most likely not.

But something had happened to those girls, and he was determined to find out what it was. With the information Selma Denning and Brianna Hayward had provided, he was retracing some of the girls' steps, yes, but they would have to dig deeper into their personal lives. One of the next steps would be to collect samples of their DNA, possibly hair from the girls' brushes, follicles intact, or cigarette butts if they smoked, anything that could positively ID them. He would also pull dental records, in the event they were dealing with a worst-case scenario.

His phone rang. When he saw the caller was his older daughter, he felt warmth invade his chest. He always had a minute or two to talk to her. "What's up?" he asked, and glanced at the picture on his desk. With bright green eyes, auburn hair, and a sizzling smile, Kristi reminded him far too much of his first wife, Jennifer.

"Hey! Look, I just got off the phone with Olivia, and she tried to convince me to talk to you about retiring."

"The female forces unite."

"Not exactly," she said, and he was certain he heard traffic noise in the background.

"Are you driving?"

"Yeah, but I've got an earbud, Dad. Hands free. So I'm safe, but don't duck the question. Are you really quitting? Seriously?"

If nothing else, his eldest had always been forthright.

"Livvie and I, we're discussing it. You know that."

"Well, for the record, I think it would be a mistake. Make that an epic mistake. And the fact that she called me tells me you're not all that keen on the idea."

Not a surprise that Olivia and Kristi were at odds. Kristi hadn't exactly been overjoyed at the thought of a stepmother waltzing into her life a few years back. But the two had been through some rough times together, and more recently they'd bonded a bit. Now that Kristi was grown, married, and had a career as a true crime writer, things between the two women seemed copacetic.

Then again . . .

"I've got to retire someday," he said. "We had this discussion."

"But you didn't get it."

"So, okay, kid, I'll bite. Why an 'epic mistake'?"

"Oh, Dad, get real! Like you would be happy changing diapers all day or arranging play dates for Ginny or worrying about picking out preschools."

"You already said—"

"Come *on,* you and I both know that you'd wither up and die if you weren't hunting down the bad guys. It's what you do."

"I might take up golf."

"Yeah, right. And I might be the first woman president."

"That would be a great idea. Olivia's pegged Ginny for Madam President number two or three."

"Very funny."

"I think she was serious."

"Well, so am I," she said, then, "Crap! Watch where you're going, dude! Oh, sorry, some ass just cut me off. Really? On Burgundy in the Quarter? Who does that?"

"Dunno."

"Jerk!" she yelled, then took a deep breath. "How do these guys get driver's licenses?"

"Maybe he doesn't have one."

She let it go. "Anyway, I gotta be straight with you, Dad. You'd wither away if you weren't on the job and, wait, don't give me any stupid excuse like you could be a PI or something. Is that what you want? Stakeouts to see if spouses are cheating on each other? Or if the president of the soccer league is running off with the team's funds? Or some insurance scam where a perfectly capable thirty-five-year-old is trying to claim disability and you're sneaking around trying to take pictures of him working out in the gym or cutting firewood? Give me a break."

He smiled. She had a point.

"Don't fall for it, Dad. You and I, we both know that your job is dangerous, but it feeds your need for excitement. You're an adrenaline junkie, and you get a rush out of nailing the bad guys and getting them off the streets. Well, maybe Olivia knows it, too, but she's fighting it. Because she loves you and she wants you to— Oh, crap, there's a cop!"

"What?"

"Gotta hang up."

Then she was gone, the connection severed. He didn't have to be wearing a detective's badge to figure out that she'd been lying to him earlier to avoid a lecture. There had been no earbud.

He dropped his phone onto his desk and told himself not to dwell on the decision to leave the department. Not today. He had work to do. He took a swallow of coffee, found it cold, and walked to the kitchen, where a fresh pot was brewing. Several cops were hanging out, reading the paper, eating a hasty breakfast, or lingering over a cup of Joe before heading out.

Turning his head to stretch the tight muscles in his neck, he poured a fresh cup and headed to his office again. He'd just settled in when he heard footsteps approach.

In black jacket and jeans, Montoya filled the doorway. "I've got bad news and . . . worse news." His eyes were guarded by his signature shades, but the set of his jaw and the grim line of his mouth indicated he was perturbed.

"What?" Bentz rolled his chair back.

"The bad news is that there was an apparent homicide last night, maybe early this morning. Working girl, lives off of Chartres, not quite in the Quarter. Mike O'Keefe took the call." O'Keefe was a street cop who'd been with the department for years.

The hairs on the nape of Bentz's neck lifted in warning. He knew where this was going.

Montoya added, "Her body was found by the super, who was sweeping up around the outside of the building when he noticed her door was open. Just a crack, but still. According to him, she never left it ajar, always locked up tight. So he peeked inside, saw her lying there, called 9-1-1. The super says he went inside, but he could tell she was dead. Didn't even try to revive her."

Bentz's gut clenched. "Anything else?" he asked, though he could guess what was coming.

"Yeah, the guy who caught the call did a quick sweep of the apartment. The victim was half-dressed, displayed, weird ligature wounds around her neck, and a hundred-dollar bill left at the scene."

Bentz's stomach dropped. "Let me guess: Franklin's eyes on the C-note were blacked out."

"Bingo." One of Montoya's eyebrows appeared over top of his shades. "Father John." With an affected Louisiana drawl, he added, "He ain't finished."

"I was afraid of that. Let's roll." Bentz pushed his

chair back and reached for his jacket and shoulder holster. "Wait a second," he said, standing. "There was something else? The worse news?"

Montoya nodded. "Or maybe the not-as-bad news, as we might have caught a break. A security camera at a parking lot near Bourbon Street, where the Denning twins were last seen, got footage of a man struggling with a woman. He subdues her and throws her into a vehicle parked at the edge of the lot. The camera only caught the rear tire and back panel of the vehicle, but it looks like a light-colored van, possibly a truck. I haven't seen the tape yet, but it's being sent over. Got a copy going to the lab to see if they can enhance."

"One woman?" Bentz strapped on his holster and sidearm.

"Yeah, don't know if it's one of the Denning sisters. Could be someone else. But the date and proximity are right. The time, too, near the time that the Denning girls' phones stopped working."

"How'd you find out about it?"

"After we interviewed the bartender, he told everyone who worked there about it, and the boss decided to review all their security tapes. I'm already checking with other businesses nearby. Maybe they've got something."

"Let's hope." He shrugged into his jacket, though he'd probably peel it off again before midday. They headed downstairs to the parking lot. All the while Bentz felt that little buzz that always accompanied a significant break in a case, a little jolt of adrenaline that came with knowing they were on the track of something. So far he wasn't sure what.

"Let's check out the apartment off Chartres," he said. "Then I need to stop by and talk to Selma Denning, check out the twins' car. By the time we get back, the tape might be back from the lab."

"If we're lucky." Montoya was already stepping through the doors to the street, where hazy sunlight filtered through a canopy of branches and reflected off the concrete. As he reached into the pocket of his jeans, he said, "I'll drive."

As if there was any question.

CHAPTER 23

"Rise and shine!" Jase set a cup of coffee on the table near the end of the couch where his father rested, faceup, mouth open, beard shadow more pronounced than it had been less than five hours earlier. Jase had already checked the news feed and had a major lead that he couldn't ignore, a possible homicide. "Come on, Ed, you know the old saying, the one you always repeated? 'If you're going to soar with the eagles, you have to rise with the sparrows.'"

"Go 'way," his father grumbled, and rolled onto his side to face the back of the couch.

"Dad—"

"Leave me the fuck alone!" Ed burrowed deeper, yanking the cover over his head.

"I have to go to work."

"Then go already! Who the hell's stoppin' ya?"

"Fine. But I'll be back, and then we need to talk."

"Yeah, yeah."

Jase turned away, then paused. "You said that I was the right one to keep."

"What?"

"That's what I'm asking. What was that all about?"

"Hell if I know. I was drunk. Or didn't you notice?"

"I noticed."

"Fine," his father said from beneath the blanket, "then you know nothin' I said made any sense. Now, just leave me alone. For the love of Christ!" He pulled the pillow over his head as if he were a three-year-old child trying to avoid a scolding.

Jase let it go.

For now.

With a final glance at the man who had sired him, Jase grabbed the keys to his truck from a table where his cell phone was charging. He yanked the phone from its cord, pocketed the cell, and then left his apartment. He could let his old man sleep it off, though it wouldn't be so easy to leave behind the remark about Jase being the chosen one. What the hell was that really about? The drunken ramblings of an old, forgetful man, or something deeper? A slipup? He should just let it go, but knew he wouldn't.

He thought about the check he'd written to his father but never mailed. He'd intended to post it today, but now . . . oh, hell, everything had already started blowing up.

Making his way down the exterior stairs at the end of the building, he wondered what he would find when he came home. Would his father still be in the apartment? Still sleeping it off? Parked on the couch with no intention of leaving? Or would he be gone? According to Prescott, Ed's truck was parked at the farm, so he'd have to find a way to retrieve it, unless Prescott brought it into town.

No doubt fireworks would explode when Edward

and Prescott came face-to-face again and Pres started going on about Ed and rehab, which Jase agreed was necessary for their father to function and survive. The trouble was, Prescott seemed to think Jase had unlimited funds, first to buy the farm and then to send their old man into some kind of treatment program. The truth was that Jase did have a bit of a nest egg, not that he was getting rich as a reporter. He'd purchased a small two-bedroom, utilized his carpentry skills to renovate, and then sold it when the market was at its peak. After that he'd invested his money in the stock market and hadn't purchased another house, as he was happy enough in his apartment. Or had been.

So, he could probably get financing and buy out Prescott, and maybe there would be a little left to help out the old man. But then he'd be flat broke, a position he'd become intimate with a couple of times and didn't much like.

Crossing the parking lot to the assigned spot where his truck was parked, he tried not to dwell on the fact that he soon might own the damned farm, a place he'd sworn to avoid, where his innocence had been buried long ago. "Don't think about it," he told himself as he opened the door of the truck. He had a lot on his plate today, starting with the apartment near Chartres where a homicide had taken place.

Then there was the 21 Killer and the series of articles Jase hoped to write about him. With Brianna's help, he reminded himself. He felt a stab of guilt, wondering if, as she suspected, helping her was actually just satisfying his own personal quest for a story.

Last night's nightmare flashed through his mind as he settled behind the wheel, a weird dream where one seductive mermaid had really been two women who looked so much alike. Arianna and Brianna. Both had the ability to tug on his emotions. Both inspired gut-wrenching guilt.

"Get over it," he told himself. He had no time for self-analysis or anything as ridiculous as trying to interpret his own dreams. He started the engine, then noticed a yellow jacket beating itself against the windshield above his dash. "Get out." He threw the driver's side door open and tried to scoop the bee to the side with an envelope sitting on the passenger seat, an envelope addressed to his father and containing the check Jase had promised.

At least now it could do some good.

The bee was buzzing and running into the glass, mad as hell as it bounced and hopped along the surface. Maybe just scared. Like so many people. Using the envelope, he scooped the stupid insect out the open door and wondered why he just hadn't squashed the yellow jacket. It would have been a helluva lot easier. One bee. Who cared?

Again, he had no time for philosophy.

He had a job to do.

Bentz's stomach turned as he slid covers over his shoes, signed in to the crime scene, and stepped into the tiny apartment off Chartres.

Within seconds a disturbing sense of déjà vu washed over him as he viewed the space with its older furniture and bars on the windows. He noticed paperback books lined up on the built-ins, the coffeepot in the kitchen filled for the next day, the smell of perfume lingering, all surrounding the reason for his being here: the dead body of a thirtysomething female victim.

She was splayed out across the neatly made bed. Half-dressed in a short skirt and open blouse, she lay there with her eyes open as if staring at the gently rotating blades of a ceiling fan positioned overhead.

He clenched his jaw, felt his stomach turn.

Crime-scene techs were busy snapping pictures, dusting for prints, searching every inch of the one-room apartment for trace evidence. None of the others seemed to have the same physical reaction to death that had been with Bentz since he was a kid.

The head tech, Rosarita Gervais, was wearing gloves, her dark hair scraped away from her face. She was leaning over the table where, as Montoya had mentioned, the hundred-dollar bill with Franklin's blackened eyes had been left. "Don't be messin' with my scene, Bentz," she warned. "You know the drill. Washington will have my ass if you disturb anything."

She was half-kidding. It was their routine. Broke the tension. But she wasn't joking about Bonita Washington, the head of the Crime Scene Unit. A brassy African American woman whose IQ was rumored to be at genius level, Washington was tough as nails.

"Got it." He gave Rosarita a nod but continued to stare at the odd C-note. He had always found the desecrated bills disturbing. Then again, what wasn't disturbing about a serial killer who dressed as a man of God and killed his victims with a rosary?

"You really got yourself a sick one here," she observed, then snorted. "Hell, they're all twisted bastards."

"Can't argue with that," he agreed. He spied O'Keefe,

the cop who'd responded to the call, and turned his attention to the burly man rumored to be able to bench press 300 pounds. "Who've we got here?"

"Teri Marie Gaines." A tough cop and a family man, O'Keefe only used his six foot four, 250- pound frame to his advantage if seriously provoked. "At least that's who she was during the day. It's the name on her driver's license. She worked as a waitress at Sylvia Black's down in the Jax Brewery," he added, mentioning the huge old brewery that had been transformed into a shopping mall. "But at night," O'Keefe continued, "she was Tiffany Elite."

"The super tell you this?" Bentz asked, his stomach roiling as he viewed the victim more closely. With smooth mocha-colored skin, Teri Marie Gaines had dark, tightly curled hair with a few golden streaks. Spread-eagle upon the bed, she was half-dressed in a tiny skirt, a bra that barely held her breasts, and a sheer blouse that was open, draped over one shoulder. Around her neck, dark ligature marks were a combination of bruising and tiny abrasions; little cuts in a distinctive pattern that Bentz suspected came from a rosary made of sharpened beads linked with piano wire or something just as strong.

Father John.

No doubt about it.

His stomach did another roll.

"Yeah," O'Keefe said, nodding. "The super, he knew what she was doing at night, and it was confirmed by the neighbor in 2-E." O'Keefe checked his notes. "Frances Kowalski."

"A customer?"

"No, don't think so." He flashed a quick grin. "Mrs.

Kowalski is a woman. In her late seventies or early eighties, I'd guess. A widow who apparently makes it her business to know what goes on in every unit in the building, night and day."

Bentz knew the type.

"She, uh, she disapproved of Ms. Gaines's nocturnal antics."

"I bet."

"Copycat?" Montoya asked.

Bentz thought of the security video from the prison. Father John had stared straight into the camera's eye, not hiding his face or features, almost flaunting the fact that he was back.

Bentz shook his head. "Doubt it."

"Yeah, me too."

Bentz turned toward the medical examiner, a middle-aged man on his knees near the body. "Time of death?"

Wrinkles appeared over his prematurely balding pate as the examiner considered. "After midnight. One-thirty to three, I'd say. Rigor's still strong and body temp suggests that she's been dead around eight, maybe nine hours. Give or take." He nodded, as if agreeing with himself. "That would be our window."

"Defensive wounds?"

"Not really. We've got some bruising at her fingers and a couple of scrapes, two broken fingernails, probably from when she tried to pry the garrote from her neck."

In his mind's eye Bentz imagined her struggle: a small woman who had expected the john, then was surprised when the tall and strapping man had slipped the rosary around her neck and started pulling, cutting off her air as he twisted his glittery weapon more tightly.

Hers would have been a fairly quick, if agonizing and terrifying death. All at the hands of a psycho who should, if Bentz's aim had been true, already be dead. If Bentz's bullet had only hit its mark all those years ago in the bayou, at least two dead women would still be alive today. A sense of guilt tried to sneak up at him, but he pushed it firmly away, kept it at bay. For now. "Thanks," he said to the examiner.

"Hey! She have a kid?" Montoya stood on the opposite side of the bed from the ME, pointing to a silver picture frame positioned beneath a lamp with a beaded shade. A small boy smiled in the picture. Judging from his wide grin, which showed off gaps and permanent teeth just breaking the gum line, Bentz guessed the kid was around seven or eight.

Montoya frowned, his gaze sweeping the room. "No sign that he lived here. No toys or kids' clothes or video games or books. Kids, they come with a lot of stuff."

Bentz nodded, then asked O'Keefe, "The super still here? He might know."

"Or maybe Frances Kowalski," Montoya suggested.

"Yeah, I'll talk to her, too."

"The super's name is Vincente. Vincente Espinosa." O'Keefe nodded to the open doorway where a skinny man lurked, peering inside.

"Got it." Bentz called over his shoulder to Rosarita. "Send me the report."

"Like you need to tell me," she muttered, raising a gloved hand to wave him off. She sent him a look that silently suggested she might want to raise her middle finger, but didn't. "Sheesh, Bentz. How long we worked together? Ten years? Fifteen?"

"Too long, Rosie. Too damned long."

"Yeah, and I love you, too."

As Bentz and Montoya stepped outside, Espinosa fluttered into motion. The super grabbed a rag from his back pocket and stepped back, trying to look busy, which was kind of tough when he'd probably been warned not to sweep or touch anything. Somewhere near sixty, his swarthy skin deeply lined, he wore a faded Hawaiian shirt and cargo shorts. His hair was pulled back into a thin, graying ponytail that heightened his receding hairline.

"You the building supervisor? Mr. Espinosa?" Bentz showed his badge, introducing himself and Montoya.

"Yeah, that's me. Folks call me Vincente."

"You called 9-1-1?"

He nodded. "I already told the other cop." Vincente's eyes were black as obsidian as he squinted against the midday sun.

"So let's go over it again. We want to hear everything you know about Miss Gaines."

"It ain't much."

Bentz managed a smile. "Let's start with when she moved in."

"Three, maybe three and half years ago?" It was a question. "You'd have to ask the owner of the building for sure. Crescent City Developers. They'd have records."

Bentz was making notes.

"She have a kid?" Montoya asked.

"Yeah, a boy. About nine or ten, I think." So the picture was a couple years old. "But he was never here. Lives with his dad."

"Do you know where we could find him?"

"Beats me," Vincente said. "I didn't really know

her. We never talked much. I just know she had a kid. Lived with his old man, out of town. Don't know where."

Someone would have to call the ex and relay the bad news that his son's mother was dead, the victim of a homicide. The kid had to be found.

"So you knew that she was turning tricks out of her apartment?"

"I didn't *know* it. But, yeah, that was the word on the street. And with the hours she kept, the people going in and out . . ." He shrugged. "It seemed likely. But hey, she was a good tenant. Gave me no grief, and she had to do what she had to do, y'know?"

"You see anyone come into her apartment last night?" Bentz asked.

"Me?" Vincente shook his head, the ponytail whipping back and forth. "Nah, I'm in bed before the sun goes down. Watch a little TV, mainly sports. The Saints, they ain't playin' now, so I have to settle for baseball. I like the Rays, y'know. Tampa Bay?"

Bentz nodded, and Vincente went on to explain how he slept soundly and even with the window open he'd heard no struggle, no fight. He had only discovered the body, as he'd told O'Keefe and the 9-1-1 operator, when he'd been sweeping up and noticed Teri Gaines's door cracked open.

The interview revealed few other details, so they moved on, up the stairs to Apartment 2-E.

Frances Kowalski wasn't a whole lot more informative, but the elderly woman in the second-floor apartment filled to the brim with religious artifacts and photos of a man Bentz assumed to be her late husband was certainly an eager witness. Whereas Espinosa had been guarded and a little reticent, Frances Kowalski was effusive to the point Bentz thought the older woman might be exaggerating, just to keep Montoya and him interested.

"About Ms. Gaines," she'd said from behind owlish glasses, the tops of which brushed thick bangs of dyed red hair. "You know, I have a bird's-eye view of her apartment. I see everything." Her lips had pursed in a sanctimonious show of disgust. "And, I hate to judge, you know—"

Bentz thought the opposite was probably true. In his experience anyone who started with "I hate to" usually relished it. Whether it was "I hate to point out," or "I hate to speak ill of the dead," or in Frances Kowalski's case, "I hate to judge," it all boiled down to some kind of self-justification to spread a little gossip tinged with a bit of self-satisfaction. In some cases, he suspected that these people actually envied the person who broke the rules and walked on the wild side.

"But she had men coming and going all hours of the night." Mrs. Kowalski's eyebrows had arched pointedly over the top of the glasses. "They weren't there selling vacuum cleaners or brushes, if you catch my drift."

He caught it.

And it stunk.

The more Bentz had talked with the woman, the less he'd liked her. Her only pertinent information was that she had heard "something" and checked her window to witness a man "in black" entering Teri Gaines's apartment. Her pale lips had pursed even more prudishly as she'd said, "I have no idea what she was doing down there." A lie. "But it wasn't good."

"It ended badly," Bentz had offered.

"Well, really?" A sniff of self-righteousness. "What could she expect?"

Unable to extract any more information from the woman, the detectives had left her to her snooping and exited the building.

Montoya reached into his shirt pocket for a pack of nonexistent cigarettes, then apparently remembered that he'd quit. Frowning, he said, "I'll tell you what. I'm glad that old buttinsky isn't my neighbor."

"Buttinsky?" Bentz repeated.

"A term my mother used for people who couldn't keep their noses in their own business. It applies here. With Frances not-a-guy Kowalski."

"I guess." Bentz noticed a news van for WKAM setting up shop on the street. "Looks like the press has caught wind of this."

"A good thing."

"I suppose." Bentz wasn't all that interested in talking to anyone from the media. Deep down, he hated dealing with the "fourth estate," though it was part of his job. He considered all reporters to be a necessary evil. The relationship between cops and press should be symbiotic, right? Each helping the other? Both groups looking out for the good of the public? But in Bentz's opinion, too many members of the press were interested in sensational journalism, creating news rather than reporting it, causing a greater public awareness, but also stirring up fear and sometimes panic. Hence, he was careful in dealing with the press and usually tended to avoid everyone who carried a press card.

The TV crew wasn't alone. Also standing near Montoya's Mustang was Jase Bridges from the *Observer,* the reporter angling for a job in the department. It had happened before, when someone from the outside had landed the position, a reporter no less. But Bentz wasn't certain that Jason Bridges was the man for the job.

"Hey," Bridges said. "How about a quick interview?"

Bentz shot him a glare. "You know the deal, Bridges. Nothing for me to say."

"Working girl, the victim?" he asked, undeterred. Obviously the homicide had already hit the wires. From the corner of his eye, Bentz noticed the approach of Brenda Convoy, a reporter from WKAM. A cameraman trailed a step behind her, shoulder cam in place.

"Look, Bridges, you're not the PIO yet," Bentz told Bridges, ignoring the TV reporter. "So talk to someone from that office. We've got notifications to make and a case to solve. Until I've got a good reason to share the investigation with the public, you're out of luck. At least with me." *And so is she,* he silently added, watching Brenda Convoy hurry along, high heels clicking unsteadily over the uneven sidewalk. In one smooth motion Bentz slid into the passenger seat of Montoya's Mustang and closed the door. A second later, without a word, his partner hit the gas, maneuvering the sporty car so that it melded seamlessly into traffic.

Pain throbbing in her ankle, Zoe pushed herself to keep moving through the woods.

Through the branches, she saw that the sun was climbing higher in the sky. She'd watched it rise, knew which direction was east, not that it helped her much as she had no idea where she was, couldn't conceive of where she would find civilization. But at least she was convinced she wasn't walking in circles. She was able to limp with the aid of a stick, and with each torturous step she put as much distance as she could between herself and the prick who had abducted her. Sick bastard. God, she wished she'd killed him. Maybe, by now, Chloe had finished him off.

Zoe's heart twisted.

Chloe.

Where was she?

Safe?

Or on the run like Zoe?

"Please, God, no," Zoe whispered through cracked lips. She pressed her fingertips to them and found them encrusted, probably with mud. Maybe even some dried blood mixed in, too. She was still naked but sunburned and bitten by mosquitoes or whatever creepy crawly things had found her bare skin.

Light-headed from the lack of food, water, and sleep, she stopped and listened again, leaned on her stick, and strained to hear. Over the sounds of insects buzzing and a toad croaking, she heard the hum of traffic, wheels spinning over asphalt. Her heart soared.

She would make it.

She'd get to that damned road and flag someone down, someone who would drive her to safety. Tears welled in her eyes and she dashed them quickly away as if anyone here in this godforsaken lowland forest could see her. She'd spent a night listening to bats and owls, looking out for gators and even bears, but finally, she was about to be rewarded. She was going to make it.

But, damn it, she couldn't tell how far away the road was.

A mile?

Two?

Five?

She wasn't certain, but she'd get there, pushing through pain, thirst, and hunger. She just had to keep heading in the direction of the sound of engines and tires.

Through the lacy branches overhead she spied an egret sailing in the blue sky, long-necked and snowy white, flying gracefully. She almost smiled as she hobbled forward and brushed the gauze of a spiderweb out of her face.

Maybe she would reach the road in fifteen minutes. Or it could take an hour.

She wouldn't let herself think that it would be any longer. Surely she'd find civilization long before nightfall and not have to spend another frightening night alone in the wilderness.

Gritting her teeth, she headed toward the sound.

Somewhere in the far distance she heard a dog barking. Rapid, thunderous barks, as if it had picked up the scent of an animal it was tracking. Poor beast, she thought, relating to the fox or duck or whatever the hound was tracking.

The dog's cries seemed to get louder and . . . closer. Her heart stopped as a horrifying thought slithered through her brain.

What if the dog was tracking her?

"No," she said, but the thought took hold.

What if the hound was owned by the psycho who had abducted her?

What if, even now, she, not some woodland creature, was the hunter's ultimate prey?

Impossible! She'd crossed the river. She'd gotten herself some distance from that horrible cabin with its dank cellar. And all that time she'd spent in the water . . . it had to make it difficult to track her. But still . . .

She swallowed hard. Told herself she was hallucinating. She was safe. Far away from the whack job with his stupid fascination about birthdays.

Right?

But the dog continued to howl, a horrid, plaintive sound that echoed through this shady forest of hickory and pine. Panic skittered down her spine.

How in the world would she, limping as she was, outrun a dog?

It's not chasing you. Don't freak out. Just keep moving. Head to the highway. Find a motorist. Get to safety.

And, for God's sake, Zoe, get there fast!

CHAPTER 24

In her practice, Brianna never stacked her clients back-to-back. Like most therapists, she gave herself at least fifteen minutes of breathing room between fifty-minute counseling sessions. She also worked to keep herself emotionally detached; empathetic, yes, but distant enough to remain objective and help each person find his or her path to emotional well-being. In the times she started to slip and become too involved, experiencing transference, she had worked through the issues with her own therapist. Generally, she was able to maintain her own mental equilibrium.

Unfortunately, her usual techniques were not helping her maintain objectivity with her last client of the day. Maybe it was lack of sleep. Maybe her worries over Chloe and Zoe were wearing away her concentration. Whatever the reason, today she found it impossible to remain emotionally detached from this widower who was heartsick at the loss of his wife, a husband who was having trouble moving on. He didn't break down, wouldn't allow himself to shed a tear, but his chin wobbled and he twisted his gnarled hands around a handkerchief so hard the thin square of cloth had become a tightly wound paisley snake.

After he left, she walked outside to her garden and felt the warmth of the morning sun warm her back. Though it was just a little past ten, she didn't have another client scheduled for the rest of the day, so she could spend more time helping Selma find her daughters.

If they're still alive.

"Don't think that way," she said, though she knew the odds of recovering the girls alive were diminishing with each passing hour. Trying to stay positive, she watched a sparrow flutter in the branches of the tree. St. Ives had also noticed the bird and made a nervous little groan of frustration at not being able to reach it.

"Stick with the mice. Or better yet, any rats hanging out here, okay?" She bent down to pet the tabby's soft head, but he was having none of it. Focused on the bird, he ignored Brianna who, at the mention of rats, thought about her shower the night before. Letting herself outside the garden gate, she walked along the narrow path between the neighbor's fence and the side of her house to the area around her bathroom window. She was an inch or two too short to see inside, but anyone near six feet tall would be able to see over the window's ledge and view the interior.

Had someone been out here last night?

Her skin crawled at the thought of it.

The crepe myrtle seemed undisturbed . . . but the fronds of a fern were twisted, a few flattened, as if stepped on. A cold wash of fear spilled down her spine.

Had there actually been someone standing here in this very spot, peering through the window, watching as she showered?

"No way," she whispered as St. Ives crept around the corner to move stealthily through the foliage. The cat stopped at her feet and looked up to meow at her. "Hey, buddy." Bending over, she picked him up, catching him squarely this time. Holding his furry body against her chest, she walked to the front of the house where her small front yard ran into the sidewalk. There was a short wrought-iron fence around the front of her property with an unlocked gate leading to the front door. Anyone could have stepped through or climbed over, but who? And why? What kind of perv?

She didn't want to think about it, but vowed to keep her blinds closed and windows shut at night. That would pose a problem in the bathroom, where steam built up when she showered. Maybe it was time to fix the exhaust fan that had given up the ghost six months earlier, and install motion detector lights outside the house. Or she could go to a local shelter and rescue a dog, a *big* dog that would cause any prowler to think twice about trespassing. She was definitely warming to that idea, as long as the dog got along with cats; well, at least with one overweight yellow tabby.

"That's a must, isn't it?" she said to St. Ives, as if the tabby could read her mind, or understand her words. "But it could be time to expand the family. What do you think? Hmm?" She buried her nose in his soft fur and he began to purr as she carried him inside and made a mental note to install the lights and fix the fan.

For now, the dog would have to remain on her wish list.

She had work to do today. The first order of business was to do some checking on Jase Bridges, find out a little information on the reporter. Just who was he? Certainly far more than the hell-raiser she remembered from her youth. Letting St. Ives climb onto the bookcase, Brianna located her laptop, dropped onto a corner of the couch, and plugged in. Just as she settled in, her cell phone dinged, letting her know that she'd missed a call. She snatched it and saw that she'd actually missed two: one from Tanisha and another from Milo Tillman. "Not now," she said aloud. One thing at a time.

Although she told herself that she was checking out Jase Bridges to screen him for Selma, she had to admit that she found him more than a little fascinating. Sure, she'd like his help in finding the missing Denning girls. But there was more to her interest, a spark that had ignited when she was little more than a girl, a spark that, she sensed, could flare if she let it. She toyed with the idea. Her love life had been dismal since Max. What would it hurt?

"Don't go there," she warned herself. Getting involved with a man right now was a distraction she didn't need. More than that. Getting involved with Jase Bridges would be a mistake. A big mistake. At least until Selma's daughters were located.

But she did need to know more about him, especially if she agreed to work with him. "Forewarned is forearmed," she reminded herself, remembering one of her mother's favorite phrases.

He'd worked for several newspapers, including the *Savannah Sentinel,* before landing at the *Observer.* Nowhere did it mention that he'd ever been married, which corroborated what he'd told her. Not that it mattered, she told herself. And yet, she couldn't help feel a small sensation of satisfaction.

"You're hopeless," she said aloud, then looked up to find St. Ives sitting on a shelf, flicking his ringed tail and staring at her as if he agreed.

"Son of a bitch!" Jase whispered under his breath as he glowered at the computer screen. His oath seemed to go unnoticed in the newsroom, where a steady hum of typing, conversation, philosophizing, and joking was the norm. Fluorescent lights suspended from the high ceiling of this converted warehouse offered a fake illumination that vied with the natural light pouring through a bank of massive windows facing the street. Centuries-old brick walls contrasted with the rows of sleek monitors and computers that processed the online version of the *Observer*.

"Trouble?" Meri-Jo Williams asked from her desk barely six feet from his. Meri-Jo, always competitive and all of twenty-three, considered herself a dyed-in-the-wool journalist, fighting sexism to find her niche in the hardscrabble world of news. All bullshit.

"Nothing," Jase said.

"Didn't sound like nothing." Her drawl, accentuated by the arch of a single, perfectly plucked eyebrow, accused him of the lie.

No way was he going to tell her that the document on the computer screen was personal. The last thing he needed was Meri-Jo breathing down his neck.

After being shut down by Bentz at the homicide crime scene, he'd spent a little time talking to the building's superintendent, extracting the basics for his story, along with some sketchy information on the victim, Teri Gaines. He'd been careful not to cross the line, hadn't pushed to view the crime scene or anything that would, at this point, piss off anyone in the department. He needed to do this job, of course, but it would be downright stupid to step on any toes in the New Orleans Police Department if he wanted to join their ranks.

"Wait. You're working on the murder of the prostitute, right?" Meri-Jo was interested because she wanted his job. She knew he was thinking of leaving, and she made zero bones about the fact that she coveted his position as the crime writer. She wanted it now. Or sooner. "Trying to tie this one in with Father John?" She waved a hand, as if shooing away a bothersome fly. "Right? That psycho who dressed himself as a priest and killed hookers." She gave a fake shudder. "What a douche."

"That's one way of putting it."

"The truth, Bridges. The only way I 'put it.'" She hooked her fingers into air quotes and glared at him as if he'd somehow offended her. Meri-Jo prided herself on being a fact-finding, truth-seeking, hungry-but-honest reporter who took her job more than seriously.

"Yeah, right," Matthew Kennedy said as he cruised by with what was probably his second super-sized Diet Coke of the day. "That's you, Meri, taking journalism to a whole new level." Pushing sixty, with an I've-seen-it-all smile and a nose for self-important BS, Kennedy had been with the newspaper through three or four incarnations and still, he survived. "Thank God you're keeping us old war horses on the straight and narrow."

"Shove it, Kennedy."

"My pleasure," he said, and sauntered off.

"God, he's *such* an asshole." She was perturbed, her

truth-and-justice feathers seriously ruffled. But before she could launch into a diatribe about "old reporters not giving the new, innovative generation a chance," her cell phone chimed and she snatched it from her desk, checked the screen, and turned her back to Jase.

Good.

Now he could absorb his discovery in private.

And absorb he did as he flipped from one page on his screen to another. After putting together his story on the homicide of Teri Gaines, he'd searched for information on his own family and dug up documents he had never seen before.

In truth, he'd always believed in "letting sleeping dogs lie" where his own history was concerned, having trusted that his father and grandparents had told him the truth about what had happened in the past. He'd been too young to remember his mother, though once, in the farmhouse attic, he'd come across a family album tucked between old books and bedding. Inside, he'd found a black and white photo of a wedding. His father, dressed in a dark, western-cut suit, stood next to a soulful-eyed girl in a white lace dress and veil. Their hands were clasped, rings evident as they stood under a simple altar.

Jase, being a rambunctious boy who accepted what grown-ups told him as fact and later, as a teenager who was always in trouble, had never really had too many questions about his mother or, for that matter, the brother who had died in Texas. He'd been too caught up in himself. It had seemed odd that Marian Selby Bridges, purportedly heartbroken at the loss of a son, had deserted her husband and two boys, leaving them to fend for themselves. However, his occasional questions about his mother had always evoked anger from his father or anguish from his grandmother. As an adult, he'd sided with his father in the belief that any woman who'd abandoned her kids and never once contacted them didn't deserve the title of mother, and she certainly didn't need to be located. He'd made a couple of lame-ass attempts to find her in his late twenties, but when the job had been more involved than he'd wanted, he'd let it go.

Was she alive? Dead? He'd been interested, yes. Hell, any kid would have questions about the woman who had given birth to him. But he hadn't felt the urge to dig up any of the family dirt. Who knew what he would find? His mother's rejection only confirmed that he didn't need a woman who would walk out on him in a heartbeat, a woman who might require the same kind of care and attention that his father was now demanding.

Truth be told, Marian Bridges didn't deserve to know the kids she'd left.

And then there had come the time when he'd met Arianna Hayward. From that point forward, his life had been turned upside down and inside out. His own secrets had crippled him emotionally, he figured. Deep down he was scared of the truth because he knew how dark, how innocently evil it could be.

No more.

Today, things changed.

With the speed of the Internet, his connections at the newspaper, a few phone calls, and some incredible search engines, he'd dug deeper than before, deeper than he probably should have.

But now, he knew for certain that the old man had lied. About Jase's life. A web of lies that had grown with the years. Well, hell, what had Jase expected? He hit the Print button on several documents and tried to keep his rage in check.

It was time to call Edward Prescott Bridges on his crap.

Tossing the documents into his briefcase, he headed outside, but as he was walking out the glass doors, he nearly ran into Brianna Hayward heading into the offices of the *Observer*.

"Hey! I was coming to see you," she said. In sunglasses, her dark hair caught in a loose bun, she looked a little messy and sexy as hell as she stopped short and he stepped outside.

A woman with pale hair and a pissed expression was walking a dog past the building. Jase had to hop over the beagle's tether to avoid tripping.

"Hey!" the blonde said irritably as beads of sweat glimmered over her compressed lips. "Watch where you're going!"

"Sorry." He backed away just before he became entangled in the leash.

"Jerk! Some people!" She half-trotted briskly ahead, the dog straining and pulling her forward. "Get a life!"

"Still making friends," Brianna observed drily.

"Always." He watched the dog tug its owner around a corner at the end of the block, then turned his attention to Brianna. God, she was beautiful. A carbon copy of what Arianna would have looked like, had she survived. His jaw clenched a bit, and he remembered his resolution to stick to business with Brianna.

Too late.

Jase felt drawn to her, wanted to know more about her. Because of Arianna and his guilt? Of course. His emotions played a big part in it, but there was more to his attraction. Something about the way she angled her face up to his, her eyes guarded by the oversized colored glasses, her chin a little point, her lips wide. He was near enough to observe a dusting of freckles across the bridge of her nose. Silently he told himself that being this close to her was dangerous.

"I think we need to talk, Bridges," she said.

More than you know, he thought.

She added, "But probably, considering the heat and lack of privacy, not here in the street."

Good idea.

"Your office?" she suggested.

Bad idea. The conference room was currently occupied, and his desk wasn't exactly private. He cringed inside, thinking about Meri-Jo being so close, always with half an ear cocked in his direction, sometimes doing her own research on stories assigned to him, trying to one-up him. She was such a pain.

Brianna started for the door, but he grabbed the crook of her arm. "Not here."

"No?"

"Too noisy, too much going on." He offered a wry smile. "The *Observer,* it's a happenin' spot."

"If you say so."

For the moment, his fury at his father had abated, and his intention to drive home like a madman to righteously confront the old man seemed less important. It could wait. And maybe that was a good thing. Jase needed to cool off before he tore into Edward. Realizing he was still holding on to her elbow, he let go. "There's a coffee shop across the street, at the corner. They make a mean cappuccino."

"And that will be more private?" A skeptical eyebrow lifted over the rim of her sunglasses and her pink lips twitched a little.

"They've got a shady spot outside, an inner courtyard. No one will bother us."

"Okay."

"And if I remember correctly, I owe you a drink," he said.

"That's not how I remember it."

He ignored her remark and said, "Play your cards right, I might even spring for a beignet."

Now both eyebrows had lifted and her lips, a glossy pink, curved into a smile. "Big spender."

"That's me." Her grin widened and he felt an unlikely pull on his heart.

"Fair enough, Bridges. You're on!" With that she turned away and started toward the shop. Sunlight burnished her hair to a coppery sheen and the hem of her skirt swung above her knees as she walked. In two quick strides he fell into step with her and told himself he was being a fool and that his brother had been right. He should avoid her.

Too late. She glanced up, gave him an amused smile, and he was sunk. Aside from his attraction to her, he was intrigued about her change of heart. What had happened to make her trust him? As they stepped into the shop, he figured he was about to find out.

They ordered at a long counter that ran along one wall. Behind them, all the tables were taken by patrons sipping iced tea or coffee while plugged into the establishment's free Wi-Fi. The buzz of conversation and coffee-making filled the space with a constant din. Jase took care of the bill, as promised. Once they'd picked up their drinks and food, he guided her through an open doorway to a veranda that looked as if it had once been an alley. Surrounded on two sides by the craggy brick exterior of century-old buildings, the narrow street had been gated with wrought iron on either end to form a courtyard. Potted palms and an indigo awning helped shade and cool the area.

The courtyard was quiet and peaceful as the few customers seated at the outdoor tables were huddled close together and lost in their own conversations. Jase nodded toward a small table with two chairs pushed into a corner, the most privacy the space provided.

"Better," Brianna said, scraping back a chair. "Out here I can actually hear myself think."

"Careful, that could be dangerous."

"You don't know how right you are about that." Her smile faltered a bit. Once seated, she shoved her sunglasses onto the top of her head so that she could look him in the eye. "So the reason I came looking for you," she said, and once again he was taken aback at how direct she was, "is that I want to take you up on your offer. Of help in finding Zoe and Chloe Denning."

"And the 21 Killer?"

"God, I hope I'm wrong about that son of a bitch." She stuffed a straw into her glass. "I mean, I don't believe Donovan is 21, no way. But I hope to high heaven that the 21 Killer is not in New Orleans and that . . . I hope he didn't target Zoe and Chloe." Sadness darkened her eyes, and she bit her lip for a second before her shoulders straightened. "So," she said, obviously turning her thoughts from the fate of the missing twins. "Here's the deal: You help me find Zoe and Chloe, and I'll give you an exclusive to my side of the story. But there's a catch."

"There always is." Leaning back in his chair, sipping his black coffee, Jase watched the play of emotions that crossed her even features.

"We have to run everything by Selma, their mother. And if . . . I mean, *when* the girls are located, you'll need to get their approval, too. My deal is only good for what *I'm* doing now."

"In exchange for my help?" he clarified.

"Right, with all your resources." She drank some of her iced tea, then unwrapped her beignet. "You have access through the paper to all sorts of news information that I don't."

"Just about everyone who has the Internet does."

"Yeah, yeah, I know. But you guys—" As she licked powdered sugar from her fingers, he tried not to stare. "You get it first. You know, lightning quick." She snapped her fingers to make a point. "And that's just to begin with." Another swallow of tea. "I'm willing to bet you have sources in the police department. And I'm not talking about the usual statements and reports generated by the department. My guess is you have someone inside."

"A leak?"

"Call it what you will." A lift of her shoulders. More tea.

"I'm trying to land a job there," he reminded her.

"Regardless. And you're not employed by the City of New Orleans yet. In fact, you're still on the payroll of the *Observer,* still trying to ferret out the news and get it printed, including the story on the Denning twins *and* 21.

"I did some research on you, Bridges. You're pretty good at what you do. You dig deep. Aren't afraid of stepping on toes. You go after the truth, guns blazing. So, yeah, I decided I want you on my side."

"Is it a side? Aren't you working with the police?"

"Trying to. They're resistant." She pointed to his donut. "You going to eat that?"

"Yeah." He unwrapped the pastry. "Eventually." He grinned.

"I've been to Baton Rouge and the PD here in New Orleans, told them what I know and stirred up the pot. But what have they done?" She frowned. "They aren't exactly excited about the prospect of keeping me in the loop, if you know what I mean. I'm not really sure they can legally, so I'm out." Absently swirling her straw through the ice cubes in her glass, she added, "And you know what? It really doesn't work for me."

That much he believed. Brianna was a woman with a purpose, and he was beginning to see that she was not easily derailed.

The tip of her tongue traced her lips, licking away some powdery sugar. He looked away, finding the motion too stupidly distracting. Man, he was in trouble. He spied a pigeon searching the cobblestone floor for crumbs, then turned his attention to his donut, biting through the maple glaze to the bacon-flavored cake beneath.

"Look," she was saying, "I don't want to get in the cops' way; that was never my intention. I just want to help find the twins. But face it; the cops don't want my help. Not here in New Orleans or in Baton Rouge." She sighed. "I don't think they trust me or my motives."

"Because you're related to Donovan Caldwell and you're trying to prove that he's innocent?"

"That's the main reason, I guess, but there are others. I'm pretty sure Detective Bentz thinks I'm a nut job." She flashed a smile and then took a final bite, polishing off her beignet. "You know, he figures if I'm not completely off my rocker, then at the very least I've got tunnel vision. So blinded by motive that I can't see the truth. You heard him the other day, right? At the police station?"

"Everyone on the floor heard you."

She pulled a face. "Maybe not my finest hour. I probably should have used some finesse, but damn, I was sick of being stonewalled."

"Don't blame you."

"So, Bridges, do we have a deal?"

He couldn't help but wonder where this would lead, and his brother's warning about staying away from her sliced through his thoughts. But as he stared across the table, studying a face that was so like her sister's, he heard himself say, "Deal." Reaching across the table to shake her hand, he wondered if he'd just made the biggest mistake of his life.

CHAPTER 25

The dog was barking his head off, baying and causing a ruckus. "Hush!" he yelled at old Red, but his voice failed him. Though he was grateful that the dog had found that little bitch's scent, he didn't want to warn her or anyone else who might be in this part of the forest.

But the hound wasn't listening to him, and once again, he wanted to kick himself, wishing he'd taken the dog to obedience training. But hell, Red had been a stray. He was lucky the beast could track at all.

And Red had definitely picked up Zoe's scent. The dog was running up ahead, bounding through the sweltering forest, startling birds, rabbits, and God only knew what else. It was all he could do to keep up with the mutt. Huffing and snorting as he lugged his gun through the undergrowth, he was sweating like a pig.

"Red!" he tried to yell, his voice a whistle. "You shut up!"

That wasn't happening. The dog darted ahead, crazy from the scent.

From the sound of the dog's baying, he guessed they were closing in on her.

About damned time! Once he collected Zoe, he'd be able to end this, in the right birth order, kill each of the twins and be on to the next quest, whatever the hell that would be. Myra, she would tell him. She was the one who decided. He just followed directions. And that would have to change. Who the hell was Myra to be forever bossing him around, making him take all the chances, suffer all the consequences? Even now, his face and neck ached, and his legs, too, had suffered from all of the attacks those two little bitches had inflicted.

And yet, he kept on obeying her.

Myra was the one who had planned all this, the one who had bought the property with the cabin, who provided him with just enough money to keep going. The work he had was spotty, which was good, as it allowed him some free time to do this, to hunt for the twins who were about to turn of age, to spare them the pain that he knew existed.

Ungrateful sluts!

Why did they fight him?

Didn't they understand that he was doing them a favor? Saving them?

A tree limb slapped him in the face and he cursed, stumbled, and felt the sting under his eye, a reminder of the pain that Chloe had inflicted.

Despite his discomfort, despite the heat and the pain running through his body, he grinned inwardly. Chloe Denning would never again have the opportunity to do him harm. No more. She'd been dealt with. After he'd captured her that last time, chasing her down to that barbed-wire fence, he'd made sure she would never thwart him again. Oh, she was alive, but just barely, and that was good enough.

Until he captured Zoe.

Then there would be no reason to hesitate.

The ritual would be quick. Orderly. Complete.

Thinking ahead, pressing through the deep woods, he licked his lips in anticipation of running Zoe to the ground and hauling her back to the cabin.

What satisfaction that would bring.

He couldn't wait.

The trees thinned a bit, and he spied his dog leaping through the tall grass. Squinting, he thought he made out a movement ahead of Red, a person stumbling through the weeds.

"Gotcha," he said, knowing that the dog had flushed Zoe out of the forest.

Perfect.

It was just a matter of time before he reached her, and he was going to savor every sweet second of his revenge. She looked frantic, hobbling feverishly. The dog barked again and she glanced over her shoulder, only to turn and try to run in the opposite direction.

As if she had an escape route.

As if she actually thought she could get away.

And then he heard it.

The distinctive hum of traffic.

What?

Heart pounding, he focused on the space between Zoe and the horizon, and spied a pickup truck traveling beyond the fence line. And after the truck came two cars. And a semi heading the opposite direction.

"Fuck!" he swore, the sound a rattling rasp. He sprang

into action, running forward, calculating the angle between Zoe and the road. He couldn't let her reach the
highway. Wouldn't.

He was gonna cut her off, tackle her before she got
to the road. Then he'd haul her back to the cabin, pre-
pare her, and finally take her life. It would be all over
soon.

But if he didn't reach her before she flagged down
the driver of a passing vehicle?

Oh, shit!

Myra would be beyond pissed.

Adrenaline firing his blood, he shot across the brush-
covered land. His legs pumped as each breath was
drawn in and expelled through his bruised windpipe.
Faster! Faster! He'd been an athlete in school, a hunter
afterward, and could run miles without difficulty. But
it was hard to run in hunting boots, packing a gun and
being beaten as he had been. Still, he should be able to
overtake a wounded girl.

Pushing his muscles, pumping his arms, he focused
on Zoe, ignored the pain, and ran flat out.

He'd make it.

He'd stop that little bitch.

Or, damn it, he'd die trying.

Selma Denning was a wreck. The poor woman nearly
shattered into a million pieces when Bentz and Montoya showed up on her doorstep. At their arrival, she'd
been certain they'd come to report one of her daughters
dead.

"No, no, we're just here to ask a few questions," Bentz
assured the distraught woman.

At that point, she let the detectives into her home. Sitting on a floral rocker by the window, the woman chain-smoked while she answered questions about the twins. Most of the information confirmed what Bentz had already learned from Brianna Hayward. Though it had obviously been difficult for her, she had come up with recent pictures of the girls as well as two hairbrushes. With little success, she fought tears as Montoya placed each brush into a bag labeled with the girl's name. The notion that the police might need DNA samples to identify her daughters was nearly too much for her.

Bentz got it. He'd been in her position when his Kristi had been abducted years earlier.

"I just want them back," Selma whispered, crushing out her third or fourth cigarette in an overflowing ashtray.

"We're doing all we can."

She stared into space, unblinking, her mind somewhere else.

"Do you mind if we have a look at their car?" Bentz asked. She nodded numbly, but didn't move from her chair. Instead, she reached for her half-empty pack of cigarettes on the table where her phone and the ashtray sat. "I mean, now," Bentz clarified.

"What?" Her hand paused midair. "Oh, yes . . . sorry. It's out back in the lot. One of the visitor's spots."

"We'll probably have it towed to the garage," Montoya said.

"Oh . . . but if the girls return . . ." Her voice faded. "Sorry. Certainly. I'll get the keys." She retrieved a set of keys and then led them outside to a lot that was surrounded by low-growing shrubs. Roughly half of the spots were taken by vehicles. "The manager will be glad if you do take it. I'm . . . I'm, um, not supposed to have any extra cars here for longer than, I don't know, five hours or so. But the manager, Stan, he's cutting me a break. You know, because of the situation." Her voice caught and she cleared her throat, then pointed out a fifteen-year-old Toyota. Selma Denning stood there smoking another cigarette as Montoya and Bentz gave the car a once-over.

They found nothing out of the ordinary. A pair of sunglasses along with the registration and car owner's manual in the glove box. A phone charger, pack of gum, and mess of tissues and gas receipts in the console. A warm, half-drunk soda in the cup holder. Gum wrappers and half a dozen French fries under the front seats. In the back, two jackets, a collapsible umbrella, and some trashy magazines were tossed over the faded seat. Montoya checked the pockets of the two jackets and found lip balm, a bracelet, and a ticket stub from a movie dated six months earlier.

Nothing that looked as if it belonged to anyone but the twins.

A total bust.

Still, they called to have the car towed, just in case. Leaving Selma with their cards, the detectives headed across town to a two-storied home built at the turn of the previous century.

As he searched for a parking spot, Montoya's cell phone rang from its spot in the empty cup holder. He picked it up, saw the caller ID, and clicked the cell off. "Speaking of my family. Second call I got today. They're all thinking I should be hunting for Cruz," Montoya said as he slowed for a red light, his fingers tapping the steering wheel. Cruz was Montoya's brother, a bad ass who had recently lost his Harley to a fleeing nun. The desperate woman had stolen it, and Cruz had taken off after her. "No one's heard from him, can't reach him, so they all have decided that I, as the one cop in the family, should drop everything and chase him down."

Bentz smothered a smile. Montoya's tight-knit family was always bothering him in one way or another. "Did you tell them you've got other things to occupy your time?"

"Like a full-time job nailing bad guys, as well as dealing with a wife and kid? Even though Abby's on hiatus from her photography for a while, she still expects me to be home and spell her with Ben and, you know, she needs a break. Geez, he's only three months and hasn't figured out sleeping through the night yet. We're all sleep deprived." He snorted and frowned, brackets lining his mouth. "So someone else in the family can go looking for Cruz. He's a big boy anyway, a grown man." Frowning at the traffic on the street, he finally found a parking spot close to a fire hydrant. "It's okay, right?" he asked, but didn't wait for an answer. "We're cops. The good guys."

"If you're willing to risk a ticket."

"From someone on the force? Bah. Look, if I get one from some meter maid who doesn't know the drill, I'll fight it. Like I said, 'We're the good guys.'" He was already out of the car and locking up. They made their way under an arbor and through a garden of exotic tropical plants to a two-storied front porch that ran the width of the building and was decorated in finely detailed wrought iron.

They were met at the front door by a pretty if harried

looking woman who seemed a little nervous when they introduced themselves. Erin Denning, Carson's second wife, was petite with short reddish hair, an upturned nose, and wide, worried eyes. She could only have been five or six years older than the twins, her stepdaughters, and, Bentz already had learned from Selma, was raising Carson's two sons, Carson Junior, "CJ," a rambunctious four-year-old with red hair, and his little brother, Jayden, whom Erin carried on her hip. She led the detectives through a spacious foyer with inlaid marble to an office with double doors and a glass desk, where her husband sat before three computer monitors and two television screens. These days Carson Denning was a day trader and worked from home.

"Detectives," he said after introductions. Though he grinned widely, there was barely a trace of happiness in his eyes. "Tell me you've found my girls."

"Not yet," Bentz said, and he saw what little light there was in Carson's pale eyes fade. "We have a few questions about your daughters."

"I see. Let's step outside." His lips folded in on themselves and he motioned the two detectives to walk out a side door that opened to a veranda where a variety of lush ferns and palms offered shade. Overhead lights had been strung to create ambiance in the evening. Water spilled from a stone waterfall into a basin where goldfish and koi swam slowly, their scales catching the sunlight. Bentz looked up, noticed a screen stretched between the wings of the house so that no bird could fly in and make a meal of the brightly colored fish.

"Look," Carson said, "whatever it takes, whatever I can do, just say the word. You have to find my daughters. My divorce from their mother was not amicable; it's hard for us to be civil to each other, but my Zoe and Chloe . . ." He let out a shuddering breath and stared at the fish darting beneath the water's surface. "They're special. I'll do whatever I can to help find them." He sat on a bench and clasped his hands between his knees. "That being said, the less my wife, Erin, has to do with this, the better." He looked up quickly, frowning. "I mean, she's fond of Chloe and Zoe, of course. They're, well, they're contemporaries of hers, but because she's related to Selma, it's . . . touchy."

I'll bet, Bentz thought, though didn't admit that he, too, had been through a messy divorce where family members were compromising partners. That, however, had been long ago; water under the emotional bridge.

"And really, other than my meeting Erin because of Selma, she had nothing to do with the divorce. Nothing." He nodded, as if agreeing with himself. "The truth of the matter was that Selma couldn't get over the loss of her twin, Sandra. That was the nail in the coffin of our marriage, though she wouldn't believe it. I don't mean to sound harsh, because it was a horrible ordeal that she went through, to lose someone that close to you. But it affected everything she did, all aspects of her life, of *our* life as a family. It was too much." He stood, stuffed his hands deep into the pockets of his slacks, and bit his lower lip. "Since no amount of private counseling sessions seemed to have helped, I was hoping that twinless twin support group might be the ticket. I'm glad she joined. But about the girls, what can I do?"

"We just want to double-check some things with you, ask about their acquaintances, anyone you might know who might have been with them that night after they peeled off from the group of friends."

"I wish I could. But . . . I didn't talk to them that day, hoped to celebrate their birthday after the fact, when they could come out here. I thought I'd take them to dinner and buy them a drink sometime after the initial celebration died down." He shrugged. "They're kids. They want to be with people their age."

Bentz and Montoya asked about Zoe and Chloe's friends and, it seemed, Carson's impression was nearly identical to his ex-wife's. Neither one had cared for the most recent boyfriends, Zach Armstrong or Tommy Jones. "Oh, they were fine, I guess," Carson said. "Just not going anywhere as far as I could see. What the girls found so fascinating about them was lost on me."

Within forty minutes, they'd learned everything they could. As Bentz stepped out on the front porch, Carson stopped him, asking, "Are you doing everything you can to find my daughters?"

A good question. What was everything? The Missing Persons Departments of both New Orleans and Baton Rouge were working together, and the press had been informed that the girls had gone missing. The FBI had been called in, and half a dozen cops from each city were canvassing the area, talking to acquaintances, checking on leads, including the security video taken near Bourbon Street. Bentz and Montoya, homicide cops, were working the case as well, mainly because of Bentz's experience on the original investigation of the 21 Killer. There was still no proof that 21 was behind this, especially since most believed that they'd locked up the killer when Donovan Caldwell was sentenced, but there was also no denying the crime pattern.

"We're doing the best we can," Bentz assured Carson, then asked him to call if he thought of anything that would help.

Once in the car and heading back to the station, Bentz said, "Twinless twins?" He snorted and shook his head as he opened his window a crack. "You know, I think there's a support group for just about anything you want these days." Before Montoya could add his two cents, Bentz's phone jangled.

He slipped it from his pocket, recognized an LA area code, and answered, "Detective Bentz."

"Hey," Jonas Hayes said, his voice grim. Bentz imagined his ex-partner's face set, his features hard, the harbinger of bad news. "I wanted to give you a heads-up before you heard it somewhere else."

"Heard what?" Bentz asked.

"About Donovan Caldwell." A pause. "He's dead."

CHAPTER 26

Brianna's cell phone rang just as she and Jase were heading back to the offices of the *Observer*. She pulled the phone from her purse, saw that it was Milo again, and didn't answer. Though she wanted to connect with him, she needed a little privacy to talk to the reticent member of the twinless twin group, a man who rarely shared, but sometimes called her for advice. It was weird. He did not make an appointment, didn't want her to be his counselor, and rarely shared during the group meetings. And yet, sometimes he sought her out. Brianna wouldn't have bothered dealing with him if he weren't a part of the group. As it was, she felt obligated, as a twinless twin herself, to give comfort or advice or just lend an ear.

But not right this moment.

He's called twice. Maybe he's in trouble. You need to talk to him.

As they reached her car parked on the street, she noticed the time on the meter had expired.

She and Jase had already decided to work out of his

apartment, on his computer. "What time works best for you?" she asked.

"I've got a few things to deal with right now. Give me a couple of hours?" His gaze delved a little deeper into hers and her stupid heart had the nerve to flutter. "Work for you?"

"Perfect."

He gave her his address and she repeated it back to him. "You said apartment 3-C."

"That's it." One side of his mouth twisted upward. "Okay, I'll see you then." He rapped on the roof of her car twice, then headed into the building that housed the *Observer* offices. She watched his tall frame disappear through the glass doors and couldn't help but wonder about running into him again after all these years, after half a lifetime of believing that she'd never see him again. Not that she'd given it much thought since college. A high-school crush was just that, a first little palpitation of the heart that one remembered fondly but left back in school.

Then why did she experience the same rush now? Why did she realize that her cheeks were warm and it had nothing to do with the Louisiana sun moving slowly across the sky?

"Because you're an idiot," she told herself as she settled behind the wheel. She didn't have time for schoolgirl fantasies, not when Selma's daughters were missing. "Get it together." She jabbed her key in the ignition. As her little car started, she forced herself to concentrate on the importance of meeting with Jase. They had to find Zoe and Chloe. And in the process, she believed that they would prove that Donovan Caldwell was *not* the 21 Killer.

In the hours before she was to meet Jase, she needed to gather and copy her notes, make a few phone calls, and emotionally gird herself. She'd already discovered dealing with Jase was complicated. Not only was she fighting her attraction to him, but there was something else going on between them, something she didn't understand, an underlying tension that she couldn't pinpoint.

Was he interested in her?

Or was it something else, something a little darker?

As she checked her mirror and nosed her Honda into traffic, she noticed a parking enforcement officer turning down the street. Well, maybe it was a good omen that she'd narrowly escaped getting a parking ticket. Maybe her luck was changing. Maybe today was the day Selma's daughters would be found.

Or maybe not.

Maybe the girls would never be located.

"Don't even go there," she warned, glancing into the rearview mirror.

When her phone rang again, she saw Tanisha's number and promised herself that she would return the call the second she got home. And Milo's, too. And she would check in on Selma. Yeah, she didn't have a lot of time before she met up with Jase again.

At that thought, she actually smiled.

"Wait. What?" Bentz said, his cell phone pressed to his ear. He couldn't believe what he was hearing from Hayes, who'd called him from California.

Donovan Caldwell was dead?

No! Not at the very moment Bentz was starting to believe he might be innocent of the murders of his sisters and wrongly convicted of being the 21 Killer.

"You're kidding, right?"

"No joke." The tone of Hayes's voice was flat, all business.

"But he's locked up."

Montoya, cutting through an alley, shot Bentz a look.

"I know," Hayes agreed. "Housed in a private cell. Well, at least it's been private for a few days. There was room for another inmate, of course, but his most recent cell mate was released a couple of days ago and for some reason, some red-tape clusterfuck I think, the other bed was unoccupied. Despite all the prison over-crowding. So the past few nights, Caldwell's had the cell to himself."

"Okay. So what happened?" Bentz asked as Montoya gunned his Mustang onto a major arterial again. Staring out the side window, Bentz barely noticed the sidewalks of New Orleans flash by. The storefronts and pedestrians and cars were a blur as he tried to wrap his brain around what Hayes was saying. In his mind's eye he saw Donovan Caldwell, the odd older brother of the murdered twins. Donovan had been out of step with society, a bit of a recluse, even a little nasty. He had harbored a hatred of his sisters but refused to take the blame for their horrific deaths, maintaining his innocence.

"Looks like suicide," said Hayes. "I mean, the guy was in the cell alone, but who knows what goes on in the middle of the night in the big house? Guards can be bribed. Some inmates have more privileges than others. You know? It's really too early to tell."

"Movie stuff."

"It happens." Bentz nodded, thinking of the time difference. California was two hours behind New Orleans, so there hadn't been much time for an investigation. Yet.

"I don't have all the details," Hayes was saying. "But apparently he had some sort of tiny shiv, sliced his wrists, but had the guts and determination to leave a message before he bled out."

"A message?" Bentz felt a niggle of apprehension skitter through his insides. "What was it?"

Montoya wheeled the Mustang around a final corner to the station and slowed for a couple of runners who cut across the street. As he did, he sent his partner another "What gives?" look.

"He managed to write 'I'M INNOCENT' in block letters on the wall of his cell. Written using his own blood."

"Jesus," Bentz whispered, a deep sadness stealing over him. He thought of the man everyone believed to be the 21 Killer now dead, at his own hand. Some people would celebrate, believing that a serial murderer had been taken off the streets for good; that he no longer would be chewing through taxpayers' money; that, if he offed himself, all the better. *Good riddance to bad rubbish!* But if they were wrong? If Caldwell wasn't 21? If he'd sliced his own wrists in resignation because he couldn't take the fate he'd been handed? So out of his mind and desperate that he would take the time to leave a final proclamation of innocence as he bled out?

"A guard found Caldwell this morning," Jonas was saying. "He was rushed to the hospital, but it was too late to save him. DOA." He paused for a second. "Look, because you called about the 21 Killer, I thought you'd want to know."

"I do. Thanks."

"Yeah, gotta run."

Bentz hung up.

"Bad news?" Montoya asked as he pulled into the lot closest to the station and drove the Mustang into a vacant spot.

"Not good." Bentz had held out a tiny iota of hope that Donovan Caldwell would eventually confess, that he would admit to being 21. Now, that wasn't going to happen. Ever. Nor would he ever be free from prison, vindicated and released because of the conviction of another perpetrator.

Guilty or innocent, Donovan Caldwell was dead. A statistic. And Bentz, climbing out of the car and heading into the station house, was more determined than ever to either exonerate an innocent man or prove that the right suspect had been tried, convicted, and sent up the river for life.

Once home, Brianna was greeted by St. Ives, who meowed at her insistently until she fed him half a can of "tuna delight" from her refrigerator. Once his needs had been met, she started gathering her notes and information for Jase. She made two copies of everything she'd given to the police in Baton Rouge and New Orleans. She still wasn't certain how her working relationship with Jase was going to play out, but she figured she needed a duplicate set just the same. As the printer chugged out pages, she made the call to Milo. After four rings, the phone went to voice mail.

Brianna decided to leave a message. "Hi, Milo. This is Brianna Hayward, returning your calls. Sorry I missed you. Hope everything's okay. Call back if you'd like." After she ended the call, an uneasy feeling came over her, and she stared at the phone a minute, almost willing it to ring. Maybe it was just part of the pitfalls of her profession, but whenever a client phoned and she wasn't able to return the call right away, she worried. In her line of work, she dealt with people who suffered from depression and anxiety and all forms of neuroses, some more dangerous than others. She had no idea why Milo was calling her; perhaps it was nothing important, but still, she worried.

He'll call back.

Don't make a mountain of a molehill. It was two lousy phone calls, nothing to get worked up about.

And yet she did.

So when the phone rang in her hand, she expected the caller to be Milo Tillman. Instead, Tanisha was on the other end of the line. "Didn't you get my messages?" she demanded.

"Yes, sorry." She rinsed out the cat food can at the sink. "I was going to call back when I had a little time to talk. I've just been busy today. So, what's up?"

"Obviously you haven't been online."

Obviously? "I've been out. Why?" Drying her hands, she glanced out the window over the sink and watched sunlight play upon the backyard.

"I called earlier just to ask you about Selma; see how she's doing. We're really not that close, you know, even though I tried to keep her company that night after the meeting. I'm not getting much from her."

"Nothing's changed. Nothing that I know of. I was about to call her."

"Then you don't know."

"Don't know what?" Something in Tanisha's tone gave her pause. "Did something happen?"

"I just saw it on Twitter, from a friend in California. Breaking news."

"What?" From the tone of Tanisha's voice, Brianna knew it wasn't good.

"Donovan Caldwell? The 21 Killer?"

"He's not the killer," Brianna said automatically, then caught herself. "What about him?"

"He's dead, Brianna."

"He's what?" she whispered, disbelieving.

"Donovan Caldwell. He's dead."

"What? No!" She was shaking her head, as if Tanisha could see her. "But that's impossible."

"I'm telling you, it's true. I double-checked."

"Oh, dear God," she whispered, her knees threatening to buckle. "But he's . . . he's in prison." Leaning against the counter for support, she gathered her wits. "Wait a second. He can't be dead. He's in his thirties and healthy. I just saw him. There has to be some mistake." But she was already forcing her legs to move and crossing into the living room, where she'd left her laptop.

"Hey, I'm just letting you know."

"But how? Why?"

"Don't know. I don't think the details are out yet. At least not that I've seen online. Just that he was pronounced dead on arrival at the hospital."

"It's just so hard to believe."

"I know."

She nearly fell onto the couch and fired up her laptop. Her fingers quivered over the keyboard as denial slithered through her brain. This couldn't be. There had to be a mistake. Just speculation. A hoax. Donovan Caldwell, the loner cousin she'd barely known, couldn't be dead.

"I don't know any details," Tanisha said again. "I thought you might."

"No." Trembling inside, Brianna squeezed her eyes shut. She had failed him. All her promises of justice came to mind, mocking and cold. "This is the first I've heard of it. He is . . . was my . . . but . . . I mean, I didn't know him growing up . . . not really." Her family and his had been separated by distance and disinterest, busy people, busy lives. But still, she remembered her aunt Cathy, a teacher, and her uncle Greg. They'd divorced after the loss of their daughters and the ensuing media circus, their son being tried and convicted for the crime. In a way they'd lost all three children years before, but now, with Donovan's death, it was final.

Why the hell was it taking so long for the computer to engage?

Finally, the screen lit and she was able to type in Donovan Caldwell's name.

Her heart nearly stopped when she saw his picture along with several news feeds, two of which had the story. As Tanisha had indicated, the news of his death was just going viral. Brianna felt hot tears rush to her eyes, if not for the man and his loss of life, then for the injustice of it all, the frustration of her own impotence. In her heart she never believed that he killed Delta and Diana, the sisters he claimed to dislike, but now it didn't really matter. Brianna had failed him by not proving his innocence before he died.

Not just you, Brianna, but the system. The cops. The attorneys. The press. Everyone who helped convict him.

Tears streaked down her face. "They're not saying how he died?" she said, scanning the first article.

"Not that I saw. But you can't fit much on Twitter."

"I still can't believe it."

"I know. Look, I gotta run. Still on the clock. I'll call you later."

"Do . . . and thanks," Brianna said, still reading as Tanisha hung up. Once disconnected, she continued to search the Internet, but so far the details of Donovan Caldwell's death were sparse.

But Jase possessed the resources to find out more.

She would go to him first. Then she would try the police, though she figured she would hit a brick wall there. Jase was her best bet.

So why the hell hadn't he called with the news about Donovan Caldwell? Why Tanisha?

Granted, Tanisha Lefevre worked at a job where she was continuously on the Internet, but still, shouldn't crime reporter Jason Bridges have access to even more information, just as quickly? Probably even faster?

"I guess you're going to find out," she said, dashing her tears away and packing up her laptop, iPad, and the notes she'd printed out. Though it was earlier than the agreed-upon time to meet, she decided to head to his apartment. If he wasn't there, she would wait.

Rand Cooligan's acid reflux was acting up again. Big time.

Driving toward New Orleans, he kept one hand on the steering wheel of his pickup and searched the console with his free hand. He was pretty damned sure he'd left a bottle of Tums in the truck, but so far no luck. He rummaged around the rat's nest of lipsticks, receipts, gum, sunglasses, and whatever else Barb decided to leave in his truck, *his truck,* and didn't find one stinkin' antacid. For the love of St. Mike, couldn't she keep her crap in her own car? Wasn't that why they'd bought the damned Ford Explorer from her cousin? So she could have her own vehicle?

"Damn it all to hell," he growled, the radio playing some country song he didn't recognize, the interior of the cab cooled by the cross breeze as he drove this stretch of country road. Thinking the bottle could have rolled into the backseat of his king cab, he glanced over his shoulder but saw nothing other than his son's baseball bag and Barb's jacket. No bottle of Tums. No little, half-used roll of any kind of antacid.

Damn, his gut ached. Burned. He'd probably have to pull over at the next convenience store or gas station and—

Son of a bitch!

He stood on the brakes.

"Jesus, Mary, and Joseph!" The truck shimmied and fishtailed, sliding and spraying gravel as the tires hit the shoulder. Staring through the bug-spattered windshield, he saw her standing butt-ass naked in the middle of the road and waving frantically. A naked girl! No, a woman! She looked like she'd been through hell. Her skin was burned and grimy, her hair matted against her head and so dirty he couldn't really tell the color. Blood was visible on her neck, and her face was twisted in sheer, full-blown, nutso panic.

"What the fucking hell?" he said under his breath,

his heart thudding wildly. For the love of Christ, he could have hit her. Killed her. And killed himself. Let alone what would have happened to the vehicle.

She was hobbling toward him. Still waving, propped up on some kind of tree branch that she used a crutch. What the hell was this? A shakedown? He looked around, saw no one else, then let the truck idle as he climbed from the cab and stepped onto the sunbaked asphalt.

In obvious pain, her ankle swollen to the size of a small melon, she hurried awkwardly toward him.

"Please, please help me," she said, her voice a crackling whisper. "Please, before he comes." She was scared spitless.

"Who?" He looked around. "Before who comes?" Again, there was no one, just a hound dog baying and bounding through the field nearby.

"Him!" Hobbling on her crooked tree limb, she hitched her way past him more quickly than he'd expected and made her way to the passenger side of his truck. "The freak. He's coming!" she added hoarsely. "Please. Just take me away from here. Now!" She wasn't waiting for an invitation.

"Hey, slow down. You're okay," he said, though she was definitely not. Not by a long shot. Whack job. Probably high on something. And scared out of her mind. Hallucinating maybe. Could be dangerous. And where the hell were her clothes? "Wait, you can't just—"

She'd reached the cab and was opening the door.

"Whoa! Hey, look!" He rounded to the passenger side. "What's going on here?"

"You're helping me, that's what." Those frightened eyes stared straight at him, her terrified gaze boring into his soul. "And you're saving my life, and maybe getting a damned medal of honor or bravery or whatever it is they hand out to citizens doing a good deed. But we have to leave now! He's . . . he's after me. And he's got Chloe! I mean, I think so. Oh, Jesus, we have to go! Now!"

"Who's Chloe?"

"My sister! Where have you been? Under a rock?" Without any assistance she grabbed hold of the interior handle and, with a squeal of pain, hauled herself onto the passenger seat. Automatically, from years of being warned about the evils of peering up a girl's skirt, he turned his head so that he wouldn't see her privates as she hoisted herself up.

This is crazy, he told himself, but slammed the door shut behind her and hurried around the truck. How the hell did he know she wouldn't manage to climb into the driver's seat and take off? He'd left the keys in the ignition, engine running. And even if she wasn't going to take off and drive, there was his rifle, in its rack. It was secured, yes, but not locked. She could grab it and point it at him and—

Oh, shit!

He hauled himself inside, settled behind the wheel, wondered how hopped up she was.

Biting her lip, she peered out the open window and scanned the horizon. "What are you waiting for? Let's go!"

"Okay, okay. Just calm down."

She whipped her head around and stared at him. "I am *not* calming down. There's a murdering psycho out there, and he's coming. So what the hell are you waiting for?"

Something had scared her. To her core.

What, he didn't know.

But he yanked his door closed. An announcer on the radio was trying to sell him a new car. He snapped off the squawk box. "There's . . . there's a jacket in the back," he said, keeping his eyes averted. Jesus, her tits were right there. Streaked with mud. Skin flaming around her nipples, burned, he guessed, as that part of her hadn't ever seen the sun. Where the hell were her clothes? Why was she running naked? How'd she hurt herself? And Christ-A'mighty, was there really a homicidal maniac chasing her, or was she just completely out of her mind? For the love of God, her sunburned breasts were so close he could touch them. But he didn't even look, just stared straight ahead and tried to figure out what kind of crap he'd just stepped into. Was she a psycho? Or on the run? Maybe from a bad home life?

"You want to go to a hospital?" he asked as she reached around and slipped Barb's plus-sized jacket over her small frame. Then, probably because the Silverado's insistent alarm system was dinging, she strapped on the seat belt. He did the same, keeping one hand on the wheel.

"No, not the hospital. The police. Or my mother's. I . . . I don't know. But we have to get the hell out of here." She looked over at him, then at the console. "That yours?" she asked, pointing at the half-drunk bottle of Diet Coke that was still in one of the cup holders from the last time Barb had driven the truck.

"No, it's my wife's. Been there a couple o'—"

"Good enough." She twisted off the cap and brought it to her parched lips. Then she swallowed, draining the whole dang bottle of what had to be flat, warm syrup. As she did, she kept her gaze in the side-view mirror, as if she really thought someone was following.

He checked his mirror. Nothing on the road behind. Not even a jackrabbit. What kind of a lulu was she?

"You're going to New Orleans, right?"

"Close. I'm picking up some hay about five miles out."

"Take me to the city." Some of the bristle had left her, and she blinked against a sudden wash of tears. "Now, for God's sake!"

Oh, Jesus. He hated it when a woman cried. Barb could just start to well up and it was all over for him.

She slapped at her eyes.

"Sure. Sure." But he hadn't engaged the gears yet, wasn't certain if hauling her anywhere was the right thing to do.

"Then please hurry. He's out there. I saw him." She sniffed, some of the starch returning to her. "I think he has a rifle."

The muscles in the back of Rand's neck bunched. "A rifle?"

"Yeah, a rifle and a dog. Don't you get it? He's hunting me." She was starting to freak out again. "You have to take me to the police or to my mom or . . ." She spied his cell on the dash, connected to the charger in his cigarette lighter. Without asking, she picked it up and dialed.

"Hey, wait a sec—"

"Please. Just drive!" she ordered, jamming the phone to her ear. "Oh, come on, pick up. Mom, for God's sake!" she said into the phone, all the while looking in the mirror. "He'll shoot us both, you know," she told

Rand. "The dog was on my scent, and he won't let me get away. He won't kill me right away, but he'll kill you. After he shoots out your tires or somehow disables your truck." Then into the phone, she moaned, "Oh, Mom, answer the damned phone for Christ's sake!" Then, more calmly. "Mom, it's Zoe. I'm okay. Coming to New Orleans. Your house, okay? But then we have to go to the police. I . . . I think he's still got Chloe. Call me back. I'm at—" She looked at him again and he rattled off his phone number, which she repeated. "I'm on my way. Be there in—?" Again she pierced him with a glare.

"Twenty minutes. Maybe thirty, depending—"

"Twenty minutes." She hung up and cradling her phone in her hands said to him, "So are you going to drive or what?"

Still he hesitated, unsure.

She went ballistic. "What? You don't believe me?" she demanded, frantic. "Why the hell do you think I'm running around out here naked? For the love of God, don't you know that people are looking for me? Isn't it all over the freakin' news?" When he didn't respond, didn't admit that he only watched sports, she said, "My name's Zoe. Zoe Denning."

From somewhere nearby the dog started baying again.

"Oh, God! He's here! I told you! Shit!"

In his mirror, he caught sight of the dog, closer now, bounding through the grass and weeds, running straight at them. Worse yet, not fifty yards behind, a tall man was cutting across the field. Dressed head to toe in camouflage, sunglasses shielding his eyes, a rifle gripped in his hands, he was moving with a steady if ungainly gait.

Shit! The girl was telling the damned truth.

In the mirror, he saw the hunter stop, hoist the stock of his rifle to his shoulder, and take aim.

"Get down!" Rand ordered, and hit the gas.

For the love of God, what the hell was this?

His pickup lurched forward, tires chirping.

Craaaack!

The sharp report of a rifle split the summer air.

The first bullet pinged off a fender.

"Faster!" she yelled as he tromped on the gas.

Then the hunter took aim again.

The Silverado's engine whined as it sped forward, accelerating, faster and faster, from a dead stop, forty, then forty-five.

"Who is that guy?" he demanded.

"I don't know."

"And he's chasing you?"

They were going sixty now.

God, what was this?

And how the hell could he take the next corner at seventy miles an hour? Shit . . . he had to slow or they'd never make it.

"Don't slow down, you moron!" she ordered. "He's coming! What the hell do you think you're doing?"

"Saving your damned skin."

Blam!

The rifle fired again.

CHAPTER 27

Brianna was stunned. And shocked. And devastated. And mad that she'd heard the news after it had started to run rampant over the Internet. Donovan Caldwell was dead. How had it happened? Had he been murdered in his sleep? Had some kind of heart attack or stroke . . . Geez, he was way too young for that. Maybe he'd fallen and hit his head. Suicide? Oh, God, please no . . . but what?

With no answers, she headed out the door only to hear her phone ring when she was on the porch.

She stopped dead in her tracks and dug her phone from her purse. Expecting the call to be from Rick Bentz or Jase or anyone associated with the 21 Killer case, she glanced down at caller ID.

Milo Tillman.

She was disappointed; didn't want to deal with whatever Milo was going through. She had more than enough on her plate already. She considered not answering as she was too emotional, her thoughts wrapped around Donovan, her heart heavy, but she gave herself a quick mental shake. As upset as she was about Donovan Caldwell's death, she could spare a few minutes for Milo.

"Hello?" She held her bag and keys with one hand and pressed the phone to her ear with the other.

"Hi. Uh, Brianna." He sounded a little out of breath, as if he'd been running, though it could have been breathless anxiety. She'd always gotten an awkward sense when she was near him; that her presence was unnerving to him, and coping in a group was especially difficult for him. "It's Milo. Tillman."

Of course she knew that, but she let him go on as she locked her door, then spied St. Ives stalking a chipmunk through the azaleas. *No, you don't,* she thought, and set her bag down to grab the cat before he pounced. Not that he would have much of a chance of catching the chipmunk, which darted into a crack between the rocks on her path.

"What can I do for you, Milo?" she asked as she retraced her steps, unlocked the door again, and deposited the tabby inside. *Be good,* she mentally ordered the cat, who wandered off in search of a patch of sunlight.

"I, uh, just needed to talk. I was hoping we could meet."

"Today?" Again she locked her door and headed to her car.

He cleared his throat, still sounded as if he needed to catch his breath. "Yeah, it's . . . it's important."

But so were a million other things.

"I'd hire you," he said quickly, as if he understood she was going to decline. "You know, so you'd be my counselor. That's what you offered, right? To everyone in the group? Back when we started up."

She had. But now was just not a good time. "Well, yes. Sure," she heard herself saying as she bent down to pick up her bag again. The chipmunk, or one just like him, scampered over the rocks to the edge of her garden. "I'd be glad to have you as a client," she said, checking her watch.

"I could come over now, to your house. That's where you have your office, right?"

"One of them, yes. But now won't work," she said. "I'm already booked this afternoon."

"But . . . well, I just need to talk to you." His anxiety was taking over.

"How about tomorrow? I'm not near my calendar, but I think—"

"No, I, um, I'm busy. I need to see you today," he insisted. And then, as if hearing the desperation in his voice, he added, "Sorry. I mean, if it would work for you. It's really important."

She managed to unlock her car with her remote. It beeped in response. "What's going on, Milo?" She opened the car door and tossed her bags onto the passenger seat, then slid into the warm interior.

He hesitated for a beat.

She waited.

Finally, he went on in a raspy voice. "It's about my twin." He was nearly panting now. "There's something you need to know about her."

Bentz rubbed the kinks from the back of his neck and heard his stomach grumble from lack of food. Upon returning to the station, he'd checked on Samantha Wheeler and made certain she was safe. It was time to double up on surveillance of her place. If Father John was back, he would eventually go after her, and she was aware of that fact. Dr. Sam had agreed to take some time off, allowing some of her older shows that had been taped to be aired until she could set up shop remotely at a secure location. She'd already worked things out with the radio station.

One problem dealt with, if not solved. Who knew who would be Father John's next victim, if not Samantha Wheeler? Another prostitute? It was likely, if the killer kept with his MO of years before. Today, at a press conference, the public would be informed that the serial killer was at large again. Already, the FBI was sending agents, which, this time around, Bentz welcomed. He could use the bureau's intelligence and resources in tracking down the sick bastard he'd thought would never be a problem again.

But he'd been wrong.

Just as he feared, he'd been wrong about Donovan Caldwell, the poor son of a bitch. Jonas Hayes had sent pictures of Caldwell's cell, complete with a dark pool of blood on the floor and bed, and the eerie crimson message written on the wall opposite his bunk: I'M IN-NOCENT.

Was he?

And was the real 21 Killer now stalking the streets of New Orleans?

Bentz turned back to his computer monitor and clicked on the Play arrow. He was viewing the security footage shot at the parking lot near Bourbon Street, where a camera had caught a tall man, his face hidden, arguing, then subduing a shorter female and forcing her into the back of his van, a white Dodge it looked like. The lab had enhanced the videotape and printed individual photographs from its frame. Although the man's face was turned away, Bentz could have sworn he looked familiar. As for the victim, he had only to view the last picture taken of Zoe and Chloe Denning to know that the girl on the video was one of the twins. Which one, he couldn't be certain, but since the tape was in black and white, he guessed that he was looking at Chloe, as the victim's dress didn't appear to be dark enough to be black.

The edge of the license plate was visible. Louisiana plate. A bit of a pelican and the starting letters KF, but that was all.

Not much, but something. He'd already called the DMV and was searching records. Once he had a list of potential vehicles, he'd double-check to make certain the girls didn't know any of the registered owners. A long shot. But, again, better than nothing.

When his phone rang, he picked up without checking caller ID. "Detective Bentz."

"This is Detective Phillipa Osgoode from the Phoenix PD." The woman's voice was all business. "You called the other day about the missing Reeves twins, Garrett and Gavin."

"That's right," he said, reaching for the sheaf of papers. "We've got a situation where twin girls have gone missing on the eve of their twenty-first birthdays." He explained about the ongoing investigation and how Brianna Hayward, Donovan Caldwell's cousin, had come up with a theory she thought might exonerate him. Unfortunately, Caldwell had died earlier this morning in his jail cell in California.

Osgoode told him that she was aware of the 21

Killer. "The Reeves investigation is still open," she said, "but I just don't think our missing twins fit your guy's MO, what with them both being male."

"That was my thought," Bentz admitted. Osgoode promised to keep him informed of any developments, and they ended the call. He took one last look at the photos of the brothers who went missing in Arizona, then shoved the file to the bottom of the stack of papers. He didn't think the Reeves brothers were victims of 21.

Unfortunately he couldn't say the same for the Denning twins, now days past their joint twenty-first birthday and still missing.

Not a good sign.

Not a good sign at all.

Jase drove to his apartment at the speed of light. His rage, temporarily abated while dealing with Brianna, had returned to a low, seething burn. Now rather than going off half-cocked, he was calmer but still angry as hell.

Forced to ease up on the accelerator as traffic slowed near the St. Louis Cathedral with its three spires knifing upward into the hazy sky, he drummed his fingers on the steering wheel. A throng of tourists had spilled onto the streets around Jackson Square, walking and talking throughout the musicians, mimes, and dancers positioned on corners and steps and sidewalks. Jase usually enjoyed watching the street performers, cases open, and hats on the ground for tip collection, but today, the scene was lost on him.

He told himself to calm down, try to think rationally and deal with his father in a civilized, adult manner.

But that probably wasn't going to happen.

Not the way he felt, not knowing his whole damned life had been a lie.

The sluggish traffic started moving again. He flipped down his visor and felt his jaw clamp tight, his fingers clench the wheel in a death grip. Who the hell did Edward Bridges think he was, manipulating his kids, lying to his family and playing the victim? What kind of piss-poor excuse of a man would keep the truth from his own sons?

The same kind of man who would bury a body and keep his mouth shut for years. A man who would lie to protect his own son, to protect you.

Jase cursed as the guilt that he'd never been able to outrun wrapped a little tighter around his lungs, so tight, he had trouble drawing a breath. For so many years he'd lived his own lie, and yet he was willing to tear his father limb from limb for doing the same.

But it had to end.

Today.

Another five minutes and he was pulling into his assigned space in the apartment's parking lot. A wayward thought crossed his mind as he cut the engine. Maybe he'd luck out and the old man would be gone.

No damned way.

He was through with lies.

Even his own.

He jogged across the dusty lot and startled a lizard sunning himself. As Jase passed, it scuttled beneath the fronds of a fat fern near the staircase. Taking the steps two at a time, Jase was up the two flights to the third floor in no time flat. As he stepped out of the stairwell, he found his father leaning over the porch railing, smoking a cigarette as he watched the traffic roll past.

The door to his unit was open wide and Ed, who had obviously showered and shaved sometime during the day, nodded as he spied his son.

As if nothing was wrong.

As if he hadn't turned Jase's life inside out.

"We need to talk," Jase said without preamble, then looked down the long walkway and spied a woman pushing twins in a stroller two doors down. "Not out here." He headed inside.

"Figured as much." Ed snuffed out his cigarette before following.

The living room was tidy. The blanket Ed had used the night before had been folded and stacked neatly on the end of the couch, the pillow resting on top.

"Now, before you go all nuts about me and the drinkin'," Ed said, holding up a hand as he followed Jase into the kitchen area. "Let me explain."

"That's what you think this is about? Your drinking?"

"Well, yeah. Didn't you say that—" Ed's eyes narrowed.

"That'll wait, Dad. Let's start a little farther back, before last night." Jase reined in his temper as best he could. With all his effort, he slowly and silently counted to ten, opening and closing a fist to release some tension.

"So what's this? You gonna punch me out?" Ed asked, settling into a chair at the small table near the slider.

"Thinkin' about it."

The old man cocked an eyebrow. "What's going on, son? What's got you so riled?"

"Mom." Jase let the word hang in the air.

"What? Her?" Ed shook his head. "She's not your worry. That two-timing—"

"Stop!" Jase yelled. "Don't! Just don't, Dad." He gripped the edge of the counter. "I've heard it before. And it's a lie."

"A lie? Sheeeit. No way, that woman—"

"That woman is my mother and yes, she left you. I don't know why, but it sure as hell was not because her son died. She left and she took him with her."

Ed froze, his eyes shifting from side to side.

"He didn't die, Dad, and you know it," Jase said through barely moving lips. "I found no record of any Edward Bridges Junior in any birth records, nor does he have a death certificate that I could locate."

"We had a boy."

"Yes, you did. Actually, you really did have three sons, Dad." Jase let go of the counter, the impression of its edge still on his palms. "And the youngest one? The one who was supposed to have died? Ed Junior, you said. Born a couple years after me? An infant when Mom took off?"

Ed's face went ashen and his eyes suddenly appeared haunted. He licked his lips nervously. "Yeah, that's right," he said, but there wasn't any conviction behind his words.

"No, Dad, it's wrong. And he didn't die, did he? That brother? He survived. When Mom took off, she took him with her. That's what you meant last night, when you slipped up. After all these years, you finally screwed up and mentioned that you chose me and

Prescott. But the third son, the baby, he left with Mom, didn't he?"

Ed didn't answer, but located his near-empty pack of Camels in his shirt pocket.

"Didn't he?" Jase yelled.

His father looked about to argue, then let out a sigh. "All right," he said sadly. "Son of a bitch. Yeah, that's 'bout how it happened," he admitted, sliding a cigarette from the pack. "You're right, son, and I guess, hell, I suppose it's time you knew."

"Well past time. So what happened?" He'd rounded the counter and stood looming over his father, who seemed suddenly a broken man.

"Your mother," he said the words as if they tasted foul. "She was a piece of work, y'know."

"I know how you feel about her. Cut to the chase."

He swore under his breath and walked out to the back deck, where he lit up.

Jase followed, knowing full well what was to come. But he wanted to hear it from the old man's lips.

Ed drew deep on his Camel and let the smoke drift out of his nostrils as he looked into the trees that separated this side of the building from the street. "Okay," he admitted. "Marian, she did take off with the baby, but he wasn't younger than you. Well, at least not by much. And his name wasn't Edward Junior. You're right about that. His name was Jacob, but I figure you already know that. Just like you already know that he was your twin."

CHAPTER 28

He drove like a madman. When he'd seen that his shots had missed, that Zoe was getting away in the pickup, he'd run back to the cabin, left that miserable Chloe locked in the basement, and jumped into the car that he'd brought from town. He'd ditched the van, hidden it in the garage until he could repair it, but he still had the car . . . Myra's car. The 2001 Ford Focus had barely been driven and blended well with other vehicles.

The good news was that Zoe hadn't gotten far. She'd been too stupid or delirious to realize that she'd doubled back. He doubted it had been a ploy to get him off the track; it was easy enough to get turned around with all the bends in the river and the forest blocking one's sight. She hadn't known that the river itself was like a snake, twisting and turning on itself, so she'd only ended up a quarter mile away from the cabin. He'd whistled to the useless dog, jogged back to the canoe, and had been in his car within fifteen minutes.

He'd even managed to make the call.

Sure, he was a few minutes behind her now, but he

was willing to bet that she would head straight to mama's condominium, which, because he'd planned it, was only a stone's throw from his own place. He thought of his house in the city, the little place with computers and phones. A respectable spot. The best part about it? The city house was far from the cabin that was titled in Myra's name, where that bitch Chloe was waiting for the end she knew was coming. Damn, though, he needed Zoe.

Myra had been adamant when he'd called her. Their conversation, if that's what you wanted to call it, had been hot. Angry. It ricocheted through his head, over and over again

"Get her!"

"But she's seen my face."

"All the more reason to stop her before she can identify you. What kind of cretin are you?"

"It's too late."

"Too late?" she'd said in a low voice that was more chilling than when she screeched. "It's *never* too late. Now, find her, capture her, take her to the cabin, and finish what you started."

"But—"

"Don't argue with me. You know I'm right. I'm always right."

He'd tuned her out then, just as he often did. He hadn't even had to disconnect the phone. He'd learned over the years how to deal with her when her demands and accusations had bruised his brain, burrowing deep. It wasn't as if she had to keep repeating herself, he heard her day and night. Until he'd learned how to ignore her voice as it rattled through his brain. He wondered if he'd made a mistake. Maybe she was the one who needed to die. But . . . no! He couldn't think that way. Remorse was just as sudden and hot as his anger. Resolved to stay on track, he pressed the accelerator and headed to the city.

Miraculously, Zoe thought, the shot had missed.

No glass had shattered.

No tire had blown.

No metal on the body of the truck had been pierced.

But the driver, a farmer-type complete with trucker hat, plaid shirt, worn jeans, and boots, had finally gotten the message through his thick skull that the beast was hunting them down. Now the farmer was scared shitless, just like Zoe.

"For the love of God, what kind of trouble are you in?" he demanded as he took a corner too fast and the pickup skidded into the oncoming lane. They narrowly missed a brightly colored Volkswagen bus filled with screaming, happy kids and balloons flying from the open windows, a birthday party that had nearly become a disaster. Fortunately, he didn't careen into the bus. "Why is that son of a bitch shooting at you? At us?"

The truck shuddered as he righted it, tires screeching.

"I don't know why!" she screamed, bracing herself and believing that any second she would feel the sting of a bullet piercing her skin or exploding in her brain. "All I know is that he wants to kill me and my sister in some weird ritual that involves zero clothes and red ribbons and being hog-tied and all kinds of weird crap. He's probably got Chloe and . . . oh, Jesus, I didn't think he would kill her first, it all has something to do with birth order, I think, but now that I've gotten away, God only knows what he'll do." She didn't want to think about it. . . . Now was the time for action, not worry.

The farmer shook his head, eyes on the road. "This is all some kind of crazy."

At least he didn't want to talk her ears off for the twenty minutes it took to reach the outskirts of town. Now, with the city of New Orleans rising before them, her heart leaped with joy at the thought of seeing her mother again, and relief to know that the psycho was far behind her.

But most likely so was Chloe.

And that leaping heart turned to stone.

Zoe didn't want to believe that she had sealed her sister's fate by escaping. But then, she didn't know what had happened to Chloe. Maybe, just maybe, her twin had escaped, too. There was always the chance! Not for the first time she sent up a desperate prayer for her sister's safety.

The phone jangled in her hands and she let out a sob when she saw her mother's number.

"Mom!" she answered, her voice cracking.

"Oh, baby, where are you? I can't believe you're safe. Oh, my God, Zoe!" Selma said, her voice broken by a sob.

"I'm almost home. I'll be there soon. Ten . . . maybe fifteen minutes at the outside?" She looked at the farmer for confirmation. He nodded, then held out his hand for the phone. Reluctantly, Zoe handed him the cell.

"Your mother?" he guessed, and Zoe nodded. Into the phone, he said, "This is Rand Cooligan. I've got your daughter with me and she's fine . . . er, safe. But you'd better get the police involved. There's some idiot taking potshots at her, shooting at my truck, and she's got a wild tale to tell . . . yes . . . no, no, as I said, she's okay . . . Yeah, soon. I know, I know. Just hang in there . . . Yeah, I know the area . . . uh-huh. Ten, fifteen minutes on the outside. . . . What? . . . No, I'm sorry. Just the one. Zoe. Yeah, sure. Here ya go." He handed the phone back to Zoe. "She wants you to stay on the line 'til we get there. Can't say as I blame her. You can talk all ya want. I know where we're going, and the phone's all charged up."

"So all these years I had a twin brother and never knew about him?" Jase stared at the old man as if he'd never really seen him before. His cell phone pinged, indicating he'd received a text message. He ignored it.

"That's about the size of it." Ed drew hard on his cigarette, lost in thought.

"So where is he? And where is Mom?"

"Don't know about the boy. But Marian? She's dead." He slid a glance at his son, then continued to gaze through the branches of the trees to the street below. Cars and trucks rolled past and a kid crouching on a skateboard skimmed along the sidewalk. A normal afternoon, for some.

"You kept in touch with her?" Jase was astounded. He thought of the one picture he'd seen of her, the haunted woman getting married.

"Nah." He shook his head. "She had a cousin, in Pocatello, Idaho. That cousin called me years ago and gave me the news. Marian, she got sick early, don't know what it was. Ended up in a nursing home. Died there. Buried in that town's cemetery or cremated, I don't know and I don't really care."

Jase felt as if he'd been punched in the gut. Though he'd expected the news. He'd even mollified himself as a child, believing that his mother had to be dead or else she would have returned or reached out to him in some way. Still, the realization that she was really dead came as a shock, as if some part of that little boy still held on to the hope that if she were still alive, he would see her again, feel her arms surround him, smell her perfume. Silly. Stupid. He thought he'd grown out of that fantasy, but hearing that she was actually gone, that he'd never look into her face if for no other reason than to ask, "Why? Why did you leave me?" hit him harder than he'd imagined.

He felt his jaw work and he cleared his throat. "I didn't find any mention of her death certificate."

"You were probably lookin' in the wrong name."

"I searched Marian Selby and Marian Bridges."

His father slid him a glance. "Next time try Wilcox. Helen Marian Wilcox Selby Bridges and then whatever else she went by. Probably got hitched a few more times, for all I know, all I care. She was married a few months when I met her. Went by her middle name. Never liked Helen, she claimed. We got together and that first husband, he didn't like it none, but gave her a quickie divorce and . . . oh, hell, you know the rest."

"No, Dad! That's the problem. I don't. Not by a long shot. And everything I believed, everything you told me, it wasn't true." His chest felt tight as bit by bit everything he thought he'd known about his mother was unraveling into a string of lies.

"Well, now you know as much about your mother as I do. Feel any better?"

The bastard. "And your son? What about my damned twin?" Jase asked, and realized he was gripping the railing, his knuckles white.

"I told you. Don't know where he is, whether he's alive or dead." His father dropped his cigarette and crushed the butt with his boot heel. "Don't care, neither. I did what I could for you and Prescott. Raised you best as I could. Yeah, it wasn't perfect, not by any man's measure, but I tried and I was there for you. Stood by you when you needed me. 'Til you were raised. 'Til you inherited." Ed scowled, and in the disgusted twist of his lips, Jase could see his father's old disappointment that he'd been skipped over, bitterness over the will that left his father's money to Jase and Prescott.

"Ah, shit." Ed stared down. "I can't change the past, Jason, and I'm not sure I would if I could, but there it is. I don't know about Jacob, never heard, and really never cared. You and Prescott, you were my sons. I don't think I coulda handled another."

"You don't know anything about him?"

"Nothin'." He kicked his cigarette butt off the deck under the railing, leaving a streak where the blackened tobacco had swept the concrete. "And that's the way I'd like to keep it."

"Not gonna happen, Dad. I'm gonna find him. Pres will want to know he has another brother, too."

"Prescott?" Ed snorted his disbelief. "He's got more'n he can handle with that wife of his. Lena bosses him around like a bitch mother dog and he's the whipped puppy. Got him gettin' rid of the farm, sellin' insurance, and hopin' to live near the preacher." His graying eyebrows drew together. "Two kids and a third on the way. What's he thinkin'?"

"What were you?" Jase demanded. "You had three."

"Expectin' only to raise two," he corrected. "Didn't know your mo—that she was havin' twins until about fifteen minutes after you were born and out popped another. Biggest surprise of my damned life."

"And not the best?"

"Hell, no," Ed admitted. "The last thing I needed was another mouth to feed."

So angry he could spit nails, Jase leaned in close. Despite the old man's recent shower, Jase could still smell the scent of old cigarette smoke and stale liquor seeping through his father's pores. "This is where it ends, Dad. All of it. The lies. The secrets. No more."

Ed snorted and raised an unruly, disbelieving eyebrow. "Yours, too, boy? You gonna start tellin' the truth from now on? Or is it just me that's got to bare my damned soul?"

"All of us are, old man." Jase didn't hesitate. "You. Me. Prescott. A clean slate."

"All of it?"

"Every last lie."

Their eyes met. Clashed. Silently accused.

"I don't know about Pres," said Ed. "He might not agree."

"He might not have a choice."

"You're up on a pretty high horse, son. Careful now. That's how the mighty fall."

"Fuck you, Dad."

Jase's cell phone pinged again. Another text. He yanked the phone from his pocket and read the news, from Kennedy in his office.

Assume you saw this about Donovan Caldwell. Guess the guilt finally got to him.

A link was included with the message. Jase clicked it open and quickly skimmed a breaking story about the death of the 21 Killer whose life had ended early this morning in his jail cell. "Son of a bitch," he whispered, and for a second his father and all their family drama was forgotten as he searched for more information about Caldwell's death. Did Brianna know? What did it mean about the Denning girls? Had Donovan Caldwell been the 21 Killer and if so, who had abducted Zoe and Chloe? His only hope was that, if they hadn't been taken by 21, if Caldwell had been convicted of a crime he'd committed, that the twins were still alive.

"Look, Ed," he said, unwilling to give the lying bastard the title of father. "I have to go to the office. But we're not done here. Just wait. Don't go anywhere."

His father found another cigarette in his pack and jabbed it between his lips. "That in there," he said, nodding toward the kitchen where Jase had left the envelope with the check that he hadn't mailed. The old man actually smiled and a light of interest flared in his eyes. "That for me?"

Jase didn't answer. Couldn't. The old bastard pissed him off too much. He made his way out the door and put thoughts of Edward Bridges and their sorry past behind him as he headed to the stairwell. He had enough time to go to the office, get more information about Donovan Caldwell's death, and check in with Bentz at the station before he returned and dealt with Brianna.

His guts twisted a little at the thought.

But his anxiety wasn't due to Caldwell's death. No, he thought as he climbed into the cab and fired up the engine of his truck. His worries were from a far deeper and more intimate source. He rammed the truck's gears into Reverse, backed out with a squeal of tires, and threw the truck into Drive.

How was he going to tell her the truth about her sister?

Squinting against the glare of the lowering sun, he slid his aviator sunglasses over his eyes and wondered how the hell he would ever admit that he'd been there the night Arianna Hayward was killed.

CHAPTER 29

Chloe knew she was going to die.

Here, in this hellhole of a basement, all alone.

No one would ever know. Not for years.

The freak had left her for hours, maybe a day, maybe even two, she didn't know. It was dark and dank in the basement. Water dripped in a rhythmic tapping noise, and the smell of water seeping through the walls was ever present.

And she was alone.

No phone.

No water.

Her hands were tied behind her back and somehow connected to her feet, so the more she moved the more uncomfortable she became. Her muscles were sore from straining, the rope cut into her ankles and wrists, and her joints ached. Sometimes she wished she would just die so that it would be over.

She'd nodded off from time to time, but her fear and anxiety kept her on edge and awake. That and the overpowering sense of thirst. She was hungry, yes, but more intense than the emptiness in her stomach was the scorched bitterness in her dry throat and parched lips. How she wished for a single drop of water. For anything wet. One moment's relief.

But it wasn't happening.

At first she'd plotted her revenge and ultimate escape. There were tools on the table and resting on holders in the wall. A knife, she thought, maybe a saw, certainly a screwdriver, any number of weapons to take the freak's life. And she'd do it, too. If she ever got the chance again. But as the seconds and minutes and hours ticked by in her head, and the pain, discomfort, and despair took over, she thought less about revenge and murder and an eye for an eye, and more about the solace of death, the peace of giving up.

There was her family to consider, but her dad had more children and a new wife, her cousin of all people. Mom would be devastated and heartbroken, but she would have Zoe. If Zoe survived. Oh, God, please. Let Zoe be free of this. If Zoe did escape, she would return for her twin, Chloe was certain, but when? And how? Would she still be alive?

She tried not to think of what might happen, to keep up her flagging spirits, to sing, at least in her mind as her throat was dry as a desert. But in the end she quit trying and just prayed that it would end soon, that her pain would be over, her battle finished.

The people she'd wronged came to mind, and she remembered thinking she loved Tommy. How long ago it all seemed. As if it had happened to another person, in another lifetime.

She closed her eyes and turned her thoughts to Zoe, the twin she loved and sometimes hated. "Be safe," she whispered, then let out a long breath. Maybe it would be her last.

As she drove, Brianna told herself that she was imagining things. She was *not* being followed. That truck that seemed to be on her tail as she drove toward Jase's apartment was probably just headed in the same direction.

"Ridiculous," she said. But she kept checking her mirror and, sure enough, no matter which direction she turned, a few cars back, or sometimes right behind her, a light-colored pickup, no, maybe a beat-up van, was following her. Sometimes the vehicle hung back, but she figured that was the driver's attempt to remain un-detected. "You son of a bitch." She recalled the other times she'd thought she was being followed: the night she'd sensed someone looking at her through the bath-room window, the crushed shrubs near that same win-dow, the footsteps behind her on a staircase. So she wasn't going crazy.

No, it's worse. Some anonymous jerk is following you.

"Why?" she asked aloud, and checked her mirror again. She turned into a narrow alley where shadows from the surrounding buildings fell over the street. Sure enough, just as she was exiting the alley, the van en-tered. It seemed familiar, but she couldn't quite place it.

Hadn't she seen Elise get into a similar van, when Ashton was picking her up from one of the support group meetings? Or had it been Desmond, the quiet one, whom she didn't quite trust, his eyes always flat, as if guarding his feelings, his face often without expression? The few remarks he'd made had been slightly misogynistic and had really gotten Tanisha's back up. She'd made sure to put him in his place on more than one occasion, saying flat out that she didn't like him. But that was no surprise. Tanisha liked only a few women and even fewer men.

Had Desmond ever married? Had he once mentioned a wife or fiancé or girlfriend? Not that she remembered, though his lack of a relationship would not explain why he might be stalking her. She looked in her mirror again, noticed the van two cars back, and felt her stomach grind. Who was this guy to follow her? Invade her life? Make her uncomfortable?

It had to end.

She was in no mood to have some creep get his voyeuristic jollies from observing her, and who knew how many others.

If she could draw him close enough to see his license plate, take a picture with her phone, then Jase would help her figure out the creep's identity, enough solid information to go to the police.

In heavier traffic, only a mile from Jase's apartment, she slowed and switched lanes, all the while hoping he would drive closer, maybe even drive alongside her so she could get a glimpse of his face. No such luck. With the sun slanting against his dirty windshield, she could only make out dark glasses and a baseball cap pulled low over his eyes.

Sweat beaded on her upper lip as she wound her way through afternoon traffic to Jase's neighborhood. She had to do something. Now. After a quick maneuver onto Jase's street, she found a place to tuck the car. She pulled into the space near a fire hydrant in the shade of a live oak with Spanish moss waving from its limbs. Quickly, she climbed out of her Honda and hid behind the tree, where she could take a video of the van driving by. She knew the driver might flee if he got wind of what she was doing. Even worse, he might try to confront her, but then there would be plenty of witnesses on this busy street. Plenty of passersby that she could turn to for help. She'd be fine.

Either way, she had him.

The van pulled onto the street and headed in her direction, then slowed when the driver didn't immediately spy her Honda.

She was already filming from her iPhone, but catching the numbers of his grimy license plate wasn't as easy as she'd thought it would be. When she'd finally gotten the footage, she focused the camera's eye on the driver, but because of the angle of the sun, its rays bouncing off the glass, she couldn't see who he was.

Until the van stopped in the middle of the street, blocking her Honda from exiting its illegal spot. Then he looked at her full-on and she recognized the man in dark glasses, scrubby beard, and hard expression.

Milo Tillman.

What the hell? Milo was stalking her? Why?

"Hey!" she called. "What're you doing, following me?"

The passenger side window was already rolled down, and he motioned for her to come closer.

She did. "I told you I would meet with you later."

"It couldn't wait."

"What can't? You said you wanted to talk about your twin."

"I have to," he said, and he sounded desperate. "I . . .

it's bad." A car pulled up behind his van, and the driver honked impatiently. "It's about—" He glanced in the mirror as the car behind him, a silvery BMW, sped into the oncoming lane.

"Hey, buddy!" The driver, a thirtyish guy with spiky hair, yelled, "Drive, asshole! You're clogging up the whole street!"

Brianna wasn't interested in the other driver. "I know," she said, forcing Milo's attention back to her. "It's about your twin."

"Yeah, I really need to talk," he admitted. "Finally. I'm ready. I need to talk to somebody about Myra."

Zoe fell into Selma's arms.

Right on the small grassy area in front of her mother's apartment building, she dropped the farmer's phone and held fast to her mother. While Rand Cooligan stood uncomfortably by, she sobbed wildly and clung to her mother, relishing the smells of Selma's perfume and smoke, the scents she'd grown up with. She squeezed her eyes shut tight and still the tears ran freely. During the phone conversation that had lasted from the second Selma had called back until this very moment with the afternoon sunlight streaming and people staring as they walked past, she'd learned that no one had heard from Chloe. Her twin was still missing. Zoe's heart cracked. All her hopes that her sister had escaped had been dashed, and now, she was certain that Chloe was still in the psycho's clutches.

Or dead.

Dear God, she couldn't, wouldn't think that was

possible. If Chloe had died, Zoe was certain she would sense it. She would just know. Surely.

Her soul ripped a little at that thought, that she, like her mother before her, might spend the rest of her life without the comfort of her sister, the person she'd known since before birth, the sibling with whom she'd grown in the womb. Was it possible that the very part of her that was her center, how she defined herself, would be lost to her forever?

No!

She swallowed back a sob of despair.

"Oh, baby," her mother whispered, tears running down Selma's cheeks as she held her daughter in a surprisingly strong grip. "Thank God, you're safe. Oh . . . honey." Looking over Zoe's shoulder as they held each other close, Selma said to the farmer standing awkwardly nearby, "Thank you, thank you."

He nodded, looked away, then cleared his throat. "She said something about a twin sister," he said, and Zoe felt Selma's arms tighten around her.

"Chloe." Zoe sniffed loudly and blinked against the wash of tears. "We have to save her. He's got her."

"Who?" her mother asked.

"I don't know. The freak. This tall psycho who kept us in a basement out in the middle of nowhere and sang the birthday song and wore nothing but a rubber apron. A psycho freak! He's got her and . . . and we have to save her."

"We . . . we will," Selma said.

"Look, Mrs. Denning, if I can help, I'd like to," Rand said, looking over his shoulder as if he expected someone to be listening in. "She's right. There's a madman on the loose. I saw him from a distance, and he was huntin' down your daughter, here, trying like hell, er heck, to shoot her. Had a dog runnin' her down. Now, I know this isn't really my business, and I don't understand what the heck's goin' on, but I'm a witness and I'd like to see that SOB nailed. That bastard meant business. You've called the police?"

Shaking her head, Selma said, "I . . . I was on the phone with Zoe."

Rand spied his phone and plucked it from the ground. "Yeah, right, okay. But now, why don't you get her cleaned up and we'll all go to the station?"

"He's right," Zoe said, sniffing. "But we have to go now. I . . . I'll take a shower later." It sounded like heaven, but there was no time. If the freak had Chloe, if she hadn't escaped—

Don't even think it!

Zoe was still clinging to her mother. "We have to tell them about Chloe ASAP." Tears clogged her throat again and she blinked hard, tried to think. "If he still has her, she's not safe. I mean, he kept saying he had to kill me first. It was all part of his twisted ritual and . . . he kept repeating it, when he wasn't singing the birthday song. First me, then her. I thought she would be safe if he couldn't kill me first."

"That's crazy," her mother whispered, horrified.

"I know, but he was really a nut job. But now I'm really scared for her. The way he was shooting at the truck. Aiming right at us. Now I'm not sure. It could be that all bets are off. Maybe he'd break his stupid ritual and . . ." She couldn't say it aloud, didn't want to admit that the monster might kill Chloe. Didn't want to think that maybe he already had.

Swallowing back her fear, she tugged her mother toward the apartment. "Let's make it fast. I've got some old jeans here and . . . a sweater or something. I'll grab them while you grab your bag and the car keys."

"I told you Detective Bentz was busy," Nellie Vaccarro's sharp voice heralded another visitor.

Bentz, who was on the phone with Hayes in LA, glanced up to find Jase Bridges standing in the doorway of his office. "Thanks," he said into the phone. "Keep me posted."

"Will do," Hayes promised, and hung up. He'd called to tell Bentz that according to all outward signs, it appeared that Donovan Caldwell had killed himself. Rumors of suicide had been swirling since they'd found the body, and now detectives and crime-scene techs were beginning to confirm their suspicion. Of course, they would keep it all under wraps pending interviews with prisoners, guards, family, and friends. Also, before confirming suicide, the investigators would want to see the autopsy report, just to make sure there wasn't any internal trauma to his body that hadn't been evident, and that there were no toxins or drugs in his bloodstream. None was expected. The prevailing theory was that Donovan Caldwell had found a way to take his own life rather than spend his remaining years behind bars.

"Come in," Bentz said to Bridges, then pocketed his phone. When Nellie Vaccarro appeared in the doorway, her pink lips compressed, he waved her away. "It's okay," he told her.

"It is definitely not 'okay.' I take my job very seriously, Detective Bentz," she reminded him almost primly. She had a lot to learn about how this place ran. One bustling little receptionist wasn't going to change things.

"I know, Nellie. I appreciate it, but Jase here, he's okay. Might even end up being hired by the department. So, trust me, this time, it's all right." In truth he wasn't overjoyed at seeing the reporter, but there was no reason to make a stink. After he'd given Bridges and the reporter from WKAM the brush-off at the crime scene, Bentz had determined that he could use a friend in the press. Bridges, being considered for the Public Information Officer position, was as good a choice as anyone.

"If you say so."

"I do."

With a final don't-get-used-to-messing-with-me look at Bridges, Nellie walked quickly down the hallway.

For his part, the reporter didn't seem the least bit perturbed by her discomfiture and got right down to business. "I need some answers, Bentz."

"About the homicide off of Chartres?"

"That, too," Bridges said, "but the reason I'm here now is that I'm working with Brianna Hayward."

Bentz nodded. Not surprised. "You want to know about the 21 Killer," he surmised. "I've talked to Ms. Hayward, heard her theories."

"And I found out that Donovan Caldwell died early this morning or late last night. I figure you, as an investigating officer of the original case, might know a little more than most."

Bentz didn't respond.

"Tell me about Donovan Caldwell. What happened?"

Bridges prodded. "How did he die while incarcerated? An accident? Natural causes? Come on, he was a young man. There's talk of suicide."

"Twitter at its best," Bentz muttered.

"It's happened before."

"Look, the investigation is ongoing. I was just talking to Detective Hayes from the LAPD. He was my partner for the years I was on the force. He tells me nothing is certain yet. There will be an autopsy. Lab tests. You know how those things go. The final report could take weeks."

"Won't they rush the autopsy?"

Bentz shrugged. "It's not really an emergency. And they'll be extremely thorough. Caldwell was convicted of heinous acts, didn't have a lot of fans in prison. The Department of Corrections will want to make sure everything was on the up-and-up."

"You've heard Brianna Hayward's theory," Bridges pressed on. "Do you really think Donovan Caldwell was the 21 Killer?"

Bentz wanted to stick to the company line, that of course the LAPD had gotten their man, but in light of recent findings, he wasn't a hundred percent certain. Before he could come up with a suitable answer, he heard a ruckus out in the hallway.

Once again, Nellie's sharp voice could be heard over the usual hubbub of cell phones, voices, printers, and the air-conditioning fans.

"I'm sorry, but Detective Bentz is with someone right now."

"Tough! I have to talk to him. Now." The woman's voice sounded close to hysteria. Lately, it seemed, it was the story of his life.

"If you can wait—"

"No way! This is a damned emergency. My name's Zoe Denning and my mom says Detective Bentz has been looking for me."

"Denning?" Nellie repeated as Bentz shot to his feet and Jase Bridges, who hadn't yet sat down, stepped into the hallway.

"She's my daughter," another voice said as a shriek loud enough to wake the dead in the neighboring parishes ricocheted through the station.

Bentz grabbed his sidearm and ran out the door to the hallway, where a terrified Zoe Denning cowered as she stared, wide-eyed, at Jase Bridges. The girl was a mess, with stringy hair, her skin burned and streaked with mud. But she was alive. And in a panic.

"It's him!" she cried. Frantic, she scrambled backward, trying to get away from Bridges. "He's the psycho who grabbed me! Him! For the love of God, somebody get him!"

CHAPTER 30

"For the love of God!" Zoe screamed at the sight of the freak. "He's the one! He's the perv who's got Chloe!" What the hell was he doing here? At the police station? All cleaned up and . . . "For the love of God! Arrest him," she said, panic flooding through her. This was wrong. So very wrong.

"Miss—?" The cop who followed him into the hallway looked at her as if she'd lost her mind. "Are you all right?"

"Do I look all right? Did you hear me?" she said, her voice rising, anger and rage beating through her.

"Miss—?" The damned cop again.

"Where the hell is my sister?" She glared at the cleaned up version of the psycho. "What did you do with her?" She started to launch herself at the man, attack him, and force him to tell the truth, but Rand, the farmer, stopped her short, restraining her with a big hand suddenly clamped over her shoulder.

"Slow down," the farmer said into her ear. "Something's not right here."

"You're damned right about that!"

The object of her wrath held up both hands, palms out, fingers splayed, his face earnest. "Not me."

"Yes! You!" Somehow this creep was trying to trick her, trick the cops with his clean, respectable façade, but she wouldn't be fooled, not after days of being held captive. "Where's Chloe, damn it! Where the hell is she?" Zoe was nearly hyperventilating, her mind spinning, only vaguely aware that other people in the department, other policemen and women were clustering around them. Voices. Phones. Shuffling feet. Stares. Her heart thudding, she was sweating, in a near panic at the sight of him.

The cop who was looking at her said, "You're identifying this man as your abductor?"

"Yes!" Zoe nearly screamed. What was wrong with them? Why was he standing here all innocent-like. As if he didn't know. "It's . . . it's . . . him! Where's Chloe, you bastard? Where's my sister?" she cried, but as she said the words and her panic at the sight of him subsided a bit, she realized that something was off. Not right. Even though she wanted to pummel the jerkwad with her bare fists, to gouge out his eyes, she wasn't sure. The face, oh, God, the face was the same and the build, but all cleaned up? Not a scratch on his face, not a bruise, not . . . wait, there was a little scar, but it was old and . . . what the hell? The psycho didn't have an old scar there but he sure as hell had fresh ones. Her throat closed in on itself as she stared at him, tried to get her bearings. Could this guy be, what? A doppleganger, another twin? Oh, Geez, was that the deal? The freak was actually a twin himself? She thought she might have a heart attack right then and there just staring at him.

Little nuance—differences—jumped out at her. Her stomach dropped. "Do you . . ." No, she wouldn't talk to the guy. To the cop, she asked, "Does he have a tattoo? On his arm? There should be a tat!"

To her amazement, the guy nodded and pushed his sleeve up past the bend of one elbow where the inky image of a rattlesnake was coiled around his biceps. "Only one I've got."

"No, no." She was shaking her head, disbelieving, trying to wrap her near-crazed mind around what she was seeing. "That's not right!" she whispered, attempting to get a grip on herself "Not a snake . . . this is all wrong." Remembering the mountain and a bloody heart on her captor's arm, she felt sick inside. She was wrong. This wasn't the creep. The man standing before her had a straighter nose and, of course, that tiny scar, faint but discernable, from years past. She was sure the freak didn't have one there. Finally, her heartbeat slowing, the truth that had been dawning taking hold, she admitted, "The tattoo was way different, like that of a mountain and a bloody heart, some weird crap like that." Oh, God, she wanted this man to be her would-be killer, to see him in custody, in handcuffs and shackles, behind bars or worse. She tried to think straight, to push past her pain and exhaustion, her hunger and dehydration, but she couldn't and felt her knees start to give.

For the first time she noticed how many of the cops had left their desks, their expressions interested and wary, some with hands on their weapons as they collected around the tense group clogging the hallway. All staring at her.

"What . . . what about some kind of mole?" she

asked in desperation. "On your . . . ?" She turned her gaze to the cop who had walked out of the office with the freak. "On his butt cheek."

Selma took in a swift breath. "You saw him without clothes?"

"Except for a rubber apron. Yeah." But if this wasn't the guy, then, oh God, Chloe was still in the maniac's clutches . . . or worse.

"You want me to drop trou? Would that convince you?" the guy demanded and before she could answer, without batting an eye, turned around and let his pants fall from his buttocks. The cop stared at them all as if they were all ceritifiable while more and more people gathered around.

"Hey! I don't think that's necessary, Bridges!" the cop said as some Hispanic dude with a goatee and diamond stud earring swaggered around the corner and stopped short.

"Whoa! What the hell kind of freak show is this?" he demanded, eyeing the gathering crowd. He acted like a cop, too—kinda—but he was wearing a black leather jacket and a bad-boy attitude that were at odds with him being a part of the force.

"This is Zoe Denning," the first cop said, and then to Zoe, his face all serious intensity as he motioned to the guy who had just shown his buttocks. "Is this your abductor?"

"No," she admitted, as the guy pulled up his pants and, his expression no longer of surprise, adjusted his shirt. "No, it can't be. But—"

"But," he said, his eyes darkening, "I look enough like him to be his twin."

* * *

"You want to talk about Myra now?" Brianna said, disbelieving as she stared at Milo. "I really can't. I have an appointment."

"Here?" Milo asked, and looked at the apartment building. "Your appointment is here?" He eyed her suspiciously.

She checked her watch. She wasn't scheduled to meet with Jase for another fifteen minutes, but she wasn't certain she wanted to spend the time alone with Milo; there was just something about him that she didn't trust.

"You followed me. And you came to my house and looked in my bathroom window."

He didn't answer, but actually blushed, as if embarrassed.

"While I was showering!"

"No . . . no . . . I'd rung the bell. Really. I wanted . . . I needed to talk to you and you didn't answer. I saw lights on, so I walked around the house and . . ."

"Looked at me while I was showering? Is that what you're telling me?"

"You were out of the shower. You had a towel around you."

"Doesn't matter! That's voyeurism, Milo. I could have you arrested! I *should* have you arrested! You can't go around peeping in windows."

"You wouldn't!" He was nervous now, his tongue darting around the corners of his mouth.

"I'm not sure about that." She was furious and wanted to let him have it with both barrels. "You scared me to death!"

"I just . . . I just didn't know how to talk to you." He seemed sincere and confused and upset. "I'm sorry. Really. Please," he said. "I just want to talk about Myra. I thought you cared about the whole twinless twin thing . . . I . . ."

A horn blasted as a minivan rolled down the street.

"Okay," Brianna said. "Just find a parking spot. I'll wait."

"You could just hop into the van."

No way would she jump into a van with a guy who had admitted to peering through her windows, a man who, at some level, made her more than nervous. She clicked off her phone's camera but put it in alarm mode, should she need to call for help. She considered moving her Honda, parked as it was in a tow-away zone, but decided this hastily convened meeting would only take a few minutes. Twinless twin or not, it was all the time she could give him.

It took Milo five minutes to park his vehicle and walk back to her spot near the tree, and she couldn't help but second-guess her own sanity at having agreed to this. She glanced around the area, just to make certain she wasn't alone.

A woman pushing a baby carriage while trying to walk some kind of big dog, a lab mix, she thought, was on the far side of the street. She also spied a man leaning over the rail of the third-floor porch. Smoking a cigarette and staring at her. Hard. Or was it her imagination? Were her nerves jangled because of Milo and the fact that Donovan Caldwell had died today. It was all kind of weird. Outré. Unnerving. Silently she told herself she was just a bundle of nerves and jumping at shadows, not in small measure due to Milo Tillman, her own personal stalker.

Was it even safe to deal with him?

What if he had a weapon?

What then?

She glanced up at the apartment building again and saw the gray-haired guy still watching her. Friend or foe?

Dear God, she was letting her imagination run wild with her. Now she was seeing evil in someone doing nothing threatening. But as Milo approached, she felt herself tense.

"Let's go somewhere where we can sit down," he suggested. "I think there's a café two blocks down."

Like this was a date or something? Two friends having coffee? No way!

"I'm sorry," she said. She needed to keep her relationship with this man professional. She'd crossed the barriers before and blurred the lines several times. Max had been a mistake, and she probably was more involved with Tanisha and Selma than she should be. They'd become friends. But Milo? The Peeping Tom? No way. His excuse for peering through her window was flimsy at best. "I really don't have a lot of time. So what's going on? What's happening that couldn't wait until our next meeting?"

"I, um, I lied about that," he admitted, and her gut clenched.

"You lied?"

"About needing to talk about Myra. Well kind of . . . and about watching you." He scratched the back of his neck nervously. "I think you're in danger."

"Me?" What was he talking about? Where was this going?

"I've followed you," he admitted as a car left the parking lot of Jase's apartment building, nosing into the street where the traffic was picking up.

"I know." She glanced up to the third floor of the building. The smoker was still there, observing the ground below and, she felt, keeping an eye on her. All the better considering.

"And I've seen you with him."

"With who?"

"Jacob."

"Jacob?" she repeated, confused. "I don't know a Jacob."

He stared at her as if she were nuts. "But I saw you together. You know, after the meeting. The other night?"

"I don't know what you're talking about."

Milo's face grew hard. "It was later, you remember, after the meeting where Selma told us about her daughters going missing?" An earnest look crossed his face, but of course she still didn't trust him. "You went to dinner, I think, or out for drinks with Tanisha and Selma after the meeting and Jacob, he was waiting for you by your car."

Now she got it. Milo was mixed up. That was it. Or he got Jase's name wrong. "His name isn't Jacob." When he didn't respond, she added, "He's a reporter. Jason Bridges."

But Milo's face had changed. Any confusion in his expression had been chased away by anger. "What he is, Brianna, is a liar. His name is Bridges, yeah, but he's Jacob and he's a murdering son of a bitch. He killed Myra."

* * *

He drove as if Lucifer himself was on his tail, taking corners too fast, putting Myra's Ford through its paces, and all the while he was on his cell phone, listening to Myra berate him, reminding him over and over again that he'd failed. He'd left the city in a rush and now was flying toward the cabin, fields and farmland flashing by.

"You're out of options. You need to kill her." Myra's disappointed voice had been cold. Calculating. As if she'd just stepped out of the grave. But insistent, so much so that he heard it even when he wasn't on the phone with her.

He'd failed. He knew it now. Actually he'd known it the instant he'd missed his second shot and the pickup had sped out of range. He'd made the mistake of thinking he could fix things, that he could still hunt Zoe down, but had realized that returning to New Orleans had been a mistake.

He'd messed up, bungled the plan big time, and Myra, that bitch, wasn't going to let him forget it. He remembered the night he'd nearly killed her, how he'd wrapped his fingers around her thin throat and squeezed, listening to her squawk and gasp, watching her eyes bulge first in disbelief and then in terror.

She'd cheated on him and he'd caught her and confronted her and killed her. Snapped her lying, cheating neck the minute she'd turned twenty-one. Myra with her blood-red lipstick so much like the ribbons that tied his mother's hair. And those red teddies with their seductive garters, again reminding him of Mother's damned ribbons. The two women he'd loved had both been bitches and he'd taken care of them, hadn't he?

He'd shown Myra. Shown Mother. Shown both of those lying sluts. His mother should never have left his father and Myra, God, she'd spread her legs so easily for another man . . . She'd deserved to die!

No, no, wait. He couldn't have killed Myra. Never. His head pounded with blurred memories of strangulation and ribbons and hatred and . . .

Stop! That was wrong. He'd gotten it all wrong. Mixed up dreams with what had really happened.

Right? Of course! Myra, his beautiful Myra was alive and had just been on the phone and read him the riot act for not doing as she commanded, for letting Zoe get away.

"We'll deal with the first one later," she had said in the awful, ever-present voice. "She can ID you and the damage is done there, but you can take care of her after the heat has died down. For now, idiot, concentrate."

He felt his back muscles bunch. Hated it when she berated him. Even now, reviewing the conversation they'd had earlier in the day . . . or had it been another time?

"For now, just kill Chloe," she had insisted, "so that's one less mistake to worry about and then get the hell out of town. Leave the van. Take my car. Lie low. You still have money, right? You've been careful with your mother's estate?"

He thought of his mother with her wide eyes, thinning hair, and red, red ribbon tying it back. The nursing facility had been expensive, would have eaten up all of her savings, which at the time had been substantial, so she, too, had to die.

She was a bitch anyway.

He didn't mind helping her along, putting a little too much medication into her protein drink.

"Money's not a problem," he'd said aloud and wondered from her lack of response, if Myra had been listening. That was the way with her. She often didn't reply to him and it pissed him off. "But what about you? If I kill Chloe and leave New Orleans, what about you?" He'd come back here because of Myra.

"I'll always be with you, Jacob," she'd cooed, soothing him, once again present. Sometimes he wondered if she even existed the way she toyed with him. "You know that."

He smiled. She'd been angry with him, but forgiving. So he would do as she had bidden. Kill Chloe, make sure that little kicking bitch was dead, and then he'd blow town and bide his time.

He could wait for Zoe.

He was a patient man.

Bentz didn't believe for a second that Jase Bridges was capable of murder, but as they sorted everything out in a conference room, the reporter himself came up with an outlandish theory in which he described finding out just this very afternoon that he had a twin brother he hadn't known about, nor met. He'd only discovered the truth earlier in some kind of purging confession from his old man, who was also a drunk.

Montoya, who'd come a little late to the party, was skeptical. "Whoa. Wait. All these twins? Seriously?" he wondered aloud. "The twin girls who were taken, the mother who's a twinless twin, and now Bridges hav-

ing a twin brother he didn't know about. What's going
on? Are we on some hidden camera show?"

Bentz didn't have time to argue the facts. There was
another girl missing and now, they had a place to start
looking. The farmer who brought Zoe Denning into the
station was a local who knew the area.

Zoe's description of the isolated cabin in which she
and her sister had been held coupled with Rand Cooligan's knowledge of the terrain and the spot where he'd
found her running through the field had helped. The
police had narrowed the possibilities to six tracts that
met the description of a small, run-down and isolated
shack with a long, possibly quarter-of-a-mile lane and
forests bordering the river. Four were dismissed as
Cooligan knew the owners.

However, Bentz didn't think just because the farmer
could vouch for the land holders that put them in the
clear, so he was dispatching deputies to those parcels.
The other two he would personally visit.

"There's the Shepherd place," Rand said in the meeting. "Small one-room house, been abandoned for five,
maybe six years. Never seen anyone going in or out,
and the gate's padlocked, rusted shut. I know cuz me
and my boy went hunting that way just last fall."

"And the other place?" Bentz asked.

"The Tillman place?" Rand shook his head. "The
owner, Sigmund Tillman, was an older guy. Oh, gosh,
he's been dead now, what? Twenty years. Left the place
to his daughter as I recall."

"But she doesn't live there?"

"Nah. And she's dead, too," Rand said, thinking hard
and nodding. "Murdered. Far as I know they never caught
whoever did it."

"Tillman?" Selma whispered, her eyes rounding. "There's a man named Tillman in our support group. Milo. His twin sister's name . . . Oh, God, I should remember this."

"Myra," Rand said.

"Okay, we'll start there." Bentz looked at Montoya. Another twin? Well, why not? To his partner, he said, "Let's roll."

CHAPTER 31

"Jacob killed your sister?" Brianna repeated, and wondered how far off the rails Milo was. Jason had a brother named Prescott, she knew that, but not one named Jacob. Even if there was a brother who looked identical to Jason, why would he have killed Milo's sister?

A cold feeling slid down her spine as the words *identical to Jason* slipped through her mind. Her heart froze. Was it possible? Did he have a twin? Hadn't Jase said something about his mother leaving after his infant brother had died?

Was it all a lie?

She glanced up at the balcony where the tall, gray-haired guy had been smoking. He was still there, lighting up another cigarette and staring at her through the smoke he exhaled. Her skin crawled. Why the hell was he staring at her, and why was he standing so close to Jase's apartment? She'd thought it was because he lived in a neighboring unit and that still could be true, but as she moved slightly so that her line of sight was obstructed by the stairwell, she noticed Jase's door was open wide though his truck was nowhere to be found on the street or in the lot.

Not a big deal.

Or was it?

"No one could prove it. Myra just disappeared. Here in New Orleans, around the time of our twenty-first birthday," Milo was saying. "We were going to celebrate together, but never go the chance. When all this talk about Selma's daughters being abducted when they were turning twenty-one happened, I wondered, of course, but—" He shrugged, sunlight and shadow playing over his face as the wind rustled through the branches overhead, causing the leaves to turn. "Then I saw Jacob and that's when I tried to get into contact with you."

"You did a piss-poor job of it," she said, thinking of him standing outside her window. Her cell phone jangled in her hand. Jase's number flashed onto the screen. "I need to take this. I'll just be a second," she said, though Milo had started to protest.

"Hey, wait, I want to tell you—"

"I said, just a sec." With an uncompromising look in Milo's direction she held up a hand, saw that he'd snapped his mouth shut ostensibly to pout, then thought, *Too damned bad,* and turned her back on him.

"Hi," she said, expecting Jase to launch into the story surrounding Donovan Caldwell's death.

Instead, he said, "Zoe Denning is alive and here at the police station."

"What?" she whispered, not thinking she heard correctly. "Zoe?" Tears of relief sprang to her eyes and she leaned against the trunk of the live oak for support. "What about Chloe?"

"Not yet . . . we don't know. Are you at my apartment yet?"

"Yes."

"Wait for me. I'm driving. On my way." And then he launched into a bizarre tale of his learning he had a twin brother who could be the 21 Killer or a copycat or his own kind of freak because Zoe had first misidentified Jase as the killer. She listened in shock as the tale unfolded. ". . . and so the police have narrowed it down to a couple of places. They're checking out a cabin owned by Myra Tillman first."

"Wait. Tillman?" she repeated, and from the corner of her eye saw Milo's head snap up. "That's got to be it," she said, pieces of the puzzle starting to tumble into place. "I'm . . . I'm with Milo now."

"What?" Milo demanded, but she listened to the story Jase spun and once he was finished, said, "Milo says that Jacob killed his sister. Never proven because he skipped town."

"To become the 21 Killer in Los Angeles."

"And he came back here, not because of Rick Bentz," she said, as the pieces finally clicked together. "But because of Myra."

True to her word, Brianna was waiting for him.

Jase tore into the parking lot, threw himself out of his pickup, and stepped onto the sunbaked asphalt. She'd crossed the parking lot to meet him and his heart soared stupidly at the sight of her. He felt the urge to throw his arms around her, to ignore the fact that the secret he bore would keep them apart forever, but, of course, he couldn't. He had to restrain himself.

He took one step toward her when from out of the shadows of live oaks, a man catapulted himself at him. "You bastard!" the man screamed. "You killed her!"

"Milo!" Brianna cried as Jase feinted to the side and his attacker hit hard against the side of his truck.

"What the hell is this all about?" he demanded, grabbing the guy's arm and pulling it around his back.

"You killed Myra."

"Not me, pal."

"I thought I explained," Brianna said. "Stop this!"

"Fuck!" Face red, eyes bulging, Milo was forced hard against the hot front panel of the truck. "It's just you look so much like the bastard."

"I know." Jase gave the guy's arm a little tweak.

Milo squealed and his knees buckled.

"We good now?" Jase asked, feeling sweat run down his face, his adrenaline punched up. "Because I've had a long day and I'm itching for a fight. What'd'ya say?"

Milo didn't respond.

"Okay, then—"

"No! Don't. I'm good. Good." Milo was nodding furiously. "Good."

Jase didn't let go.

"You sure?"

"Yeah, man, I'm sure. Look, I didn't mean anything. You just look so freaking much like the guy I've been searching for . . . hell."

Jase released him and stepped back, but he remained wary, ready to pin the guy again and call the cops. "I don't have time for this," he said. "The guy you're looking for, my brother, the police think he might be at a place your sister owned around here."

"What?"

"A cabin by the river?"

"That old place?" Milo was shaking his head. "I thought . . . I mean, I think my uncle or cousins ended up with it."

"Deed's in the name of Myra Tillman, owes a ton of back taxes. State's about to step in."

Brianna asked, "How do you know that?"

"Connections. I called the office on my way over here." He stared hard at Milo. "I suggest you go to the cops and explain everything you know about what happened to your sister. Talk to Detective Bentz when he gets back there. You got that?"

Milo wanted to argue. Jase saw it in the shorter man's eyes.

"Okay," he acquiesced, still scowling and rubbing his arm.

"I mean it."

"I said, okay!"

"Good." To Brianna, he said, "Let's go. I think it's time I met my brother." He was starting for his pickup when a shadow crossed his path. A premonition of dread tightened his muscles as he looked up to find his father standing on the other side of a live oak.

"Don't you have unfinished business?" the old man asked as he flicked a knowing glance at Brianna.

"Not now, Dad," Jase warned.

"No time like the present."

"I said, not now. Not when the police are about to take down the twin I never knew I had, the sicko who is probably the damned 21 Killer."

"Always chasin' a story," the old man said, unperturbed by this bit of news, that his own son could be a serial killer.

"What's he talking about?" Brianna asked.

Edward's old eyes twinkled.

"We've got to go." He rounded the pickup to the passenger door. "Come on, Brianna."

She looked from his father to him and back again as she followed him. "What's going on, Jase?"

His old man chuckled. "Tell her on the way," he suggested, and patted his shirt where the envelope Jase had left him poked out of his pocket. "Jase here knows all about how your sister died."

"What?" she asked, her eyes, so like Arianna's, turning on him. He didn't wait, just grabbed her arm with one hand and opened the door of his truck with the other.

"You're a bastard," he said to the man who sired him. "You know that, don't you?"

"So I've heard." Ed reached for his near-empty pack of Camel straights. "But I'm gonna fix that right now. You think you killed a man, don't you?"

Jase paused, his hand on the hot door handle of his truck. He remembered knocking a guy senseless with one hard punch.

"It wasn't you, son. Oh, yeah, you hit him hard. Cold-cocked the son of a bitch. But he didn't die from it."

"Wait. What? We buried him."

"Buried who?" Brianna asked, staring at him in horror.

"Tell her." Ed lit up.

Jase drew in a deep breath. Wasn't he the one who'd said there would be no more secrets, hadn't he vowed as much to himself? But not like this, not for his old man's amusement. "The man who killed your sister."

"What?" she cried. "But Arianna drowned."

Jase was sick inside remembering. "I know. And . . . and it's my fault. Come on, let's go. I'll explain."

"What the fuck is going on here?" Milo said, hearing all of the conversation.

Ed chuckled again and let out a stream of smoke. "This here," he said to Milo, "this here is Judgment Day. Oh, and, son?" he said to Jase through Jase's open window. "That grave up at the farm?"

Jase froze. "What about it?"

"Doesn't exist," the old man said. "All that's up there is an old tarp filled with rocks. You didn't kill no one, boy. If you don't believe me, ask Prescott."

"What the hell is he talking about?" Brianna demanded as Edward Bridges let out a long, self-satisfied laugh that was almost a cackle and ended with a coughing spate.

Jase started the truck and peeled out of the lot.

All of the ghosts of the past seemed to chase after him as he started talking, his confession as dark as the middle of the night. As she backed into the corner of the cab of the truck, listening in stunned silence, he admitted the truth.

"I loved Arianna," he said and caught the pain in Brianna's eyes. "It was a long time ago of course."

"Of course," she whispered, a sharpness in her voice as they both knew how long Arianna had been gone.

"We would meet at the river late at night. She'd sneak out and I'd be waiting." It had seemed so innocent, or at least no more dangerous than being in trouble with her parents.

As the miles rolled beneath the tires of the truck, he added, "It hadn't gone on all that long. A few weeks. One night I showed up later than expected because of car trouble and when I got there—" He cleared his throat remembering how they'd swum beneath the moon and the stars. It had been exciting, almost dreamlike until that particular night, the one that changed all their lives forever. "When I got there," he continued feeling the weight of Brianna's gaze, seeing, from the corner of his eye how horrified she was, "Arianna wasn't alone."

"What do you mean?" she asked and he heard the hesitation in her voice over the rumble of the engine.

"There was a man with her. An . . . an assailant."

"A murderer?"

"Rapist." In his mind's eye he remembered walking through the forest to see Arianna lying on the river bank, her body white and naked, a faceless man atop her. She'd been whimpering, sobbing softly and painfully as her rapist had grunted in some kind of sick pleasure. "I went ape-shit," Jase said. All the anger he'd felt at that moment came flooding back. "Jumped the guy and tried to beat him senseless. Or . . . or thought I had. It's all a blur. It's like when people say they 'saw red.' I don't remember hitting him, but I did, and he turned, kind of roared and twisted. That's when I saw the knife, the one he'd used to subdue Arianna."

"Oh dear God," Brianna whispered, her voice breaking.

Without thinking, Jase had attacked, sprang on the back of the man who had turned in the darkness, a blade flashing. He'd jabbed quickly, connecting with Jase's face and slicing, creating the scar Jase bore today.

"He cut me." With one hand, he indicated the scar. "Got his licks in." The truth was they'd fought, struggled. "We went at it and somehow I managed to connect, a blow to his nose while holding his other wrist away from me. The guy was stunned and dropped the knife before crumpling into a heap." His jaw worked as he remembered the scene, how the bastard, his pants at his ankles had slumped to the ground and Jase had given him one final kick. All the while Arianna had screamed and mewled, scrabbling in the darkness for her clothes.

"How come I've never heard of this?"

"Because it was covered up. That's the way Arianna wanted it."

"I don't understand."

Neither did Jase. Never had. Never would. "I—I was certain I'd killed the bastard and stupid kid that I was, once I saw that Arianna was safe, or as safe as she could be, I took her home, she begged me to not tell a soul and I lied and told her I wouldn't. Then I asked my brother and father to help me. Since I was convinced I'd killed a man, I wanted my dad to go with me to the police, but Ed would have nothing to do with it."

Brianna had wrapped her arms around herself as if to ward off a chill, or protect herself somehow as Jase took a corner a little too fast and the tires screeched in protest.

"Dad," Jase spat out, remembering how stupid he'd been, how scared, how young. "He swore he'd buried the body under a tree on the farm, and I believed him. It was a mistake and a lie, but that's what he told me. The tree?" he glanced at her, "It's still there, kind of a reminder, I guess. And now Prescott, my brother, he wants me to buy the place. Tree and all."

"Your brother was part of it?"

Jase's jaw grew rock hard. "Seems as if."

Jase stole a look at her, saw the revulsion on her face, the same revulsion he felt. "So now Ed says I didn't kill the guy?" Jase couldn't believe it. "What kind of man would let his son think he was a murderer?"

"The same kind that wouldn't let his kid go to the cops and plead self-defense," she said, her voice cold as ice. "What happened to my sister?" Brianna asked, staring at him as if he were Satan incarnate.

"I went back to Arianna, once things were settled with Dad and Pres. I pleaded with her to go to the hospital, or the police. Or both, but she was frantic, insisted that no one, not even you know."

Brianna let out a soft moan.

"Trust me, I tried to talk her into it, but she wouldn't hear of it, wanted to pretend it didn't happen, made me swear I wouldn't say anything and I didn't. Ever again."

"Except to your father and brother," Brianna said in an accusatory whisper.

"Right." His insides churned at the memory and he finally forced out his final confession, "I kept my silence. Even after she drowned three days later."

Brianna seemed to wilt into herself. "She never said anything," she whispered. "Arianna, oh, dear God, she was my twin. We shared everything and she thought she had to hide the fact that she'd been raped from me?" she said.

"I don't know why she didn't tell you," he said as he drove past the city and into the countryside beyond. If he'd expected to feel release at unburdening himself, he'd been wrong. All he felt now was guilt. Deep, burrowing guilt. But hadn't it been with him all along? How many nights had he dreamed of Arianna's death? A hundred? A thousand? Each version was a little different, none the truth, but all the while he swam in a river of guilt and he never could save her. In all the scenarios in the dreams as in reality, she died. He felt sick inside. Had Arianna taken her own life? Had her drowning been an accident? He doubted anyone would ever know the truth.

Brianna's reaction only made it—his guilt—burn hotter.

"I'm sorry," he said, and he meant it. God, how he'd meant it. "I should have forced her to tell your parents or you or the police or someone."

"Or you should have, instead of relying on your sorry excuse of a family and saving your own damned skin."

Every muscle in his body tensed. He stole another glance at her and saw her lips curl in disgust.

"You son of a bitch," Brianna whispered, her eyes narrowed and filled with a new-found hate. "You son of a freakin' bitch."

CHAPTER 32

Brianna was stunned. Shocked. Everything Jase had told her rang true, but still, her heart tore as she thought of her twin and what Arianna had endured. Alone. Afraid to confide in anyone, even Brianna.

Fighting tears, she stared straight ahead through the windshield as the Louisiana countryside flew by in a blur.

Jase had lied to her. If not by commission, then omission until now and that thought soured her stomach. She didn't dare glance his way as he drove a good ten miles above the speed limit, all the while remaining silent, letting her digest everything he'd finally told her. From the corner of her eye she witnessed his own anguish and anger. His jaw was set, his hands clenched over the steering wheel until his knuckles blanched, his eyes focused on the road ahead.

Was everything he'd confessed the truth?

She blinked.

Why would he lie?

He wouldn't, she thought as she heard the sounds of sirens in the distance. His body language said as much.

So, she was forced to believe him and his tale, no, his confession, for that's what it seemed like. So Jase had not only been secretly romantically involved with her sister, but he'd witnessed Arianna being attacked, saved her, killed a man, then held his silence as Arianna had requested.

Why? Oh, God, why?

Dying a little inside, Brianna imagined her sister, in pain and shame, dealing with fear and indecision and unable to reach out. Not even to her.

Brianna's throat swelled and hot tears welled in her eyes. Why couldn't Arianna trust the one person who had been with her since their conception, the person closest to her with her secret? Why carry the burden herself?

Arianna, oh, dear Lord, I am so, so sorry I wasn't there for you; that you couldn't trust me enough to confide in me.

Her stomach roiled and she began to shake.

"Pull over!" she cried as the truck sped across a bridge spanning a small stream. "Pull over, now!"

Jase cast a glance in her direction, got the message and once they were off the bridge, eased onto the shoulder as Brianna scrambled to unbuckle her seat-belt, forced open the door and as the pickup ground to a stop in the gravel, flung herself outside. She landed in the dry grass, litter and loose gravel where she took three steps, doubled over and lost what little contents had been in her stomach. Tears ran down her face as she retched violently. Again.

She dropped to her knees as the truck idled and a long shadow fell over her. Jase's shadow . . . Dear Jesus, how fitting. Hadn't his damned shadow been cast over her all her life? Squeezing her eyes shut, she tried to block out not only his image but all the pain, the truth, the horrid thought of her sister dying alone and bereft. Guilt consumed Brianna for she knew in some small way, she, like Jase, had failed her twin.

"For what it's worth," he said, his voice raw, "I'm sorry."

"Go away!"

"I can't—"

"Just leave me the hell alone!"

"Brianna!"

"I—I can't even think about this," she admitted, on the edge of hysteria.

"Then don't."

"But I can't freakin' stop!" She was sobbing now and when he tried to help her up, take hold of her shoulder and pull her to her feet, she threw out her hands. "Don't touch me," she warned, then finally looked him full in the face again and saw the agony wrenching his features, the regret pulling at the corners of his mouth. "Don't!"

He let his arm drop. "Get in the truck."

"No!"

Again her stomach turned over, but she fought the urge to dry heave and was able to finally straighten.

"Please," he said softly as over the fading scream of sirens, a motorcycle whined in the distance. "Get into the pickup."

"I. I. I just can't."

He grabbed her then and she fought him, wildly, violently hitting him, wanting to kick and scream and rail at the heavens in her guilt and frustration. Jase held her tight, refusing to let go, allowing her hands to beat his chest impotently, almost as if he welcomed the pain she inflicted as if it were somehow a kind of penance. A balm for all the guilt and torment he, too, had suffered.

Slowly her sobbing subsided and she let her balled fists fall to her sides as she realized what she was doing, how her anger was misdirected.

Still he held her, drawing her even closer, whispering to her. "Let it all out."

What the hell was she doing fighting ghosts, charging at windmills, focusing her own pain in the wrong direction? For a second she listened to the rhythmic beat of his heart, slow and steady. Comforting. And she closed her eyes to drink in the smell of him as her thoughts swirled not only with images of Arianna, but of Zoe Denning, Selma, and Chloe, she finally stopped, her strength gone.

Chloe. That poor girl.

Brianna blinked suddenly. Opened her eyes to stare up at the man looking down so intently at her. His eyes were filled with pain and all his pride seemed to have dissolved in their struggle. "I said, 'I'm sorry,'" he repeated so sincerely, her heart nearly broke.

"So am I," she admitted, then pushed herself out of the arms that held her so intimately against him. What was she thinking, letting him comfort her? "Just drive," she ordered, as the motorcycle roared by. "Just . . . get in and drive."

She made her way to his damned truck and hoisted herself inside without his assistance. As he slid behind the wheel and engaged the gears, her heart bled one more time and in this instance she realized her pain was because of the torture he'd obviously been through ever since witnessing Arianna being attacked.

From the opposite direction, a huge truck piled high with bales of hay rolled by but she barely noticed as Jase eased the truck onto the pavement then hit the gas.

Dashing the tears from her eyes, Brianna squared her shoulders and fixed her gaze through the bug spattered windshield, staring forward to the ever-lowering sun. Whatever fantasies she'd had about Jase Bridges had to be squashed. Forever. The teenage crush. The sexy dreams. The daytime thoughts. All had to be abolished.

Right now she'd concentrate on their destination: the Tillman farm where, she hoped beyond hope, they would find Chloe.

Alive.

From her underground jail cell, Chloe heard him arrive, the excited yips of the dog, the heavy tread on the floor above. So this was it. He was back to kill her. She wondered about Zoe and prayed that her sister was alive. *Please, God, save her,* she thought as she heard the latch on the lock click open, then the scrape of the ladder as he was readying it to be slid into this rotten-smelling prison.

God, she hated it here, and it pissed her off to think that she would die here, rot here, her body left for who knew how long. She thought of her family, not just Zoe, but her mom and dad. She'd been so mad at her dad for leaving them, for marrying her damned cousin, for having a new set of babies who were her brothers and her second cousins or something as ridiculous all rolled into one, but now, in this darkness, knowing she was about to die, she forgave her father and wished that just once more she could see all the members of her family again, including CJ and Jayden, who were innocents in her father's drama.

The hatch opened fast. Trap door hitting the floor above.

Chloe startled, jumped, and her bonds pulled tighter, pain streaking down her shoulders, agony ripping through her back muscles. At least the torture would end with her death.

Quickly he descended. Faster than usual.

She closed her eyes, didn't want him to see that she'd given up, that her fear had evaporated into acceptance. *Just get it over with,* she thought.

"Well, it's not your birthday," he said as both booted feet landed on the floor, "but it is your lucky day."

Her heart pounded and for the briefest of seconds she thought he might let her go. No such luck. "Today, bitch, you die." He said the sentence without inflection, without a lick of emotion. "So let's get ready."

She peered through the slit of a nearly closed eye and saw him cutting lengths of the red ribbon, for what purpose, she had no idea. She wanted to scream at him, ask him about Zoe, but she didn't. What did it matter? Her curiosity would die with her in this subterranean hell.

He was whistling now, that same damned birthday song, as if reliving his intention of killing them on their birthdays though God only knew how many days had passed since she'd actually turned twenty-one. She had no idea of time but belatedly realized that her sister must be dead. He'd been adamant about Zoe dying first, so if he was back here, it meant that part of his mission had been accomplished.

Bastard!

Sadness welled deep within her, but no tears came. She'd cried them all and now . . .

He turned and reached down, intent on placing the ribbons around her in some precise manner. For his ritual. But he had to move her, it seemed, adjust her so that the rope binding her was perfect, the ribbons in place. As he leaned closer, she looked up beneath the veil of her lashes, to his bruised throat, evidence of her miserable attempt to kill him.

It hadn't worked.

He was tough.

But the inside of his throat was vulnerable.

If she could somehow reach it—

He placed a hand on her and she saw his neck stretched over her.

She could bite him! If she had the guts, all she had to do was clamp her teeth down on his Adam's apple. He'd never suspect . . . Oh dear God. Could she? Yes!

Quick as a snake striking, she lunged with her whole body, her mouth open wide.

"What?" he cried as she bit, sinking her teeth as far as she could into his throat.

"AAARrrrrrgh!"

He squealed as she clamped down hard. Blood— thick, salty, and warm—rushed into her mouth and ran down her own chin as he stumbled to his knees, then stood and tried to shake her off. Flesh ripped beneath her sharp incisors.

"You fucking bitch," he hissed, his voice destroyed, red spit flinging from his mouth.

She held on, clenching her teeth together as he roared and threw his head, this way, then the other. Screaming and stumbling, he flailed, trying to pull her off him, but she suffered his blows, thinking all the time of Zoe and knowing she would never survive.

Well, damn it, if she was going to die, this fucker was going with her!

He threw himself against the wall, rattling her bones and snapping her head back. But she didn't let go, her jaw locked as she slithered down the wall and in a horrible tearing of flesh, part of his throat ripped and she nearly chocked on the thick piece in her mouth.

He fell to the side and gurgled, thrashing as blood spurted from the gaping hole in his neck. And over the noise of his death throes, she heard other sounds, sirens screaming in the distance, and on the floor above, the damned dog barking like crazy.

Please, she thought desperately, unable to move, bound as she was. *Please, please save me.*

He was moaning, a rippling sound, coughing on his own blood, gasping wetly and lying not ten feet from her, the red ribbon unraveled over his body and drenched in his blood. Overhead she heard shouts and footsteps, the dog's barking quieted, men shouting.

I don't want to die.

"Down here!" a deep voice cautioned.

"Careful!" Female voice.

"Police!" Deep voice again. "Bridges, come out!"

"Help me!" she yelled, though her voice was faint and she had to spit against the remnants of the freak's skin, muscle, and blood in her mouth and then as the thought gagged, causing her body to spasm and her bonds to tighten. She nearly passed out.

"Holy shit." A man from the room above. "We've got a victim!"

"Police! Bridges, come out with your hands up! Throw down your weapons."

"He's dying," she said, and hoped to hell she was right, because she was certain she, too, was leaving this earth. With shouting and footsteps overhead and the rasping final gasps of the man next to her, she closed her eyes and let the calming blackness roll over her.

Bracing himself, his side arm drawn, Bentz yelled into the dark cavity beneath the Tillman farm's cabin floor. "Bridges!" he ordered for the third time in as many minutes. "Lay down your weapons! Put your hands over your head and come out!"

No response. Just darkness and the dank smell from a basement that should never have been carved out of low-land soil wafted upward.

Damn it.

A low moan issued from the basement.

"Let's go!" Montoya, as usual, was pulling at the bit.

This time Bentz agreed and as his flashlight beam washed over the small room below, he saw the dark stain of blood running to a drain in the dark cement. The bruiser of a man who appeared identical, at least facially, to Jason Bridges lay on his side. His throat had been slashed and a dark gaping hole existed where once had been his Adam's apple. As if his neck had been ripped apart by a hungry wolf. "Jesus."

Nearby, lying on her back, blood smeared over her

lips, her body naked and bound was Chloe Denning. Unmoving. Her skin so white as to be nearly blue, her eyes open.

His heart sank.

They were too late.

"Get the paramedics! Now!" Bentz yelled to Montoya as he swung into the opening and dropped onto the blood-soaked cement floor.

He reached Chloe, checked her pulse and fought the nausea that always found him at a homicide scene.

"Come on, come on," he whispered to the still girl, willing her heart to beat. But his pleas were for nothing.

If Chloe Denning was alive, she was hanging on by the thinnest of threads.

"Hey! Can't you read?" a policeman shouted as Jase, ignoring the barricade of police cars and stretched yellow tape, strode through a swarm of cops and EMTs. He was headed toward the small cabin where he now knew his twin brother was holed up.

If Jacob was alive, he was going to meet him. If the son of a bitch was already dead, then he wanted confirmation that his twin had actually existed. Damn. How had he not known? Where the hell was all that twin karma and connection he'd heard about, that Brianna spouted, when he'd needed it. Anger fueled his strides and clenched his fists as he made his way along a patchy, weed strewn lane. Determination drew him toward the shabby structure that was little more than a shack while lights bars on the parked vehicles flashed wildly against the surrounding fields and forest.

"Didn't you hear me? Stop. There! Right now!" A cop, identified as Deputy Bill Morrison, was yelling and approaching fast.

From somewhere behind him Jase heard Brianna's voice. "Jase! Don't! Please." As if she were actually frightened for him. The same woman who had tried to beat him to a pulp only minutes before, the same woman who had iced him out on the rest of their short journey to this God-forsaken scrap of land. *Now* she cared?

"It's all right." Another voice. Belonging to Rick Bentz. "Stand down," he told the other cop as he walked from the direction of the cabin toward Jase.

"But—"

"I said, 'It's all right.' Stand the fuck down!" Bentz glowered at the deputy and the younger cop, turning a bright red, holstered his weapon. To Jase, Bentz said, "You shouldn't be here."

"I need to meet my brother."

"Too late." Bentz was shaking his head.

"Then to see him." Jase met the reservation in Bentz's eyes. "I have to."

"I don't think—"

"I *have* to."

A muscle worked in Bentz's jaw and he glanced over at his partner. Montoya hitched his goateed chin toward one of the two ambulances on the grounds. The other was taking off, wheels spinning, lights flashing, siren wailing. The second was in no hurry.

"This way," Bentz said and headed toward the ambulance where the back doors were still open, a body bag within. With a look to one of the attendants, Bentz said, "We need to open it up."

The EMT hesitated, then unzipped the bag, the sound a hiss that curled through Jase's soul as he found himself staring into a face so like his own that if it weren't for the unshaven jaw, mussed hair, and sightless, fixed eyes he might have been looking into a mirror. Blood was everywhere across a hairy torso and his neck, hell, it looked like it had been ripped apart by a wild animal.

Jase's knees weakened.

This was his twin? The brother who had been conceived with him, who had grown with him in a bitter womb? A hundred thoughts flashed through Jase's brain, pictures of a mother he didn't remember, memories devoid of this person, so like him, so damned opposite.

All the breath left his lungs in a rush and he felt as if he'd been hit, a hard jab to the solar plexus. "Son of a bitch," he whispered, knowing the truth, feeling something stir deep inside him, a connection that was quickly severed with the reality of who this monster was.

His brother, the twin he'd never known, Jacob Bridges was, indeed, the 21 Killer, a psychopath who had killed at least three sets of twins and probably more, a soulless monster who bore his own face.

Bile rose up his throat and he took a step back. With a nod from Bentz, the attendant quickly zipped the bag and slid it into the back of the ambulance.

"No. Hell. No." Jase shook his head, as if negating the truth could make it so. "Damn it!" His knees wobbled a bit but he somehow remained on his feet and a second later he felt slim fingers surround his.

"It . . . it'll be all right," Brianna said, squeezing his hand. He turned to look at her, felt a glaze of tears over his eyes and blinked it back to see that her gaze, too, was shimmering, a tiny drop rolling down her cheek. "It'll be all right."

His heart swelled for the briefest of instants and he saw her smile. Bravely, he thought and he couldn't do the same.

Brianna was lying of course.

It would never be all right.

Never.

But at least it would be over.

EPILOGUE

October

J ase found a beer in the refrigerator and cracked it open, then took a deep swallow. As he stepped onto the back porch of the farm house, he stared across the rolling acres to the tree where for years he'd believed a body had been buried. He'd been wrong. As his father had pronounced all those months ago, and as Prescott had confirmed. The old man had taken off, cashed the check, and Jase hadn't heard from him since, but Prescott had explained that the assailant who had raped Arianna had been an associate of Ed's, someone to whom the old man owed money.

The guy hadn't been dead, but had agreed to disappear; Ed's debt was then forgiven, any rape charge unable to be pinned on a faceless man. Prescott didn't know the rapist's name, and Ed would take that bit of information with him to the grave.

Nonetheless, Jase had gone to the police and told his tale. Though the clock on the statute of limitations had run out on any charges that might have occurred during the fight, Jase had lost any chance he'd had of getting the job with the police department.

As well as any chance he'd had with Brianna. She hadn't spoken to him since he'd stood over the dead body of his brother in the body bag, and he didn't really blame her.

So he'd bought out Prescott and moved here, his only companion a red hound dog that had been found on the Tillman property, probably belonging to his brother. The dog warned him when visitors arrived and was content to curl up at his feet in the evening. Good company. As much as he wanted now.

At least Chloe Denning had survived. She'd been traumatized, of course, but she was going to live while his brother, Jacob, the 21 Killer had not. The police had finally closed the case on that one with the evidence collected at the cabin, including the red ribbon that matched ribbon found on previous victims in California. In searching the cabin, the police had also discovered the grave of a woman buried within the walls of the cell. DNA testing was back, the woman was the owner of the property, Milo's sister, Myra, the woman Jacob had loved and murdered; though according to both Chloe and Zoe Denning, he'd acted as if Myra were alive and the brains behind his crimes. The police had located his cell phone, again in Myra's name, but never charged or minutes purchased. The phone was little more than a prop.

His twin had been a bona-fide psychopath. Crazy and sadistic. Ritualistic. A killer who had taken the life of his lover, Myra and maybe, just maybe their mother. Before he turned his attention to twins. The theory was that because he'd killed Myra when she was turning 21, he tried to replay the scenario with twins, all because he knew he, too, was a twin. Yeah, the Denning girls were right, Jacob Bridges was a freak. As well as his damned brother. Go figure.

Jase had finally come to terms with that sorry fact as well as resolved, in his mind, Arianna's death. Had she committed suicide? No one would ever know, but his guilt was lessening. He doubted he could have saved her from herself or the accident. No one could have. Not even Brianna.

Now as he sat on the porch rail and drank his beer, Jase watched the dog chasing squirrels near the tree where he'd been certain his own victim had been buried.

He was still pissed at Prescott for that one. The old man? Well, he was who he was and Jase would never forgive him, but Prescott? Really? He wasn't certain the fences between his only surviving brother and himself would ever be mended and it hurt a little when he considered his niece and nephews. Maybe someday . . . damn he hoped he could watch those two and the new baby, another boy, grow up. Somehow he'd have to find a way to forgive Prescott for his lies and secrets.

We all have our own secrets. You kept yours, didn't you?

And he'd spent the past few months trying to purge those very demons, the secrets, from his life by burying himself into work. He'd thrown his back into repairing fences and cleaning out buildings during the day and worked on a book at night. He figured he had an intimate take on the 21 Killer and already had some publishers interested in the story. That is, if he had the guts to go through reporting all the ritualistic murders knowing full well that his own twin brother was the monster behind the bizarre homicides. If he needed help, Kristi Bentz, the detective's daughter was already a true crime writer and she'd suggested a collaboration. He was considering it. Who knew?

As for his job at the *Observer*? He'd let it go. Let Meri-Jo have the crime beat. He didn't need it any longer. Didn't want it. Time for a fresh start.

He figured he needed some time to himself, to adjust to this new life, to figure out where he'd go from here. It would be a lie to say that he didn't think of Brianna, but he tried to keep that at a minimum.

The dog was barking again and this time the hound's attention was focused on the lane.

Jase pushed himself upright and walked around the wraparound porch to the side of the building where the late-afternoon sun was bouncing off the windshield of a small car driving toward the house. He squinted and told himself that he was hallucinating, because the compact sure looked like a Honda, and the woman behind the wheel was a dead ringer for Brianna Hayward.

No way.

He drained his beer and left the empty on the porch.

Barking and yipping, the hound bounded over the dry grass of the field before slithering under the bottom fence rail while Jase cut along the path leading to the parking area near the garage.

The Honda ground to a stop, and sure enough, Brianna climbed from behind the wheel.

His heart did a stupid little thump. God, he was an idiot.

"So," she said, shielding her eyes with the flat of a

hand as she approached. Wearing a T-shirt, skirt, and sandals, she was as gorgeous as he remembered. "You're a cowboy now."

"Yes, ma'am." He couldn't help but grin. "Seems to me someone suggested I wasn't cut out to be a buttoned-down type."

"You aren't." She hesitated. Bit her lip. Seemed about to turn away from him and flee back the way she came before she squared her shoulders and looked him straight in the eye. "Listen, Bridges, I don't know how to say this, but . . . I've thought about everything that happened." Her mouth turned down and she squinted a bit, still held his gaze. "It was bad. Really bad."

"No argument there."

"And I desperately wanted to blame you for not being straight with me, for everything that happened, for my sister's death, for all of it. You know, just call you the bad guy and file it away forever. But . . ." She let out her breath. "I was wrong." She hesitated, one thumb nervously rubbing her forefinger. "And I've done some major soul-searching and yeah, some counseling. Even shrinks have shrinks, you know, and I think . . . Dear Lord, I *hope* I'm getting past it."

"Just like that?"

"No, not just like that." She shook her head, her hair highlighted by the late-afternoon sun. "It took a while." She sighed and nodded, agreeing with herself. "And I was pretty awful to you."

"You were. But maybe I deserved it."

"No one does. I was just lashing out. Stupidly and I'm sorry. Life's too short, you know, for carrying around all that negative energy." She shoved her hair from her face. Her eyes clouded for a second, and she closed them, as if she suddenly doubted her reasons for coming out here and needed to gather her strength.

"And?" he prodded.

"And—" Her eyes opened again. Clear once more. A smile toyed at the corners of her mouth and she seemed calmer. "Look, I'd really like to start over, get to know you." She rolled those expressive eyes and sighed. "Sounds corny I know, but I believe in saying what I think."

"I remember. Direct."

"Yeah, and so I have a confession."

"You do?"

"Mmm. You might not believe this," she said, her cheeks turning pink, "and I hate to admit it, but the truth is I had a major crush on you in high school."

"I know."

"You know?" Her smile fell away. "Are you kidding me, Bridges? I bare my soul, make this big proclamation, and you say you *know*?"

"Yep." The breeze ruffled her hair and played with her skirt. He tried not to notice.

"Okay . . . so, with the whole Arianna thing, it was too much, that you knew how she died and you had an affair with her . . . and see how complicated it is? I don't want to dwell on it anymore." Her gaze was suddenly tentative. "And the thing is, as I said, I want to start this, thing between us, whatever it is," she made a gesture from her to him and back, "over again."

"Really?" He found it hard to believe. Damned hard after the way she'd reacted to him when he'd finally told her the truth.

"That's all you've got to say?"

"I'm just surprised."

"So you don't want to?"

"No, no. Of course I do," he admitted and took a step closer to her. She didn't back away and he figured that was a positive sign. "But I've got to warn you."

"Warn me?"

"It might be dangerous."

"How's that?"

He felt his lips twitch. "I have a strong feeling you might want to pressure me into joining that twinless twin support group."

Never," she said, and laughed, shaking her head. "Trust me, you wouldn't fit in."

"Okay. Then it's a deal." He told himself he was making a huge mistake, but figured what the hell? She was right. Life was far too short to dwell on the past. "So, what do you say? How 'bout a beer?"

She grinned a little wider, her smile as sexy as ever and one of her eyebrows arched playfully "A beer? Sure." Then she winked at him. "As long as you're buying."

Rick Bentz fingered his badge, turning it over and over as he sat at his desk in his office at the department. It was quiet now, twilight stealing through the slats of the window on the far wall. He still hadn't quit his job, though he'd played out the scenarios of leaving and staying in his mind a dozen times over.

His quitting the department wasn't Olivia's choice, nor was it Montoya's. It was his alone and, damn it, he was torn. Things had quieted down since their last major case. The 21 Killer, Jacob Bridges was dead. A good thing. Justice served. The one sour note in the case was Donovan Caldwell, who had been, as it turned out an innocent man, just as he'd protested to the very end when he'd written his last plea in blood on his cell wall as he'd bled out. Not that he'd been a great guy, but his end . . . not right. That bothered Bentz. A lot. The Caldwells had not only lost their twin daughters but their son as well, due to a mistake in the system.

Wasn't fair.

Then again, what was in life?

The other sets of twins who Brianna Hayward had thought were his victims, the brothers in Phoenix and the sister and brother in Dallas had turned out not to have been in the psycho's path, nor had 21 turned up in New Orleans because of Bentz. But he'd ended up here anyway and at least now he would harm no more innocents.

Thank God. Jacob Bridges had been a nutcase. According to the Denning twins he'd talked constantly to the already-dead Myra, acting as if she were calling the shots when he'd killed her years before. And his fascination with red and ribbons. Hard to believe he was the twin brother of Jason Bridges, who seemed grounded and normal despite his own not-so-great upbringing.

Twins, but diametrically opposed in personality.

"Hey!" Montoya poked his head into the office. "You goin' home or what?"

"Yeah."

Montoya's gaze narrowed in on the badge. "Uh-oh. What're you doin'? Oh, hell, don't tell me you're thinking of quitting again?"

"Always. But I can't. Even if I wanted to."

Montoya flashed his knowing smile. "Because of our boy Father John?"

"Maybe."

"No maybe about it," Montoya said, walking into the small office and hooking one knee over the corner of Bentz's desk. "That bad-ass is under your skin."

"The one that got away," Bentz said, nodding. The thought still ate at him, but no longer to the point that he needed to down a beer as he stared at the arrogant bastard on the prison's tape. So far Bentz hadn't repeated his slip-up with alcohol, didn't intend to again.

Montoya pointed out, "The bastard's been quiet for few months now and it was years between his killings."

That much was true. After the murder of the nun in the prison and the prostitute in her apartment, Father John had seemed to stop his bizarre murders. Inexplicably he'd ceased. Again. Why? Didn't make sense. Also, though he'd once been an obsessed stalker of Dr. Sam and her radio show, he hadn't called in, hadn't taunted her. But of course, he could still be listening. From some dark lair.

This time, the killer was being coy. Careful. Why come back and flaunt the fact that he'd survived by killing the nun and prostitute only to disappear again?

Didn't make sense.

"Maybe the son of a bitch is dead. You know the prostitute could have been killed by a copy cat. That's the way the department would like to spin it," Montoya said. "To avoid another panic by the public if they thought Father John was stalking the streets of New Orleans again."

Bentz reached over, clicked his mouse to his computer and the darkened screen illuminated, freeze-framed on the smiling, nearly gloating image of Father John looking up at the camera right after killing the nun. "The department's spinning it in the wrong direction." He pointed at the image. "You and I, we know, this guy, he's the real deal."

"Or maybe a twin." Montoya's dark eyes flashed.

"Don't even joke about it."

Montoya gave a quick nod. "A major bad dude."

"One I have to catch."

"We," Montoya corrected, though they both knew it was Bentz whose shot had missed its mark in the bayou all those years before. "We."

"Okay. We."

Montoya's grin grew wide and wicked as he reached into the pocket of his jacket and pulled out his signature shades. "We'll get the bastard."

"Promise?"

"You got it." He slid his sunglasses onto the bridge of his nose. "The bastard doesn't stand a chance."

Chuckling, Bentz slipped his badge back into its case. "Come on, let's get out of here. It's almost Halloween and that means the baby's birthday party, so I've got major dad duties to perform."

"And you love it."

"Yeah." No reason to lie. "I do."

Montoya laughed as they walked out of the office and down the hallway, but Bentz didn't quite let go of his dark, worrisome thoughts about Father John.

He hated that son of a bitch.

As the moon rose over the bayou, he climbed into his new cabin situated over the water. The night was sticky, the mosquitoes thick. He'd been quiet. Leaving well enough alone, but the itch was with him again, the need firing his blood, the sound of bullfrogs and crickets reminding him it was time to hunt.

He switched on the radio and listened to her voice, low and sexy, offering up advice over the airways. He thought of calling her. It was so much easier now with cell phones, but he waited and eyed the cassock hanging from its hook. Detective Bentz would be expecting that move and there was no way Father John was going to be outfoxed by the cop who'd nearly killed him. Oh, no. Their dance wasn't over. Not yet.

"Just you wait," he whispered into the night.

Closing his eyes for a second, he listened to the sounds of the bayou and heard a fish jump as he reached for his rosary, the beads winking blood red in the lantern's glow. For a few minutes, he ran the string lovingly through his fingers. But it didn't feel quite right, he thought, opening his eyes to the night. Finding his file, he set to work, sharpening each bead to a razor-sharp point, making certain that the wire he'd used to string the beads together in their unique pattern was strong.

Sooner or later the urge would overtake him again.

He could only fight it so long.

And then it was simple: He would have to kill again.

Dear Reader,

I hope you enjoyed *Never Die Alone*. I'm lucky that I can revisit some of my favorite characters.

Recently I was asked to write a sequel to *Deep Freeze* and *Fatal Burn*, two of my most popular novels. This new novel, *After She's Gone*, takes up about a decade after the first two books end.

In *Deep Freeze*, Jenna Hughes along with her two daughters has escaped the glam and glitz of Hollywood. Little does the ex-actress know that an obsessed fan, one with murderous intent has stalked her all the way to the shores of the Columbia River and the small town she now calls home. Not only is she in danger, but both of her daughters, Cassie and Allie, too, are in the maniac's brutal plans.

Fatal Burn takes up where *Deep Freeze* leaves off. In this story, Dani Settler, a tomboy and friend of Jenna's daughter Allie, goes missing. The bloody trail turns instantly cold and the police as well as her father are stymied. While Travis Settler frantically searches for his daughter, Dani is running out of time and must rely solely upon her wits to keep herself alive against her would be hate-filled killer.

After She's Gone, a brand-new book, will be in the stores in January 2016. This book takes up nearly a decade after *Deep Freeze* and catches up with Allie and Cassie Kramer, both who have tested the waters of acting in Hollywood with varied success. Allie, the younger sibling is much more famous that her older sister. Jealousy and rivalry have been parts of their lives and culminate when Allie goes missing, and Cassie, never all that stable to begin with, is suspected in her sister's disappearance. Is Allie dead? The victim of her sister's jealousy? Is she part of an elaborate publicity stunt? Or is she now the victim of her own insidious stalker with his own malevolent intent. Catch up with the Kramer sisters and find out in *After She's Gone.*

For those of you who are into my Grizzly Falls series that features Detectives Alvarez and Pescoli, you'll be glad to know that in late 2016, there will be two more books available. Expecting to Die takes up where Deserves to Die left off, with a very pregnant Regan Pescoli debating whether she'll stay on the force or throw in her badge and stay home after her baby is born. Unfortunately an old nemesis plans to take the choice away from her and all her carefully laid plans, as well as the lives of her family, are threatened. Things only get worse in Willing to Die where Pescoli and Alvarez battle a foe who is willing to sacrifice everything to extract a deadly revenge.

I think you'll like the stories. At least, I hope so.

If you'd like more information on these books or any other I've written, please check out my website. At www.lisajackson.com you'll be able to see what's new and read excerpts from upcoming as well as already published books. Also, you can like me on Facebook at Lisa Jackson Fans or follow me at readlisajackson on twitter.

Keep Reading!
Lisa Jackson

In this explosive new thriller, #1 New York Times
*bestselling author Lisa Jackson delves into the deep
bond between two sisters and their shared dream that
becomes a harrowing nightmare of madness, hatred
and jealousy . . .*

Cassie Kramer and her younger sister, Allie, learned
the hazards of fame long ago. Together, they'd survived
the horror of a crazed fan who nearly killed their
mother, former Hollywood actress Jenna Hughes. Still,
Cassie moved to L.A., urging Allie to follow. As a
team, they'd take the town by storm. But Allie, finally
free of small-town Oregon, and just that little bit more
beautiful, also proved to be more talented—and driven.
Where Cassie got bit parts, Allie rose to stardom. But
now her body double has been shot on the set of her
latest movie—and Allie is missing.

Police discover that the last call to Allie's phone came
from Cassie, though she has no recollection of making
it. Instead of looking like a concerned relative, Cassie
is starting to look like a suspect—the jealous sister
who finally grew sick of playing a supporting role. As
the tabloids go into a frenzy, Cassie ends up on a Portland psych ward. Is she just imagining the sinister figure who comes to her bedside, whispering about
Allie—a visitor of whom there is no record? Is someone trying to help—or drive her mad?

Convinced she's the only one who can find Allie,
Cassie checks herself out of the hospital. But a sudden
slew of macabre murders— each victim masked with a
likeness of a member of Cassie's family—makes Cassie

fear for her safety and her sanity. The only way to end
the nightmare is to find out what really happened to
Allie. And with each discovery, Cassie realizes that
no one can be trusted to keep her safe—least of all herself . . .

Please read on for an exciting
sneak peek of Lisa Jackson's
After She's Gone,
coming in January 2016,
wherever print and eBooks are sold!

Portland, Oregon

He watched.
Carefully.

Paying attention to every detail as the rain sheeted from the night-dark sky and streetlights reflected on the wet pavement.

Two women were running, faster and faster and he smiled as the first passed into the lamp's pool of illumination. Her face was twisted in terror, her beautiful features distorted by fear.

Just as they should have been.

Good. Very good.

The slower woman was a few steps behind and constantly looking over her shoulder, as if she were expecting something or someone with murderous intent to be hunting her down.

Just as he'd planned.

Come on, come on, keep running.

As if they heard him, the women raced forward.

Perfect.

His throat tightened and his fists balled in nervous anticipation.

Just a few more steps!

Gasping, the slower woman paused, one hand splayed over her chest as she leaned over to catch her breath beneath the street lamp. Rain poured down from the heavens. Her hair was wet, falling in dripping ringlets around her face, her white jacket soaked through. Again she glanced furtively behind her, past the empty sidewalks and storefronts of this forgotten part of the city. God, she was beautiful, as was the first one, each a fine female specimen that he'd picked precisely for this moment.

His heart was pumping wildly, anticipation and adrenalin firing his blood as an anticipatory grin twisted his lips.

Good. This is so good.

Silently he watched as from the corner of his eye, the first woman raced past him just as he'd hoped. Eyes focused ahead, she was seemingly oblivious to his presence, but, in his heart, he knew she realized he was there, observing her every movement, catching each little nuance of fear. He saw determination and horror in the tense lines of her face, heard it in her quick, shallow breaths and the frenzied pounding of her footsteps as she'd flown past.

And then she was gone.

Safely down the street.

He forced his full attention to the second woman, the target. She twisted her neck, turned to look his way, as if she felt him near, as if she divined him lurking in the deep umbra surrounding the street.

His heart missed a beat.

Don't see me. Do not! Do not look at me!

Her expression, at this distance was a little blurry, but he sensed that she was scared to death. Terrified. Exactly what he wanted.

Feel it. Experience the sheer terror of knowing you're being stalked, that you are about to die.

Her lower lip trembled.

Yes! Finally.

Satisfaction warmed his blood.

As if she heard a sound, she stiffened, her head snapping to stare down the darkened alley.

That's it. Come on. Come on!

Her eyes widened and suddenly she started running again, this time in a sheer panic. She slipped, lost a high heel and she kicked off the other, never missing a step her bare feet still slapping the wet pavement frantically.

Now!

He shifted slightly, giving himself a better view, makes sure that he didn't miss a thing.

Perfect.

She was running right on target.

At that moment a dark figure stepped from a shadowed doorway to stand right in front of the woman.

Screaming, she veered a bit, slipped and nearly lost her balance, only to keep on running, angling away from the man.

Too late!

The assassin raised his gun.

Blam! Blam! Blam!

Three shots rang out, echoing along the empty street, fire spitting from the gun's muzzle.

She stumbled and reeled, her face a mask of fear as she twisted and fell onto the pavement. Her eyes rolled upward, blood trickling from the corner of her mouth. Another bloom of red rose darkly through her white jacket.

Perfect, he thought, satisfied at last as he viewed her unmoving body.

Finally, after years of planning, he'd pulled it off.

Allie McIntyre was dead.